"One of the best authors
in contemporary romance.
SUNRISE SONG will add new fans
to Kathleen Eagle's loyal readers."
Deborah Smith, author of *Bridges*

❧ ❧

"I love you," Michelle repeated, as though she were teaching him new words.

"I'm not sure I know what that means." Zane looked down at her, inviting her to read the candor in his eyes.

"I think you do."

"I know how to *make* love." He slid his hand up her side and cupped her breast. "Do you want me to make love to you, Michelle?"

"Do you want to?"

He looked into her eyes, lifted his chin slowly, lowered it slowly.

"Why?" she asked.

It was a woman's question. He had only a man's answer. "I can't get close enough to you any other way."

WINNER—
Midwest Fiction Writer of the Year!

"The premier voice in women's fiction today . . .
No one writes of the human heart
in more compelling terms
than this gifted author."

Romantic Times

KATHLEEN EAGLE

SUNRISE SONG

AVON BOOKS
An Imprint of HarperCollinsPublishers

This is a work of fiction. Names, characters, places, and incidents are products of the author's imagination or are used fictitiously and are not to be construed as real. Any resemblance to actual events, locales, organizations, or persons, living or dead, is entirely coincidental.

AVON BOOKS
An Imprint of HarperCollins*Publishers*
10 East 53rd Street
New York, New York 10022-5299

Copyright © 1996 by Kathleen Eagle
Cover art by Hiroko
Inside cover author photo by Robert Knutson Photography
Library of Congress Catalog Card Number: 95-94923
ISBN: 0-380-77634-0

First Avon Books printing: March 1996

Avon Trademark Reg. U.S. Pat. Off. and in Other Countries, Marca Registrada, Hecho en U.S.A.
HarperCollins® is a trademark of HarperCollins Publishers Inc.

Printed in the U.S.A.

10 9 8 7

This book is dedicated in memory of those whose names appear on the monument at Canton; in gratitude for those who keep culture and tradition alive for those who come after them; in honor of my sons, David and Christopher, for their courage in seeking new visions in the old way.

ACKNOWLEDGMENTS

The background research for this novel was challenging, since there's been very little written about the Hiawatha Insane Asylum for Indians, established in Canton, South Dakota, and operated by the Bureau of Indian Affairs from 1902 until 1934. A newspaper article written by Harold Iron Shield for the Dakota News Service caught my attention, and the juxtaposition of a turn-of-the-century Indian cemetery between two fairways on a South Dakota golf course conjured an image that begged for a story.

I am grateful to Mary Sterud, caretaker at Hiawatha Community Golf Club in Canton, for taking the time to be gracious and informative when we visited the cemetery during a golf tournament. I am also indebted to Brigid Shields of the Minnesota Historical Society, and Colleen Kirby, librarian at the South Dakota State Historical Society, for their invaluable help in researching the background for *Sunrise Song*. Finally, I want to express my appreciation to my son, Christopher Eagle, for helping me write about *hanble ceya* without compromising his own deeply personal experiences.

✣ Prologue ✣

Canton, South Dakota
Spring 1973

From the upstairs bedroom window in her Aunt Cora's house Michelle Benedict watched another old duffer step up to the fourth tee of the nine-hole golf course across the road, crouch over his club, and do that funny little golfer's dance as he lined up his shot.

She decided to watch him blow it.

For blow it he surely would. The ghosts from the cemetery were working on him. She could tell by the way he hesitated, focus straying as he adjusted his green cap, then started over with his golf dance.

From her vantage point she could see the four flag fluttering in the warm prairie wind. It looked like an easy shot, but from where she stood, all nine of the course's holes looked easy. Not that she was much of a golfer, but Hiawatha Golf Club's flat layout contained only one real trap, and that was the Indian cemetery between the fourth and fifth fairways.

"Damn, I landed on 'sacred ground' again," she'd heard more than one golfer say. Some cursed it; others joked about it. But ever since she'd inherited her aunt's house, Michelle had taken a serious interest in the old cemetery. She had some strong feelings about it. Strange feelings. Defensive feelings, even though she didn't know a soul who was buried there. It just didn't seem right to build a golf course around a cemetery. Especially not *this* cemetery.

The old duffer finally swung his club back and took a whack at the tee. The ball sailed into the clear blue sky like a pop fly. The golfer touched the bill of his cap and watched the white dot travel. Michelle knew exactly where it was going. She could feel it. She could almost hear the wail of those ghost singers in her ear. The west wind would have its way, and the ball would land on one of more than a hundred unmarked graves behind the screen of shrubs.

According to club rules, the golfer wasn't supposed to drive his cart into the scraggly enclosure or play the ball out or otherwise disturb the ghosts. He was supposed to take a two-club-length drop.

Some golfers did. Some didn't. To most of them the sunken plots probably just looked like big divots, and it wasn't as though any of the town fathers were buried there. Just a bunch of crazy Indians planted for all eternity right in the middle of Hiawatha Golf Club. Crazy Indians who had once lived under the watchful care of Dr. Tim Hubble, Aunt Cora's husband. The asylum, along with Dr. Tim and Aunt Cora, were gone now. Only the cemetery remained, along with a house full of fussy furniture and boxes of Dr. Tim's papers.

And there was Michelle, of course, full of fond memories of her aunt and funny feelings about what lay across the road. Forty years had passed since the last grave had been dug over there, but still . . .

There must be some family members somewhere, she thought. Maybe they'd be interested in Dr. Tim's records. Maybe they didn't know about the golf course. Maybe they'd agree with her that this just didn't seem right.

The wind nudged the ball, sliding through the zenith of its arc, toward the hedge. Michelle smiled. The ghosts were in the game today. Another golfer was about to visit the Indian cemetery, sure enough. The old duffer shook his head and rammed the club into his bag as the ball dropped out of sight.

Pine Ridge Sioux Indian Reservation, South Dakota
Summer 1928

A pale gray owl appeared suddenly, startling a young vision seeker out of his prayerful reverie. It dropped from the night sky, like one of those rockets the boy's brother had seen in battle during the Great War, and fell on a mouse, the hunter snatching in silence, the prey crying out its distress. A few quick wing flaps lifted the two back into night's dark bosom, leaving the boy to ponder in his hilltop seclusion.

It was a sign, the boy decided, for he was named for the small owl whose rarely heard call heralded spring. Pagla, the boy's grandfather called him, and even though it was not the name that was recorded for him on the Indian bureau's rolls or in the boarding-school teacher's book, Pagla was who he truly was. So his grandfather had said, and so it was. When he left the hill he would tell the old man about the owl. It was one thing he must be sure to report.

It was his grandfather who kept the vigil for him on the flat below his hill and tended the fire that would burn until Pagla returned. His grandfather was a holy man, much respected by those among the Oglala people who still kept the old ways. He had prepared the boy for this, his first *hanble ceya,* which he had chosen to do on his twelfth birthday. It was his decision, Grandfather had said, and one not to be taken lightly. Together they had made prayers in the sweat lodge, and Pagla had fasted, carefully preparing himself. He knew the risks they both took in making this vision quest, for the spiritual practices of the Lakota had been banned by the government in Washington, and many people, like his brother, Adam, had forsaken them.

The Lakota were dreamers, Adam had told him. Maybe in times past a warrior could be a dreamer, but no more. A dreamer might fill his lungs with gas and

die without ever seeing the face of his enemy. The white
man's wars were not won by counting coups. Those
days were over, Adam said. Nothing to be gained by
taking risks. No one sang a man's praises when he died
in battle so far from home. They would not even know
what name to sing, for he would be only one among the
thousands. And no one would care for his widow and
orphans. Not these days. It was time to stop dreaming,
start facing reality, Adam said. Forget the pipe, forget
the songs. They'll only get you into trouble.

Pagla dreaded trouble. He'd seen enough of it already.
There was trouble at school when he and his friends just
barely shared a little joke in Lakota, some story they'd
learned from their parents or grandparents. There was
trouble when he couldn't explain himself in English.
There was also trouble at home with not enough food
to go around, not enough blankets, never any money,
and everyone getting sick all the time. And there was
trouble with Adam, who'd been searching for this thing
he called reality in the bootleg whiskey he'd acquired a
taste for in the army.

After three days alone on his hill, Pagla had accustomed himself to hot afternoons and bone-chilling
nights. Hunger was nothing new, and patience had been
instilled in him long ago. But the mysteries that surrounded him were more formidable in darkness than
they were in daylight. Each morning the light came as
reassurance, and he told himself that he was a man now,
and he could see that he was the equal of all that lay
before him. He would not worry the next time the sun
went down.

But he did. The time between sunset and moonrise
was the worst. He had to pull his blanket over his head
to keep the gnats from worrying his face and the mosquitoes from driving him to his feet. He prayed for the
night breeze, but when it came it rattled the grass, and
the sound sometimes fooled him into thinking that something was coming toward him. He would pop out of his
blanket and peek over his shoulder, then scold himself
and duck back under cover, where he'd feel something

crawling on his neck. Then he'd shiver. And he'd shake. And he'd shoo the creature away and try to get back to his prayer for his brother, who couldn't stop drinking sometimes; for his grandfather, who couldn't stop coughing sometimes; and for moonrise. Come on, moonrise.

In darkness the familiar voices of the prairie confused him with their new secrets. They reminded him that he, too, had secrets. The government agent had warned his grandfather about keeping secrets, and some of his own relations echoed the warning. "Give it up," they said. "If you don't listen, they will send you away." But his grandfather said that *hanble ceya* would give a man strength and wisdom in the face of these threats. You can never tell what the white man might do next, Grandfather had said. Nothing was unthinkable anymore.

Even so, *too much* thinking could drive a man crazy the way things were now. A man must still the noise in his head, calm his heart, open his ears in the darkness, and listen. Just listen. Strength and wisdom, Pagla reminded himself as he listened to the prairie voices. The harmless night wind rustled the grass. The friendly crickets sang their song. All that moved was one with the night, even the fire that burned on the flat below his hill.

The prairie voices transported the boy in a dreamlike state. He did not anticipate human intrusion. He heard nothing amiss, sensed no danger until a loop was suddenly dropped over his shoulders, slack jerked, ground yanked away. He responded with the lethargy of one awakened from a deep sleep, momentarily unable to find his arms or legs. But it was too late for his arms. He managed one kick before his ankles, too, were tied together. A man's voice pronounced him "heathen bastard," and a burlap sack was pulled over his face.

Weakened from fasting, terrified, desperate for air, Pagla lost consciousness.

❧ I ❧

Standing Rock Sioux Indian Reservation, South Dakota
Spring 1973

Zane Lone Bull woke up scared.

It took him a moment to catch his breath, get his bearings, and realize that the eerie moaning coming from the back room was just Uncle Martin having another one of his dream fits. Zane rolled to his side and sat up on the tattered sofa, planting his bare feet on the hard-packed dirt floor of the two-room cabin he shared with his uncle. The pre-dawn moaning was enough to give a person a bad case of the quivers. The old man sounded like some tortured soul calling out from the grave.

The dog barked outside the door. Zane dropped his chin to his bare chest and raked his hair back with splayed fingers. He had enough nightmares of his own to contend with, but he figured poor old Uncle Martin's monster had to be a real beaut. That thought merged with the predawn chill, blanketing his body with invigorating goosebumps. Countless miserable, sweaty nights had given rise to his appreciation of nip-in-the-air goose bumps. He snapped his jeans and reached past the cold wood stove for the shirt he'd left hanging on the back of a kitchen chair. It was still dark, but he knew where everything in the cabin was. There wasn't much to keep track of. He fished a cigarette and matches out of his

6

shirt pocket, lit up, and headed for the back room.

"Uncle, wake up." Zane dropped into a squat beside the bed. He couldn't see a damn thing, but his hand homed in on the warmth of the old man's shoulder. "You're okay, now. Nobody's gonna hurt you."

Martin made a pitiful sound that might have come from a small child. In a way, Zane realized, it did.

"Yeah, I know. I know how it is." But when the old man reached for him, Zane instinctively ducked away. He'd do the comforting on his own terms, and ending up in one of Uncle Martin's desperate headlocks was not among them. "I don't know who it is or what it is, but I know *how* it is. Whatcha gotta do is put that ol' *gigi* on the run."

Parking his cigarette in the corner of his mouth, Zane flipped the switch on the big flashlight he'd put beside Martin's bed and beamed the light into the shadowy corners of the tiny room, one by one. "Is he gone already? Must be one chickenshit *gigi* if he took off that quick. Maybe we better try smokin' him out."

But the offer of a drag on Zane's cigarette was lost on the old man, whose eyes were still wide with fear.

"Yeah, you're right." Zane studied the lengthening ash. "This ain't good for you. I never used to smoke much before I went to 'Nam. Now I can't quit. Not that I've tried all that hard."

Still wide-eyed, Martin watched Zane savor the lungful of smoke he'd been offered. Almost as good as a cup of coffee, and equally necessary. But Martin never indulged himself in either of Zane's morning rituals. He only watched.

"What are you thinkin' about, old man? What's goin' on inside that head of yours?"

Martin sat up and swung his legs over the side of the bed. Summer or winter, the old man slept in long johns and socks. Always kept his boots close to the bed at night. Wouldn't go to sleep unless he knew they were there.

"I envy you sometimes, you know? You don't ask no questions, nobody tells you no lies. Just keep to your-

self.'' Zane's knees cracked as he rose from the floor.
''I'm learnin' from you, Uncle. Always did learn the
hard way, but at least it's some kinda way, huh?''

Martin leaned down to put his boots on, his gray
braids dangling over his knees.

''Just keep to yourself,'' Zane repeated absently,
watching his uncle go through his predictable motions.
He headed for the front door in his droopy underwear,
snatching his frayed straw hat off a nail on the way out.
Zane had to chuckle. Martin wouldn't even make a trip
to the outhouse without that hat.

Pale daylight had begun to define shapes in the front
room—the bronc saddle in the far corner, the water
cooler on the little kitchen table, a 1971 calendar on the
clay-chinked wall. Zane didn't mind doing that year over
again. This time he wasn't spending it behind bars.

Martin's nasal whine, an innocently warped version
of a Lakota a cappella, soon rose beyond the door. He
was singing up the sun. Wordless, toneless, it was still
a reassuring sound. It reminded Zane that he was home,
finally. Nothing fancy, but he didn't need fancy. He
needed freedom, safety, and some peace of mind. With
those requirements satisfied, he could make do.

''Let's go over the hill and get us some breakfast,''
Zane suggested when Martin came back inside. He
didn't know how much the old man understood, but he
knew his uncle would follow him whenever he got ready
to go. Nevertheless it pleased him to carry on this one-
sided conversation, to have someone of his own to talk
to first thing in the morning.

''You think they're up yet over there?'' Zane stuffed
his pickup keys into his front pocket and grabbed his
shirt off the chair. ''I'll be takin' a run down to Rapid
today. Takin' that hot-blooded Arab back to the owner.
I put a nice handle on him now, gave him the full thirty-
day Lone Bull training program. How long do you think
it'll take that Hausauer to ruin him?''

Martin was choosing a threadbare plaid shirt from a
plastic basket full of folded laundry. He rubbed the

saggy seat of his longjohns over his butt cheek, scratching.

Zane laughed. "Yeah, that's what I say. Drugstore cowboy, that one. Don't know why he bothers with the horses. All he needs is the snakeskin boots and the turquoise jewelry. But, hell, he pays good. Long as we get our money, we don't care whether he rides that gelding or cooks him up for dinner."

Martin was concentrating on a stubborn shirt snap.

"I've seen people eat worse stuff than that; I ain't lyin'. There's no limit when it comes to turning the human crank. You name it, there's somebody somewhere . . ." *Who'll eat it.* Wants to eat it. Has to eat it. Has one item on the menu, and whatever it is, it's more than there was the day before. Zane had been there himself, and so had his uncle. He had to think that only one of them remembered.

"So you don't have to worry about any of that, and neither do I anymore. Live our own lives, mind our own business, same-old-same-old, no trouble, no sweat. No blood, either. And no tears." Another clever allusion lost on a man who didn't know rock and roll from church music, but that was part of the beauty of it. When Zane laughed, Martin laughed. He clapped one hand on the old man's back, opened the door, and saluted the greening prairie, the growing intensity of blue in the sky, and the brown dog lolling his tongue at him. "This is paradise, right, Soup?"

The rest of Zane's family lived in a little frame house about half a mile south of the cabin. Way back in the shadow time of his early life, Beatrice Lone Bull, the woman he called Unci, Grandmother, had taken him in. He had some vague memories of a different house and a different place, but Unci had always been there along with her mute son. She'd answered few questions about the other place, but he knew there were family connections to Rosebud and Pine Ridge Reservations. Beatrice had brought her two boys to Standing Rock and moved them all in with the Tusks, her sister Cecilia's family.

The only unusual part was that they never went back, not even to visit.

The cabin he shared with Uncle Martin was the first home he remembered clearly. It had housed a lot of people in those early years before they'd built the frame house. Eventually the numbers had thinned out. Zane had joined the army. Cecilia's husband and one of her daughters had died, and two daughters had left home. But son Randy had a habit of bouncing in and out of the nest, and two grandchildren had taken up residence. Meanwhile, Cecilia and Beatrice stood their ground like two solid tent poles. The family depended on them as surely as they did the allotment of land and the two little houses they'd built on it. But the two women were long past aging. One was old, the other ancient.

"Ain't that right, Uncle?" Zane said as they crested the rise that separated the two houses. "They're old as the hills, but they still make a damn good pot of cowboy coffee. Hey, looks like Randy's back."

Randy Tusk was like a turtle, the way he towed his shelter around. He was the proud owner of a dinky trailer, easy to move with his '55 Ford pickup whenever he felt like taking up residence in town. The little propane heater wasn't too reliable, which often put a crimp in his claim on independence, especially in the winter. Lately he'd taken up the political causes that Zane had championed for a brief, futile time after he'd gotten his discharge. Zane was tired of fighting for lost causes.

The door on the side of the trailer swung open, and Randy tumbled out. He offered Martin a sleepy smile. "How's it goin', Uncle?" Then he turned, and his slender hand was engulfed in Zane's brawnier one. "Hey, Z."

"What've you been up to, little brother?"

Randy's fingers went to work trying to tame his night-wild hair. It had been at least a month since he'd refused Zane's offer of a haircut, saying he was going in for braids, like old Martin. He squinted into the morning sun. "You heard about the latest at Wounded Knee?"

"Nope." It wasn't exactly a lie. It had been almost a

week since Zane had scanned the front page of the *Rapid City Journal*. "I did my time. I got nothing to show for it. You carry a gun for somebody else, I don't care who it is, sooner or later you end up with their spit on your face." He rubbed his chin against his shoulder as if to rid himself of the insult. "I don't much care for the way it tastes."

"There's ways, Z. There's other ways."

"I don't wanna hear about 'em before coffee." The three men headed for the house, where the smoke rising from the chimney signaled warm promise. "I'm goin' down to Rapid, take back that Arab," Zane told Randy. "Wanna come along?"

"Haven't you heard? They don't like Indians down there very much these days."

"First thing I did when I got out of the pen, I took the RED POWER bumper sticker off my pickup.

Randy grinned. Obviously Zane had noticed the new FRYBREAD POWER proclamation pasted on the side of his trailer. "Did that make a difference?"

"Haven't had my tires slashed since."

"Good for you." Randy got the door, and they both stood aside in deference to their elder uncle. "The answer's in the courts, Z."

"Yeah, right." Zane's hand on Randy's thin shoulder forestalled him from following Martin inside. He wanted to let Randy go his own way. He really did. But Randy had mentioned the wrong word. "I've been to court," Zane reminded him quietly. "What could I say but, 'Sure, I busted that asshole's face.' Didn't give a damn about him being a deputy sheriff. He was using Indians for target practice."

Randy grabbed Zane's shirtsleeve. "There are other courts, Z. Other judges."

"That one gave me two years, and I did all but two months of it. I get out, I take a look around, and not one goddamn thing has changed. Jesse's still dead, and nothing we said, nothing we did made any difference. The courts don't work for us. The cops, the feds, the Bureau of Indian Affairs, none of it works for us. The war over in Vietnam made more sense to me. At least there you know why people are shootin' at you. It's because you don't belong there.'' He jerked his chin in the direction of the square-topped buttes on the eastern horizon. "I belong here. I ain't messin' with nobody anymore, and nobody's messin' with me.''

Randy looked up, his face inches from the one he'd been looking up to all his life. "This is a shithole, Z. All we got left is a shithole, but you wait. If somebody decides there's money to be made in shit, they'll be lookin' for a way to take this, too. All I want you to do is talk to Cedric. Listen to what he has to say about challenging some of these real estate titles. Before all these old people die off, if we can just find some—''

"Somebody ought to show you a real shithole.'' Zane sighed, avoiding his brother's eyes. He knew the kind of invitation he'd see there, the enduring willingness to follow him anywhere. "Ah, maybe not.'' He laughed and waggled Randy's shoulder like a rubber bone. "But will you come down out of the clouds once, hey? They'll be callin' you Hits His Head On The Sky.''

The two men laughed. Handing out advice made Zane uncomfortable, and they both knew it. What little he gave went to the man he called his brother, and it was always the same. "You could go to college yourself, Randy. You always liked school. You'd do real good.'' He smirked and wagged his head. "Cedric barely made it through a year of law school, and he thinks he knows it all.''

"I think he's on the right track. I've been checking some of the agency enrollment records, the BIA rolls. Going back a ways, it gets real interesting.''

"Not to me. I ain't listed on no BIA rolls. No state records, nothing. Far as I know, I was never actually born.'' A grin crept slowly into his eyes. "Hatched, maybe. Like a damn rattlesnake.''

"But you never really checked, did you?''

Zane imitated a warning rattle, his eyes glowing with mischief.

Randy shook his head. Family was important to him,

but so were ancestors and origins, words Zane brushed off like corral dust from the seat of his pants. "Maybe you ought to."

Zane shook his head. "Like ol' Beatrice always says, it's no good asking too many questions. So I stopped asking a long time ago."

"You boys get in here and shut the door," Cecilia called out from the kitchen. "You'll be gettin' this ol' grandma's cough started up again."

"What is Auntie Beatrice to you, Z?" Randy asked as he ducked through the doorway. "You ever ask yourself who—"

"We've got the same last name, and she's the only woman who didn't end up throwin' me out on my ear after I'd been around her a while." Zane followed Randy into the dim interior, where the air was heavy with wood smoke and the smell of coffee and two layers of lard—the ghost of last's week's frying and the promise of this morning's.

He grinned at the withered woman who sat by the stove, painstakingly peeling potatoes. Beatrice reminded him of the everlasting pile of rummage in the church basement, wrinkles in a hundred shades of brown and gray. "Ain't that right, Old Woman?" he asked her vacant eyes good-naturedly as he adjusted her sweater over her shoulder. "You stuck by me. Guess I can do the same for you." He glanced at Randy. "It's like talking to Uncle Martin. I don't know if I'm gettin' through to either one of them anymore."

Randy shrugged. "I knew my dad's background because he was from here, but I went down to Pine Ridge—"

"Jesus, Randy." Zane shook his head. "It's hotter than hell down there now, and I ain't talkin' about the weather. They've got Wounded Knee surrounded by weekend warriors just itchin' for combat ribbons."

Randy shrugged off the warning and strode into the kitchen, sidestepping the mattress in the corner of the front room where the two grandchildren were peacefully nestled under a pile of star quilts. He greeted Cecilia, who paused in her preparation of unleavened skillet bread to give her son a prune-lipped peck. He was more interested in the big white enamel pot of coffee on the stove.

He handed Zane the first cup. "I went to the agency, not to Wounded Knee. Couldn't get in, anyway. They've got that whole area blocked off. But I heard that some of your old friends are there, holed up behind some kind of makeshift barricade."

"Yeah, well I wish them luck." The good kind, he added mentally, if there was any around for those who stuck their heads up in the air when they heard gunfire. He'd stood his ground shoulder to shoulder with some of the people he figured to be at the Knee. He'd gone to Southeast Asia to defend everybody's so-called inalienable rights. He'd come home to South Dakota, tried to defend the same rights, and found out what it meant to be alienated. He tapped a fist on Randy's shoulder. "But more than that, I wish you'd stay out of it."

Randy sipped noisily at his coffee. "You ever wonder why that woman has no land?" He nodded in Beatrice's direction. She was just sitting there, hunched over a half-red, half-white potato. "No lease checks coming in. Nothing."

"She sold it, long time ago," Cecilia put in as she turned the slab of heavy bread in the big, black skillet.

"Uncle Martin doesn't seem to have any, either," Randy persisted. "His father must've died pretty young, and he was from Pine Ridge, right? You'd think Uncle would be getting lease checks from Pine Ridge."

"Before the Indian Reorganization Act, they used to be able to sell allotted land outright. They needed money, sold the land." Zane cocked a reproving eyebrow. "You ever heard of the Depression, Randy? The Dirty Thirties? *Everybody* was poor then. Even white people. The ol' lady did what she had to do, whatever that was. Right, Auntie?"

Cecilia moved the skillet off the stove.

"If he got land from his dad, you think she could have sold it? You think they'd let her?" Randy asked.

"Don't give him any of that." Zane favored his aunt with a conspiratorial wink as she handed him a plate for his breakfast. "He needs a lesson in what it means to go hungry. You really spoiled him bad, Auntie."

Cecilia giggled like a young girl.

Randy took the pancake turner out of his mother's hand and filled his own plate. "I've been checkin' some of this stuff out, hey. I think some of those sales weren't really sales at all. And I'm thinkin' if the right kind of lawyer gets hold of the right kind of records . . ."

"I don't even wanna hear about it," Zane said. Randy glared, affronted, and Zane responded with an upraised palm. "Hey, I've done my time. I deserve a life, for crissake."

"Who doesn't?"

"Nobody." Zane took a stab at conciliation. "Everybody deserves to do a little livin' once in a while. So let's you and me go down to Rapid and kick up our heels tonight."

"You can have Rapid. I've got places to go, people to see."

Zane shrugged as he carved up his skillet bread, trying to remember a time when he might have said the same thing. He understood the feeling of discontent, the need to be on the move, the readiness to fight, but Randy was probably more particular about his battleground than Zane had been, and he probably had a better idea of who his enemies really were. Zane hadn't always been too fussy.

"If I can come up with the kind of records I'm talkin' about, some kind of proof . . ." Randy set his plate on the table and stood next to his chair, waiting for Zane to glance up from his food. "If I do, will you even look at it? Just take a look?" He dragged the folding chair away from the little Formica table and sat down, pressing his face close to Zane's, like an unrelenting pup. "Just take me seriously for once."

Take me with you, Randy had pleaded once when Zane was home on leave. *Tell them I'm old enough. They'll believe you.*

"Take a look for what?"

Randy shrugged. "For the hell of it."

"The hell of it is"—Zane used his fork to drive his point in Randy's direction—"it won't matter. Get that through your head; you'll save yourself a whole lot of trouble."

"Can't." Randy scooted his chair over, lining himself up with his plate. "I gotta pick up where you left off. We're warriors, remember?"

"I hung up my guns, little brother. Ain't feedin' you no more fairy tales, no more pipe dreams. This is it." He poured a dollop of corn syrup on his blue plate and dipped a forkful of bread into it. "I've seen worse. Believe me."

"I never thought they'd kick the fight out of Zane Lone Bull."

"Don't give me that hangdog look." Zane laughed. "All right, then, go on. Bring me your paper dragon, *misunka*," he said, addressing him indulgently as his younger brother. "I'll tear off its wings for you."

"Nah, you'd rather go down to Rapid and get yourself laid. Or screwed." Randy gestured for the surrender of the syrup. "Which is it?"

Zane slid the bottle across the table, his cold glance warning the younger man off the subject. There were certain aspects of his life that were not open for discussion, not even to Randy. Military life had taught him to value his privacy. Prison life had driven him to guard it like a hellhound.

"Just kidding," Randy mumbled. "I'll be staying around for a while. Maybe I'll have something to show you when you get back."

Head held high, the leggy gray gelding circled the corral as if he were practicing for a performance. Zane watched him in the side mirror as he backed the trailer up to the gate. He preferred a horse with more chest, but he liked the Arab's style. He didn't mind riding a good horse for somebody else, but he planned to be training his own registered stock someday.

At the top of the big mirror the reflection of Zane's would-be helpers appeared on the hill. Nine-year-old Sissy and her seven-year-old brother Jojo would add a few minutes to his departure time, but what the hell? Zane was back to living on Indian time. His little niece and nephew were already tumbling down the well-worn path, racing to see who could get to him first. He'd have to find a task for each of them or he'd have a fight on his hands.

Randy's sister, Chickie, had dumped the kids off on their grandmother shortly after Zane had been released from the pen, which was over a year ago. She'd promised to come back and get them before school started. They'd only seen her twice since then, and both times her parting comments had started with "next time I come back . . ."

Zane wondered if Chickie knew what she was missing. Maybe she really believed her own bullshit. To some extent he supposed everybody did. But it wasn't right to feed it to the kids.

He took the halter and lead rope off the pickup seat and greeted the pair with a broad grin as they came running to him. "You guys wanna help me load this big, bad broomtail into the trailer? He's goin' home today."

They jostled for position, but Sissy managed to outreach her brother for the halter. Jojo grabbed her arm with one hand and a handful of her black ponytail with the other.

Zane pulled them apart. "Leave her alone, Jojo. I told her not to be fightin' you, and that goes both ways."

"I wanna put the halter on," the boy whined.

"You can lead him over to the trailer." He flipped the lid on the toolbox he'd built in the back of his pickup and produced a wooden brush. "I want him to look real nice when his owner sees him. Somebody could brush him for me."

"I will!"

"I will!"

"Lucky thing I've got two brushes and the horse has two sides."

The gelding had come to Zane broke to ride but bad-mannered, like some rich man's kid. Zane looked the animal in the eye as he approached. From the first he'd respected the Arab's intelligence, and in one month the horse had learned to trust Zane's soft-spoken commands and his big, gentle hands. The horse stood quietly, allowing its trainer to claim mastery by hooking an arm around its sleek, arched neck.

"I could comb his tail out, Uncle Zane," Sissy offered as she slipped the halter over the gray's ears.

"Be sure and watch out he doesn't kick you."

Zane lit a cigarette and stepped back to let the two children show him what they'd learned. He was learning, too. The part of his life he'd spent in the army and in prison had been devoid of children. It was like fourteen years of winter. The worst part was, a guy got used to it. He supposed it was like any other rut. Sterile as it was, the routine became treacherously comfortable.

"Get his belly, too, but watch his ears."

"If he lays them back, he's gettin' mad," Sissy recounted dutifully.

" 'Atta girl."

They went by their mother's last name. Footloose Chickie had never been married and didn't want to be. Cecilia and her brood were all Tusks. Zane was a Lone Bull only because Beatrice had taken him in. She wouldn't talk about his father, although he suspected she knew who he was. She'd shown him a picture of his mother once, a long time ago, and then she'd secreted the moldy old photograph away, which meant it was probably lost. The old woman couldn't remember much of anything anymore.

He remembered the little spots on the woman's face in the sepia-tone portrait. "Silver tears," Beatrice had said. Woman-talk, Zane judged. Even then—he figured he'd been about Jojo's age—he'd known it was nothing that fancy, just mildew. What had happened to her? Did she run away? Did she die? What?

The old woman had offered him no more clues. Only
the curling photograph of a white woman. She'd *looked*
white, at least in the picture. He figured she'd gotten
herself knocked up by an Indian guy and didn't want
anyone to know. Getting into a fix like that was probably
a whole lot worse back in the Dirty Thirties than it was
in the Age of Aquarius. The guy was probably related
to Beatrice somehow, or maybe he was some kind of
dissident or criminal. A bloodline that wasn't worth
claiming.

Or maybe Beatrice really didn't know. As far as she
was concerned she had two sons, the younger one an
abandoned half-breed who called her grandmother, the
older one a retarded mute who couldn't call her anything. "It's no good asking too many questions," this
woman who'd raised him had often said. "They might
take you away. They can do that any time they want.
Got to be real careful."

And she had been. Whatever secrets she'd once
known were long since forgotten. Zane had decided it
was better that way. There was no changing the past.
No use bucking history. Since time had a way of trans-
forming a schemer into a visionary, one generation's
deeds and misdeeds easily became the next generation's
treasured legacy. Who needed the sordid truth? Not Zane
Lone Bull, not anymore.

Ask me no questions, I'll tell you no lies.

Good advice. He'd learned it at the knee of a woman
who was already old and wise when she took him in,
and now he'd lived long enough to understand what
damn good advice it truly was. The past was a load of
crap. Nightmares and regrets. He'd committed enough
of his own misdeeds. What little past he had was plenty.

And the future? Hell, that was whatever went down
between daybreak and nightfall. It was what Uncle Martin greeted with his song. Over in 'Nam guys had it
down to so many days and a wake-up. In the joint guys
did so many calendars. Zane didn't own a watch, and
he didn't use a calendar. He used his head. If he'd managed to stay alive and hang on to his sanity from day-

break to nightfall, he figured he was doing okay.

Nowadays he was doing better than okay. He was free to go. He could walk as far as he wanted to in any direction. He could get on a horse and ride, hop in his pickup and drive. Just go whenever he wanted to go. Do whatever he wanted to do. The only thing he'd ever been much good at, besides shooting off his mouth or his gun and generally raising hell, was breaking and training horses. He'd taken up beading and leather work when he was in the pen, and people said he was pretty good at that, too.

Making a living with such talents hadn't struck him as a likely prospect when he'd finally been handed his parole, but with the help of Rapid City western wear shop owner Marla Ferrell he was doing just that. She'd introduced him to the kind of people who paid him real cash money to teach their spoiled horses some manners. Her store was a good outlet for his belts, jewelry, and beaded tack, and when he felt like hanging out in town for a night or two, she was willing to share her bed. She asked him no questions, he told her no lies. It worked out fine.

The Hausauer place was just north of Rapid City, a picturesque spot with a view of the Black Hills, which formed a jagged blue-black buttress for the southwestern sky. It had once been a cattle ranch, but there wasn't a cow in sight along the two miles of gravel road that led to the brand-new two-story house. Zane passed the driveway and swung around the house toward the pristine outbuildings, which included an indoor arena. Zane envied the Hausauers their facilities, thinking it was a shame they were going to waste. The big white barn was the only one serving any apparent function. Two horses stood in one of the corrals outside. Zane had just backed the trailer close to the steel corral gate when he saw the old man emerge from the house.

The Hausauer patriarch was the only real cowboy in the family. He was still shaped for the saddle, but the way the joints were rusted in the old man's hips and bowed legs, Zane figured Butch would need a crane to get him seated.

"My son ain't here," Butch reported as he watched Zane back the gelding out of the trailer, smooth as silk. "Was he expecting you today?"

"I don't know. The deal was thirty days' training, and that's what it's been."

Butch shoved his gnarled hands into the pockets of his quilted jacket and peered past the brim of his brown Stetson. "Did he pay you up front?"

"Half."

"I'll take care of the rest if you want to show me what he can do now. This one's all looks and no brains if you ask me."

Zane nodded and handed Butch the lead rope. "He's touchy." He hauled his saddle out of the back of the pickup. "Head shy for some reason. He'll take the bit, but you gotta go real easy with the headstall."

"Bill hasn't got much patience. He wants to be able to put a key in the ignition and take off. You and me, we know it don't work that way."

Zane nodded again. As long as the old man was willing to pay him, it was just as well Bill Jr. wasn't around. He'd rather deal with someone who had the experience to appreciate what he'd accomplished. He saddled up the gray, rode him into an empty pen, and put him through his paces, moving him easily through his gaits, reining him through tight turns, backing him from one end of the pen to the other, all for the old rancher's amusement.

"I'm a quarter horse man myself," Zane said as he brought the gelding to an abrupt stop a foot short of the old man's well-worn boots. Butch didn't budge. "But this guy's sure fast, and he won't play out on you."

"He's never handled that good, I'll tell you."

"You've got that right." Zane swung down from the saddle and offered the reins. "Like to give him a try?"

"My arthritis is actin' up again. Could mean rain. We could use a nice spring rain." Butch rubbed his elbow absently as he scanned the cloudless blue sky. "Old cattleman's habit, I guess. Wishing for rain. My boys don't have much of a taste for it."

"Rain?"

"Ranching. The spread I started out with is down southeast of here. Down around Pine Ridge and Rosebud." Butch squinted up at Zane, studying him for something. "I 'spose you know that country pretty well."

Zane glanced toward the Hills and gave a noncommittal shrug. "I'm from Standing Rock."

"I was thinking there were some Lone Bulls down where we're from."

"I suppose you'd find a *lone bull* in just about any pasture you wanted to visit this time of year. All kinds of bulls around here, huh?" Zane smiled, thinking it was too bad Randy hadn't come along. He would have offered the old man a more serious response.

But Zane's joke was lost on Butch, who, like Randy, wanted to nail down those connections. "Lone Bull rings a bell. 'Course, I know a lot of them people down there. Have for years. Good cowboys there." He handed Zane several twenty dollar bills. "Like you. Indians always did make damn good cowboys."

Zane pocketed the money without looking at it. The old man wasn't likely to try to shortchange him. "You tell Bill to let me know if he wants me to take on any more. Can't take too many at a time, and I've got quite a few lined up."

"Blooded horses are about the only livestock he's interested in these days. Keeps talkin' about land deals and mineral rights." Butch shook his head, surveying the grounds as though taking inventory. "You build something solid, you turn it over to your kids when you think you've been workin' hard long enough and it's time to take it easy, you'd think they'd appreciate it and hang on to it at least." He gave a disgusted snort. "But, hell, they don't know the value. They don't understand the sacrifices you've made."

"Kids these days, huh?" Zane dumped his saddle back in the pickup bed. "That's too bad."

"Maybe you'd be interested in coming to work for us."

The old man made it sound like a genuine offer, but Zane knew better. Bill Jr. was running the show these days. "I don't think so. Sounds like your operation's pretty much up in the air." Zane offered a handshake. "Besides, I got a family to look after, and this is too far from home."

Zane parked his pickup and trailer in the alley behind Boots and Saddles, Marla Ferrell's upscale Western shop, and dragged half a dozen beaded breast collars off the bench seat. Four of them were on order, which meant he'd be leaving town pretty cashy this trip.

Marla squealed like a pig headed for mud the minute he walked into the shop. Anticipating her next play, he filled her arms with his beadwork. He'd let her put her hands on him later.

She smiled, disconcerted only momentarily. "Didn't you bring me any belts? I sold the last one to a woman from Denver. She called and wants four more."

"I got tired of making belts."

"The temperamental craftsman," she cooed, tapping his chest with a long pink fingernail. "So difficult." She flashed him a coy smile as she set the breast collars on the shelf behind the display case full of silver trophy buckles. "Such a turn-on."

He knew his engaging wink would go a long way.

She directed his attention to a tall glass case containing some of his work. He'd found ways to make strings of beads look like cascades of water. Plenty of time to experiment with stuff like that in the joint. Marla called it an art, and she'd had a sign made using a facsimile of his blocky signature, as if he were some kind of celebrity.

"See, I put your picture in the display. The one I took that time we rode to the top of Harney Peak. That deliciously dark look of yours says it all. Brooding artist who sees through the eyes into the soul." She opened a drawer and produced an envelope, handing it to him with a flourish. "And I raised the prices, which is reflected in the amount of your check. Most of your buyers are women, you know."

He shrugged as he tucked the envelope into his shirt pocket. "Most of the waist sizes haven't sounded too promising."

"Gifts for their husbands, crafted by someone they want to fantasize about. Supper's on me." She headed for the front of the shop, casting him a Mae West look over her shoulder. "After that I have a fantasy of my own I'd like to try out on you."

He chuckled. "Did you find a black-and-white pinto yet?" She was always talking about the TV Westerns she'd followed. *Bonanza* was her favorite. Zane hadn't seen much TV. His cowboy heroes rode the big silver screen.

"Not one with the exact same markings as Little Joe's. These things must be done right." She flipped the red CLOSED sign that hung in the window, then turned to him, smiling. "But there's no end to my fantasies, and they all involve getting you naked."

"God, you're shameless, Marla."

"I have nothing to be ashamed of." She locked the door. "I'm going to Albuquerque early next week on a buying trip. Wanna ride shotgun?"

Bracing his elbows on the display case, he watched her put her shop to bed a little early, clearing counters and straightening displays, rising on booted tiptoe to return a hat to its peg, angling for a quick assessment of her short, dark hair and her bright makeup as she passed a full-length mirror. She was attractive in a hard-edged way, the same way he was. There was a chiseled leanness about her that was more than physical and that struck him as a female version of his own sum and substance, with no soft parts of any kind. If she'd been born a few years earlier they could have been twins, maybe.

It was an irrational notion, but it disgusted him.

Abruptly he pushed away from the glass box. "That picture is the closest you'll ever come to showing me off to your business friends again. I feel like shark bait around those people.''

"They think you're refreshingly straightforward, exotic and''—she gave him that licentious smile again—"a little dangerous, which is very exciting.''

"Why do you get such a kick out of telling people I'm an ex-con?''

"Because I know it doesn't embarrass you, and it's such a wonderful conversation starter.''

"How do you know it doesn't embarrass me?''

"Nothing embarrasses you. You don't care what anyone thinks. That, among other things, is what I like about you.''

Neither her complacency nor the fact that she missed the point of his question surprised him, but he had to work at distancing himself from a vague feeling of displeasure, a troublesome aversion to the cool impudence in her eyes.

She slipped her arms around his waist and looked up at him invitingly. "What do you like about me?''

He offered a sardonic smile. "Your sensitivity.''

"Don't you mean my honesty? We both want the same thing, so why play games?''

"You're right. That's what I like about you.'' He was too old for games. "If supper's on you, I'm havin' steak.''

"I know just the place.'' She slid her hands over the back pockets of his jeans. "I'm easy, but never cheap.''

They went to a reputable steak house and had to wait in the bar for a table. Zane hadn't eaten since breakfast. The aroma of grilled meat expanded the hollowness in his gut. He laid claim to a bowl of peanuts. He didn't drink much anymore, but he was on his second beer and feeling fairly mellow when Bill Hausauer appeared at their table and magnanimously claimed that the next round was on him.

"The ol' man says you really did a nice job with that gelding. I'm anxious to try him out.'' Bill hooked his thumbs in his belt and took a wide, territorial stance. An easy smile brightened his baby-pink face. He had the look of a man who spent a lot of money he'd done nothing to earn. Chunky jewelry, spotless white Stetson, western-cut clothes that no real cowboy would wear. His hands reminded Zane of soft white bread dough. "He paid you what you needed?"

"And then some. You got yourself a real nice colt."

"If he handles good, I can probably throw some more work your way. I'll put in a good word for you with some people I know. How would that be?"

"Tell them to get in touch with Marla. My schedule's gettin' pretty tight." Zane tipped the neck of the brown bottle and let a long draught slide down his throat.

"Oh, yeah?" Hausauer chuckled. "Well, that's real good. Keeps you busy, and staying busy keeps a guy out of trouble. Too bad those bucks down at Wounded Knee haven't got nothin' better to do than take over some little church and insult the American flag by turning it upside down."

"That's not an insult," Zane said quietly. The surrounding bar talk bubbling over the steel guitars was beginning to get to him. "It's a distress signal."

"Looks like an insult to me. What do you mean, distress signal? They started the trouble themselves."

"An upside down flag is a military distress signal. You look healthy enough, Bill. Did our Selective Service pass you up?" Bill dismissed the notion with a guffaw. Zane figured old Butch had a friend on the draft board. "Well, even if you'd been a Boy Scout . . ."

"I don't really give a damn what they do down there. They're only hurting their own people. I know lots of good Indian people who don't want nothin' to do with that AIM bunch. I get along with Indians just fine."

"Zane was over in Vietnam," Marla put in.

"Fought for your country," Bill observed almost appreciatively.

Zane wished the man would either sit down or move on. He didn't like having people stand over him.

Bill elevated himself on the balls of his feet.

Zane glanced down at the unscarred alligator wing tips on the man's cowboy boots.

Bill's heels sank back to the floor. "I went to high school with some Indian boys who went over there. Couple of 'em didn't come back. Those are the guys they dishonor when they show disrespect for the flag. Guys like you." He noticed a waitress dressed in a little cheerleader skirt and gave her an imperious high sign. "Hey, bring this table another round, honey. This man is a goddamn war hero." He wagged a pale, chunky finger under Zane's nose. "I'll be sending you some more horses for sure."

Zane ignored Hausauer's friendly parting gesture as he drained the last of his beer. He set it down with a resolute *thunk*. "Let's get out of here."

"But what about—"

Zane smiled as he scraped the floor with his chair legs. "I'll show you what I can do with a good fire and anything that's raw."

Marla's eyes brightened. "The mind boggles."

Zane woke up in the early morning hours. Rain splattered on the pavement outside the bedroom window, but he realized that it was the noise Marla made in her sleep that woke him. It was halfway between purring and snoring, a grating sound that pushed him closer to the window and the patter of the rain. He decided he'd sooner wake up to poor old Martin's tortured moans than this woman's snooze tune. He wasn't sure why.

Business had been good, food tasty, sex adequate, all thanks to Marla. But since he'd slept all he could, he was ready to leave. And she was easy to leave, which was the only part that bothered him. He really wanted to *want* to stay, to feel some regret as he eased himself from her bed, not, he realized, out of consideration for her peaceful state, but out of a lack of need for any parting words. Or touches. She'd touched him all he wanted her to. He carefully claimed his clothes from a mixed pile, shaking hers away without handling them. He got dressed in the bathroom and left the apartment with hat in hand. He wanted to feel the cold, cleansing rain on his face.

He liked cold water. It woke him up, made him feel alive and alert. It felt good to leave the lights of the city behind, roll the pickup window down, and smell the infusion of rain and South Dakota clay. Back roads were the only roads here, threading the way between huge pieces of prairie like a quilter's running stitch. Zane found comfort in the vastness of it, a sense of infinite privacy. If he turned on the radio, he'd find only static. It was either too late or too early, and he was beyond the reach of most signals. Quiet sounded good. He was almost home.

Gray dawn drifted reluctantly over the jagged horizon. A light drizzle gathered on the windshield. Zane slowed down when he saw the light at the side of the road. The headlights looked like bewildered eyes cocked askew on the slope of the ditch. It didn't surprise him when he got close enough to recognize Randy's pickup. Zane had offered a loan toward the purchase of tires with a little more tread. Randy had said he was working on a trade with somebody, but he'd obviously pushed those baldies beyond the limit.

Zane parked on the gravel shoulder, stretched his back as he emerged from the pickup, adjusted his hat to shed the drizzle, and headed across the road. He wasn't eager to find his brother passed out on the front seat. Not that he hadn't been there himself a time or two, but once the party was over, so were the laughs. The passenger door hung open on the far side, but he didn't see anybody in the cab. Johnny Cash was singing "Folsom Prison Blues" for a pair of wet crows perched on the right-of-way fence. If Randy was working on a remedy, he was sure trying to top off his blowout with a dead battery.

"Where's the owner of this piece of junk?" Zane demanded officiously. "The wrecker's here, so get your ass in gear." He reached through the open window on the driver's side, hit the lights, and shut off the radio. Then he noticed the keys in the ignition. Then the blood on the split vinyl seat. His skin tightened at the back of his neck as if somebody had opened a door behind him and walked out, abandoning him to the cold. He stared at the blood, then followed its trail slowly, moving only his eyes. Zane knew blood when he saw it, blood from a wound, a bad one. He knew death when he smelled it. In the shadowy grass beyond the open door a scuffed boot toe pointed skyward.

"Jesus."

Zane's throat sealed up like a zipper. Morning shadows narrowed his field of vision. All he could see was the boot. His first thought was that it was past time his little brother had a new pair. The sole was almost worn through.

He pushed away from the closed door and headed for the open one, absently wondering whose legs were carrying him. In his head he called on God, but he couldn't open his mouth, couldn't say his brother's name until he saw his lifeless face.

❧ 2 ❧

Zane had been planted in the church basement near the foot of the coffin since the previous night's community feed. From his vantage point he could keep an eye on everybody and stay close to the body without actually looking at it. Cecilia had insisted on putting her son's remains on display even though much of the lower left side of the face had been blown away. The undertaker had fixed it up with a bandage and arranged the corpse so that viewers saw mainly the right side. Most people refrained from doing too much rubbernecking. They'd seen their share of murdered Indians.

Zane couldn't get past his initial urge to transform himself into some kind of protective cover for his brother, even though no more harm could have been done. He hadn't wanted anyone else to see what he had seen, the pulpy, purple flesh, the cheekbone exposed, the sightless, fish-eyed stare, all starkly bared to the cleansing rain. Whenever he closed his eyes he saw it all again. He felt the cold drizzle, heard his own pulse thudding in his ears.

"Rain In The Face," Zane had heard distantly, as though someone else were speaking, mocking his voice as he knelt in the wet ditch grass. "What are you doing, getting yourself soaked out here? What happened?" He'd laid his hand over his brother's eyes and counted the bullet wounds. Face, chest, gut. "Who did this, *misunka*? Did you see? Did you know?" Then, softly, close to the bloody ear. "Did you suffer long?" And then, more woefully, more dramatically than he would have thought he had a heart for, "Oh, God, how much did you let him suffer?"

Too much. Randy had managed to get himself out of the pickup, but somebody had taken the time to make sure the job was done and done and done.

Randy the Runt. A premature baby and a sickly kid for half his life, he'd defended himself with the threat that his brother would avenge him. "When Z finds out. When Z gets back. You want a big Z carved on your ass?" He'd always had too much mouth and not enough muscle.

The Indian cops were on the scene first, but the FBI was called in immediately. The reservation was their jurisdiction whenever a felony was committed. Agent Obi Flynn had made a list of names. Friends, relatives, people Randy had worked with before he'd gotten laid off from his last job at a gas station in McLaughlin. Flynn hadn't been too concerned when nobody could name any enemies. He was more interested in the friends and relatives, anyway, especially those who had been in trouble before. Like Zane. Zane's friend, police sergeant Gabriel Star from Rosebud Reservation, had told him confidently that Randy had not been murdered by a kinsman. "I'd bet money," Gabe had said. "He didn't have anybody around here gunnin' for him like that."

Agent Flynn was taking names, but Zane would be surprised if any ass got kicked.

A shadow fell across the crack he'd been studying in the cement floor. He glanced up and found himself smiling. Cecilia was bringing him more coffee, her every step focused on avoiding a spill. He reached for a folding chair and dragged it up close. "You don't have to bring coffee every time you wanna sit next to me, Auntie."

"Nobody else wants any."

"Pilama," he said, thanking her as he took the cup

carefully from her hands. Their shared need had nothing to do with coffee. She knew that no one else felt her loss the way he did.

"All he ever wanted was to be like you," she said as she eased her squat, barrel-shaped body into the chair. She had been dogging him with reminiscences, pitching them out randomly. There was no need to connect them together. Zane took each piece as it came, acknowledging it with a nod. "When you were fighting in the war, he tried to enlist," she said distantly.

The glass mug warmed Zane's palms. "He never told me that."

"He was ashamed because they wouldn't take him." Her memory sounded flat, devoid of any emotion her son's disappointment might once have stimulated. "He couldn't pass the physical."

"He's just lucky he didn't. I'd have given him a real swift . . ."

Zane glanced over his shoulder at the folded hands in the coffin. So Randy had been 4-F. He'd never known that. Never asked. Fuckin' 4-F, the GIs had called Randy's kind. Only Randy would have offered to trade his draft status for one of theirs, and plenty of guys would have taken him up on it. An M-16 would have looked like a rocket launcher in those waxen hands.

They'd always been slight for a man's hands, but now they looked fragile, like the hands of a Japanese doll Zane had seen in a shop once. Every once in a while the chest in the coffin seemed to rise, as though on a breath. He knew his eyes were playing tricks on him, but he'd begun to torment himself by willingly embracing the illusion.

Zane shook his head. "He was too smart for that. He would've made a damn fine lawyer, teacher, you name it."

"Whatever you did was what he wanted to do. He was always telling people how his brother was a sergeant, and that it was the sergeants who were really in charge of the army."

"Sounds like something I might have said once." He

noted the grease slick floating in his lukewarm coffee. "In another life."

"Another life," Cecilia echoed. She leaned forward, peeking past Zane for a look at her son. "I won't mind much when it's my turn."

"I will, if yours comes before mine." With a jerk of his chin he indicated Beatrice and Martin, who sat against the far wall, side by side. Martin was gnawing on a piece of frybread while Beatrice dozed, chin to chest. "You think they really understand what's happened?"

"She didn't want to leave the house, but I hated to leave her there alone. When I told her you and Martin had already gone, then she came on." Cecilia nodded thoughtfully. "She understands enough so she's sure scared."

"Yeah, they both are. All those cops trying to ask them a bunch of questions, barkin' up the wrong tree, as usual."

"It don't matter. Whatever they do, it won't change nothing. Now look at those two," she said, directing his attention to Jojo, who was ducking in and out of the stairwell, jabbing at Sissy, then daring her to catch him. "Pretty soon he'll be crying."

"Jojo, come here at once," Zane said. The boy grinned, ran a few steps in place, revving up, then scampered across the room, circling chairs and skirting adult legs. Two feet short of his goal he stubbed his rubber-capped toe and tripped into Zane's waiting hands. "Your sister's gonna whack you good if you don't quit doing that. Aren't there some kids playing baseball outside?"

The boy braced himself between Zane's knees. "Yeah, but they make me stand way out there, and they won't let me bat."

"They will if I tell them."

"I don't wanna play baseball. I wanna ride horse."

"I don't have a horse here for you to ride. Want a gum?"

Jojo shook his head.

Zane tucked a green package into the side pocket of

the boy's handed-down jeans. "Well, here, keep it for when you do. Maybe if you give those kids some of that, you can play."

"I don't wanna play with those guys. They called me—" Jojo stretched his neck to whisper a confidence. Zane directed him toward his left ear, where his eardrum was still intact. "They called me little pee-pee boy," Jojo whispered.

"Should we think of something to call them?"

Jojo nodded vigorously as he suspended himself between his uncle's thighs, which served nicely as parallel bars.

Zane covered the small, soft hands with his big callused ones. "What do they sound like when they run their mouths like that?"

The boy rolled his eyes as though it might help him think up something really good. "I know what they *smell* like."

"Wha . . . what does *he* want?"

Jojo turned to see what had caught Zane's attention. "That's the FBI agent," the boy said, pleased to be able to identify the man who was standing in the stairwell doorway. "He wears a gun under his jacket."

The man's beckoning gaze fell on Zane.

"How do you know?" Zane asked Jojo quietly as he rose from his chair. He didn't like being summoned by a cop, but he liked the idea of the agent's presence at this particular gathering even less.

"He showed me." Jojo pointed vaguely in the direction of the churchyard. "Just a while ago outside. Want me to ask him if you can see it?"

Zane patted the boy's shoulder. "Grandma's gonna get you some Kool-Aid, okay?"

"I don't want—" A sharp look from his uncle ended Jojo's protest. "Okay, but I'm gonna be peein' in red pretty soon."

"Jeez, no shame, that guy." Zane pulled another pack of gum from his pocket. "Give this to your sister."

Obi Flynn shoved his hands into his pockets and

stepped inside the door as Zane moved in and cut off
his approach to the coffin.

"He looks real good, considering," Flynn offered,
craning his slim neck slightly. "Don't know why you'd
want to keep the lid open with all these kids around,
but"—he shrugged, turning on a smug smile—"you
people have your own way of doing things, that's for
sure."

"You came to show us a better way, did you?"

Zane stood his ground, blocking a closer look, protecting his brother's privacy even though he knew Flynn
and others had already invaded that to the satisfaction
of any curiosity that came with their territory. They'd
kept the body and held the funeral plans in limbo. But
now that his brother's corpse was in his charge, Zane
stood guard. Flynn would not be invited to pay his respects when Zane knew the man had none.

Flynn waved off the suggestion. "No, no, I don't
mean to interfere. Couple things I wanted to ask you
about is all."

Zane didn't move, didn't blink.

"I know it's a bad time, but I've got a job to do, and
I'm sure you're just as anxious as I am—"

"Get to the point."

"Well, it's about this letter . . ." Flynn glanced over
his shoulder, sliding one fidgety hand over the widely
separated ribbons of brown hair that clung to his scalp.
"Can we maybe go upstairs? I never could handle funerals."

"You picked a strange line of work, then."

"Death is a fact of life. That's not what bothers me.
It's all the—"

Zane led the agent upstairs and out the little white
clapboard church's modest front door. The baseball
players' voices drifted from the backyard on cool April
morning air. The hills surrounding the little town of
Bullhead wore a new spring green mantle, dappled by
moving cloud shadows. The meadowlarks tweedled
cheerfully.

Zane rested his backside against the wooden railing

next to the steps and folded his arms. "Is this better?"

"Yeah." Flynn squinted as a thin cloud shroud slid eastward, unveiling the sun. He smoothed his striped tie, then slipped his hand inside his suit jacket. Zane was tempted to warn that he wasn't as easy to impress as his young nephew, but the man withdrew a pack of Kools. "I'm not much of a churchgoer, I guess."

Zane declined the proffered cigarette with a shake of his head, a direct stare. He had no desire to smoke with this man.

"You and me, we've been down this road before, as I recall. With me lookin' for answers and you holding out." A cigarette now bobbed between Flynn's thin lips. He flicked open a sleek steel lighter. "You never told me all you knew that time, either, and you were the only one we managed to nail."

"*Convict,* you mean, even though the *deputy sheriff*"—Zane glared at Flynn, his tone mocking the designation—"or whatever the hell it was they were calling Gunderson, he had it comin'. But Jesse Strikes was the one who got *nailed* pretty good."

"That was a real tough call. That deputy had every reason to believe she was armed."

"I was armed," Zane said, recalling one of the charges against him. "I could have blown the sonuvabitch away."

"Why didn't you?" Flynn eyed him through a veil of smoke. It was an odd look that seemed to accuse Zane of shirking his duty.

Zane looked away. "I didn't think he'd shoot her. I threw down my weapon. I told her . . ." He chuckled mirthlessly, remembering his brief bout with infectious idealism. "I thought I was back in the land of the free, the home of the Lakota brave, where some sort of rules applied. You surrender, the shooting is supposed to stop." He glanced back at Flynn. "I figured Wounded Knee was past history."

"It is. It oughta be. You people wanna demonstrate, fine. Take a lesson from the college kids. Have a sit-in someplace. Give everybody a flower. You people, you've gotta take over Alcatraz or a federal building right in the middle of DC, or Wounded Knee, for crissake.'' Flynn gestured with his cigarette. "In your case, a courthouse. You carry guns, people are bound to get hurt. You of all people should know that, Lone Bull. I know what your military record was like. Now you've ruined that with a prison record, which is a crying shame, but you people have a way of doing that. You just can't—'' The cigarette hand gestured again in apparent exasperation, as though Flynn were lecturing a kid who'd let him down. "What do you think they're gonna accomplish down there at Pine Ridge? What can they possibly—''

"Nothing." Zane's tone was as expressionless as his eyes. "That's my expert opinion on that one, Flynn. Now what about this job you have to do?''

"I'm not so sure they're not related somehow.''

"What's related?''

"That business at Wounded Knee and your brother's murder. Down there you've got the traditionals and the protesters against Chairman Wilson and the legitimate tribal government. It's Indians killing Indians," Flynn said matter-of-factly. "That's what a case like this usually boils down to, too. They get to partying, and somebody accuses somebody of sleeping with his woman, and pretty soon they're chasing each other down the road, shooting out each other's tires. This time . . .''

Zane's gut knotted. He tightened his grip on the railing until the corners of the wood dug into his hands. "I didn't smell any booze.''

Flynn spat a stream of smoke toward the far hills. "Don't imagine you would. It was a very messy scene. Very messy.''

"What do you want here, Flynn? My brother is dead. You kept his body for nearly two weeks. You did your tests. Did you find alcohol in his blood, or what?''

"Inconclusive.''

"What's that supposed to mean? You don't have an open-and-shut case of drunken Indians killing each other off?''

"There's no such thing as an open-and-shut case." Flynn dropped his cigarette on the cement step and ground it beneath his dusty black shoe. "He wasn't really your brother, was he? More like a cousin or something."

"Like you said, we have our own ways."

"Why didn't you take the deal we offered you, Lone Bull? You could have saved yourself some hard time and me some trouble. There was damage to that courthouse, there was theft of public records, there was—"

"Murder," Zane added quietly. "Jesse's brother had been beaten to death by three rednecks who turned out to be Duane Gunderson's friends. They got off with aggravated assault in that same courthouse. We were trying to say that we didn't think it was quite right." Zane looked down at the toes of his boots. "And I let Gunderson blow a hole through Jesse's chest."

"That's the kind of thing that happens when you take the law into your own hands."

"Get off it, Flynn. What do you want from me?"

"All you have to do is tell me what you know."

Zane sighed. "You've searched every gopher hole in our pasture. You've scared the shit out of those old people, and all they know is that somebody murdered their boy. And that's all I know. My brother's dead."

"Was he an AIM member?"

"He never said."

"Any chance he mouthed off to some of Wilson's goons down at Pine Ridge?"

"I don't know. I didn't follow him around."

"Yeah, but he was into some kind of Indian troublemaking. If you'd stoop to enlighten me just a little . . ."

Zane barked a sharp laugh. "That's a tall order, Flynn. I wouldn't know where to start."

"Try Michelle Benedict."

Zane shook his head. "Never heard of her."

"From Canton, South Dakota?"

He shook his head again. "Never been there."

"I'm interested in your brother, Randy." Flynn withdrew a pale blue envelope from inside his jacket. "So was she, according to this. We found it in his pickup." He made a production of unfolding the letter and clearing his throat, as though preparing to offer an entertaining reading.

" 'Dear Randy, I'm so glad you called. As I said in my last letter, it would be best if you could come to Canton instead of meeting me in Rapid City. There's so much here that I want to show you. Whenever you can arrange the trip would be fine. You're the only one I've heard from so far. I'm easy to find. It's the big white house on the gravel road west of the golf course. Hope to hear from you soon. Yours truly, Michelle.' " Flynn handed Zane the letter. "What do you think that's all about?"

"He never mentioned her." Genuinely intrigued by the smooth, feathery script and the pretty name as much as the invitation, Zane rubbed the pad of his thumb over the blue vellum, then brought it close to his nose. "Nice."

"Yeah." Flynn extended his hand. "Smells like either sex or politics to me."

Zane's smile did not touch his eyes. "You're quite a bloodhound, Flynn."

"Could be Randy had something going with somebody's wife."

"Not in Canton." He laid the letter in Flynn's hand. "Rapid wasn't his kind of town, either."

"I've got a few leads to follow up on a little closer to home. And, of course, Pine Ridge, but it's a little hot down there right now." Flynn pocketed the letter. "First things first."

"Which means what? Check out all the relatives?"

"Sounds like you know your Indians pretty good, Lone Bull. You might have been a good BIA cop. Too bad about your criminal record." Flynn nodded toward the basement window as he backed down one step, then another. "Too bad about Randy, too. I mean that. But, as usual, nobody around here's tellin' me a goddamn thing. Call me if you think of anything that might help us.''

''Yeah, sure thing.''

Zane popped a cigarette into his mouth as he watched the black car back into the gravel street. Too bad Flynn didn't wear glasses, he told himself, half smiling as he struck a match. Then his ears would have served some purpose.

The following day they buried Randy on the hill near Auntie Cecilia's house. The old woman's melancholy keening had dwindled to a soft hum. It was raining again, and the wind drove the water into Zane's face as he shoveled mud into the grave he had dug himself. He'd had help, of course, and the spring ground had been soft, the night cool, and the moonlight comforting. He'd told himself he was carving a safe place where his little brother would find shelter from the wind. He'd wanted to do a nice job. He hadn't done the kid too many favors in his short twenty-six years of life, hadn't set him much of an example. The least he could do was lay him to rest properly.

That, and maybe find out who Michelle Benedict was. He'd called Information from the store in Bullhead and found out that she wasn't listed as having a phone in that big white house west of the golf course in Canton, South Dakota. Not that everybody had to have a phone. Zane didn't. But he figured that most white women who wrote letters on scented blue paper had phones. He doubted that he'd find too many Indian women in the little town in the southeastern corner of the state, far removed from Indian country.

Pretty, feminine handwriting on crisp, blue paper with a small, pale pink flower at the top. He'd always been a sucker for stuff like that. When he was in 'Nam he'd gotten letters on paper kind of like that from a woman he'd never met. Jackie something, who'd seen his picture in *Stars and Stripes*. He'd only written her once, when he was half-shot and feeling sorry for himself. He'd told her a bunch of lies about how great the cookies she'd sent him were. Three weeks later he'd received another box of macaroon rocks and another letter. The letter mentioned the number of prayers she'd offered up for his safety, her concern for American Indians, and her preference for the Beach Boys over the Beatles. None of that had interested him, but the pink paper had given him a serious hard-on.

Because he'd been seriously *hard up*. He wasn't now, he reminded himself. But that damned Michelle Benedict letter wouldn't leave Zane alone. It was like some blue-winged fly, bothering around his head while his hands were too busy to shoo it away. The cold rain should have driven it away, but it didn't. The act of filling in a grave should have numbed his mind, but it didn't. It was his brother's grave and his brother's unfinished business.

It was no good keeping a dead person's stuff around, the old people said. Auntie Cecilia had already given away most of Randy's clothes, and Zane knew nothing he could say after the funeral would stop her from burning that little trailer Randy had towed around so proudly. His tipi, Randy had said. Portable accommodations for a man who had places to go and people to see.

But why had that man been planning to see a white woman who lived west of the golf course in Canton, South Dakota?

Zane finished his work, shook hands with the mourners, and led the two old women back to the house. Before they reached the door Cecilia insisted that he get the gas can from the shed.

"It's raining," he said. "We can do it tomorrow."

"Now," she said.

And he did as she asked, because the *wanagi* would not rest until the details were taken care of properly.

❧ 3 ❧

Zane found the old white house without any problem, but when he knocked on the front door, there was no answer. The VW hatchback in the driveway was an indication that somebody must be around, or would be. *Had* to be. He'd just made a hell of a long drive, and he wasn't heading back down that road without some answers.

If she'd gone out, no choice, he'd have to wait for her to return. He turned his back on the door, tipped up the brim of his black cowboy hat and watched the activity on the golf course across the road. Somebody in white pants took a windmill swing at something in the grass. When the guy started walking, Zane figured he must have made a hit. Nobody cheered. Pretty quiet game, Zane mused.

Pretty peaceful out here. Just plain pretty when you got right down to it. Before he came looking for the house, he'd taken the time to drag Main. He'd never been to Canton, and he always liked to check things out, see what Main Street had to offer. The little town looked like a hundred other South Dakota communities with its neat brick houses, trimmed-up yards, its requisite grocery store, bowling alley, grain elevator, couple of gas stations, couple of bars. He hadn't noticed the school or the library, but he knew they'd be there. The kind of places a person generally went to town for, the kind of town that was the backbone of South Dakota commerce. He'd driven past all that, admired the greening alfalfa fields that skirted it and the freshly turned plots that would soon be planted with corn.

The golf course was on the outskirts of town, too. The Big Sioux River curled in from the east and wound its way south, headed for the Missouri. High wooded bluffs overlooked the river and the golf course, creating a tranquil scene, all blue and green, basking in spring breeze and late afternoon sun. The big white house seemed to preside over it all.

Zane was beginning to feel a little foolish. He hadn't told anybody at home what he was up to. It sounded too harebrained. But it didn't seem to matter how many times or how many different ways he'd told himself how stupid it was to drive clear across the state, there he was. He wasn't sure what he was looking for, but something in the pale blue letter had jogged some obscure memory, a gut instinct that drew him to the town.

It wasn't the woman's name. He knew he hadn't heard *that* before.

It was the name of the town, mentioned in hushed tones in the periphery somewhere, sometime in the past.

Canton.

The name gave him the shivers.

Determined to shake off his uneasiness, he hopped off the porch and followed a well-worn path around the side of the house. He stopped, stood quietly in the shade, and took in the homey backyard scene. The lilacs in bloom, the fresh green cottonwoods, the bird feeder, the clothesline strung between two T-shaped poles, and the young woman with long brown hair that glinted red-gold in the sun.

She was the centerpiece, standing with her back to him as she joined two pairs of pale blue bikini panties together on the line with one clothespin. He couldn't see her face, but he liked what he saw from the back. Long fingers, graceful hands, slender hips, bare feet padding through spring green grass.

A colorful array of tie-dyed T-shirts, striped towels,

long dresses, and short skirts flapped in the breeze. The fact that he was looking right at her underwear when they hadn't even met brought him an unexpected smile. Without being invited into her bedroom he'd already learned that she slept in a soft white cotton nightgown on a double bed covered with flowered sheets, that she hadn't burned her bras, and that there was probably another pair of sexy bikini panties beneath her bell-bottom jeans.

She started humming as she bent to the wicker basket at her feet, her voice sweet but a little off-key on the refrain from McCartney's "Yesterday." Her hair slid across her face like a silk curtain, and when she tossed it back, she saw him. She froze for a moment, then straightened, tipping her head to one side like a curious child.

"Are you Michelle Benedict?"

Her smile was tentative. "Yes."

"You, uh . . . you wrote to my brother, Randy."

"Randy Tusk, yes. I'm surprised he didn't call first. I mean—" She glanced behind him, as though she expected someone else to appear in the shadows. "It's a long drive from . . . Standing Rock, isn't it?"

"Hell of a drive." Seeing no objection in her eyes, he moved in closer. "Randy's not with me. I came instead."

"Oh. Well. Would you mind if I . . . I just have three more—" She took a quick peek at the basket and held up slim fingers, two straight branches, like the top of a winter sapling. "Two more things to hang up. I guess I have no more secrets. It's all right here in plain view."

Not quite. He smiled. "Need some help?"

"Oh, no. I'm almost finished." She snatched up a ball of checkered cloth and snapped it into a dish towel. "I'm surprised Randy didn't call."

"You're not listed."

"The phone is still listed under my aunt's name, but Randy knows the number."

Zane shoved his hands into his back pockets, eyeing the pale sliver of belly flesh that her reach to the clothes-

line exposed above her beltless, low-riding jeans.
"When did you last hear from him?"

"Quite a while ago. I thought maybe he'd lost interest."

"Are you married or something?"

"No." Her blue eyes flashed a curt challenge.

"You don't happen to have a jealous boyfriend or—"

"I don't see why that's any business of yours."

The air of innocence dissipated for him. Her quick
shut-down hit him in the face like a cold splash of reality. "Just tell me what you had going with my
brother," he said quietly. "Plain and simple."

She scowled. "I've never met Randy. He answered
my ad."

"Your ad? Randy?" It was hard to pick from the wild
guesses that suddenly sprang to mind. "Just what are
you selling?"

"Just what are you looking for?" She planted her fists
firmly on her hips. "Better yet, Mr. Tusk, what—"

"It's Lone Bull." He yielded to her indignation with
a step back. "The name's Zane Lone Bull. We're not
technically brothers. More like cousins, but we were
raised in the same . . . by the same . . ." In his unexpected rush to volunteer, Zane suddenly felt as though
he'd dropped some critical cover. He shifted his boots
in the grass and eyed her cautiously. "What were you
advertising for?"

She stared at him, poised to jump away.

"Look, I'm not gonna cause you any trouble." One
hand signaled his bid for a truce. "Like you said, I drove
a long way. I'm just trying to find out—"

"Actually, I was looking for someone named Lone
Bull."

He questioned her claim with a double take.

"That was *one* of the names, anyway. Tusk wasn't
on the list, but Randy did say that he was related to the
Lone Bull family. Could you be related to someone
named James Lone Bull? He died here—" She glanced
above his head, searching her memory. "I think that one
was about nineteen-thirty or so."

"I wouldn't know."

"Well, I think Randy's looking through some kind of records. Or he plans to. He said he was doing some research of his own, and the last time we talked he seemed quite interested in the records that I—"

"He's not interested anymore," Zane told her flatly. "My brother's dead."

Her bright eyes clouded. "I'm so sorry."

He heard her sincerity, saw it in her eyes, felt it in the way she touched his elbow instinctively, warming him even through the barrier of his sleeve. The gesture was regrettably fleeting—his regret and her openness prompting a delicate silence, an exchange of questioning looks.

"Would you like to come inside?" she asked.

He smiled softly and raised a finger. "Just one more thing." He tipped his finger toward the basket.

She drew the flowered sheet up by one corner. He took another corner, and together they tossed it over the line.

"Why did you come?" she asked.

"I read your letter. You said you wanted him to come here rather than meet you in Rapid City. I wanted to find out why, and I couldn't find your phone number."

"I could have taken the hospital records but not the"—she pointed toward the house with a clothespin—"not the cemetery, which I thought he would want to see. James Lone Bull is buried in the cemetery across the street. That's where the hospital was. Well, the asylum."

"Randy was looking for hospital records?"

"I don't think he was to begin with." She peeked over her arm at him as she pinned the sheet. "I've been looking for the relatives of the people who are buried over there, you see. That's why I put that ad in the reservation newspapers, along with some of the major ones. Rapid City, Mobridge, Bismarck. Next I thought I'd branch out, maybe Denver, Albuquerque, Minneapolis." She turned to him, looking almost apologetic. "Obviously it wasn't what you thought."

Zane glanced away. Her unspoken apology made him

uncomfortable, since he probably owed her one. "He never mentioned you," he explained. "And he never kept too many secrets from me."

"How did he die?"

"I found him by the road. Somebody shot him."

"Oh, my God." She touched three fingers to her lips, as though an oath had escaped them. "And you're trying to find out who?"

"The FBI agent who's *supposed* to be trying to find out who—" Zane shook his head. He wasn't going to get into that. Her image of the FBI was probably created by Hollywood, same as most people's. Big heroes. "Anyway, this agent is the one who found your letter in Randy's pickup."

"I'm surprised he hasn't called me. I mean, if he's investigating a . . ."

"Murder," he filled in when she hesitated. "That's the right word for it."

"I've never known anyone who was murdered." She reached for the empty basket, picking it up by one handle. "*Almost* known, I mean. *Wish* I'd known. We talked over the phone a couple of times, and he sounded very nice."

Zane nodded, trying to picture Randy with this woman. Kindred spirits, maybe, but they would never have made a couple. Too much alike, he realized, secretly embarrassed for jumping to conclusions. They were light and dark versions of the same kind of innocence. He had a feeling she was going to trust him the same way Randy had. It was something he'd never asked for, never earned, never understood, but he always figured a guy took what he could get.

"I'm really very sorry." She started walking toward the house, and he followed. "The FBI has my letters? Wow."

"It's not a real big 'wow.' Office Obi is a busy man. He'll probably shelve this case before he gets to you."

"How could he do that?"

"Easy." He formed an imaginary ball between cupped hands, then reached for the sky and made a hook shot. "Two points. Say, wasn't there a song about Officer Obi?"

" 'Alice's Restaurant,' " she said, offering a bright smile. "Arlo Guthrie. Do you like folk music?"

"I'm a country music fan myself. But I remember this guy in, uh—" He caught himself. This wasn't Marla. Talking about the guys he knew in the joint might not get him anywhere with this woman. He shrugged, a little disconcerted by the notion that there might be anywhere to get. "This guy I once knew used to joke around about Officer Obi, and then he'd sing a little of the song. Couldn't sing worth a damn, but it was funny the way he did it." He opened the screen door, stepping back to let her precede him. "You have a nice voice."

"I didn't know anyone was standing there. I'm sure it was just as funny the way I did it."

"No. I really wanted to hear you sing the words."

"It's kind of a sad song when you think about believing in yesterday." She deposited the basket near the back door and led him through an old-fashioned gray and white kitchen into an equally old-fashioned fussy parlor. "I shouldn't have asked Randy to come all the way down here. I could have met him in Rapid."

He took a seat in a big maroon wing-backed chair. "Would there be anybody who might not like the idea of you meeting up with some Indian guy?"

She laughed. "I can't think of a soul who would care." She was hovering over him, making him feel a little uncomfortable for having seated himself, even though it wasn't his custom to stand on ceremony. "I'm sorry," she said. "I guess that's not what you want to hear. You want a suspect, don't you."

"Maybe someone does care, and you don't realize it. Maybe some guy you thought you were all through with. Maybe he didn't show you his jealous side."

She tucked one bare foot beneath her bottom as she sat down, finally, on the flowered sofa. "Maybe you're the real detective."

"Not me." He braced his elbows on his knees, spreading his hands in search of an explanation. "I thought maybe he'd want me to come down here for him and . . ." He sighed, annoyed with himself. "I don't know what. Somebody gets wasted like that, he leaves a lot of things unsettled. Indians are kinda careful about the *wanagi*. Don't want 'em hanging around too close, especially if they're unhappy. Not that I necessarily go along with all that, but just to be on the safe side, it's best to take care of the stuff they leave behind."

"And you thought I might be some of your brother's"—she paused, then gave the word a testy emphasis—"stuff?"

"Never know."

"He seemed quite interested in family history." Scrutinizing him, she leaned into the sofa's arched, wood-trimmed backrest. "Are you?"

Zane shrugged, his eyes expressionless.

"The cemetery is just across the street," she reminded him.

"All I saw coming in was a golf course."

"With an Indian cemetery smack in the middle of it."

He glanced toward the front window, shook his head and chuckled. "I don't know much about the game, but I'll bet the *wanagi* are screwin' up a lot of putts."

"Randy said he thought there might have been a James Lone Bull somewhere on his mother's side of the family, which . . . Would that be your side?"

Still focusing on the window he ignored the question.

"He was interested in the hospital records, more than the grave site," she added.

He shifted his gaze her way. "And what would you be doin' with some old Indian guy's hospital records?"

"Have you ever heard of the Canton Asylum or the Hiawatha Asylum for Insane Indians?"

Canton. He'd definitely heard something about Canton. But the only Hiawatha he remembered was part of a book he was supposed to read in high school. He'd read the interesting stuff, but that must have been one he couldn't get into.

He shook his head.

"Would you like to stay for supper? It won't be

fancy, but it's either here or Dairy Queen.''

He took a deep breath. Nothing cooking yet. He smiled. Nothing ventured—he gave a nod—supper gained. "Here's good. Thanks.''

He wasn't going to ask about her records. It wasn't the kind of thing that interested him, not the way it had Randy. Randy always wanted to know exactly how he was related to everybody. If somebody told Zane they were related, he just nodded, didn't ask any questions. Randy was his brother. Randy's mother was his aunt, her sister was Unci, his grandmother, and together the two old ladies had mothered him. It worked out fine, and he didn't want any of it to change on some technicality.

Beatrice's long-dead husband had been a Lone Bull from Pine Ridge. Randy was really reaching for relatives with this one. But that was Randy. Always looking for connections. Technicalities. For himself, Zane figured if he looked for the details, he'd probably find even less family than he thought he had, so he just left well enough alone.

Michelle made sandwiches from some chicken she had in the refrigerator. She let him make the coffee. He watched her out of the corner of his eye, cutting the sandwiches diagonally, securing them with toothpicks as if she were about to deliver them to a corner booth, arranging the plates with fresh fruit and potato chips. He could feel her watching him as he poured ground coffee into the basket, eyeballing the amount. He brushed a few spilled grounds to the edge of the counter with the flat of his hand, thought better of adding them to the basket, and decided on the sink. A sink with running water was a handy commodity. He figured on getting with the program one of these days.

"You make wonderful coffee," she told him later as they shared their supper on the front porch.

"Surprised?"

"A little." She savored another sip of his wonderful coffee and smiled. "You caught me by surprise from the beginning, and you don't seem to know when to quit.''

He peered past the brim of his hat and treated her to a twinkling eye. "You want me to quit now?"

"Not before dessert. I made cookies this morning."

"For yourself?"

"For a bake sale. A fund-raiser for the library. They just renamed it after my aunt, Cora Hubble. This is her house." She leaned back in the big green porch rocker, a sad smile tilting the corners of her mouth. "I lost my aunt this winter, so I do understand what it's like for you now. Not that it was such a shock. I mean, she'd lived a long life. She died peacefully in her sleep." She looked at him, found him listening intently. "This may sound screwy, but in most ways she was closer to me than my mother is."

"Doesn't sound too screwy to me."

"That's why I love this house. She's still so much a part of it. She'd lived here since before World War I. Her husband was a doctor, and he was in charge of the asylum I was telling you about." She pointed to two gray gambrel roofs visible beyond the golf course greens. "It was over there, where those barns are. The Commissioner of Indian Affairs closed it down back in the mid-thirties. They tore the original building down in the late forties. There's a new hospital back behind there now. Just a regular hospital."

"Not for us wild and crazy Indians," he said with a touch of humor, a conspiratorial wink.

She shook her head. "Just an ordinary little community clinic. There aren't any reservations close by, so I'm not sure why they put the asylum here in the first place. But Dr. Tim—everyone called him that, even Aunt Cora—he was quite devoted to helping Indian people." She set her half-eaten supper on the table between the two rockers. "Dr. Timothy Hubble. Have you heard of him?"

Zane shook his head.

"Your brother didn't recognize the name either. I guess people forget after a time. Anyway, after Dr. Tim died, I started spending most of my summers with Aunt Cora. I went to the university in Vermillion, so I was

nearby, and she was always . . .'' She gestured with open
hands, her face alight with fond memories. ''Such a
wealth of stories. Just like, well, Indian people love to
tell stories, don't they?''

''Some do.''

''My aunt was like that. She was a teacher in a little
country school, and her husband was a country doctor.
They never had any children, but they had each other
and their work, and they both believed very strongly
in . . .'' Her expansive gesture melted away, and she
smiled regretfully. ''Anyway, I'm her heir, and I want
to handle their property the way I think they would want
it handled. So, when I found all those boxes and boxes
of hospital records stashed away in the attic, I
thought . . .''

She turned to him, searching his eyes for a spark of
interest to match hers. He couldn't work up much of an
interest in any dusty records, but he didn't mind listening. Not as long as he had something pleasant to look
at.

''I don't know if Aunt Cora even knew about them,''
Michelle continued. ''I don't think anyone has been up
there in years. She caught me exploring up there once,
years ago, and she said that we mustn't disturb Dr. Tim's
things. But I don't think too many people know about
that cemetery. Frankly it bothers me that they built that
golf course around it. So I thought I'd try to track down
some descendants of some of the people whose names
appear in these records and on that monument over
there.''

''And do some consciousness-raising?''

''Not exactly. But, you know, *you* didn't know about
James Lone Bull being buried down here, and there's a
chance you might be related to him. Randy was quite
curious. I mean, I wonder how many people even know
about it.''

''Or care,'' he allowed before popping a potato chip
into his mouth. ''They're dead, right?''

''Right, but I just thought that if there were some
relatives somewhere . . .''

"They might wanna dig 'em up and take 'em home?"

"There might be something of interest to them in some of these records." She ejected herself from the chair. "Would you like to see the cemetery before it gets too dark?"

Not really.

But he was an unexpected guest, and he could neither fault her hospitality nor ignore her request. She was just *dying* to show him a burial plot with his name on it.

He set his plate on top of hers and stood, towering over her. "I'd like to take a walk and stretch my legs. Guess that's as good a direction as any."

"I'll get my shoes."

A ragged array of native prairie shrubs loosely marked the perimeter of the burial ground. Strangely there were no headstones, no markers, no "cemetery" sign. There was only the chill Zane felt when he stepped into the place where spirits dwelled.

Get real, he told himself. It was a normal temperature drop with the sun just setting at their backs. He could tell where the graves were by the grave-size depressions lined up row on row in otherwise flat ground. He couldn't help paying attention to where he walked, sticking to the strips of taller, greener grass that grew between the depressions.

His caution didn't escape his eager guide's notice.

"You're not worried about ghosts, are you?"

"Hell, no." He pulled the brim of his hat down a notch and flashed her a smile. "Do I look like the superstitious type?"

"You don't look like any type, but you did say you like to be on the safe side." She was leading him toward a big stone wedge on the far side of the grassy lot. "Personally, I don't worry about them, but I think they might exist. I feel Aunt Cora's presence in that house, although it doesn't scare me. In some ways it's a little agitating, but not scary."

"Agitating?"

"It's like she wants me to find things, do things."

"Sounds pretty scary to me."

"She would never steer me into harm's way. She was the kindest, most . . ." She glanced up at him, as if she expected him to back her up. "Maybe I just think I feel her presence because I miss her."

"Could be."

"Of course, I've had more time than you've had to accept"—They'd reached the stone, and she laid her hand on it, dubbing it—"this reality. That's really hard."

"Maybe you oughta do what we did." Zane turned to look back at the house, much of it hidden in the distance by ponderosa pines and Russian olives. A second-floor window seemed to stand guard like an unblinking eye. "Burn everything that belonged to her, including her house."

"You did? Even Randy's *house*?"

"He lived in a little trailer." Still staring at the house, he recalled the way the flames had licked Randy's silver turtle shell from the inside out. "We burned it. My family is still pretty traditional."

"I could never do that." She, too, regarded the old house. "I'm not sure I want to sell it, either, but I live in Rapid City. I'm a teacher."

"Just like your Aunt Cora," he remarked absently as he turned to the monument. "Your school out already?"

"Almost. This is a long weekend for us."

"This doesn't look that old."

Almost against his will he scanned the big brass plate that was bolted to the stone. Listed in three columns under the bold heading NAMES OF INDIANS BURIED IN HIAWATHA ASYLUM CEMETERY were over 120 names, each with a date. No births were memorialized here. Only deaths.

"They just put this up a couple of years ago," she said quietly. "I didn't realize what it was. As much time as I've spent at the house across the road . . ." She pulled a wind-tossed lock of hair away from her mouth as she looked up at him. "This was all just grass. Of course, I see it now, where the graves are, but I never came over here.''

''You don't play golf?''

She shook her head.

''You can bet none of these guys did, either.''

''Aren't you the least bit curious to know whether this man was your—'' She pointed toward the Lone Bull name toward the bottom of the third column. ''What relation would he have been to you?''

''Just another crazy uncle.'' He gave her a cocky smile. ''How many beds you got over there?''

Evening shadows softened her questioning expression.

He shoved his hands in his pockets and scanned the purpling sky. ''How would you feel about loaning one out for the night? If it wouldn't agitate Aunt Cora's ghost too much.''

''Agitate?'' Michelle chuckled. ''Without a chaperon, she would be scandalized.''

''Yeah, well, I'm a big boy. I think I can defend myself if you get fresh with me.'' He shrugged. ''Or I could lock myself in my pickup and freeze it out.''

''There's the Gateway Inn,'' she suggested, pointing back down the highway.

''No, thanks. I'll be takin' off early anyway.'' He forgave her sensible brush-off with a quick smile. ''You're absolutely right. You don't know anything about me.''

She cast a quick glance at the names on the plaque, as though she were checking in with them for some kind of affirmation. ''I know you wouldn't hurt me.''

''How would you know that?''

''You're not the type of man who would harm the innocent.''

''Are you innocent?'' He was just being cocky. He'd already made up his mind she was. There was something about the way the ruby-trimmed evening glowed in her eyes.

''I had nothing to do with your brother's death,'' she told him. It was a suspicion he'd almost forgotten.

"And I have no clues to offer. No jealous lovers or *ex*-lovers."

He tipped his head slightly, studying those eyes. "If they're not, they should be. Innocence is rare these days."

"You can use one of the bedrooms upstairs."

"Thanks," he said. "I could really use a good night's sleep before I head back. And I promise not to get in your way."

"I trust you."

He wondered who she was trying to convince. "Trust is almost as rare as innocence," he said, and on that assessment he gestured, inviting her to lead the way back. "You said I didn't look like any type."

"You don't *act* suspicious." She offered a bright-eyed smile as she strode next to him. "Your eyes aren't undressing me."

He returned a smile with a hint of craft. "But I've already taken inventory of your underwear."

"And passed the test," she noted easily. "You kept your cool."

"A guy never knows when he's being tested."

Once inside the front door he removed his hat, preparing to press for another favor. He felt exposed, realizing that she was getting her first really good look at him. Like his uncle Martin, he seldom parted with his hat.

He plowed his fingers through his flattened hair. "Would it be okay to use the shower?"

"There's one upstairs." Having made her decision to let him stay, no amenity seemed too much to ask. "I'll get you some fresh towels," she said, and he followed her, gallantly snatching the laundry basket off the kitchen floor.

He never passed up a chance for a hot shower. It was one of the few things he'd missed since he'd moved back home. Public Health had been putting in wells on the reservation, and there was promise of bringing indoor plumbing even to the more isolated homes. Fund-

ing from HUD was also available for new housing, and
Cecilia was on all the waiting lists. Meantime, Zane enjoyed running water in other women's homes.

He took off the beaded turtle amulet he always wore
on a thong around his neck. Unci had made it for him
when he was a baby; that much she'd told him. He
wore it for luck. Long life was the promise she'd said it
held, but *luck* was the word he favored. It came his way
on occasion. He'd served two tours in 'Nam and returned with only one visible scar, a flesh wound, high
inside his right thigh. Lucky bastard, his buddies had
called him then, and he'd figured if he'd used all the
luck he'd had coming in the instant that piece of shrap-
nel had torn into him, so be it. An inch higher, a little
to the left, and they'd have shot off his passkey to other
women's—

Not this one, he told himself as he set the turtle on
the back of the sink. He'd promised not to get in her
way, and he wasn't going to. He imagined her standing
up in front of a class, Jojo and Sissy sitting in little
desks in the front row, and he liked the picture. He decided to preserve her that way in his head. Carrying on
in the tradition of her kindly old aunt for whom the
town library had been named. "Not my type, *keya*," he
told the turtle. "Maybe I don't look like any type, but
she sure as hell does."

He slept well, woke up early, and thought he would
leave without disturbing her, but she'd beaten him to
the punch and made him breakfast. He didn't question
the gesture. He ate his fill quietly and found himself enjoying her strong coffee, her gentle, sleepy-eyed smile,
and the way her bare feet sounded on the linoleum. He
wondered whether she'd had trouble sleeping with him
in the house.

It amused him to catch her stealing quick glances,
searching for some kind of reassurance about him when
she thought he wasn't looking. What was she unsure
of? Her safety? He figured he'd taken the test and de-
served a passing grade on that one. His readiness if she
decided she was willing? Hell, he was a man, wasn't

he? And she was a damn sweet-looking woman, even if
she wasn't his type.

But there was something else about her, something
he hadn't encountered before, not close-up. Something
he thought he could really get to like if he weren't careful. He didn't know what to call it, but it had a
potential-for-satisfaction kind of feel to it, like seeing a
light in the distance and knowing there was a fire
within reach.

He'd fallen prey to this sort of world-weary tender-
ness when he'd helped her bring the clothes in off the
line. They'd worked side by side in the hush of spring
twilight, filling their arms with a hodgepodge of cloth
that smelled wind-washed, felt cool and dusky damp.
He'd confessed that he visited the closest laundromat
fairly regularly, but he didn't mention the old folks and
kids he generally had in tow.

He smiled into the steam from his coffee, recalling
the way she'd snapped the underwear off the line first
and stowed it in the bottom of her basket, while he'd
played the discreet gentleman and gone for the sheets.
She'd repaid him by making his bed with them, and
he'd drifted happily off to sleep on that fresh-air smell.

But he had been the one who'd taken the white
nightgown off the line. The little tucks around the neck
peeked out now beneath a blue cotton wrapper. He
imagined that the nightgown must smell like her skin
by now. He wanted to get close enough to find out, but
those glances of hers didn't come across as a come-on.
He'd had a good share of experience with women and
their ways, but this one he couldn't quite figure. All he
knew for sure was that she wasn't like Marla, nor, for
that matter, was she like him. She wasn't used up.
There was real fire there.

To his surprise she had managed to spark a little curiosity in him, and when he got home late that
afternoon, he mentioned James Lone Bull, just to see
what kind of a reaction he got. Cecilia said she had
enough ghosts of her own to deal with, and Beatrice
stared at him. But the stare wasn't quite blank.

He knelt beside the old woman's chair. "Was that your husband's name?" he asked in Lakota. "Uncle Martin's father?"

She wagged her gray head. She could have been saying no or loosening up a stiff neck. He couldn't tell anymore.

"There's somebody named James Lone Bull buried down in Canton. Little town way southeast of here," he told her, gesturing toward the kitchen table. "Strange place to put an Indian hospital, even back then, back in your day. Hiawatha Insane Asylum." He looked at her as he said the name, and he detected a flash of recognition in her eyes. "You've heard of it, haven't you."

She stared at the turtle amulet exposed by his open shirt. "No good," she said in Lakota.

"What's no good, Unci?"

Beatrice shook her head. "No good, Cinks."

"I'm no good?" It had been a long time since she'd called him "sonny," an endearment that never failed to rub him a little raw inside. "Your son's no good," he surmised. "I'm your son, and *I'm* no good."

On a sigh he pushed himself to his feet. "Jesus, woman, I don't know why I bother. You gonna talk like that, it's better you don't have too much to say these days."

"Don't go bothering around that place," she said tonelessly.

The warning surprised him.

"It's a bad place?"

"Leave it alone," she muttered distractedly. "Leave it alone."

He cursed himself the next morning for letting the old woman's words bother him throughout the night. It was just that she rarely made much sense anymore, and when she did, it came off as a message that might have been chiseled on the back of that dreary stone marker sitting in the middle of Canton's deceptively orderly little golf course.

Leave it alone.

Hell, that was exactly what he planned to do.

After all, he was a busy man these days. Too busy to be a damn referee, but he had to settle a squabble between Martin and Jojo before he even had his first cup of morning coffee. It was Martin's job to care for the chicks they were incubating under a heat lamp in the chicken house. If Zane had his way, he'd get rid of the damn chicken house altogether. He'd hated chickens since he was a kid. But Cecilia had always raised them, always would.

He lifted Jojo and set him on the corral rail. "You can't go in the chicken house, okay? You leave the door open and this sneaky ol' Soup's gonna get in there and kill the chicks." With a jerk of his chin he directed the boy's attention to the shaggy brown mutt who sat at his feet, one ear cocked toward the fenced shack. "You want him to kill those little chicks?"

Jojo scowled. "Uncle Martin's still in there."

"He's feeding them. And you can feed them, too, but only when I'm here. I don't want you goin' in there alone with Uncle." Zane tapped Jojo's knobby little knee with the edge of his gloved hand. "Get the two of you in there together, there's no telling what kind of trouble we'll have. In a couple of weeks, those chicks will be big enough so you can play with them a little more. Deal?"

Jojo shrugged, hitching one shoulder all the way up to his ear. "How did Mom get a name like Chickie? Her name's Carmen. Carmen sounds better than Chickie."

"Your grandma caught her messin' around in the chicken house. I ain't lyin' just to make a point, now; this is true." Zane pulled a serious expression and sketched the incident in the air with one expressive hand. "Grandma reached in there and drug her out by the ear. That little girl's hair was so full of feathers, she looked like a fancy dancer. She smelled like chicken crap, and she was squawkin' just like a chicken."

Jojo giggled.

Zane nodded. "Sure as hell, we thought she'd turned into a chicken. Had to call her Chickie after that."

The boy's small hand claimed the big gloved one still resting on his knee. "How much younger is she?"

"Than me? Five years."

"Why didn't she come to Uncle Randy's funeral?"

"I don't know." He'd wired her the money for a bus ticket. He wondered what she'd done with it. "She never was much for funerals." Truth was, she liked parties better. But who didn't?

"He was her brother," Jojo said. "I thought we'd get to see her."

"You know how she is. You'll see her when you see her. Hell, I used to be like that, too." But he hadn't left any kids to wonder when he was coming back.

"Grandma says you got straightened up down at that prison you were in."

Zane pulled on his hat brim, eyeing Jojo with mock skepticism. "She thinks so, huh?"

"Well, she says you decided it wasn't so bad to stick around home a little more."

"Yeah, I guess I did."

"Maybe they should put our mom in prison for a little while."

Ah, Jesus. "You don't wanna wish that on her, Jojo. She'll come home one day." Zane was glad for the excuse to smile when he heard the house and the chicken coop doors slam almost simultaneously. Time to saddle up. "Besides, you got your sister, your grandmas, you got your uncles, you've got all kinds of cousins."

"You ain't goin' back in the army?"

"Nope." He lifted Jojo off the fence. "Not even if they beg me pretty please."

"But what about the war?"

"Looks like we lost it."

Zane pretended not to hear the footsteps sneaking up on him. Small arms suddenly tackled him from behind, belting his middle. "Easy, there, Sissy girl. You goin' out for wrestling?"

"Wrestling's for boys, Uncle," the voice behind him scolded.

"If I run the horses in, you guys wanna go for a ride?"

"I want my own horse," Jojo said as he slid to the ground. "I'm too big to ride double."

"Sorry, partner." Zane nodded at the chestnut gelding who was sniffing at the empty grain trough on the far side of the corral. "All I've got's two gentle horses and this knothead I'm working for Tom Deiderich. You can ride with Uncle Martin, or would you rather ride with Sissy?"

"Uh-uh."

"You got a problem riding with your uncle?" Zane asked casually, just making sure.

"I'll ride with Uncle Martin," Jojo decided. "But I get to sit in the saddle."

"Go for a ride?" Zane asked Martin as he approached. The old man grinned. "It's gonna be a short one. I haven't even had my coffee yet, thanks to you two gettin' into it over a bunch of damn chickens. But what the hell, it's a beautiful morning."

And he caught himself humming as he saddled up and rode out. "It's a beautiful morning . . ." He didn't know the rest of the words, wasn't much for listening to pop radio. He thought about Michelle, humming the Beatles while she hung her clothes out.

He told himself to forget about Michelle as he nudged the chestnut's choppy trot into a canter. He headed over a grassy rise, leaving his three "tails" to wait for him by the corral.

Zane figured that Jojo was just letting him know that he thought he was too big to ride double, but it was hard to know how far to trust Martin. On his good days, he was just a simple guy who couldn't talk. When Zane was a kid Martin had been his overgrown buddy. They'd had good times together on Martin's good days. But some days Martin would get scared or confused and do stupid things, like grab somebody and hang on. And he hadn't always been careful about where he grabbed.

A hazy memory of one particular incident always brought on a not-so-hazy feeling in Zane's gut, sort of a rush of nausea. He refused to bring the memory into focus, although he knew what it was. He just didn't want to see it in his head.

He was a *man*, for crissake, and his uncle was not, not really.

Martin had cried that time. That much Zane remembered clearly. Cried like a big, overgrown baby when Zane, hot-faced and mad as hell, had yelled at him. Called him names neither one of them had really understood. Something had changed between them that day. It was the day Zane had become the one in charge.

Martin could sure make a person feel uneasy sometimes. Close up a guy could feel that something was going on within the old man's silence, kind of a pitiful palpitation, a continual dull ache. It hurt a little to care about him sometimes. The kids probably felt it, too. Zane always left it up to them. If they weren't in a mood to trust Martin, Zane always gave them another choice.

Without telling them in so many words he let them know that he understood how they felt. A guy like Martin could be deceptive. He had the body of a man and the mind of a child. He was both, and he was neither. He was terrified of doctors, who had never been able to do him any good, anyway. Beatrice had once speculated that Martin's inability to speak was his way of protecting himself. From what, she couldn't or wouldn't say.

Just another crazy Indian.

Back at the cabin that night he played cards with Martin by the light of a kerosene lamp. Zane hadn't had much luck teaching him gin, but Martin was no dummy when it came to playing poker.

"Maybe we should go to Vegas, huh?"

Martin screwed up his face as he studied his five cards.

"Nobody'd ever guess what a fox you are, would they? I'd play it cool. You could just play it straight. We'd be rakin' it in." Zane eyed the five red bicycle designs. "What the hell have you got there?"

Martin glanced over the top of his cards, looking all innocent.

"Yeah, well, I'm gonna pay to see." Zane tossed two wooden "farmer" matches into the pile in the middle of the table.

Martin proudly presented his hand. Two pair, sixes, and nines.

Zane laughed. "Christ. You left me matchless."

He threw in his hand and lit a cigarette in the lamp chimney. In the timeless yellow fireglow, through the lazy drift of smoke, he squinted speculatively at his uncle. "Are we related to anyone named James Lone Bull?"

There was that look again, the same one he'd seen in Beatrice's eyes. Awareness where there were no connections to understand it. Anxiety where there was no judgment to soothe it.

Only a hard-hearted sonuvabitch would persist.

But, damn, that look, there was some *life* in it.

"You know that name, don't you? James? Who was he?" On impulse Zane went to the old steamer trunk where he kept an assortment of handy stuff, including paper and pencils. Most of the paper had long-forgotten mimeographed messages on one side. He put several pieces on the table in front of Martin, clean side up. "You wanna draw something for me, Uncle?" He took out his pocket knife, whittled a point on a yellow pencil, and handed it over. "Here. Draw me something."

Martin bent to the task, taking more care than he usually did. He liked to draw, but he usually created intricate, repetitive patterns. Pretty, but meaningless as far as Zane could tell. This time Martin created a stick figure.

"Jesus, that's real good. That's better than . . ." Zane tapped his finger on the drawing's head. "Is this James Lone Bull?"

Martin looked Zane in the eye and put his hand over his mouth.

"You don't have to tell me, but maybe I can guess. Like guessing what cards you've got, huh?"

Martin put pencil to paper again. A heavy line surrounded the stick figure.

"What's he doing? Is he in a box? Like Randy?"

Martin kept drawing.

"Was he related to us? Was he in a hospital, maybe? Jeez, if you'd just shake your head or nod or something, Uncle. Long time ago there was this hospital in Canton."

Martin looked up briefly, then went back to his work again.

Zane took a long, slow pull on his cigarette, then tried the word out again. "Canton hospital for, uh . . ." *For guys like you?* "For crazy Indians."

Martin stared at Zane's face with an intensity that made him half wish he had a mirror handy.

"Not you," Zane said quickly, which made him feel like the worst kind of hypocrite. "I didn't mean—"

The hell he didn't. He felt bad when Martin laid the pencil down and sat there, hanging his head over his accomplishment.

Zane sat back in the kitchen chair, searching the log rafters for the reference to a time, a date he'd shrugged off for lack of any reference to him, his world, his own interests.

"Jesus, I can't remember when it was she said that place was shut down." He reached across the table, tapped his uncle's arm with a gentle fist, and flashed a between-us-guys grin. "She gave me the whole damn history lesson. I should have been listening as close as I was looking. Real pretty. Kind of soft-looking, you know what I mean?"

Martin gave no indication that he did.

"I met this woman down in"—back to the word proven to elicit a response—"Canton. This pretty woman I met lives in *Canton*. A bad place, Unci said."

Martin looked up.

"Is it a bad place, Uncle? Do you remember . . ."

Martin took up the pencil again and drew one heavy line, then another, harder. A series of heavy black slashes formed a rectangle filled with small boxes that might have been windows, or rooms in a house. Or cells,

Zane thought. Storage boxes for living, breathing people.

Wild and crazy Indians, like Zane Lone Bull. Or Martin Lone Bull.

Or James Lone Bull, whoever the hell he was.

But as he watched his uncle labor over his drawing Zane had the feeling he was bound to find out.

❧ 4 ❧

Pine Ridge, South Dakota
Summer 1932

Rachael Trainor gingerly lifted her head off the ground and squinted in the direction of the thudding retreat.

"You stupid . . . *horse*!"

It wasn't much of an insult, but considering how little breath she had left to expend, it was something. The bay kicked up his hooves in reply. He was already a quarter of a mile down the rutted road, and Rachael was looking at what she should have called the animal. A black-tailed horse's *ass*. Not that it would have bothered him, but it might have soothed her sore bottom if she'd managed to gasp out that last word.

She lifted her shoulders and slid her elbow into position for support.

"Yeow!"

She'd just managed to jam her elbow into a patch of cactus. Thrown on the ground, abandoned, and now stabbed. What next? She groaned miserably and rolled to the opposite shoulder, scanning the scrubby grass for more hidden menace as she pushed up on a shaky hand. Oh God, she hurt. She didn't think she'd broken anything, but everything hurt, including her pride.

Not three hours ago she'd informed her skeptical

brother, Edward, that she was still just as good a horsewoman as ever—withholding, of course, the small detail of the number of years that had passed since she'd actually been on a horse—and he'd finally let her take that *beast* for the day.

"Stick to the roads," he'd said, and he had drawn her a map. There was, however, no point in wondering where she was at the moment. His map had ceased to make sense a long time ago, maybe because she'd taken a little detour to catch the breathtaking view from the top of a butte.

She eased herself into a sitting position and twisted her arm, trying to get a look at her elbow. Bloody, bony pincushion it was now. And her bottom. Ohhh, her poor, aching arse!

But it was her left ankle that actually failed her. She had gotten it twisted in the stupid western stirrup on her way to the ground. She was just lucky she wasn't being dragged across the prairie, battered by a pair of horse shoes of her way back to Edward's place.

She'd seen a cabin along the way—she didn't think it was too far back—but getting there would be the trick. A couple of hobbling test steps brought on a wave of nausea, not to mention sharp pain. She needed help. But the endless rolling stubble and the infinite, dry-eyed sky offered her no sympathy, no promises, no prospects.

Where the devil was that little cabin?

There was nothing to do but limp along and pray like crazy. Dear Lord, she needed some *help*.

As a registered nurse, Rachael was trained to help, and being helpful was part of her nature. She and her brother, Edward, had been raised on the notion that the good people were those who served, and she wanted very much to do good. Edward, being older and politically well-connected through their father, a representative in the Massachusetts legislature, had received his appointment as the Indian agent at Pine Ridge Reservation twelve years ago. Rachael had completed her nurse's training in Boston and spent five years working with patients in two of the largest asylums for the insane on the East Coast, including the government program at St. Elizabeth's in Washington, D.C., before applying for a position that would put her closer to her brother.

She hadn't told Edward about her plan until after she'd accepted the job. She'd intended to surprise him, and she'd succeeded. He wasn't altogether pleased. The Dakotas were desolate country, hard hit by drought and economic depression. White residents were moving out in droves, headed for better prospects in states like Washington and Oregon. But the Indians were stuck there. According to Edward, they were selling off everything they could, living on pipe dreams and the charity of the federal government, and quietly going crazy.

He could assure her that she would have patients. But patience? He'd give her six months, he said, a year maybe—she'd always been more stubborn than most— to come to her senses and go back East, where she really ought to consider one of the marriage proposals she'd turned down. Charlie Rutledge, Edward reminded her, was an old friend whose family's deep pockets had only profited from bad economic times. He would have been a good match, and she was *nuts* to refuse his ring.

Edward had no idea what a bore his friend Charlie was, being one himself, nor did he truly appreciate the extent of her stubbornness. She was stubborn about her work and as devoted to it as Edward truly was to his. And she was strong. A woman had to be strong to work with patients who were often quite sound in body if not in mind.

Ah, but she also had to know her limitations, and *this* woman wasn't strong enough to hobble back to the agency on a sprained ankle. Or dumb enough, or desperate enough—yet—to try. Maneuvering awkwardly, she sat herself back down on the side of the road and elevated her leg on a rock. If she took her short riding boot off she knew she wouldn't be able to get it back on, so she loosened the buckle at the ankle.

Oh, for a chunk of ice!

She leaned back on her uninjured elbow, closed her eyes, and tried to think of a way to attract any attention

that might be out there somewhere. *Human* attention.
She wasn't sure what had scared the horse.

Stupid horse.

"So there *was* a rider."

Rachael dropped her head back and opened her eyes.
A brown-skinned man towered above her like a tree,
clouds slipping past the crown of his battered brown hat.

"Who's now a footer," he amended, clearly amused.
He circled her, forcing her to lift her head so she could
keep track of his activity. She wondered how he'd managed to sneak up on her, especially since he was leading
a horse. Unfortunately, it wasn't hers.

"That bay's halfway to Nebraska by now," he told
her as he jackknifed his long leg and planted his booted
foot beside hers on the rock. "Did he throw you?"

"I'm afraid so."

"Do much damage?"

"I don't think it's too—" She sat up, wincing as pain
bolted her foot to the rock. "Yes, actually, there's damage. I think my ankle may be sprained. And this . . ."
She rotated her wounded arm, craning her neck for a
closer look. "I should have worn long sleeves."

"Prickly pear," he noted. "Looks like you found
yourself a good patch of it."

"It really stings."

"It won't keep you from goin' back where you came
from," he observed dryly. "Can you walk?"

"A little bit." She took her throbbing foot down and
grabbed the rock for leverage. "The question is, can I
stand?"

His hand appeared beneath her nose. It was large, dark
brown, callused, thoroughly masculine, mercifully oblig-
ing. It swallowed her right hand up completely, his iron
bar of a wrist serving as her left-hand hold as he peeled
her smoothly off the ground. Once erect, she balanced
on one foot like a hopscotcher preparing for her next
move.

He made it for her, easily sweeping her into his arms.
"My place is just down the road."

She had no choice but to grab his shoulders and hang

on. Her nose bumped into his hat brim, but he didn't seem to notice, didn't even glance at her face, suddenly so close to his. She heard the air fill his chest as he drew a deep breath, as if he were bracing himself for something, or perhaps against it. She did the same. There was an exotic, sweet oil scent about him, not at all unpleasant, nor was the unexpected closeness.

And that, more than anything, was what surprised her. She sensed the power in his arms and shoulders and a peculiar transfer of energy where their bodies touched. It flowed warmly into her back, her arms, her legs, not unlike the feeling she got when she mounted a horse. Her view of the world was instantly transformed. She was suddenly on top of it, and anything she wanted seemed within reach.

"You wouldn't happen to have any ice at your place, would you?"

"Did, but it all thawed." He risked a glance at her, a touch of humor lurking in his dark eyes. "Several months back."

"A girl can wish," she said lightly.

"So can a man." He lifted her, carefully managing her injured parts while she grabbed a handful of mane and dragged her right leg over his unruffled horse's bare back. Then the big man vaulted up behind her, his arms encircling her as he took the reins. "Where you headed?"

"I was just out for a ride. Truthfully, I'm not sure where I am. I'm not really familiar with the area." She glanced over her shoulder for a brief glimpse at the sharply hewn angles of his face. "I'm Rachael Trainor."

The man's eyes turned frosty. "The agent finally got himself a wife?"

"Good heavens, no. Pity the woman who takes my brother on for a husband." If there were unofficial sides to be taken, Rachael had little trouble shrugging off her priggish older brother for diplomacy's sake. "It's probably too late. Edward is horribly set in his ways."

"Don't go to the agency much, myself. Waste of time. They got no ears."

"So that's what's wrong with dear old Edward." Rachael laughed readily. "But what do you suppose is the purpose of those big flappers on the sides of his head?"

"Couldn't say. Indian men are built different."

"Really? How intriguing." As was her Good Samaritan, she decided. "My new job may prove even more interesting than I anticipated."

"Don't be too sure," he warned, his voice deep and warm just behind her ear. "No matter how we're built, seems like we're not so interesting unless we've got something can be turned into cash." He paused, then added on a soft and distant note, "Or unless there's a war on."

"Did you serve in the war?"

"Sure did." He switched to a lighter tone. "Learned to get around in Paris on a *voulez-vous*."

"Handy phrase."

"Oh, yeah."

It seemed remarkable to be trading such banter with an Indian man, riding with him on his horse, headed for a primitive-looking log house in the middle of the desolate prairie on a sunny summer afternoon. Remarkable because, for one thing, he sounded just like a man. Rachael didn't know exactly what she'd expected. Interesting people, certainly, but not an engaging man who talked, well, just like a *man*.

Indian people had been coming to Edward's door since she'd arrived a week ago, but he had introduced her to few of them, and she'd heard even less conversation. Some of the people brought along a translator, for Edward spoke only a few words of Sioux, or Lakota, the correct name for the people in this region of South Dakota and their dialect. Rachael had heard a number of school-age children interpreting for their parents or grandparents. Occasionally a group of men would come to the agency and sit on the porch with Edward, and he would ask her to serve coffee. Conversation seemed sporadic and stilted, much as her own conversations with her brother had always been. She thought perhaps Ed-

ward had finally found some birds of his detached
feather.

But the man sitting close behind her, his left thigh
subtly lending support for hers, did in no way remind
her of her brother. Edward was stuffy, his sense of himself leaving him no room to gain a sense of anyone else.
Edward was completely predictable and utterly humorless. Intuition told her that this man was none of those
things.

And her own response to him was unconstrained and
astonishingly unmistakable. Every nerve in her body
seemed to be sitting up and taking notice.

She was also busy taking notice of his home—his
place, he'd called it. They were approaching an empty
split-rail corral. A black dog lifted its head briefly, then
stretched and went back to sleep in the bare reddish dirt
on the shady side of the house. There was a clothesline,
a washtub on a wooden stand, an outhouse, a languish-
ing garden, and a couple of farm implements Rachael
couldn't have identified if she'd been asked to. She did
know a wagon when she saw one, and the old black
Model T Ford. But the place seemed pretty quiet.

"Who else lives here with you?"

"Nobody right now."

For some reason, that bit of news alarmed her. "I
think I could get back to my brother's place on my own
if I could just—"

He didn't seem to be listening. The ease with which
the man sprang on and off the horse was impressive, but
it was the one thing about him that did not surprise Rachael. His readiness to help her dismount suddenly did.
Wary and short on alternatives, she planted both hands
on the animal's withers. "May I borrow your horse?"

He squinted up at her, his hands bracketing her as he
laid claim to the animal's dun-colored hide. "If *this*
horse took off for Nebraska, I'd be up a creek. He's part
of a team and the only transportation I got."

"What about the automobile?"

"Ain't had that runnin' since—" Resting his chin on
his arm, he cast a wistful glance at the vehicle. "Since

my little brother poured molasses into it, thinking it would work the same as oil.''

"You can't get it fixed?"

"Even if I could get the parts, who'd fix it?" He put a tentative hand on her waist, and they eyed one another. The same hot wind that swept a stray wisp of hair across her dry lips also lifted his brown shirt collar. "I'm not about to hurt you, Rachael Trainor. I've got the parts to fix up your arm, and I think you might wanna take that boot off.''

"Not if I'm going to have to walk back to the agency."

"My wagon's runnin' fine."

"You'll take me back, then?"

He nodded. The sun shone over her shoulder, straight into his hooded eyes as he waited patiently.

She answered, finally, with a nod, then swung her good leg over the horse's neck and slid into the man's arms. Nose to nose, she deemed it an appropriate time to mention, "You haven't told me your name."

"Adam Lone Bull."

"Lone Bull," she repeated.

"Lone Bull. Spelled like it sounds."

He kicked the back door open and carried her into the house. From hot, windy daylight into cool, dark interior. He elbowed the door shut, enveloping them in stillness. Her heartbeat grew resonant. His breathing sounded stormy. He paused, obviously contemplating his next move.

She didn't see many choices. The cabin was neatly kept if starkly appointed with an iron bedstead, a quilt-draped bed, a wood stove, a plank table, and several wooden chairs. Her roving eye came full circle, back to his face, his eyes on her, watching her take inventory.

She apologized for her boldness with a soft smile. "I believe my brother has spoken of you. Quite a decorated soldier from what he said."

He deposited her in a chair. "I'm sure that's not all he said."

"He said that you'd been one of the more progressive

men among the Sioux and that people listened to you. But he says that now . . .''

"Now I'm just another drunk." He plunked another chair in front of her, then dropped a folded towel on the seat. "Put your foot up here."

"Edward would never admit to it, but he does exaggerate sometimes." She sat back, watching him, letting him take charge of her injured foot even though she was trained to take care of it herself. At the moment it was her job to withstand pain in more of her parts than she cared to acknowledge. She let him help her lift her foot and permitted him to ease her boot off. "All I know is, you're not drunk now."

"Nothing around to drink." He knelt beside the chair and carefully peeled her sock away, exposing her swollen, purpling ankle. "This looks pretty bad. Could be broken."

"I don't think so." A sharp jab of pain called her a liar when she moved her big toe, but she held her lips tight against all but one admission. "I'm a nurse."

"That's your new job?"

"I've been a nurse for some time. My new job is *head* nurse at the asylum in Canton. I'm supposed to start next week."

A quick glance betrayed his sudden interest. "How're you getting there?"

"By train. I'm just paying my brother a short visit to make sure he's behaving himself."

"A simple thing," he murmured as he turned his attention back to her foot. "Brothers deserve to be visited."

"Mine might take exception to that notion, but I didn't ask. I just told him I would be—ouch!" He'd stood up quickly, jarring her footrest, turning away from her as though something about her had offended him. "Where are you going?"

"Outside."

Abruptly he shut her up alone in his cabin. She drew a deep breath and discovered comfort in its earthy odor. She realized a sense of safety, relief from the wariness she'd felt when she'd looked on the place and its owner from the outside.

She tipped her head back and noted the sod roof. The wind whistled through a crevice somewhere, but it didn't touch her. Neither did the baking sun. She could have been out there on the side of the road, but instead she was safe inside, thanks to the man who'd correctly guessed her brother's description of him. Fast becoming another degenerate drunk, Edward had said.

Rachael saw no sign of degeneration, but she sensed some deeply embedded sadness, not about his person, but in the solitary room that was his home. It wasn't a function of the austerity of the place. It wasn't the fact that the twentieth century had apparently thus far bypassed the place, along with most of the reservation. It was really nothing visible, but it was there. Something that thickened the air, some grief residing in the clay-chinked walls.

"Who else lives here with you?"

"Nobody right now."

Adam returned with a pail of water, which he set on the floor beside her chair. He soaked a stringy towel, wrung it out, then dropped his hat on the table and bent over her outstretched leg.

She gasped when the towel touched her foot. "That *might as well* be ice!"

"Ice is what you asked for." He lifted her heel and tucked the wet towel beneath it. "I am one of the lucky ones. I have a deep well."

"I see that."

He cast her a brief, doubtful look.

"Do you have any alcohol?" The cold pack provided, she was on to the next need as she examined her elbow. "Or peroxide. Any kind of disinfectant. This stings like crazy, but I can't see what's . . ."

"Take your hand away and let me see," he said, taking her arm in his hands.

She started to protest that his hands were not clean, but she held her tongue and watched him pluck out nee-

dles finer than her hair with a hand so steady it did not
touch her skin.

"The smallest needles will pop out when it festers,"
he predicted. "I've lit the cook stove and put water on
to boil. Will that meet your standards?"

She nodded quickly.

"There's no alcohol here," he assured her.

"I'm not the agent's agent."

Reluctantly he smiled. "Only his sister."

"Will it be a problem for you, taking me back? If my
brother threatens you in some way . . ." The look he
flashed her denied her brother any such ability, but she
felt compelled to explain her concern. "I've heard some
of the talk—eavesdropping a little bit, since I've come
here to work, and it helps to listen in once in a while—
the talk about traditional Indian ways versus the progressive policies that were supposed to change your
lives, especially now that you've been granted full-
fledged citizenship, so I gather that some of your people
are on one side and some on the other, and that my
brother thinks that you've switched sides." She looked
up at him, found him listening, waiting. She smiled. "To
me, it's all still talk. I don't know what his beef is with
you, or yours with him. What I know for sure is that I
have a sprained ankle here, and if you hadn't come
along . . ."

"You have more than that."

"Well, along with a badly bruised bottom."

His eyes brightened. "I got another towel."

"Actually, I think if we could keep changing this,
keep applying the cold pack . . ." She reached for the
towel, confessing quietly, "My tender pride has suffered
enough injury."

He chuckled. "Sit on your pride then, and we'll tend
to your foot."

She leaned back and let him unwind the towel. Every
movement of his hands fascinated her. Rugged as they
were, they were also remarkably deft. Of all the phy-
sicians' hands she'd observed, she could recall none

gentler, none more sure. Where was the Sioux warrior in this man? Where was the savage?

"How did you come to live alone?" she asked. "I don't see that as common here. Not that I've visited any homes, but from what I've observed just in passing . . ."

Once again he admonished her with a glance.

"I'm sorry. I didn't mean to pry."

"Yes, you did. But it's not your fault. It's in your nature to pry." He forgave her with a knowing smile. "My wife died six years ago. She had tuberculosis. We had a baby, but he died, too. My mother stays here sometimes, but for now she is with her sister. My grandfather and my brother were"—his voice seemed to drop into the bucket along with the towel—"hospitalized."

"Where?"

"In Canton. My grandfather died there two summers ago."

"I'm sorry."

"I wanted to bring his body back here. A dead man could no longer be a threat to them, I thought, so I asked for his body." He scooped up the towel and twisted it hard. The water splashed his Levi's on its way back into the bucket. "But I was told that he was already buried. 'Interred on the grounds,' they said. They told me what it would cost to dig him up and bring him back on the train, and if I would pay in advance . . ." There was a faraway look in his eyes, a humorless smile on his lips. "I told them I would do it myself, but they couldn't permit that. Too far, they said. There are health codes and procedures, they said. These things must be handled properly."

"Who's *they*?" she asked gently. "Edward?"

"Trainor gives the answers. I don't know where they come from." He draped the cool towel over her ankle. "I told him they owed me this much, but he said the Indian Bureau wasn't the same as the War Department. There's no telling where the answers come from."

"I didn't realize that the people here took part in the war."

"Many of us volunteered when the recruiters came

around. And when they came around selling the war
bonds, our parents bought all they could because we
were in a fight. This was something they understood.
But the dead were not brought home, and this was something my grandfather did not understand. To leave the
dead behind, where their enemies might find them and
desecrate them so that the souls would not rest . . .''

He sat on the floor, his forearms draped over his
knees, and he spoke past her, looked past her, addressing
something in the log walls. ''I told him that was a load
of hooey. I saw what happened to men who were hit by
mortar fire. You can't desecrate a body any more than
that.'' He shifted his eyes to claim hers. ''You understand that, being a nurse.''

''Yes.'' It wasn't quite true. She'd seen terrible damage done to the human body, but not on the battlefield.
Still, she understood. She worked with patients whose
minds had somehow been desecrated. The damage was
invisible, but the agony was not.

He rubbed his beardless chin on his shirt sleeve. ''I
don't know what they did to him in Canton, but I know
I should have brought him home.''

''I'm sure they tried to help him there.''

''Are you?'' His tone was doubtful, distant.

''Dementia is very sad. There's little hope of bringing
the mind back. Sometimes we can diminish the agitation,
deter some of the violent episodes.'' She saw the anger
in his eyes, and she added gently, ''Try to make them
more comfortable. We surely do that.''

''My grandfather was not demented.''

''When you're close to someone, sometimes it's hard
to believe . . .'' Or maybe not. She watched him rise to
his feet. ''Who committed him?''

''His guardian,'' he said, embittered, adding crypti-
cally, ''his benevolent uncle.''

''Your grandfather's uncle?''

''Uncle,'' he said with an odd laugh. ''Uncle Sam.
Used to be known as our Great White Father.''

Whose agent, Rachael realized, was her brother. Edward was stuffy and self-righteous, but she had never

known him to misapprehend his responsibility or take it lightly. He had not mentioned to her that his responsibility included institutionalizing the mental patients she would soon attend, but she saw now that it did, since, as he had explained to her, Indians were wards of the federal government. She didn't doubt that that particular task weighed heavily on him.

"And your brother?" she asked. "How is he?"

"I haven't seen him in over three years." He took her look of surprise for reproach. "I *have* tried, but they say to me, 'Due to his current level of agitation, family visitation is prohibited.'" His own level of agitation subsided, and he reproached himself. "I've tried, but not hard enough. I say I'm going to see him anyway, but I wait for a better day. It's a long way to Canton, and the money to get there is hard to come by."

"That's true enough," she offered. "After I get started there and become familiar with his case, I'll certainly write to you and tell you how he's doing. Unless . . . would a letter be . . ."

"I can read." He mocked them both with a humorless smile. "Me, I'm a good boarding-school Indian. I can read and write and do all kinds of amazing tricks."

"I didn't mean to sound rude. I suppose you think that's part of my nature, too."

"What I think . . ." He turned away from her. "I've probably said enough to get myself committed. That's what I think."

"In my professional opinion you are as normal as any man, Mr. Lone Bull." She reached up and touched his shirtsleeve, bringing his head around again. She smiled. "And less tedious than most."

"Most men bore you?"

Her smile brightened. "Those who have no ears certainly do."

"Maybe it's time you looked for one who's built differently."

"A man built to listen," she mused. "Fascinating concept."

He studied her, his gaze falling not into her eyes, but

on her lips. Part of her wanted to cover them up, but another part of her was tempted to moisten them, make him do more than look. Then she wondered what in the world was *wrong* with her. She knew right well what he was thinking, and she was just sitting there *letting* him think, letting him churn up all this heat and letting herself . . .

"Where's the stove?" she asked. He blinked, finally. "You said you'd put some water on to boil, but—" She gestured toward a wall rack and a workbench, which appeared to serve as a kitchen. "I don't even see a cook stove."

"It's out front under the shade I put up for the summer," he told her, his interest clearly elsewhere. He straddled a third chair, scooting it closer to her, folding his arms around the back of it and tipping it on two legs as he leaned into the prospect of counting on her favor. "If you did write to me about my brother, I'd want to be told the truth. You understand? No hogwash."

"I would tell you the truth as I saw it. Of course, I'm not a doctor."

"That's one point in your favor. Point number two"—he held up two fingers. "You're not a white man."

"I'm a white *woman*."

That made him smile. "Do you wear a white nurse's dress?" She nodded, and he touched the crown of his own luxuriantly thick hair, which he wore trimmed above his ears. "A little cap?"

She laughed, nodding again.

The humor faded from his eyes, but the warmth of it remained, along with the risk of hope. "Are you capable of telling me something that is true, Rachael Trainor?"

She gave a resolute nod. "Certainly."

"No hesitation." He lowered the chair's front legs to the packed earth floor. "That's a good sign. I'll get the water before it boils away, and we'll clean up that arm."

"I appreciate your help. You have a gentle . . ." She glanced away, feeling oddly atingle simply because she'd almost said *touch*. "I don't know what I would have done if you hadn't come along."

"Your brother would have come looking for you."

"Would he come here?"

"He's been known to show up here. When he thinks I have something he wants, he comes looking for me." He snatched his hat from the table, then stood there studying it, fingering the shapeless brim. "We used to get along pretty good, him and me."

She groaned, amused by the concept. "We used to fight like cats and dogs, him and me. But he's the only brother I've got."

"Mine is only a boy of fifteen. *He's* the gentle one, my brother is. Our mother spoiled him. I used to give him a bad time about being the baby boy, but he would never get mad at me. He would just say"—he looked up, seemed surprised to find her listening, then shrugged, half smiling—"that I was the warrior in the family and he was the peacemaker."

"There must be quite a difference in your ages, then."

"I'm aging rapidly," he said as he put on his hat, pulling the brim down low. "Thirty-two. My brother was just a little guy when our father died, not long after I came back from the war. Then my wife died, my son. My little brother was a comfort to me. He was very close to our grandfather. They shared . . . certain things." He shoved his hands into his pants pockets. Half his years seemed to drop away, replaced by long-forgotten enthusiasm. "You'll see for yourself that there's nothing wrong with him. You'll see."

She smiled. "What's his name?"

"When you see him, call him Pagla. Say it for me."

"Pag-la," they recited together.

He nodded jauntily. "Good. It means . . . it's a small owl. Unlike me, my brother did not spend much time in school, and he speaks little English. My grandfather decided that one 'progressive Indian' in the family was enough."

"What name would be on your brother's records?"
"Martin Lone Bull."

When Adam Lone Bull delivered Rachael to her brother, the two men exchanged little more than the warning glances of passing rival males. Adam didn't even get down from the wagon seat and spared little interest as Edward awkwardly helped Rachael down. The big man was probably embarrassed for her scrawny brother, she decided. Considering the meager support Edward had to offer her as she hobbled up the wooden porch steps, she decided it was a good thing he hadn't been on the scene when she fell. He could never have lifted her off the ground the way Adam had done. Too late she realized that her rescuer had gone unrewarded but for her thanks.

"If he hadn't come along, I'd still be sitting there," she told her brother.

"I was about to send someone out," he assured her. "The horse came back on his own."

"That stupid horse."

"Hardly." Edward assisted her as far as the parlor sofa. "As I said, the horse came back on his own."

Rachael had built many a walking cast in her time, but she'd never been the tottering wearer of one. It took some getting used to. She decided to stay at the agency for an extra week, but no longer. She and Edward were beginning to get on each other's nerves. She'd messed up the order of things in his pantry, and he had questioned her about Adam Lone Bull once too often. How had the Indian behaved? Did he ask her for money? Had he mentioned any plans for his allotted land? Surely the man would have to sell it. Nobody was making it on the land these days, and Lone Bull never even showed up to claim his rations anymore. What was he eating, anyway? Rachael reported that she'd seen a garden.

"He's got himself a well," Edward said.

"Is that so unusual?"

"Water's a problem. A lot of the land allotments have

been sold off, especially since everything's dried up. But Lone Bull's father had a pretty good operation going back before the war. Cattle prices were good during the war, and my predecessor encouraged the Indian ranchers to sell their stock, make some money, which most of them did. Then they leased the land over to white ranchers, and, of course, the parcels with water are the first to go. Adam Senior held on longer than most. For his sons, he said. After the war things got tough, and then, of course, the Lone Bulls had to look after their relatives. That's the way they are here. But that's one well that never went dry."

"Adam has since lost most of his family," Rachael recalled.

"He showed a lot of promise once," Edward allowed. "It's this whole tribal thing that kills them. You can't get ahead when you're giving it all away. Now the old-timers sit around talking about their treaty claims. They've hired a lawyer to argue that they've got money coming from the government for the taking of the Black Hills. And all the progressives, which Adam Lone Bull *used to be*, they've just given up on becoming productive citizens. They might as well finish selling off their allotted land and let somebody get some use out of it."

"Then what will they do?"

Edward shrugged. "Come see me for their monthly rations. If Roosevelt gets elected, these Indians can expect some changes."

"It can't get too much worse for them, can it?"

"Whether it can or it can't, the more traditional ones are afraid of change. They're afraid of the boarding schools, afraid of their mixed-blood cousins." He laughed. "Hell, they're even afraid of me. I try to look after them, and they're afraid of me. Is it any wonder they had to build an asylum just for insane Indians? They drive themselves crazy." He shook his head sadly. "You can't plant yourself in the way of progress and still hang on to your sanity. You might as well just divest yourself of the past and move on. Those who don't"— he deferred to Rachael with a graceful gesture—"may find themselves in my gimpy sister's otherwise competent custody.''

Indeed, they *were* getting on each other's nerves.

Late that afternoon a shuffling sound in the kitchen distracted Rachael from the novel she was reading. She eased her cast-bound foot off a pile of pillows and descended the stairs quietly. She'd offered to make supper, but Edward had gone off saying he wasn't hungry and that he would make do for himself later. If he was rummaging around in the kitchen already, she meant to remind him of the cold chicken in the icebox.

But when she got downstairs she discovered an unexpected visitor.

"Adam, what are you doing"—she saw the bottle in his hand, and she let the last word drop—"here?"

He took off his hat and hung it on the back of a chair, as if he were planning to stay a while. "As you see, I'm helping myself to your brother's whiskey."

"I thought Edward had left."

"He has." He leveled her with a look that dared her to be inhospitable. "I thought you were going to Canton."

"I am." She glanced at the curtained window. "I guess I didn't hear you knock on the door."

"No, you didn't." He smiled enigmatically. "I don't knock on doors."

"You didn't think anyone was here?"

"I saw Trainor at the trading post, and I could tell he'd be gone for a while." He uncapped the brown bottle. "How's your foot?"

"It's clumsy. And fractured a bit. You were right." She sat down at the little kitchen table, watching warily as he took a drink straight from the bottle. "I'm surprised Edward keeps that around."

He winced as he swallowed. "He stocks it just for me. A few years ago, him and me, we'd throw down a couple of belts together and laugh about Prohibition. Comrades in arms, he'd say, and we traded war stories. His were different from mine. He didn't spend much time in the trenches." He moved the other chair, his hat swaying from the finial, but instead of claiming it for himself, he motioned for her to prop her cast on the seat. "We both liked Paris."

"You appear to be a very enlightened man, Adam," she observed magnanimously as she elevated her foot, adding a parenthetical word of thanks. "It seems to me . . ."

"That I should know better? Everyone knows that Indians can't handle 'spirits.' " He leaned back against the drain board and examined the bottle closely. "White men don't have any problem. They don't believe in spirits."

"There are people of all races who have problems with alcohol, which is why we have Prohibition. Would you care for a chicken sandwich?"

"I didn't come to eat." As if to prove his point, he took another drink.

"But I'm inviting you to—"

"I used to be 'enlightened,' " he told her, offering the bottle in her direction. She shook her head, and he helped himself again before amending, "Or 'progressive,' that's the word they like to use. But the light went out, and I am not making progress anymore."

"What light?"

"The white light. Bright city lights." He tipped the bottle to his lips again, and she had half a mind to tell him to take the bottle and go. But when he set it aside and smiled at her, she forgot that notion completely. "Have you been to Paris?" he asked.

"No, I haven't. Would you like a glass?"

He shook his head. "In Paris we were all just 'Yanks.' The girls were always glad to see us, and in the taverns they poured the wine for everybody."

"You shouldn't drink like that, Adam."

He grinned. "How should I drink?"

"You should slow down. You might—"

"Get drunk?"

"Well, if you do, you might get caught."

"I usually do," he said much too cheerfully. "When I drink, I get drunk. And when I'm drunk it's easy to catch me." His hand settled on the bottle again. "They tell us to leave it alone. Then they put it on the shelf and walk away, just to see what we'll do."

What he did was help himself. Again, right there in front of her. Obviously he didn't think she'd report him. And he was right. But maybe she could slow him down, distract him, encourage him to talk more and drink less. "Do you think about the war a lot?"

"I don't think about it at all." He stared at her cast, quietly adding, "But sometimes I dream about it."

"Then this drinking isn't good, Adam." She gripped the edge of the table and leaned toward him. "I'm a nurse, and I know about these things. I understand."

"You're a white woman. There is wisdom born in your skin. Isn't that so?" He laid his finger against his temple and smiled. "You don't need anything up here because you are born with the answers in your skin. You understand nothing, but you know what's good for everyone." He lifted the bottle and toasted her. "Enlightenment."

"Adam, this is crazy."

All trace of humor left his eyes. "Crazy?"

She would have called the word back, but since it wasn't possible, she ejected herself from the chair, banging her cast as she pushed its prop aside. She looked to him to protest, to tell her to sit back down, to be careful, but he only eyed her coldly as he took another drink.

She moved to his side and put her hand on the bottle. "Edward could come back any time and catch you at this, and I'm sure there would be hell for you to pay."

"I pay hell every day of my life, Rachael Trainor." He glared, daring her to contradict him. She drew her hand back, and the storm brewing in his face blew over. "Your brother doesn't intend to catch me here. He knows that I know where he keeps his whiskey." He looked at her, arching one eyebrow as if he'd just noticed some remarkable feature. "And here's his sister. Did he leave his sister on the shelf for me, too?"

"Don't be ridiculous."

"It's a trick the Lakota used to use on the battlefield,

back when we had a few horses and a little room to maneuver.'' He pointed to some imaginary high ground beyond the kitchen door. "Put somebody up on a hill as a decoy. Somebody who looks like an easy catch. If that somebody works it right, the enemy can be fooled into giving chase. Lure him right into a trap." He raised the bottle in deference to the agent's sister. "But it only works if the enemy is tempted by the decoy."

"And clearly you are tempted if that bottle is the decoy."

"I have developed a taste for the whiskey, but not the sister. I'm willing to risk losing my mind." He offered a mordant smile. "But not my balls."

"You're quite mistaken, Adam."

"It's a poor choice?" He turned the bottle, ostensibly checking the contents. "You can do more for me than this?"

She refused to be baited. "That can do you no good at all."

"But you can." He shifted his shoulders, leaning closer, tipping his head as if to confide in her. "I told you what good deed you could do for me."

"And I told you that I would write to you about your brother." She lifted her chin and looked him directly in the eye. "I will do that, and I will be truthful."

He searched her eyes for the truth she promised, then turned to the bottle again, betraying no hint of what he'd found. "I don't know what they do to people there in Canton, but I do know that no one ever leaves that place."

"Well, I'm sure that all depends. Some patients improve simply with prolonged rest."

"Rest?" He looked up at the milled molding that trimmed a pale gray ceiling quite different from his own. "Indians get plenty of rest at home. That's mostly what we do. We're known for our laziness."

She ignored his sarcasm. "Is your brother violent?"

"Never." He looked at her and repeated quietly, fervently, "Never."

"But you said yourself that you're older, you left

home when he was young, you hardly knew him until—"

. "My brother was never violent. There is no violence in him." His tone brooked no dissention. "In me? Yes," he allowed. "But not in him."

"If he suffers from depression—"

"He suffers now when he did not before."

"How do you know?"

"I know." He glanced away. Suddenly he had distanced himself, slipped into some wrinkle in his own mind. "I see him in my dreams. I see my father, my grandfather, and I see my brother."

"And the war."

"But not tonight." His focus and his confidence reverted to the brown bottle. "Not if I drink this until I pass out."

"How did your father die?"

"This is an excellent question," he admitted, amused. "One that a woman would know to ask. Maybe the skin makes less difference than I thought." Again he saluted her with the bottle before indulging in a drink.

"Tell me the answer," she urged.

The ghost of a smile touched his eyes, and his voice drifted on the memory. "My father tried to make it work. 'We have our treaties,' he said. 'We have land, and they owe us for what they took.' But he was worn down. I came back from the war, and I could see it. He'd bought that car, but most of the cows were gone. He put on a big feed to celebrate his son's victory. He had a giveaway ceremony, gave the war bonds he'd bought on the promise that doing so would bring me home safely. 'Ohan,' he said. 'They sure did.' "

He looked at her, inviting her to be his confessor. She nodded, encouraging him to go on.

"He was not the same man. I never saw him drink before. My mother said nothing, just watched. I was the big man, now. I had seen the world. I had tasted French wine. I told him, 'You're a foolish old man for giving everything away, and you're going to kill yourself with that stuff.' "

She glanced fearfully at the bottle in his hand.

"The woman thinks she has counted coups on me now," he observed with a chuckle. "Got me to make her point for her. But the stuff that killed my father wasn't good whiskey like your brother's. It was the kind that eats flesh."

"In time any of it will do that."

"Time itself will do that. Clock time. The kind of time your people brought us." He shook his head. "The war changed many things. Many people, not just my father. There was a big demand for beef, and the agents said the price was good, so we sold the cattle. Then we leased the land or sold it, and with the money we bought things. Things with batteries and motors."

"Who's *we*? Weren't you in the army?"

"My family was here," he said quietly. "Now they are gone, and I am here."

"I don't like what I see here, Adam, and I haven't been here very long. But I believe . . . I *know* that there are many, many people—white people, yes—who want to see things change. The working people in this country are suffering, the farmers, the laborers, the veterans, the . . ." She checked to see whether he was still with her. A little glassy-eyed, but still functioning. "This is an election year, and I truly believe—"

"Us Indians are citizens now, but in most states we can't vote. And even if we could—" He paused for another pull on the bottle. "That car," he said softly, drifting again. "My father was proud of that car. Proud to show it to me, show me how he could drive it. Me, I said he was a fool."

"But I know you didn't mean to hurt him."

"How do you know?" He looked at her as though he suddenly had no idea where she'd come from. "What does it matter what you know, Rachael Trainor?"

"*You* know, then. Because you have . . ." She wanted to touch him, just to reassure him, but the way he was looking at her, she didn't dare. She smiled instead. "You have ears."

"Good ones." He smiled, too, then lifted one shoulder, taking half the smile back. "Well, not so good since they fired those big guns right next to my head, but good enough. I'm a good one for listening. I went to boarding school. I heard about all the plans for making us into good Americans. We were supposed to take the land they allotted us and become cattlemen. But when the cattle are gone, then you lease the land, or you sell it, and they plow it up, and the earth our people have walked, our fathers and grandfathers have walked, that same earth blows away . . ."

He kept covering the same ground, over and over again, like a man shackled to a stake.

"The drought hit everyone hard," she said.

"My father would not sell, but he did lease the land. Then the white man who leased it moved away, and my father died. I tried to raise cattle. I tried to lease the land. I even tried to—" He could not bring himself to admit it, but she could see that he'd been willing to sell anything he had. "It was too late by then. My wife and my son were dead, and the little food it would have brought could do them no good. And my grandfather said . . ."

He was drifting away again, and she wanted to keep him with her, keep him talking until she could figure out how to help, what to do to keep him from, Lord, going off the deep end.

"Your grandfather said?"

"Nothing. Something about selling the bones of my ancestors. Something about . . ." He shook his head. "Sometimes the dreams get mixed up with the past, you know? Scares the shit out of me when that happens." He closed his eyes and turned his face from hers. "Sorry. I've said too much."

"No." She made him look at her, took his face impulsively in her hands, and forced him to rest his sad eyes on hers. "I have ears, too. Good ones."

"And lips, and tongue." The sadness in his eyes slipped into his smile. "A heart, too, I think." His eyes held hers as he turned his head, briefly touching his own lips to her palm. Then he took both her hands in one of his and slid them over his shirt to the middle of his chest. "You will tell me about my brother."

"I will write to you." Her mouth went dry. She could feel his heart thudding against the back of her hand. "I promise."

"I would not ask you, Rachael Trainor, but there is no one else. And if your promise is empty there is nothing I will lose by it."

She swallowed hard. "Not even a shred of faith?"

"In what?" He released her hands, his eyes turning cool again. "You?"

"In human nature."

"I have faith that this will make me laugh and cry and sleep like the dead. And, finally, it will make me puke my guts out." He capped the bottle. "Then I'll leave it alone for a while."

"There must be a better way." Even she could hear the hollowness in her claim.

"For you I'm sure there is. Tell your brother I said go to hell." He tucked the bottle under his arm and moved toward the door, chuckling to himself. "I'll buy him a drink there."

"I'm not going to"—he closed the door on the last of her pledges—"tell him anything."

She went to the window, her throat burning as she watched him disappear into the evening shadows. Her foot throbbed, and her head ached, and she felt sickeningly powerless. The man who had helped her was determined to harm himself. She wanted to stop him, but she didn't know how. She hated that feeling, the feeling that there was something that needed doing, but the means to do it was beyond her reach. Before the tears came she went to her room and locked the door.

❧ 5 ❧

"Good morning, Martin."

The strikingly handsome sixteen-year-old acknowledged Rachael's greeting in his usual way. He lifted his eyebrows. It wasn't much, but in the four weeks since she'd been working at the asylum, she'd made it her business to learn each patient's means of communicating. Martin Lone Bull's face was not only beautiful but expressive.

For many of the patients communication was simply a matter of speaking in English, or one of a number of different Indian tongues, or some combination. Many of them were quite rational, lucid, surprisingly docile. There were several epileptics, but Rachael had yet to witness a seizure. There were a number of people who had been patients at the asylum most of their lives. They knew the history of the place better than Dr. Tim did.

But, of course, there were the problems that were self-evident—the usual range of low- to high-grade imbecility to idiocy, various forms of dementia, organic brain disease, intoxication, and manic-depressive psychoses, and, according to Dr. Tim, the occasional constitutional psychopath. It was hard to determine from the records the circumstances under which many of them had been committed. Actually, it was hard to determine much of *anything* from the records, but Rachael hoped to improve the record-keeping over time. The demands on Dr. Tim's attention were beyond one man's capacity. He'd also hinted that some of the circumstances under which Indians could be committed for mental treatment might seem unusual, but Indian health needs were different, and she would soon learn that there were many special circumstances to be considered.

Patients were consigned to Hiawatha Asylum from reservations in all parts of the country, but there were many Sioux, who, of course, spoke the first Indian language she had come in contact with. And there were many patients who did not verbalize at all, which was to be expected. Rachael had quickly concluded that her first task was to learn each patient's particular signals. She was good at that.

"How are you feeling this morning, Pagla?" She motioned for him to stay seated on the bed as she drew up the chair and whispered with a secret smile, "*Pagla,* how are you?"

The boy smiled, too. This was progress, and it wasn't the first instance. He'd begun responding to her more than a week ago. Before that he'd offered nothing but a vacant stare.

"Dr. Tim insists upon 'Martin,' but I think he's being a stickler about that for no good reason, and I know you prefer 'Pagla.' Do you know who told me that?"

Since she didn't expect any answers, she plugged her ears with her stethoscope. As usual the boy drew back from her attempt to lift his pajama shirt. "No, I'm just going to listen, the way I've done before. Then you can listen, too, all right?"

He hung his head, avoiding her eyes as he reached for her hand and the compromise she had previously devised to allay his fears. "All right, together," she said, and she guided the instrument, his hand guarding hers. He didn't like to be examined, but he permitted it as long as she let him set the limits.

"*Wašté,*" she said. "Sounds good. *Wašté.* Your chest sounds almost clear. Frankly, I think you've just had a touch of ordinary congestion. I wish we could get some tests done and put to rest Dr. Tim's suspicions once and for all.''

Dr. Tim suspected tuberculosis in seven of the patients, but no X rays or sputum tests were done. It was not a nurse's place to question the doctor's judgment, but she'd never heard of "inactive" TB being handled this way. The doctor deemed confirming his suspicions unnecessary. He didn't have the lab facilities to do it himself, he said, and funds were short. Since he was doing all that could be done for them by enforcing rest, there was no need to take them all the way to Sioux Falls or Yankton for tests.

Rachael thought it an unusual approach. Not all of the "suspicious" cases were isolated the way Martin Lone Bull was. Some were getting plenty of sunshine in the solaria, but fresh air was certainly in short supply there. The doctor used the word *inactive* pretty loosely, she thought. But Rachael was new to the Canton program, and she'd already learned that Dr. Tim's decisions were not to be questioned outright. If she were to succeed in effecting any changes, she would have to be diplomatic about it.

"Anyway, Pagla, you remember who told me your name. It was Adam. *Ciye*. Brother. Your brother, Adam." She'd coaxed another smile from her patient. "Yes, I have met him. I really believe you understand what I'm saying. Your brother, *ciye* Adam, was the one who told me to call you Pagla. And he told me how to say it. Pagla."

She produced a thermometer for the boy, let him see what it was, and assured him with a gesture that she wanted to put it in his mouth, not his rectum, which she'd gathered from his previous responses had been somebody's practice with him. She could not imagine why.

"I want to learn more about your language," she told her patient as she supervised his handling of the thermometer, pointing her finger under her own tongue to remind him of the proper seating. "Yes, that's it.

One of the women—Alice DeCouteau? Do you know Alice? She's taught me a few words." When she wasn't crying, Alice could be quite instructive. "*Cepa.* I think that means fat. At first I thought that meant 'pregnant' because Alice pointed to her stomach, and, of course, she is pregnant, but then she said '*Cepa* like Amos,' and Amos, well . . . Amos is fat. *Cepa.*" She laid her hand on her own stomach. "Big stomach."

Pagla pursed his lips around the thermometer and leaned toward Rachael for a closer look at her flat stomach.

"No, not me. I'm not *cepa.* You can see that, can't you? And you're trying to figure out what I'm talking about because you *do* understand. I'm making a little sense, but not much." She tipped his chin up, made him look at her, gave him an encouraging nod. "Just a little. Let me try another word. Alice also said, um . . ." She stood up a little and imitated Alice's defining actions, patting her bottom, lowering it to the chair. "'*Onze,*' Alice told me, and she . . . I think she wanted me to sit."

Pagla looked surprised.

"*Onze.* Am I saying it right? Sit down? Does it mean to sit down?"

Delighted now, the boy gave a soundless laugh.

"You're laughing at me. And that's not what it means, is it, but you *are* almost—" But for the lack of sound, he might have been doing what should have come naturally to a sixteen-year-old. "You're laughing, you rascal. If I'm saying it wrong, you're welcome to cor—" The laughter in the boy's eyes vanished. "What's wrong?"

She had only to turn around, following the direction of Pagla's stare.

"What are you doing, Miss Trainor?"

"Dr. Tim!" She ejected herself from the chair, gesturing excitedly. "Dr. Tim, this boy is not unreachable. I'm sure he understands some of what I'm—"

"I know you mean well, Miss Trainor, but you are

very new to this service, and I cannot spare you to play charades.''

She turned to her patient to reclaim the thermometer. ''I'm getting vitals on the patients who—''

''I'm looking after Martin quite closely, Miss Trainor. I saw him first thing this morning, didn't I, Martin?''

The boy's eyes had glazed over.

''Severe idiocy, Miss Trainor. The boy is well beyond our reach, which, I grant you, is almost too sad to admit for one so sweet. And handsome, too, don't you think? Despite the dark skin.'' The boy stiffened as Dr. Tim patted his hair. ''But with such a sweet disposition we hardly ever have to worry about Martin's behavior, and I do keep close watch lest his physical condition deteriorate.''

''His temperature is normal, and his chest . . .'' The doctor's shuttered expression made Rachael uneasy. ''Well, as you've already seen for yourself.''

''Indeed, I have.'' He gestured toward the open door. ''Please accompany me to the hospital building, Miss Trainor. We have people coming down with influenza left and right. You have no idea how these people suffer with it, no matter what the season. And now Alice DeCouteau has broken her arm.''

''Broken her—'' Rachael had been with the woman just yesterday afternoon. ''How?''

''An accident on the slide.''

''Poor Alice.'' Playground equipment left over from a requisition for Indian boarding schools had been installed by the Indian office for recreation, which was an important part of Dr. Tim's program. ''I do hope the baby—''

''No sign of trouble there. Leave that,'' he ordered when she started to pick up the foul-smelling chamber pot on her way out of the boy's room. ''That's the attendant's job.''

''Doctor, I know we're understaffed. I can . . . I mean I just can't walk away from this. It would help if these antiquated things at least had lids.''

"The list of things we don't have is as long as my arm." As if to measure it out he used that arm to usher Rachael into the hall, then motioned to attendant Dick Hollings. "Empty the pot in here, Hollings. It's beginning to stink."

"Some of the attendants don't seem to understand the meaning of the word *sanitation*," Rachael confided as she followed Dr. Tim out the front door. It was a relief to breathe fresh air. "They'd rather sweep up in the hallways than try to clean up a patient who has not been out of his bed for God knows how long." She made a mental promise to herself that the empty lawn chairs on the porch would be occupied with patients this very afternoon.

"God isn't the only one who knows, Miss Trainor." The doctor gave a perfunctory smile as they descended the steps of the institution's "main" building, which housed two offices, kitchen and dining facilities, and two wings to accommodate patients. "Dr. Tim knows everything that goes on here."

Rachael had no grounds to doubt her colleague. She hadn't been on the job long enough to evaluate competency, but she'd determined quickly that the plant and its equipment were well below the minimum standard for a government medical institution.

She glanced at the offending playground apparatus as they walked past on their way to the newer brick building, which was called the hospital out of habit rather than function. The rolling grounds were peaceful and bucolic. The asylum's own farm boasted a dairy along with hog and horse barns. With the playground equipment in the yard, the two massive red brick and gray stone buildings might have been mistaken for one of the Indian bureau's numerous boarding schools. The swings were quite popular among the patients. Last week they'd been the cause of a fight between two of the older women, and the attendant on duty had herded everyone inside.

The hospital building had an operating room on the second floor and a hydrotherapy room in the basement.

Neither one served its intended purpose. The central portion of the building was used for employees' quarters. Rachael had a small room on the second floor. The drug room was on the first floor, along with the employees' kitchen and dining room. Wings on either side of the building housed more patients.

Dr. Tim gave a cursory inspection of the dormitory rooms, starting upstairs with the men, noting that Mr. Blue had settled down since yesterday. A paraplegic diagnosed with high-grade imbecility, Mr. Blue was consigned to mutter away the daylight hours on a mattress on the floor in one of the four-bed rooms. At night when he became "disturbed" the attendants sometimes locked him in the bathroom.

"Let's see if they're cooking down here yet." Dr. Tim led the way to the solarium, which had been designed as a sunning area, particularly for patients suffering from tuberculosis. But it was used as just another ward room in the hospital building.

"Cooking?" Rachael had yet to see the doctor take a meal in the employees' dining room.

He laughed. "Our residents in the solarium."

"It does get awfully warm," Rachael said, rolling up the sleeves of her uniform. She would have to get used to Dr. Tim's odd sense of humor.

"You do understand that we are a containment facility, Miss Trainor. We keep these poor souls from endangering society and, if at all possible, from harming themselves. There's little more we can do." He surveyed the three empty beds with their dingy linens and threadbare coverlets. The glass-walled solarium was bright, which was a cheery change from the rest of the building, but it was unbearably stuffy. There were no shades and no ventilation.

Patient Peter Magpie sat on a mattress on the floor smoking a handmade cigarette.

"Where are your roommates, Pete?"

The white-haired man jerked his thumb over his shoulder as he puffed. Peter was blind. Two of his roommates were thought to be tubercular, although neither showed any sign that the disease was active.

"In the toilet?" Dr. Tim asked.

Peter grunted.

"You want to go outside today, Pete? Play some horseshoes?"

The blind man grunted again.

"It's bound to be a long winter," the doctor warned. "Might as well get out while you still can."

Peter laughed himself into a coughing spasm, then sought relief in his cigarette.

Dr. Tim did an about-face, signaling Rachael with a subtle jerk of his head. He led the way back into the dim hall, quipping, "These are the times that try men's sanity."

"Sanitation, as well," Rachael muttered.

He turned on her suddenly, flicking his white clinic coat back, imperiously planting fists on hips. Dr. Tim was not a huge man, but ample. Pudgy hands, high waist, rounded hips, a wattle under his chin. Her father would have described him as a man with undeniable presence.

"I cannot see to every distasteful detail, Miss Trainor."

"I know that, Doctor."

"I am a crusader with few allies, and she who is not my ally is but one more thorn in my side." He leaned closer. "I do not intend to become a pincushion here, Miss Trainor."

He was alluding, as he did each time they spoke, to the dissension among some of the members of his staff, which had bothered Rachael since the day she'd arrived in Canton and met Ella Sims, head nurse at the asylum.

Head nurse? Rachael had barely managed to curb an immediate challenge to the title. She'd thought *she* had been hired for the position of head nurse.

Not right away, Dr. Tim had confided when she'd questioned him privately. There was the small matter of getting rid of Ella Sims first. He'd been at odds with that woman long enough, hoped to send her packing soon, at which time, he suggested, the job would be Rachael's. The news was only the beginning of her disappointments.

They looked in on the women on the first floor. Lizzie Buck had refused to leave her bed because her throat was bothering her, so she'd been manacled to the bed frame for safe keeping. "Ah, dear Lizzie, more flu," Dr. Tim sympathized. "Rest is what you need."

"I've asked the attendants to open the windows as far as they can," Rachael reported as they headed back to the main building after dropping cursory aid and comfort in two additional dormitory rooms. "With the bars on the windows, you can only raise them a couple of inches, but even that would help. The thing is, the attendants can't seem to see the necessity from one day to the next. So each day—"

"Yes, well, I've been superintendent here for thirteen years. I have to attend to security first, comfort somewhere down the line. I'm running the place on a shoestring, and still we continue to function." He opened the front door of the main building and stepped back to let her precede him. "We are an important part of the economy in this part of the state. Most of the people who work here are grateful for the employment. The city of Canton is delighted to have us here."

"Certainly understandable," Rachael allowed. "I intend to be of every assistance—"

"And you will be," Dr. Tim assured her. "Yes, I do think some changes are in order around here. Long overdue."

"And some of them won't be that difficult to make really," Rachael said, heartened by the sense that they were both on the same track. She followed him through the reception area, past the two administrative offices and into the dark hallway that connected the two dormitory wings with the central kitchen and dining area. She could smell cabbage boiling for supper. "I'd like to propose a few changes in the routine. I think we could improve sanitation if we got rid of—"

"The chamber pots?" He shook his head as though he'd heard this suggestion before. "We must have chamber pots. We can't have our charges wandering around at night."

"Hospital bedpans are standard for those who can't—"

He waved the suggestion away. "Unnecessary expense. The pots are still perfectly functional, and there's no money to be had for anything fancier. We pride ourselves on our ability to economize. We have consistently *saved* government money, turned a tidy surplus back to the Interior Department."

"Really?" Offhand she could name about a hundred needs on which to spend a tidy "surplus."

"Economy looks very good on our records, especially now." With a smile he reiterated, "These are the times that try men's sanity."

"Women's, too."

"Yes, indeed, the mind can only cope with so much sorrow," Dr. Tim expounded, his voice filling the long, brown corridor. "In these troubled times, with so little money to operate this place . . ." He gestured dramatically. "As I've said so often, those who control themselves will fare better than those who do not. They will be cleaner, and they will have more freedom. As for the rest, we can control their arms, their legs, but not their bodily functions."

A clatter in the back stairwell leading to the basement distracted him. A thunderous shout followed, then a snarling, unintelligible curse.

Dr. Tim shook his head. "And not their mouths, unfortunately, without resorting to measures . . ."

"The noise is part of the pain," Rachael said, her attention, too, drawn to the back stairwell. She'd been forewarned that, on occasion, a dangerous patient might be taken to the "dark ward," where he could be restrained and subdued without agitating the others. Sedatives and bromides were used first, but a patient could not be sedated indefinitely. A cold water treatment was sometimes just the shock required to gain a violent patient's submission. Rachael was familiar with the procedure. She hated it.

Dr. Tim gave a resigned sigh. "Yes, but the attendants can only be expected to tolerate so much."

The same would have to be true for the patients, she thought, but it would be imprudent for a nurse to advance such an argument to a doctor. She would make it her business to report rather than to conjecture. The overall conditions at the asylum had shocked her, but she'd managed to comment sparingly. Dr. Tim was only one man, one medical doctor with a degree in psychiatry. Most of the employees at the asylum were unskilled local residents. Dr. Tim clearly needed support from what there was of his professional staff.

Support and straightforward information. "I have had occasion to remove adhesive tape from some of the patients' mouths, Doctor. They could choke."

"Indeed they could. We must not let that happen." Again he confided, "I can't tell you what a relief it is to have you on staff. It's been so hard to get anyone to come. Thank God for Edward."

"It wasn't my brother's idea. After that government investigation a few years ago—"

"Yes, well, the damn Meriam Report on the failures of the Indian Service made everyone in Washington jumpy. They even sent me one of their meddling snoops. Dr. Know-It-All himself." Dr. Tim chuckled. "They're never accurate, you know, those reports. They're written to satisfy some politician who thinks some particular crusade will garner votes. Lately it's Indian policy. Next year it'll be something else. You know how that goes. They come, they snoop around, they go back where they came from. Some government know-nothing who has no experience in dealing with people who—"

The voice of outrage bellowed again from below the stairs.

"People who are in that condition," the doctor continued, pointing in the direction of the tortured uproar. "A man with the body and mind of a bull, unable to

reason and extremely dangerous.'' He shoved his
hands in his pockets and started slowly back down the
hall, luring Rachael along with his continuing discourse. ''A new patient. Rotgut liquor corrodes the
mind as well as the body. It's tragic. They've had to
take him downstairs on several occasions. Very difficult to subdue.''

''I believe I made some progress with Martin Lone
Bull. I'd like to continue—''

''I think it's best if you attend primarily to the
women, Rachael. Poor Alice. We don't want to see her
lose that baby, do we?'' He paused at his office door.
''Although, God help the little bugger, I can't imagine
what will become of him.''

''Doesn't she have family?''

''Who knows?''

We ought to, she thought. ''She can't have been a
patient here very long. The baby's father—''

''Who knows when and where and with whom these
people copulate? I doubt that Alice knows. With such
a deficit in her mentality, there's little potential for
morality, is there?''

Dr. Tim chuckled to himself as he turned the knob
on the office door. Then he paused, turning to Rachael, apparently expecting her to respond to his comment. She took a step back. She couldn't laugh with
him and didn't know quite what to say. She just stared
at him.

''I intend to make the best use of your skills,'' he
assured her, going back to the question of her duties
since his wit was obviously lost on her. ''I don't want
you emptying slop jars or struggling with windows or
wasting your efforts trying to coax sense from the
senseless. You have all you can handle with those who
become physically ill, as they are so wont to do. No
resistance to disease.'' He shook his head and sighed.
''They are like children, these Indian people. They remain children, despite our best efforts. They are simply a weak breed, poor souls.''

''I don't . . . I mean, they've been through so

much.'' She wanted to come up with something better, but she *was* at a loss.

"Yes, yes, they have. Those who are strong enough will take their place in society. Those who are not—'' He gestured, indicating the east wing, then the west. "Many of them are here. Unable to adjust, unable to go forward. They need discipline and care. If you were looking for needy patients, Miss Trainor, you've come to the right place.''

"Then I'd better find Alice and see how she's doing with that arm.''

"Cora instructed me to invite you to come for dinner tonight. Roast chicken, I believe. Cora can do wonders with even the scrawniest capon.''

"That sounds lovely.''

"But I do have one rule.'' He raised an imperative finger. "Once I leave the hospital I speak of my work only in very general terms, particularly around Cora. She's a gentle soul, and the details of all this—''

"It's hard to talk medicine with anyone but another medical professional.''

"So true,'' he said, his whole face radiant with his grin. "I think we'll make a good team, Miss Trainor. This is the only institution of its kind in existence, you know. This is an outpost, and we are pioneers in our field. There is no precedent but the one we set here.''

It was hard to disagree with Dr. Tim. It was impossible to dislike him, even when he said something that had a bit of an unpleasant odor if you took a moment to sniff at it. It was like an overboiled egg, Rachael decided. You simply tossed that one out and relied on the good stuff. He was, after all, the doctor.

But he was wrong about Alice. The young woman had been diagnosed with manic depression, and the doctor insisted that she was "as uncommuicative as the rest of them,'' yet she had begun to respond to Rachael.

"What were you doing on the playground?'' Rachael asked gently when she found the injured woman sitting alone in the dark hallway, cradling her casted forearm on the small mound her stomach was becoming. "Did you forget about the baby?"

Alice looked up, indignation flashing in her dark eyes. "I was thinking about the baby. Those toys, they are made for children." She lowered her lashes as her hand, poking through the white plaster, stirred over the cotton nightgown covering her stomach. "This guy wanted to play."

"He didn't want his mother to get hurt."

"He wanted his mother to do *something*." Alice sighed and glanced down the drab, empty hallway. "Sometimes I think I'm going crazy."

Rachael swallowed hard. Alice turned her head slowly and looked into her eyes, anticipating, daring some response. Rachael froze under the young woman's startling scrutiny. She felt responsible somehow. Derelict. Guilty.

The corners of Alice's mouth twitched. With her good hand she gave Rachael's shoulder a playful little push. "Come on, nurse. Laugh a little."

Disconcerted, Rachael managed a smile.

Alice leaned closer, studying Rachael's face. "You look tired. You tired of us already?"

"No, not at all," Rachael said quickly. "But a broken arm is nothing for a nurse to laugh about."

"It's my arm that's broken, and I ain't cryin' about it. Not today." Suddenly she sat up straighter on the backless wooden bench. "Eee, I felt him move. He's kickin' around in there. See, he ain't cryin'." She moved her hand over her stomach and laughed. "Again! Strong baby, this one." She reached for Rachael's hand and placed it on the side of the gentle mound. They waited together until it happened again. "Feel that?" Alice crowed.

Slight but certain quickening. Rachael nodded, feeling at once delighted and restored. "Oh, yes. This is a strong one all right."

"We call it 'growing strong' in my language." Alice mirrored Rachael's nod with her own. "You say 'pregnant.' We say a woman is 'growing strong.'"

"And you are, Alice. You're growing strong with this child." She smiled as the baby moved beneath her hand once more. "It's wonderful."

"Maybe," Alice said, her attention drifting down the hall again. "We'll see."

Rachael enjoyed her evening with the Hubbles. Cora was a vivacious woman who doted on her husband, and he returned her affection, complimented her for setting a fine table, and regaled Rachael with the long list of his wife's accomplishments in the Canton community. Not only had she initiated the campaign to start a library, but she had organized a literary discussion group and a local historical society.

Cora regretted that the couple had no children.

"But she gives so much time to other people's children that she ought to be able to claim part ownership," Dr. Tim pointed out proudly as he stirred thick cream into his after-dinner coffee. "In addition to her school teaching, Cora directed the church Christmas pageant last year, and, of course, she has the children's choir." He reached across the corner of the table to squeeze his wife's hand. "She plays the piano and sings like an angel."

"I play and sing *adequately*," Cora averred, blushing like a new bride. "Dr. Tim sings my praises lavishly, but the truth is, he's quite tone deaf himself."

"I beg your pardon, Mrs. Hubble, but when I'm right, I'm right, as Miss Trainor will no doubt agree when you perform for her."

Cora slid Rachael an apologetic glance. "If we had a child who was taking piano lessons I would be off the hook."

Rachael helped Cora with the dishes while Dr. Tim filled his pipe and slipped out to the porch. Cora had a story for every heirloom silver serving utensil and hand-painted plate she handed Rachael to dry. Her family lived in Baltimore, and she was surprised when Rachael recognized the origin of her accent, which she thought she'd lost. South Dakota was their home now, she said. They had bought land, and Dr. Tim had built her a lovely home.

"He's the angel in the family," Cora said as she handed Rachael a platter, hand-painted roses dripping with rinse water. "The angel of mercy, sent to these people directly by God. He works tirelessly, and with such meager resources, such terrible obstacles, so little qualified help, and the help he's had . . ." Cora gave Rachael a decided you-know-who-I-mean look. "Thank God you're here. He's been saying he didn't want anyone. No more nurses. That woman has simply soured him on nurses."

"Miss Sims?" Rachael had not been around the woman long enough to form any opinions. "She went on vacation shortly after I started here."

"Maybe she'll find another job."

"I wasn't told that the position of head nurse was already filled, but since it is, and since I've had very little contact with Miss Sims, I really can't—"

"You do see how difficult Dr. Tim's job is."

Rachael nodded. "The needs are almost over-whelming."

"Those who don't understand that find it so easy to be critical." Cora placed the heels of her hands on the edge of the sink and stared out the window, across a sun-parched cornfield that would yield nothing but a little silage this year, into the pink-and-purple evening sky. "I hardly know the woman," she said distantly. "I guess I don't really want to know her for all the trouble she's caused him. I've offered to lend a hand, but he won't even let me go over there. The hospital, the staff, the patients—" She sighed. "He keeps all that apart from his home life, but I told him, 'You must bring Miss Trainor for dinner. She doesn't know a soul here, and she's Edward's sister, after all.'

"Edward is so like my husband, so dedicated to his work with Indian people. They've been friends since Edward received his appointment as agent." Cora turned, her face brightening. "It's good that you and your brother are able to be closer now, especially since neither of you is married. Family is so important.''

"So I've heard." Rachael put the platter on the sideboard with the other serving pieces Cora had said she would put away later. ''Edward's considerably older. We were never playmates or anything. But he suffers his little sister's presence when he has to.''

"Well, he and Dr. Tim share many interests, including a small business venture.''

"Really?"

"Edward got my husband interested in participating in an investment group here in South Dakota. It doesn't involve a large amount of money. Who has much money to invest these days? But if you can spare a few dollars, now's the time, my husband says." Cora fussed with her upsweep, tugging at a short piece of brown hair at her nape. "A little something set aside for the future. Dr. Tim is very optimistic about the future.''

"That's refreshing. Optimism seems hard to come by.''

"Especially where these Indian people are concerned. They can't seem to adjust to changing times. But Dr. Tim will not give up. He will never give up, and if those poor souls were capable of appreciating him, I know they would. They were a majestic people, you know. In their day.''

Rachael thought of Adam Lone Bull. She hadn't really expected an answer to her letter. Maybe he hadn't received it, or maybe he had and didn't believe her assurances that his brother was doing well under the circumstances. She had chosen her words carefully in explaining the circumstances, but she had been truthful.

"I met an Indian man at Pine Ridge who's a war veteran," she found herself confiding to Cora. "I found that remarkable. You know, the Sioux enlisting in the United States Army. Too many cowboy-and-Indian stories, I guess." She laughed. "Maybe I'm the one who's out of touch with changing times.''

"Oh, Dr. Tim says they still love to fight and that

they're always fighting each other, poor souls. Nothing left of the mind, but the fight is still there, he says.''

"Interesting observation," Rachael mused.

Another peculiar bit of wisdom from Dr. Tim.

❧ 6 ❧

"Good morning, Pagla."

The boy scooted backward across his bed like a frightened crab, then hugged himself into a ball, arms wrapped around his legs, forehead resting on his knees.

"Don't you remember me?" Rachael closed the door to his room and approached him carefully. His reaction to her made her feel a little guilty. "I've been so busy in the last two weeks, and you've been sleeping so much. Every time I've looked in on you, you were sound asleep. Dr. Tim was concerned about your chest, and he wanted you to get plenty of rest, which you have done." She touched his hair, but he kept his face buried in his knees. "You must be feeling better now, hmm? You're looking—"

She was going to say fit, but she noticed the bandaged wrists he was trying to cover up with his hands. "Restraints?" She couldn't imagine why. His brother had been right. From what she had seen, the boy had no violence in him.

"Well, they've bathed you, it seems. Did you fight? You mustn't . . ." She pulled the chair close to the bed and sat down. "I've written to your brother, Pagla."

No response. The boy kept himself folded up and didn't move.

"Adam," she said softly. "*Ciye*. Brother. I've written to him about you. He hasn't replied, but he didn't say

III

that he would. He asked me to let him know whether you were all right, and I have done that. I know he must be relieved. You're on his mind, Pagla. He really cares very . . . here, let me see.'' He flinched when she lifted the hem of his trousers and found more gauze. ''Ankles, too?''

She pulled the bandage back far enough to get a peek at the bruised flesh. She had questioned the use of metal restraints rather than the leather ones that had replaced the old-fashioned apparatus some time ago in all the other institutions she'd worked in. But Dr. Tim had given his customary response. *Not in our budget.*

''I see no infection. That's good. I can't imagine why they would . . .'' There was only one ready explanation. ''You weren't trying to harm yourself, were you?''

It was not her question but the distant bellowing beyond the door and down the hall that brought the young man's head up. His eyes widened.

''It's another patient. He won't hurt you, Pagla.''

His legs shot for the edge of the bed as he dove for her arm and held tight, staring a hole in the door. The terror in his eyes unnerved her, especially when he shifted them to her face, lifting his chin. *''Ciye,''* he whispered.

Rachael was stunned. This boy *never spoke.*

''Ciye,'' he repeated, barely audible, doubly urgent.

''It's not just the fight, is it?'' she whispered triumphantly, pressing her hand over the two that clutched her arm. Dr. Tim's assessment had been much too pessimistic. ''The mind is still there, too.''

The tortured human roar reached them again, echoing distantly in its descent in the dreaded stairwell.

Rachael's throat went dry. She had yet to see the face that went with that angry outcry. Not long after she'd heard it the first time, Dr. Tim had remarked that the man was too dangerous for Hiawatha and told her to stay away from him. The ruckus he'd raised was so unsettling to the other patients that the doctor was going to ''ship that wild psychopath back to the hoosegow'' if he didn't settle down soon.

Sure enough, Rachael was witnessing the proof of it,

for Martin was terrified. But the boy had spoken! "It's all right, Pagla. It's sometimes necessary to—"

The youth's eyes widened. He squeezed harder. "Adam. *Ciye!*"

Rachael frowned. "Your brother? No." She shook her head and patted Martin's shoulder. "Your brother never sounded like that, did he? I've met Adam. In fact, he helped me when I got myself in a terrible fix last summer. I fell off a horse, you see. I was riding near Adam's cabin, and I don't know what scared—"

A tear slipped down the boy's smooth, brown cheek.

"Adam's cabin," she clarified. She'd jarred the boy's awareness by reminding him of his brother, and she wanted to bounce it a little more, but gently. "Do you understand what I'm saying? I paid Adam a visit, and he paid me one. He's a nice man, your brother. *Ciye.* He said you didn't speak much English, but maybe . . ."

The boy closed his eyes, driving another tear over the edge. His lower lip trembled.

"It's good, Pagla. *Wašté.* It's good to cry sometimes." She brushed the boy's thick black hair back from his face. "You miss your brother, don't you? He misses you. But you'll get better, and you'll go home. I really think so. This is the first time I've heard you—"

He lifted his hand toward the door. *"Ciye."*

"This is real progress, Pagla. When you make a conscious effort to communicate like this, Dr. Tim can see that your mind is not—" His grip on her arm tightened again, nearly cutting off her circulation. "What? Dr. Tim?"

Pagla stared deeply into her eyes, his terror penetrating her to the quick. A fleeting bubble stretched between his lips as he pried them just far enough to repeat his brother's name.

Rachael's heart shattered and soared, both, impossibly, at once. "I should ask Dr. Tim to bring Adam here. Maybe it wasn't advisable before, but now I think it would help—"

"Ciye . . . ena." Pagla touched his ear, his eyes pleading with her.

"You hear your brother?" She nodded encouragingly. "Lord, yes, I hear mine, too. Even when they're not around, you can hear that voice in your here." She imitated his gesture, touching her own ear. "Was yours as bossy as mine?" She pointed to him, then to herself, smiling sympathetically. "Little brother, little sister. It's not always fun, is it? They're so much older and bigger, so they think . . ."

Pagla wrapped his hands around her fingers and rested his forehead on the back of her wrist. His tears wet the back of her hand. *"Ciye,"* he said in a soft, rusty voice. *"Omakiyi ye."* And then, most surprisingly, he whispered, "P-please."

He was pleading with her for something—to see his brother, perhaps—and the need to make her understand fairly glistened in his dark eyes. "Adam?" she said.

The boy closed his eyes and nodded, mumbling something in Lakota.

"I understand, Pagla. I do." She freed one hand and lifted his chin on two fingers. "You want to see Adam, and by Heaven, you will. I think we've made a true connection today, and I'm going to note it in what there is of your record." She sighed. "The medical record system is a mess, but I'm working on that, even though I'm trying not to step on any toes. The toes around here are as tender as peas. But I will also work on getting a visitor in here for you. I'll ask Dr. Tim specifically about bringing Adam . . ."

The boy groaned pathetically at the mention of his brother's name. He grabbed her shoulders and shook them desperately until she secured his hands in hers and made him stop.

"No, Pagla. This is exactly what Dr. Tim won't want to see. Agitation. That's probably why they took that fellow you just heard downstairs, to cool him off. But you don't need that. You're doing just fine. I'm going to try to come back this week, and I'm going to work on . . ." He was hanging his head, but she lifted it again and persuaded him to look at her. *"Ciye.* I'm going to see if I can find a way for you to see him."

*   *   *

She knew that the only way was through Dr. Tim, who had made it quite clear that he rarely, if ever, permitted a patient family visits. Armed with what she considered to be her own breakthrough, she approached the doctor in his office and asked him to hear her out.

"I think Martin Lone Bull would benefit from a visit with someone from his family. I've just discovered that he does understand some—"

Dr. Tim glanced up from his typewriter, peering coolly over his reading glasses. "Has the boy been ill?"

"No. In fact—"

"Are you doing cleaning chores again?" He waggled his finger at her, tapping the top of the paper he'd been typing on. "I've told you, Miss Trainor, you must leave that sort of thing up to the attendants."

"If I could get them to do a better job of it, I would, but without—" She cut off the rest of her complaint, palm raised in the image of a submissive Madonna. "It wasn't that. I have a special interest in Martin."

"Careful, now, you must not become emotionally involved, Nurse Trainor." He smiled sympathetically. "I'm warning you, it will break your heart, which I suspect is quite tender."

"Not anymore," she assured him. "Nurses can't afford to be tenderhearted."

"Insanity runs in Martin Lone Bull's family." The oaken swivel chair creaked as Dr. Tim leaned back, folding his arms across his chest. "His grandfather died here, and now, of course, we've admitted his brother."

Rachael did a double take. "His brother?"

"That wild man, that's Martin's brother. I just don't know whether we're up to the challenge of breaking that one." Dr. Tim didn't seem to notice her astonishment. He clucked his tongue, wagged his head and seemed totally at a loss. "Very sad situation. War veteran. Shell shock never quite goes away, you know. Add to that the family history, and then the alcohol. They can't handle alcohol."

"So that *was* him. How long . . . He's been here, what? Almost a month?"

"He's a raving lunatic. 'Mad Bull,' the orderlies call him, and he is. Strong as a bull. Requires total isolation, absolute restraint. As I've said, he's quite dangerous."

"You think his drinking . . ."

"The straw that broke the camel's back," Dr. Tim confirmed. "Apparently in a drunken rage he assaulted a white man. When it happens on the reservation sometimes we end up with them." He sat up, offering a fed-up glance in passing as he leaned toward the type-writer. "Aren't we lucky?"

"So . . . is he considered a criminal or a madman?"

"Sometimes there isn't much difference, is there?" Returning to his work, the doctor checked a notebook against what he'd typed. "I don't give up easily, but neither am I willing to jeopardize anyone's safety. And—what am I missing, the date of the last . . ." He glanced up. "And I don't expect to move him out of the dark ward again soon, so you won't have to worry about him."

"Unless he comes down with pneumonia."

"If he does, I'll see to him." He adjusted his glasses and turned a page, still searching. "As for Martin, other than brother Mad Bull, I believe he has a mother, but she's shown no interest in him."

"Maybe if we . . . if *I* contacted her . . ."

A quick sigh signaled his growing impatience. Again the doctor folded his arms and eyed her over the wire rims of his glasses. "We have neither the time nor the wherewithal to beat the bushes for family members, Miss Trainor. This is not like any institution you've ever been associated with. Our patients are a different breed to begin with. They are"—he measured half an inch of air between thumb and forefinger—"this close to their savage origins. It's no wonder madness strikes them the way it does. Hard and with appalling frequency. And then I think the families just write them off. Or would if they could write. They show very little interest, Miss Trainor. Very little interest."

"But it must be hard for them. We're really quite far away from any of the reservations, and I've wondered why that is."

"Because this institution serves many tribes, and because tribalism is part of their problem. It's been very difficult to break all that up. In order to civilize them, we have to remove them from that environment. We've put the children in schools. We've tried to eliminate"— he jabbed a finger in her direction—"their religious practices, for example. Madness. Self-mutilation, among other distasteful pagan rituals. It has been outlawed, all of it, but the agents still catch them at it. Martin's grandfather was one of their high priests."

"Did he have a problem with alcohol, too?"

"Probably. They all do. We are a storage facility for the rotting apples that would spoil the barrel if not removed."

"Our patients are not rotten. They are—"

"Sick. Yes, tragically, many of them are sick, and we have no cure for their illness. But we will look out for them, won't we, Miss Trainor? They are safe in our care." He laid his forearm over the top of the typewriter and leaned closer. "Speaking of alcohol, have you detected the smell of alcohol on the person of our head nurse?"

"Miss Sims?" He had tried to lure her into this discussion before, and she wanted no part of it. She shook her head. "She avoids me. Frankly, I feel awkward reporting directly to you. I should be—"

"Replacing her soon," he finished for her. "I'm hoping she'll resign. She was appointed by the Indian Bureau, and I've appealed to them to recall her, but all that did was bring near catastrophe down on us. Instead of investigating her, they investigated all departments. They would have shut us down if they'd had a place to send our patients. Shut us down! Fortunately we have friends in Congress. Men with foresight. These people don't belong in state institutions."

"I don't understand. Because . . . ?"

His open-handed gesture indicated that the conclusion was self-evident. "Because they're Indians."

Rachael thought about all this for days. She understood now that Martin had recognized his brother's voice, that, in fact, the sound of that familiar voice may have triggered an awakening in some dormant part of the boy's mind. But what a price!

She remembered the man who had helped her, and in remembering, she heard his voice again, the soft, comforting sound he'd obviously planted deep in her ear when she'd sat in front of him on his horse. She also remembered the way he'd sounded when he'd been drinking, still soft-spoken, but his tone had more bite. Even so, it was hard to imagine that the bellowing fury she'd heard coming from the stairwell had actually come from the throat of Adam Lone Bull. The howl had hardly sounded human. She dreaded the moment when she would see for herself what had become of the gentle man who had picked her up off the side of the road and tended to her injuries.

But, of course, she had to face him, to observe his condition firsthand, and she didn't want to do it in the company of other staff members. Dr. Tim hadn't exactly ordered her to stay away from the bowels of the main building. He'd only warned her that the man might be dangerous. She would be safe, she decided. She knew he'd be restrained. She owed a debt to Adam Lone Bull, and if he recognized her, it would be a good sign.

There were those patients who didn't recognize anyone. Many of them persisted in repetitive behaviors, like rocking or waving their hands, and droned incessantly. Their minds had been reduced to the essence of pain, and their voices intoned pure misery. But there were relatively fewer such patients at Hiawatha than at other institutions for the insane. A greater number were lethargic, apathetic, and docile. Some, like Peter Magpie and Mr. Blue, were physically handicapped. Others seemed simply, utterly dispirited.

Rachael remembered Dr. Tim's comment about Adam

Lone Bull—about the challenge of "breaking" him. She wondered how many patients had raged as vociferously as he did when they were first admitted. Had Alice DeCouteau, or Tom Yells At Night? Tom had spent his entire adult life at Hiawatha, and Rachael wasn't sure why. Melancholia, Dr. Tim said. Maybe Tom had had more spirit once. More temper. Maybe he'd been "broken."

But Rachael was not a doctor. She was a nurse, and she understood the requirements of her job. Discretion was one of them. In fact, there were times when discretion was paramount.

Early evening was the best time of day to slip into the basement of the main building. Supper was over, and many of the patients were in bed by 7:30. Everyone was locked in, each room with its own padlock, and all lights were turned out at 8:00. The building was pitch dark. Rachael had suggested electric night lights, at least for the hallways, but she'd been told that attendants with lanterns did the job quite nicely without using expensive electricity. So she took up her lantern and headed downstairs.

Besides the boiler room, most of the basement was used for storage. It was dark and dank, the air heavy with soot from the hoard of soft coal that would soon be used to heat the building. There were two small rooms that were both kept padlocked. Rachael had a full complement of door keys.

She opened the door slowly, against the creaky protest of its hinges. Like most of the asylum's doors, it was a release valve for warm, fetid air and unsettling darkness. She eased the lantern through the doorway, illuminating a bare foot, which was quickly pulled back into the shadows. A small bed had been overturned, and there was a mattress on the floor nearby.

He was a dark hulk sitting on the floor with his back against the wall, tattered and eroded but still recognizable as the man she'd met at Pine Ridge Reservation.

"Adam?" She stepped inside the cell, speaking

softly, as though to a child. "Adam, do you remember me?"

He groaned, turning his head from the rude light.

"The light hurts." As she set the lantern on the floor just inside the door, she noted the camisole restraint—laced in back, blind sleeves tied so that his arms and hands were incapacitated—and the metal shackles, one steel ring around his ankle, the other fastened to a water pipe that ran along the wall.

Rachael drew a long, deep, steadying breath. If he warranted this much restriction he must have been putting up quite a fight. "I'm sorry, Adam. I didn't mean to shine that in your eyes. I came to see if you needed—"

She started closer, but his sudden outraged roar knocked her back like a bellows. Bound hand and foot, it was the only defense he had. She waited until he stopped growling and settled back against the wall before she tried again, speaking to him softly, reassuring him. But when she crossed some invisible line he scrambled to his feet, asserting his physical presence like a bear standing on hind legs to attain its most forbidding height. It was all he had, that and his furious, barrel-chested roar, and it was enough to drive her back again.

"You'll hurt yourself, Adam," she said quietly, reiterating his name in the hope of gaining his trust. But each time she crossed his invisible line, he jerked frantically on the iron pipe, straining against his bonds and yelling fiercely even after he'd lost his balance and gone down on one knee. She started forth to help him, but he sprang to his feet, white teeth bared and gleaming in the shadows. For his sake she retreated, conceding round one.

But also for his sake, she began to plan round two.

On her next visit she found him strapped to his bed. He strained against the straps to avoid her tentative attempt to touch his shoulder. His eyes fairly bulged out of the sunken sockets in his gaunt face. She spoke to him quietly and tried to offer him a drink of water, but he let it run down his face. The walls and floor were spattered with evidence of the food he had rejected. The man needed to eat. He desperately needed a bath. But clearly he would have no part of her.

She wanted to tell him that his brother was doing better, but she worried that mention of the boy would only upset him more.

"You might as well get used to the idea that I'm going to look in on you when I can." Since he refused to drink it, she used the water and her handkerchief to swab his face. "You've got to stop fighting and let us help you, Adam. Otherwise the restraints—" He almost bit her, but her hand was quicker than his jaws. They shared a long, hot stare. Finally she said, "I don't believe you'd really hurt me."

His lips parted, his eyes challenging her to try him.

She withdrew her hand and tried reason. "The restraints continue to be necessary as long as you fight. I hate them, too."

His maniacal laugh drove her from him.

But he would not leave her alone. She heard his voice, sometimes distantly in a corridor, more often in her sleep. She resisted the temptation to speak further to Dr. Tim of either of the Lone Bulls, partly because she wasn't completely comfortable with the nature of her concerns. The man who had lifted her out of an embarrassing predicament, who had set her on his horse and taken her to his cabin, *that* man had been strong and whole and perfectly sane. What's more, he'd been a caring human being, not the broken drunk her brother had described. A far cry from the "mad bull" he'd apparently become.

But the man who had trespassed in her brother's house, helped himself to forbidden whiskey and guzzled it like water, *that* man accounted for the change.

The next time she visited him she took soap and warm water with her. She found him sitting on the floor, one ankle bound to the iron pipe, but he wore close-linked wristlets instead of the camisole. He turned his face from the light as he struggled to his feet. His hair was matted, his pajamas dirty, but at least they were dry. The ubiquitous chamber pot stood within his reach, and apparently he was able to maintain control of his bodily functions.

Rachael set the lantern, the water pitcher and basin next to the wall and closed the door. "I know I haven't been a welcome sight lately, Adam, but here I am anyway. I've brought food and bathwater. I suspect you could do with both."

He scowled at her and growled a wolflike warning.

"Don't even bother to start that bellowing. It doesn't scare me."

But she had to be wary of his greater mobility. He was tethered by a longer chain this time, and he could lift his arms even though his wrists were bound. Still she drew closer. The fetid odor that pervaded the institution had long since overridden the spicy, masculine scent of the man she'd met at Pine Ridge. But this was the man, or a piece of him, anyway.

He stood with his feet wide apart like a cornered animal, ready to defend what little domain he had left. His body, perhaps, if not his mind.

"I don't know how well you understand, Adam, but I think you remember me." She knew she was within range of his unbound foot now. Another step and he could bring his fists down on her head. She kept her voice soft and steady. "You're going to have to help me so I can help you."

"Stay *away* from me, woman." He answered her surprised look with a dark, level stare and a winter-quiet warning. "Stay away from me, or I swear I'll find a way to kill you."

"I can't believe you'd do that," she said, eyeing his bare feet.

"Believe it, spider legs. I spit out their slop food, but my teeth would grind your snake-woman eyes. Believe it!" And he howled like a feral dog.

She stood her ground, refusing to respond to his outcry. Only when he gave it up did she back away, seeking the water basin. "I won't hurt you, Adam. I promise."

"Hurt? What is there left to—" But his whole body

stiffened when her intention hit home. "Stay back! Don't come near me!"

"I'm a nurse, Adam. I'm accustomed to—"

"Not to me!" He threw his head back and laughed. "The fools have sent me a woman. Don't they know what I could do to you? Don't *you* know?"

"I'm your friend, Adam. Remember?"

He howled, the laughter of one gone truly mad.

She summoned more nerve from her deepest reserve and moved closer. "I know you're terribly uncomfortable, but we are desperately understaffed here, and it's very difficult to maintain—"

"Stay away from me," he warned, sidestepping her careful approach. "I don't want you around me, woman. The smell of you makes me sick."

"If you don't let us keep you clean, you *will* get sick."

His low-pitched, satanic laughter shriveled the skin on the back of her neck.

"Touch me and I'll kill you." He bent his arms at the elbows and brandished his fists. "With my bare hands. One hand. Free one hand, and I will snap your neck like a cottonwood twig."

He could do it anyway. They both knew that he could easily hurt her with his arms, his hands, his filthy bare foot. All she had to do was step a little closer. His nostrils flared as he waited, watching her, daring her. She took the dare. She moved boldly within his range, carrying the basin in her hands and the question in her eyes. His jaw muscles worked as he tried to stare her down.

Then he closed his eyes and turned his face aside. "I want . . . *ask* you to leave me."

"Are you . . . embarrassed?" Few of the patients had the capacity for such an emotion. "You needn't be, Adam. I've seen it all."

"This is what gives you pleasure, Snake Woman?" He squared his shoulders, held his head high and flashed a feral grin. "No, no, you are Deer Woman. My grandfather warned me. Show me your feet." He pointed with a scornful jerk of his chin. "Take off your shoes and show me your hooves."

"I'm your friend, Adam." He was either talking pure nonsense or referring to some sort of tribal superstition, but she decided against questioning him. It was best not to contest anything he said. She set the basin on the floor and bent to soak a wash rag. Fully aware that she was standing in a vulnerable position, she had to choose her words carefully. "You helped me, and now I want to help you."

"You'll untie me?"

"Whoever checked those devices out at the clerk's office has the key." It was one of several procedures she intended to revise, but since the doctor seemed set in his ways, she'd have to take each reform a step at a time. Meanwhile, she justified the practice. "We don't want you to hurt yourself."

His laugh was decidedly bitter, but it was controlled. She put the warm rag in his hands. "I'll let you—" It slid through his fingers and landed on her shoe.

Antipathy frosted his dark eyes. "You want to help me? Go ahead. Do your job."

She picked up the rag, wet it again, and washed his face, which turned to stone as he stared at her. It was a relief to return to the basin for more water.

"You're not eating much," she observed guardedly as she swabbed his torso through the open front of his buttonless shirt. "The food is nourishing if not tasty. You're losing weight. You need to eat."

"Your eyes." He smiled humorlessly at her questioning glance. "I would eat your eyes."

"I can't let you do that, I'm afraid, but I came prepared to offer you something much better."

"What?" His voice dropped to a sensuous, guttural rumbling. "How would you have me pleasure you, Deer Woman? Should I feed between your legs?"

She meant to ignore the remark. There was nothing remarkable about it, really. She'd heard worse. Mental patients were notoriously foulmouthed. Her uniform generally deflected such suggestions, but this was the first one she'd heard in English since she'd come to Canton. She couldn't be sure what she'd heard in any of the Indian tongues her patients spoke.

Far from distracted, the look in his eyes penetrated her crisp white dress. He regarded her with a sense of blatantly sexual familiarity that was almost unsettling. *Almost* exciting.

She meant to ignore that, too.

She jerked his pants down and continued to sponge him, working over him quickly, treating his rising erection as she would any other part of her patient's body. He tipped his head back against the pipe and laughed as she readjusted the garment and tied the string just below his navel.

"If you'd sit down," she began, pointing to the bare cement floor.

"If I would *kneel* down—" He waited until she looked into his eyes, and then he chuckled. This time she was sure she detected a bit of humor. "—then I would be in the right position, Deer Woman."

"That would be better," she agreed, feigning absolute naiveté. "Then you could lean over the basin while I wash your hair. I have more water in the pitcher. This coal dust is—" She looked into his eyes, ignoring his affront and offering him the sympathy she knew he didn't want. "The bathing facilities are inadequate here. No continuous bathtubs. We really need—"

"They douse me with cold water," he said flatly. "Remember the water I drew for you?" She nodded dumbly. "Colder than that."

"Only when you were out of control, Adam. I've heard you. The cold shock is sometimes . . ." He didn't need these restraints now. She couldn't justify them at this moment, but tomorrow he might be a raving lunatic again. Avoiding his fiery eyes, she tested the water in the enamel pitcher. "I won't hurt you, Adam. This water is still warm."

The shackles chinked as he knelt before the basin and bowed his head like a supplicant. She felt, for just a moment, as though she had brought Goliath into the fold.

"When they come to . . ." she waited for the water she'd poured into his hair to stop dripping. Then she applied soap and began massaging his scalp, speaking to him quietly. "When the orderlies move you to the bed tonight, you must be cooperative. They restrain you only because your behavior has been out of control. When they see that you won't fight them, they'll stop using the restraints, at least during the day. At night, well . . . no one may leave the room after lights out."

He said nothing. He didn't move. He might have been a piece of statuary but for the thick, wet hair that tickled her fingers. She rinsed it, patted it dry with a towel, took a comb from her pocket, and did her best to tame it with a side part. There," she said. "Now do you understand what I'm saying about the—"

"What did you tell your brother?"

"What do you mean?"

"About the night I came into the house," he said, rising to his feet. "What did you tell him?"

"I told him nothing."

He stared, emotionless and clearly unconvinced.

"I told him nothing, Adam."

He frowned, still studying her. "Did I rape you? Is that the story?"

"Of course not. I've said nothing of the kind."

"Then why am I here?"

She touched his dingy shirt sleeve, laundered soft and shapeless but not clean. "Do you remember when you were brought here?"

"I was drunk when they picked me up, but I don't think I did anything . . ." Still frowning, he admitted to his confusion for the first time. "I know there was a fight. I don't remember what it was about, or who . . ."

"You assaulted someone, I believe."

"Maybe he got the worst of it, but I took a few hits, too." The wristlets jangled as he brought his hands up to his face and touched his lip with one finger. If he'd been injured there, it had since healed. "At first I didn't know where I was. It wasn't here. Another jail. I know I was sick. I was sick when they moved me, on the train, I think, but I . . . they kept me . . .''

Her fingers stirred over his arm, soothing, consoling. She didn't want his confusion to turn to agitation. Today he was doing well. "You'll get the rest you need here."

"It's worse than I thought." He scanned the massive rough-hewn beams above his head, the tiny barred window, the heavy door. "This is a prison."

"It's a hospital, Adam."

He looked at her, then looked away.

"You're quite lucid now. If the violent episodes subside, I think your stay here will be a relatively short one." She slid her hand over the wristlets, reminding herself that it wasn't up to her to defend their use. Dr. Tim had been out of touch, she decided. Modern leather restraints had sheepskin pads and were not punitive. And how expensive could they be?

"I'm sorry." She looked down, avoiding his eyes. "This is necessary to protect the staff, to protect you from harming yourself."

"You are a nurse in a prison," he said tonelessly. "You torment your prisoners until they wish for death, but you deny them even that."

"If we took off the restraints . . ."

"I would find a way out of here." He grabbed her arm, adding without hesitation, "I would kill anyone who got in my way."

"Why do you tell me this?"

"To scare you away. I don't want you here."

"Sorry. It didn't work." Not the way he intended, anyway. She was scared, but she wouldn't be scared away. "I will speak to Dr. Tim about you. I think—"

"I wouldn't do that." He relaxed his grip, and for a moment she thought he'd found something in her eyes that threatened to make him smile. "They'll think you're crazy, too. What kind of a prison would they send you to, Rachael Trainor? Would it smell like this one?"

Having no answer for him, she took the package from the pocket of her white sweater and unwrapped the bread she'd brought. She offered it to him, holding it close to his lips. He only stared at her.

"I made it myself," she said. "The bread and the apple butter in between. I have a room in the other building, Adam. It's a little room, too, and we employees all share a kitchen and other . . ."

With a look he questioned the possibility of any real parallel.

"What I mean is, I live here, too, so I'm close by. If you'll let me, I'll help you get better."

He looked at her for a long, open-ended moment, taking his time with his appraisal. His eyes dismantled and reassembled her without rearranging anything. As disturbing as it was for her, she was determined to wait him out.

Finally he parted his lips and took her bread into his mouth. She waited, accepting the risk that he might spit it back in her face. But he swallowed it and took another bite. His lips trembled, and she knew how hungry he must have been.

"As I said in my letter, your brother is doing well," she said quietly.

He stopped chewing and stared at her again. "What letter?"

"I wrote to you, just as I promised. Maybe you were unable to—"

He lifted his bound hands. "Do you keep my brother tied up like this?"

She hesitated, then shook her head too quickly. "Not usually. There's usually no need to. He's not violent. But he's not—" She had promised him an honest assessment, but she had to be careful not to say anything too distressing. The boy had his problems, to be sure, but now was the time to deliver all the positive news she could think of. "He is beginning to respond. You were right about speaking to him in Lakota. I've managed to learn a few words, and he's even said . . . a few words back to me."

"They said this was a hospital." He swallowed, gazing at her hand and the last of the bread. "I didn't know it was like this. My brother has been here much too long.''

''He's one of Dr. Tim's special patients, Adam. And I look in on him as often as I can. He's getting the help he needs.''

Again Adam laughed, that terrible, hollow, hopeless laugh.

He could not be expected to understand. She offered the last of the bread.

He took it in his hand. ''Will you come here again?''

''Yes. Now that I know you won't hurt me, I should report to Dr. Tim that—''

''Don't tell anyone *anything*,'' he warned, assessing her again with a piercing stare. ''Not unless that's what you're here for. To spy.''

Paranoia, she thought sadly, but she offered a reassuring smile. ''I'm here to help.''

''Will you bring the keys next time?''

''You've told me what you would do if I freed your hands.''

''And you believe me?''

''Should I?''

''I'm a madman.'' A scant, enigmatic smile played on his lips. ''Don't believe anything I say.''

❧ 7 ❧

Spring 1973

Zane wasn't planning on making a phone call. Not today. He had two kids dripping chocolate ice cream all over their pants and his pickup seat, and one old man and a dog riding shotgun on one box of groceries and two of laundry in the back. They were all headed home until Zane surprised the hell out of everyone when he pulled a U-turn and parked a few feet from the phone booth in the Cenex station lot.

"You guys finish your ice cream," he told Sissy and Jojo as he shut his door. "I gotta make a call."

He found the matchbook with her phone number on it—a cowboy's little black book—and lit a cigarette while he had the matches handy. This was the last time he was going to try. When the matches were gone he'd be ditching the phone number.

"Mmm—hello?"

Fate had stepped in. Zane smiled as he tucked the matches under his shirt pocket flap. Her voice sounded drowsy. He pictured her rousing all sleep-sotted and rumpled from an afternoon nap. "Hey, it's Zane Lone Bull."

"Zane." Her voice brightened. "I'm glad you called."

"Oh, yeah? Why?"

"I've been thinking about your brother, wondering whether they've arrested anyone. I haven't seen anything in the newspaper." She paused. "I . . . I've been watching and, you know . . . wondering."

"Like I said before, don't hold your breath."

"No suspects?"

"The feds don't feel like they have to keep me posted on the progress of their investigation." It was almost a direct quote. Officer Obi was quite a quotable guy. "Have you come across any pictures of that insane asylum in your aunt's stuff? I mean the original building."

"Actually, no. You can kind of see it in the background in some of the pictures my aunt left, but nothing really clear and close-up."

"Well, I think I might have one for you. It's a little crude, but I'm bettin' that's what it's supposed to be."

"Where did you find it?"

He drew deeply on his cigarette as he watched Martin accept a face-licking from Soup. "My uncle drew it. I have a hunch he might have been a patient there."

"Does he remember it? What does he say?"

"Nothing. He doesn't talk. He's kinda retarded, y'know? Kinda like . . ." He turned toward the street—the town of Mobridge's Grand Crossing—leaned his shoulder against the drive-up phone housing, and watched a truckload of cowboys and Indians pull up to the Last Chance Package Store across the way. "Anyway, they both acted funny when I mentioned Canton. The ol' lady, too. So I think that guy they've got buried across the street from you might be related to us somehow."

"Randy was going to check the Bureau of Indian Affairs records."

"Yeah, well, I don't know whether he ever got around to that, and I don't know as much as he did about all that who's-related-to-who kind of stuff. That was his bag, not mine."

"Most of the record-keeping at the asylum seems pretty bad," she admitted. "I was just looking at a few of the files labeled 'deceased.' I don't know how they could tell who to contact when somebody died. Half of them, you can't tell what was actually wrong with them, why they were there, or what they died of. If there's a death certificate, it doesn't say much. And for some of them, it's like they just dropped in out of nowhere. No address, no next-of-kin, nothing.''

"You've got records for James Lone Bull?''

"Yes, I've found him, but as I said, there's no—''

He reversed his stance, switching shoulders, turning back to the pickup. "How about Martin Lone Bull?''

"I don't . . . think so,'' she said tentatively. "What I'm going to have to do is drag all those boxes down from the attic. I started out just looking for the names that are on the monument.''

"Why?''

"I don't know. Maybe because I don't think they'd want to be part of a golf course.''

Zane glanced up at the mackerel sky, picturing Randy's plot, soon to be taken over by buffalo grass, and the idea of the golf course burial ground struck him as perversely funny. "Hell, that place is as close to Forest Lawn as you're gonna get out here. Maybe some old *heyoka* got the last laugh. White guys tending their graves.''

"What's a *heyoka*?''

Martin looked up from the pickup as though he'd heard his name called. "A contrary. Somebody who's crazy in a sacred way.'' Either his explanation was too weird to question, or she'd made sense of it. Zane smiled, wishing he could see the expression on her face right now. "Anyway, those guys on the monument have been dead a long time. But my uncle's alive, and all of a sudden he's not quite as retarded as I thought he was. I think these drawings he made might have something to do with him being in that asylum.''

"I can start looking through the other boxes. They're quite interesting, actually. It's like I've unearthed a piece of history. I'm sure nobody's touched them since Dr. Tim.''

"Dr. Tim, huh?'' Martin had lost interest in the dog,

who was now sniffing around the groceries. Zane stuck the cigarette in the corner of his mouth and waved his arm. "Sssst! Soup! Get outta there."

"Soup?"

"Worthless mutt," Zane muttered. "You kids stay in the pickup!" Damn, they'd smeared ice cream from hell to Texas. "Listen, I thought maybe you'd wanna see them."

"Kids?"

"No, these drawings."

He was uncomfortable with the silence at the other end of the line. Maybe he'd read her wrong.

"Maybe you'd want to help me search through these files," she suggested tentatively.

"You still got a vacancy upstairs?"

"Yes, I do, but . . ."

"Or the driveway. I ain't fussy."

"Good. Then we'll see how it goes."

He didn't have a lot of time to waste wondering what that meant. She'd offer him a bed, and if he kept seeing her, eventually she'd be in it with him. What other reason would she have for setting up this game? Not that he wasn't curious about the asylum now that his questions about it had jarred something loose in the mysterious workings of his uncle's mind. But Michelle Benedict was entertaining reading, and Zane was interested in turning a few more of her pages.

Beatrice didn't want him to go down there. She didn't tell him in so many words. She just sat there in her chair and made a monotonous humming sound, like a heater fan going on the blink. Same damn sound she'd made for days before he'd shipped out for 'Nam.

Cecilia told him just go on, then. She said he could go move in with one of his *wasicu* women for all she cared.

Sissy and Jojo fussed to go with him.

Uncle Martin carefully folded his drawings and gave them to him to take along, as if he'd drawn him a map. The way to *Heyoka*ville.

It was a hell of a long drive. Zane left at the crack of dawn, and by the time he hit I-90, he had half a mind to head west to Rapid City, where he knew exactly what the score was. He was too old for courting games. Then he chided himself for thinking he had to get laid every time he left home, and he took the eastbound lane.

Hell, some guys *stayed* home and got laid, right there in the same bed they slept in every night. He wondered what that might be like. Might even be worth buying a bed.

God, he was thinking crazy!

Hell, why not? He was on his way to Canton, wasn't he? Former site of the Hiawatha Asylum for Insane Indians. But Zane Lone Bull was crazy like a fox. He had business to attend to, curiosity to satisfy.

Recalling his most recent visit with Agent Obi Flynn, he told himself that the Rolling Stones were right. Satisfaction was hard to come by these days. Officer Obi wasn't about to make any progress in any investigation other than the one he'd been conducting regarding the disappearance of his hubcaps. "It's a government car," he'd grumbled. "Federal property. Now look, far as your brother's case goes, I've got my short list of suspects and leads, following each and every one just as far as it goes. Fact is, Randy Tusk didn't seem to have any serious enemies."

No shit.

So officer Obi's short list consisted of Randy's friends and relatives. Another crime of passion. Zane had a strong hunch that Randy's killer was not on the agent's list and that the crime had been committed by someone with a cool head and a cold heart. He wasn't sure just how he'd hatched this hunch of his or when. All he knew was that Flynn was on the wrong track, and he was having a hell of a time controlling the urge to jerk the man's head out of his ass and tell him to start looking . . .

Where? Down the road to Canton? Not likely. Flynn followed leads, not roads, and Zane was just as glad Michelle Benedict hadn't made the short list.

Randy, on the other hand, was a road man. He liked back roads, Indian-country roads, knew them like the back of his hand. He bought himself a house that he could take on the road. He ended up dead on the side of the road.

But what other road had he been following? There was something about following Michelle's letter, following Uncle Martin's drawings, following the road to Canton that was not meant for Flynn. It was meant for Zane.

Christ, he got the willies whenever his mind got to wandering crazy like that. It made him sweat and gave him goose bumps at the same time. He threw the vent fan on high and tore open his shirt snaps. The old beaded turtle was sticking to his chest like a damn wood tick.

He wasn't about to play detective. Randy was dead. Uncle Martin was crazy. Zane had the hots for the woman, and that was that.

Michelle met him at the door. "You're early."

Her eyes told him she was glad, so he knew he was on safe ground. He arched an eyebrow. "Did I have an appointment?"

"You must have left early, huh?" She pushed the door open and beckoned him inside. "I was figuring you wouldn't get here until suppertime, but I'll bet you're hungry now. All I have to do is put it together. Do you like lasagna?"

"I'm real easy to feed."

"I've been trying to do a bunch of stuff at once, and the result is"—she turned a full circle as she led him through the living room, waving at boxes and bunches of clutter and naming it—"chaos. Ignore the mess."

He chuckled. She was wearing a shapeless long blue jumper over a tie-dyed T-shirt. Her feet were bare, the soles blackened. Her hair was clipped high above her nape. It cascaded over the big barrette like a rooster tail.

"I'm glad you're here. I've been pulling stuff out of that attic, trying to see what all's up there. Mostly there's a lot of mustiness and dust, junk in the way." She nodded toward the stairway, looked at him, then glanced away. "But some of it weighs a ton, so I'm really glad you came down."

"You want me to get to it right now, or do you think maybe you could offer me something cold to drink first?"

"Sure." She backed away from the newel post. "Pop or lemonade?"

"Those are my choices?"

She shrugged. "What would you like?"

"I'd like for you to stop acting like I'm shining my headlights in your big, round eyes."

"I'm sorry. Having company makes me nervous." She looked down at her voluminous jumper and brushed at a dirty spot. "I mean, it's not that I'm a recluse or anything, but I don't entertain much."

"I'm not here to be entertained, so just relax. For a can of pop I'll haul your junk down from the attic."

"And if you're hungry I have—"

"I can wait." But the smell of meat and tomato sauce was going to make it a challenge.

His boot heels sounded imposing behind her bare feet on the hardwood floor. His nose followed the aroma while his eyes followed her into the kitchen. Truth was, he was working up all kinds of hunger.

It looked as though somebody was either moving in or moving out. There were some old tan folders on the table along with two cookbooks and several red-and-white spice tins that looked as though they'd been around too long to have any flavor left in them. "This is a nice house," he said. "Homey."

"I wish I could move it to Rapid City. I like my job there. I love the Black Hills." She poured a dollop of Joy into her palm, then turned the cold water on. "But I also love this big, old, empty house. Empty without her."

"Houses can be moved."

"I know, but . . ." She took a can of diet cola from a refrigerator that had to be almost as old as she was, grabbed a couple of cartons, and elbowed the door shut. "Well, I just don't think she'd want me to do that."

"Your aunt?" He accepted the cola with a nod, figuring he'd have to choke down a few swallows before
he could get past the saccharine taste. "So what? She's
dead. She ain't gonna kick."

"That's not the point." She started opening a succes-
sion of cupboard doors, digging out a box of pasta, a
mixing bowl, a glass. "Even if she were alive she
wouldn't 'kick.' She wasn't like that. But I want to be
respectful of her feelings."

"What feelings?" He shook off the glass as he ripped
off the pop tab. "She doesn't feel anything anymore.
You gave her a decent burial, right?"

"Right."

"Right, so that's the end of that story. You've got a
life, you do what you want with it. That goes for the
house, too." He took a seat at the kitchen table, shoved
some folders aside, and set the can down.

"What about Randy?"

She was filling a kettle with water, standing with her
back to him. In order to really enjoy the view he had to
change her clothes mentally, back to those hip-hugging
jeans she'd been wearing the first time he'd met her. She
had a nice long back, nice round bottom on her.

He took his black hat off and set it on its crown atop
some papers. "What *about* Randy?"

"Well, he's gone, too." She struck a wooden match
and lit a second burner on the stove. She already had
the tomato smell going on the back burner. The pot of
water landed on the front one. Then she turned to him.
"That's really why you're here, isn't it? That's why you
came the first time."

"That's different." Zane turned his hand in a self-
evident gesture. "He didn't just check out; he was murdered. It's like he's got one foot in this world and one
in the next. Whatever he was up to, whatever he was
thinking . . ." He shrugged it off. "You're right, dead is
dead, but he didn't leave me an empty house." Just a
big, empty hole in his gut, but that would shrink down
sooner or later.

"It's not empty."

"In a way it is." He picked up one of the dusty spice tins. Paprika. "The life's gone out of it."

"But the memories . . ." She took a wooden spoon from the drawer by the stove. "I gather you don't really expect to find out who killed him."

"I don't expect much of anything. I sure don't think the feds are tryin' too hard, but then—" He wanted a cigarette. He drank some pop instead, winced at the taste, then allowed, "I don't guess it makes much difference. They're killing people down at Pine Ridge, too."

"I heard about that. A protester, right?"

"Right." For starters.

"Are you a member of the American Indian Movement?"

"Me?" He shook his head. "I'm a stay-out-of-trouble kind of a guy, me."

"It's hard to know what to think about that takeover at Wounded Knee." She was busy mixing something up in a bowl. White stuff. She cracked an egg into it and stirred some more. "Seems like there are Indians on both sides. The AIM people barricading themselves in that church—some people say most of them aren't Sioux—and then the tribal police and the tribal chairman . . . What's his name? Wilson?"

"Tricky Dickie," Zane supplied with a chuckle. He always got a kick out of listening to white people talk about Indian politics like they really wanted to get a handle on it.

"Oh, gosh, one Tricky Dick is enough," she said. Nixon, of course, had been pretty busy lately trying to explain his way out of the Watergate mess. "It seems to me that if they just left those people alone the whole thing would resolve itself. I mean, it's not like they've taken over the Pentagon or anything."

"Leave which people alone?" He eyed her dubiously. "You know how hard it is to tell the good guys from the bad guys in that little Wounded Knee fracas? You got your state troopers, your federal agents, your National Guard, and then you've got your Indians." He counted off the factions on his fingers. "You got your full-bloods and your mixed-bloods, you got traditionals and apples—"

"Apples?"

"Red on the outside, white on the inside," he explained. "Then you got your Wilson roadblocks, your anti-Wilson roadblocks, your missionaries, and your movie stars. You think Watergate's confusing . . ."

She was listening, studying him, trying to x-ray through his sarcasm. "I guess I meant the outsiders ought to pull back and let the people themselves sort it all out."

"Wilson and his goons would just go in there and start shooting people."

"But he was elected by the people at Pine Ridge, right?"

He laughed. "The people elected Tricky Dick Nixon, too."

"Was Randy involved with AIM?"

"Funny you should ask." He set the can down carefully, rubbing his thumb over the seam. He'd wondered about that visit Randy had paid to Pine Ridge. He had more friends down there than Randy did. And more enemies. But he'd stayed away from both lately. "Not to my knowledge," he recited carefully.

"Are you an AIM sympathizer?"

He looked her in the eye, deliberately turning on the charm. "If I am, do I still get some of that lasagna? It sure smells good."

"That's only the sauce. Wait'll I get the cheeses blended in with that." She cocked her head, genuinely interested, her smile less artful than his. "So are you?"

"I've learned to keep my sympathies to myself." He drained the rest of the pop from the can in three swallows, letting the taste slide past his tongue. Then he squeezed the can as if he wanted to wring it dry. "Where can I chuck this? You need your cheese cut up or anything?"

She introduced him to a cheese grater, and she laughed when he handed her the bowl of curly white shreds, showed her the knuckles he'd scraped, and told her he was just adding some red spice for "extra zing." She made him wash his hands, sprayed him with some medicine cabinet stuff, then let him pour sauce and cheese between her layers of soft white noodles. Once they had the whole works stowed away in the oven, they went upstairs.

"Your room's all ready for you," she said, and lifted her hand toward the doorway as they passed, heading for a second set of stairs.

"My room?"

"Was that bed okay? There's another—"

"That one's fine."

His room. It was a novel concept. Almost forty years old, and the one time he'd actually had his own room, his own "house," a warden had had custody of the key.

It wasn't easy hauling boxes out of the attic. The light, the dust, and the air were all bad, and he kept bumping his head on the steep-pitched rafters. He hated cobwebs and spiders and the smell of rodent crap. He wasn't about to tell her how he felt about rats, but if one decided to show its snaky tail, she'd see for herself how fast he could haul ass.

"You want *all* these boxes down?" he asked for the third time.

"If they're too heavy . . ."

"Hell, they're not heavy, they're just . . ." He thought he heard something scratching. "You got a cat?"

"I wish I did."

"I wish you did, too," he muttered, ducking below the bare bulb, balancing two boxes, and using his foot to find the edge of the first step down. "What's the smell up here? Did they keep drugs up here or something?"

She giggled. "Mothballs, silly."

Mothballs, *silly?* He'd never known a woman who called a man "silly." Didn't quite know how to take it. "Smells like the stuff they gave me when they took out my tonsils."

"There are some wonderful old clothes up here. Aunt

Cora was quite the fashion plate in her day. Oh, speaking of . . . Zane?''

"Yeah?'' He'd reached the bottom of the stairs. He stacked the two boxes on top of four others, and then he paused, waiting on the sound of her voice. He wanted to hear her to say his name again in the same delicate, inviting way. "You okay up there, Michelle?''

He popped his head through the opening in the attic floor and found her sitting on a box cradling her foot in her lap. "What happened? Something bite you?''

"It's okay. Just a splinter or something.'' She smiled, her eyes following his ascent. "I always forget to put on shoes. I hate shoes.''

He scanned the rows of boxes, avoiding the foot, which she'd said was okay. Fresh injuries were personal. "Show me how much of this stuff you want moved, and I'll take care of it while you take care of your foot and my supper.''

"Eventually it all has to come down, I guess.''

He surveyed the shadowy shapes, curved tops, square corners, all coated with dust and filled with stuff nobody had used or cared about for decades. "That's a whole lot of lasagna, lady.''

"But from what I can tell, these are pretty much all the records.'' She patted the stack of boxes next to her as she rose from her seat. "Just three more. And if you could take them all down to the living room . . .''

They stood within inches of one another, close bodies in close quarters. He wanted to get closer. He wanted to lift her bare feet off the floor, carry her downstairs, and forget all about the damn boxes. Forget the lasagna, too, for that matter.

"What do I get with it?''

"With what?''

"The lasagna.''

"I baked bread this morning.'' She smiled, easing her way around him toward the stairs. "I'll fill you up, I promise.''

"Likewise, I'm sure,'' he muttered a moment later

when all he could see of her head was her bouncing
rooster tail.

They shared a candlelight dinner on her Aunt Cora's
fancy china, and then, at her invitation, he built a fire in
the living-room fireplace. Candlelight and wood smoke
reminded him of home, but the instrumental music playing on the stereo didn't. Soft, fluid piano. Mellow mood
music. He was game for a mellow mood.

He got comfortable with her on the floor in front of
the hearth, sipping the coffee he'd made, munching on
the sugar cookies she'd made, and sorting through old
papers. Mostly he watched her sort through them. She
was fascinated by the fact that the stuff was old, and
since the hospital had been torn down a long time ago,
she was uncovering bits of the past.

He was fascinated by the way she looked when she
was fascinated.

"Now, these are the ones I've found that are listed
on the monument." She stood a stack of files on her
knees, flipped through the tabs, pulled one out, and
opened it up. "Here's James Lone Bull. Admitted in
1928, apparently considered senile, although it doesn't
even say how old he was. Oh, here, it says he was
treated for pneumonia, looks like twice. Maybe that's
how he died." She presented him the file like a platter,
a spread laid out for him on the floor next to his coffee,
inviting him with a gesture to help himself.

He took up the top page and read the name he shared
with a man who was old and senile in 1928. It was all
over for him a long time ago—way before Zane's time.
But there was something immediate and compelling
about holding the paper in his hand and reading the
words that had been written about this elder Lone Bull.
" 'Disruptive,' " Zane read aloud. " 'Sings, tries to
dance. Requires isolation.' "

"Maybe it was a perseverance behavior," Michelle
suggested absently as she sorted through another box.
"Incessant singing. You know, like incessant head-
banging or hair-pulling."

"Jeez, maybe the guy was just trying to liven things

up a little.'' He turned the page and found James Lone
Bull's death certificate. ''Yeah, here it is, danced himself
to death.''

''What?''

He pointed to the paper, shook his head, and sighed.
''Sent him to the funny farm for doing the *kahomni* in
1928. Doctors tried everything, couldn't make him quit.
Danced himself right into the ground.''

''Really?'' She tipped her head, trying to get a look
at what he was reading. ''What's *kahomni*?''

''The dreaded Sioux circle dance. Ta-tum ta-tum ta-
tum.'' He beat out the cadence on the floor with the flat
of his hand. ''Monotonous as hell. Some people go crazy
just listening to it all night.''

''It doesn't say that.''

She was waiting for him to show her that it did. He
winked at her. ''Gotta read between the lines, Michelle.''

''This is serious stuff.'' She laid her hand on the file,
absently aligning the edges of the papers. ''This poor
man might have been a relative of yours.''

''I think he was. You know how I can tell?'' She
shook her head, trusting him again. He smiled. ''I think
I hear him laughing. He's saying, 'That's a good one,
sonny. You really had her for a minute there.' ''

The corners of her mouth twitched. ''Did not.''

''Did too. What else've you got there?'' With a thrust
of his lips he indicated the box she'd been digging
through as he set the old man's file aside. ''Any more
crazy Lone Bulls?''

''We're looking for Martin, right? I really don't think
'crazy' is a good word for—'' She pulled a sheet of
paper from one of the files. ''Look, Zane, here's a diagram of the cemetery.'' She dusted the wood floor with
her skirt as she scooted up next to him to share her find.
''Here's James Lone Bull's plot right here. We can probably go over there and figure out exactly where—''

''For what? You think I oughta put up a headstone?''
His gaze skittered across the paper she'd shoved under
his nose, then quickly homed back in on her eyes. ''I

don't wanna stir up anything across the street. I'm just thinking if I knew more about what happened to my Uncle Martin, maybe I could help him.

"When I asked him about this place"—he pulled the papers out of his back pocket, unfolded them carefully, and handed them to her—"this is what he drew. You gotta understand, Michelle, this guy's almost sixty years old. He sings the sun up every morning, but he doesn't talk. Getting him to go to a doctor is like—" He remembered the last time, when the old man had been so sick with bronchitis he couldn't stand up. But he'd clamped his jaw shut until the nurse had let him put the thermometer in his mouth himself. "To get him there, you almost have to knock him out. And they don't know what's wrong with him, besides the fact that he just hasn't got much upstairs. They say there's no physical reason why he can't talk."

"This is quite expressive, I think." She studied one of the drawings with a satisfied-teacher look on her face. "These are people, of course, and there are two big buildings. This looks like a swing set." She looked up at him, puzzled. "A swing set? Maybe this one is supposed to be a school." She held up another page and compared them. "It's in this one, too."

"Maybe it's a lot of different places all run together. Uncle Martin has the mind of a child. I'm not even sure he can remember that far back, and you get the feeling that whatever his thoughts are, one kind of slops over into another. But when I got onto this hospital thing with him, I could have sworn he knew what I was talking about. It scared him, but he was trying to show me something." He pointed to one of Martin's figures, defined with bold lines and hard edges. "See these circles? See how the arms are tied down?"

"I don't know how much they could really do for mental patients back then, or even tried to do. I suppose some of the treatment was . . ." She handed the paper back to him, then scooted across the floor to her boxes. "Let's see if we can find your uncle."

She shoved a box at him. He finished his coffee, set

the cup aside, and reluctantly started digging. It looked like the typical bureaucratic paper glut. He flipped through financial records, supplies ordered, supplies dispensed, receipts, payroll records, letters, and carbon copies of letters. The medical records may have been sketchy, but somebody had worked hard at keeping business records.

"Here's a list of transfers," Michelle announced, explaining as she scanned her find. "I remember Aunt Cora talking about this. Late in 1933 they sent a whole bunch of people to St. Elizabeth's Hospital in D.C. when the government started closing this place down. Aunt Cora was pretty resentful of that whole affair. She said the Indian people pleaded to keep their patients here. She said the people of Canton sent a delegation to Washington, and that everyone praised Dr. Tim for the work he was doing here." She glanced up from the paper. "No Martin Lone Bull on the transfer list."

"He's been at home ever since I can remember."

"I've noticed that some records seem to be much more detailed than others," she observed as she flipped through more files. "This nurse, R. Trainor, seems to have been a little more conscientious about keeping records. Oh, here!" She swung around, brandishing a folder as though she'd struck gold. "Martin Lone Bull."

"Jesus. He *was* a patient here." The name on the file not only proved it but gave Zane a queasy feeling at the same time, the same kind of queasiness he'd felt when three cocky young short-timers he'd sent out on patrol in the Mekong Delta had turned up missing. All the signs were there when he'd gone looking, plus there was that queasiness. "Prisoners," he muttered, and she questioned him with a look. "The people. They were tied up. That's what he drew in the picture."

She held the file within his reach, but she wasn't going to open it. She was leaving that up to him.

He stared at the tan folder, finally took it in his hand, and pried it open. "Feel like I'm peeking through a crack in the door to somebody's room."

"And seeing into his past," she sympathized.

" 'Taken into custody in 1928'—he looked up from the page, his eyes engaging hers briefly, inviting her to come closer and see for herself—" 'with grandfather.' James was his grandfather. Let me see James again."

She moved to his side, and they perused the clinical histories together. Cold words strung together in pithy, skeletal phrases, no heart beating anywhere on the page.

"You know what?" Zane said finally. "I'll bet James Lone Bull was a *yuipi* man or something. Look at all the times they noted singing, dancing, disturbance among the patients. Look what it says here." He pointed to a terse notation. " 'Patient practices forbidden rituals. Isolation required.' "

Michelle scowled, incredulous. "He wouldn't have been committed for practicing his religion, would he?"

"Who knows what they did to people back then for practicing traditional religion. They arrested them, for one thing. The Constitution doesn't seem to protect Indian religion."

"Really?"

"Really. Old laws that banned the Sun Dance and all the rest of the ceremonies are still in effect. Nobody gets arrested for it anymore, but people are still pretty careful, the ones who've kept the faith. Most of us never learned, not many people remember." He turned a yellowed page. "But I'll bet Uncle Martin does."

"You don't practice these ceremonies yourself?" She sounded disappointed. With a quick look he defended himself by challenging her to make something of it. She glanced away, her cheeks turning pink. "I'm sorry. I don't mean to pry."

"I don't. Nobody ever . . ." He'd never learned the way, never sought it. The old way. The Indian way. The Great Mystery. Truth was, it scared him.

When Uncle Martin sang, it enchanted him. When he watched the traditional dancers circle the arena fashioned from cottonwood boughs at a pow wow, stomping the grass, lifting their faces to the wind as though it whispered secrets for their ears only, it made the soles of his feet itch. He'd been about seven years old when he'd brought home a dead porcupine and asked Unci if she knew how he could make a roach like the one Clarence Three Legs wore on his head when he danced. The woman had snatched his road kill and buried it in a deep hole.

Hell, *it* didn't scare him. *She* did. The old woman had more taboos than Huck Finn.

"You mean actual laws?" Michelle clearly didn't want to believe this of her government. "The Sun Dance, I know, but that was because it involved mutilation."

"What does circumcision involve? At least with the Sun Dance the guy's old enough to make a choice, and it's entirely up to him. Nobody . . ."

His interest in making his point drifted as he continued to scan his uncle's records. "So little Martin was a boarding-school runaway. 'Chronic truancy,' it says. 'Speaks almost no English. Mentally deficient.' " He lifted his head slowly, repeating the remarkable notation. "*Speaks almost no English?* Hell, the man doesn't speak at all."

"He draws pictures."

"He ran away from boarding school," Zane marveled. "I'll bet they put him in here because he couldn't cut it at the boarding school. Now they put you in a reformatory if you run away. 'You wanna get sent to Plankington?' they say."

Then he remembered standing before the vice principal's big oak desk, holding his hands out, anticipating the ruler's sting. "Redfield," he mused, staring across the room into the fire. "When I was in school they used to say, if you don't behave and do your work you'll get sent to Redfield. I never asked anybody what happened to you there. It was one of those threats like, if you don't behave, the *gigi* man is gonna come after you. Whatever he'd do when he got hold of you, you knew you weren't gonna like it. But there was always this fear of getting sent away to a bad place where they kept renegade Indians."

"Did you go to boarding school?"

"Off and on," he said absently as he continued his perusal. "Here's that R. Trainor again. 'Martin prefers to be called Pagla. We have communicated using the few Lakota words I've mastered.' Smart lady," he allowed, feeling personally obliged toward the owner of the graceful script. " 'Patient is calm and responsive.' Then there's a line here that's crossed out." He held the paper up to the light. " 'Recommend family visit.' Then it says, 'Brother inquired.' Or maybe it's 'Mother inquired.' " He tilted the paper, scrutinized it, then shrugged. "Must be *mother*. Must be Unci. Wonder why they crossed that out?"

Michelle was watching him with a smug-female smile. "What makes you think R. Trainor was a woman?"

"Look at the writing." He stuck it under her nose. "Besides, nurses were women back then, weren't they?"

"I guess so."

"Not too many male nurses anyway. I'd say it's a safe bet all around." He flipped through the pages, looking for some resolution to this chapter in Martin's early life. "Doesn't say how long he was here. According to that list, he wasn't transferred when they shut down, but it doesn't say he was released. So probably five or six years?"

"Some of these people were here for years and years, and it's hard to tell . . ." She was looking through other records, combing through the words and setting some of them out for his inspection. " 'Alcoholic dementia,' " she read. "That's an interesting diagnosis."

Zane peeked over her shoulder. "You think in twelve years the guy might have sobered up?"

"Things were a lot different then. There was no Alcoholics Anonymous. I'm sure they did the best they knew how." She glanced up at him. "Don't you think?"

"What I'm thinking is that there was a time when my uncle was able to speak, and I'm wondering why I've never heard him say a simple word." The two files suddenly felt warm in his hands. "And now that I know he did time here, I've gotta wonder what they did to him."

"You make it sound like a prison when you say that he *did time*. You know, the people in Canton speak of Dr. Tim almost the way Aunt Cora did. The second coming of St. Francis of Assisi or something. And they loved her, too."

"So did you."

"So did I," she repeated firmly. "Of course, I didn't know him. But maybe we'll find some more clues in these files."

"Maybe we oughta let well enough alone." It's no good asking questions, the old women always said. Renegade Indians could get themselves taken away, or put away. Zane had been put away for two years.

Randy had been put away for good.

"I don't know what my brother was looking for when he answered your ad. Maybe he was just curious. Maybe he thought . . ." He offered her the two files. "Whatever they did to my uncle, I can't undo it."

"But you were looking for a way to help him," she recalled gently. "Not undo, but maybe to understand better."

"Okay, so he was here with his grandfather. One lost his voice, the other his life."

"Not all of his voice. Your uncle still sings."

"Only for Tunkasila," he said. When she wouldn't take them back he dropped the files on the floor between them. "Only to his god."

"Only *his*?"

He ignored her brazen insinuation.

She persisted. "If James was Martin's grandfather, what would he be to you? Great or great-great . . ."

"Who the hell knows? Martin's my uncle because that's what I call him." He looked her directly in the eye.

The stereo needle dropped on another LP. Haunting strings this time. Zane felt himself slipping into the soothing flow of unfamiliar music and the patient solicitation in her eyes.

He felt like an impostor. This whole thing was Randy's initiative. Zane didn't give a damn about tracing pedigrees.

"Look, I don't know where I came from," he told her as genuinely as he knew how. "I only know I'm here. You start lookin' at all this stuff too close, it gets complicated." She was giving him a funny look, and he realized he'd tipped his hand a little. Feeling exposed, he tried to cover with his usual shrug, his easy smile. "Who needs complications?"

"It's hard to avoid them."

He indicated the pile of boxes with a jerk of his chin. "You drag out stuff like this, you're not trying very hard."

"You drove a long way to see this stuff."

Damn that all-knowing Earth Mother look in her eyes.

"Maybe I just wanted to see you."

Her eyes turned dubious, but he continued to probe with his hooded gaze. He decided it was time to do some testing, see about getting personal on easier terms and in more pleasing ways.

"This is nice. The fire in the fireplace, the music."

"I don't have much country."

"That's okay. This stuff grows on you."

"What do you do? For a living," she added when he questioned with a quirked brow. "I don't think you've mentioned what line of work you do."

"You're assuming I work," he said, smiling when he saw that he'd thrown her off balance. "I don't have a job."

"Oh."

"Jobs can be kinda hard to find."

"Oh, I know. There's so little . . ." She wasn't satisfied. "Do you lease land or . . . have cattle?"

"I don't have any land. I'm almost forty years old, and you might say I'm still living with my mother."

"Oh." She looked to the fire for inspiration. "I thought maybe you were a cowboy."

"Do you like cowboys?" He chuckled. "If you wanted to think of me as a cowboy, you wouldn't be too far off. I train horses for people."

"Oh." She was relieved. Obviously she had her reasons for wanting him to be gainfully employed. "So you work for people who—"

"I work for myself. Myself and my family." He counted them off, starting with his thumb. "There's me, Grandma Beatrice, Auntie Cecilia, Uncle Martin, and then the two little kids, Sissy and Jojo."

"You have two children."

"Yeah, sorta. They're my sister's kids. Randy's sister's kids," he amended. "Look, don't get hung up on technicalities, okay? They stay with their grandma. They all look after me, I look after all of them. It works out." He leaned closer to her and confided, "I'm not married. I've never been married. Was that your next question?"

"No."

"There's a woman I see sometimes, but I'm not shackin' up with anybody."

"I wasn't asking—"

"You wanted to, but you didn't know how to go about it." He touched her chin, searched her eyes for any sign of objection. "And the reason you wanted to was because I've got that look in my eye. Like I'm thinking about makin' my move any time now." Her eyes were clear blue wellsprings of expectancy. He smiled. He liked taking these things more slowly than he used to. "Would that be all right?"

"Depends on what kind of a move you're thinking about making."

"A careful one," he promised, taking her face in his hands. "I don't want you to move away."

She didn't. They were sitting across from one another on the floor like two kids having a powwow. It was as innocent a pass as he'd ever made. Her eyelashes drifted downward, and he knew she watched his lips until she couldn't see them anymore, but she could feel them seeking hers. He sipped at their delicate corners, tasted them with the tip of his tongue, inhaled the flower-washed scent of her cheek.

God, she was a sweet little pot of honey.

He was sure now. He had an appetite for honey. But

he wasn't a kid anymore. He knew how to go easy on the sweets.

He lifted his head and looked down, smiling. She looked like Sleeping Beauty, just coming out of her spell.

Damn, he was good.

"Hello, Michelle," he whispered for good measure.

"Hello, Zane."

"Was that okay?"

She swallowed, gave a little nod. "So far, so good."

And he backed off, satisfied to savor her sweet-water taste. "How long have you been a teacher?"

She blinked, trying to recover her mental footing. "Eight years."

"Naw. You don't look old enough."

"Well, I certainly am. And you don't look like you're almost forty."

She looked pleased. He'd said the right thing.

She dropped folded hands into the pool of blue cotton skirt she'd bunched between her thighs, leaned forward over crossed ankles, and confided in a rush, "I don't know any real cowboys, so I don't know whether I like them. I'm not seeing anyone, but that doesn't mean I'm . . ."

"Starving for sex?" He chuckled merrily. "Hell, neither am I."

"Why are you so direct?"

"I can be indirect. Would you like that better?"

"I would like"—she spotted their cups, side by side on an unopened box—"more coffee. How about you?"

"Are you moving away?"

"I'm coming back." She unfolded herself as she reached for the cups. "Do you want anything else?"

"Mmm-hmm." He gave her his signature wink. "But there's no hurry."

His moves were subtle and delicious. A touch of his hand, a brush of his shoulder, a tempting smile. Michelle caught herself one step away from wishing he would put his arms around her and make a less subtle move. But he didn't. Maybe he wasn't that interested.

They talked long into the night, and then he went upstairs. She turned out her light and listened to his footfalls overhead, imagined him taking off his shirt, unzipping his jeans. The silly musings of an old maid. That, too, was a silly thought, for she valued herself and her independence. And she wasn't *that old*.

But she was old enough.

She lay there, counting the minutes in chunks of ten, trying not to check the illuminated face of her bedside clock, trying not to think about the man upstairs, trying not to stay awake. But sleep wouldn't come.

When she heard his footfalls on the stairs, she stiffened. Straining to listen, she nearly forgot to breathe. She had forgotten to lock her bedroom door. He would knock, she thought. He wouldn't just walk in. She would open the door, just a crack, and she would say something like . . .

He went out the back door, leaving her feeling at once stunned and utterly stupid. But no pickup door was opened or shut, no engine was started. She sat up in her bed, craning her neck so that she could see out the window overlooking the driveway.

A cigarette glowed in the dark. She almost laughed out loud. He lusted after a smoke, not her old maid's— *young* maid's—body.

Oh, God, what was wrong with her? Turning thirty was not the end of the world, and she was not, *not* an old maid. The last thing she needed in her life was some man to worry about and pick up after. Especially one who didn't have a real job.

Had he *said* he wanted to be part of her life?

No, he had not. He'd said he wanted something else but there was no hurry, and he'd said he was seeing another woman. That didn't sound promising, even if she were interested in him. Which she was not. Not very.

He moved out of sight. She slipped out of bed and approached the other window, taking care not to get close enough to let him see her. It was bad enough that *she* knew what she was doing. He strode across the front lawn, bathed in bright moonlight. He wore no jacket, shirtsleeves rolled halfway up his sinewy forearms. The late-night spring chill didn't seem to bother him. He crossed the gravel road, leaving a trail of smoke as he dragged on his cigarette, fueling himself. He was headed for the cemetery. His action intrigued her as much as it surprised her, but she resisted the foolish urge to follow him.

He had to be out of his friggin' mind, walking around on people's graves in the middle of the night. The only thing worse than stirring up Indian *gigis* was stirring up crazy Indian *gigis*. He couldn't sleep, needed a cigarette, and figured the woman probably wouldn't want him smoking up her ruffled curtains. He'd had no thought whatsoever of taking a walk, no plan to cross the road, no reason to pay a nighttime visit to a place that gave him the creeps even in broad daylight. His damn legs had just started walking.

He knew exactly where they were taking him, too, even though he'd hardly looked at the diagram. He didn't have to remember where her finger had pointed, didn't have to count plots. He was drawn to it, and steeling himself against it only made it worse. It was as though some big magnet were sucking him across the grass toward one of the telltale depressions in the northeast corner of the burial grounds.

Uncle Martin's grandfather. A *yuipi* man, sure as hell. Zane didn't believe in that stuff, never had.

Jesus, he hoped they'd nailed the coffin lids down tight back then.

"I just want you to know, straight out, I don't talk to dead people, and I don't exactly believe in ghosts. So what am I doing here?" He lit another cigarette and hunkered down as though he intended to share a smoke. "You tell me."

He'd come to see a woman. He liked her, thought there was a good chance he could score with her. Simple as that.

"Probably not much point in discussing this with a

dead guy. I guess you don't get horny anymore, being a stiff.'' He chuckled, then stopped and listened. An owl chortled at him from the top of one of the big, shadowy cottonwoods beyond the shrubs. The night wind rattled the new leaves.

Zane blew a puff of smoke into the grass. "Hope you haven't lost your sense of humor. I've got the same last name as you.'' He didn't dare say the name out loud. Not with that owl sitting up there. He was pushing his luck as it was. "I guess your daughter-in-law gave me her last name when she took me in. Beatrice. She wanted to be a grandma, so that's what I call her. She hardly ever talked about her husband or you or anybody from . . ."

The owl crooned overhead. Did it speak of death? Or was it *pagla,* the small gray owl who announced the coming of spring?

Zane's heartbeat kicked into high gear.

"I guess what I want to know is, what were you doing here? What was Uncle Martin doing here? Okay, so he's kinda off in the head." Jesus, about now he should talk about anyone else being off in the head. "I mean, he acts like a big kid, but . . . what's he trying to tell me about this place? What happened here, *mitunkasila*?"

The word felt right. A strange calmness claimed him, affirmed him, fortified him like a steadying hand.

"Okay, Grandfather, what is it you want with me?"

❧ 8 ❧

Michelle was just getting breakfast started when Zane appeared in the kitchen doorway. She poured a cup of coffee, turned, and nearly spilled it on him. She hadn't heard him move in close behind her. In silence his physical presence seemed all the more imposing, like a butte rising from the flatlands. He wore black well—shirt, hat, plain leather belt marking a low waist. He'd just showered, and he smelled of Aunt Cora's lemon soap. Michelle imagined the taste of it on her tongue as she set the mug in his big palm. He nodded his thanks.

"Eggs and bacon?" she offered.

"I've gotta be hittin' the road."

"If you eat here, you won't have to stop for a while."

"This is all I need." He sipped the coffee, then jerked his chin in the direction of a stack of folders on the kitchen table. "So where are we with this?"

Which *this*? Michelle wanted to ask, but she wanted him to say something promising without her asking. She felt silly, her face growing hot as she stared a hole through a pile of folders. "Those records are yours, Zane."

"Mine?"

"I don't know whether the state library would want any of the rest for the archives or anything. I suppose I should ask.'' She laid her hand on the pile. ''But since this has to do with your family . . .''

He laughed. ''Yeah, we really need this for the family archives.''

''You're the one who came all this way. You ought to''—she turned her palm up, push the stack with her fingertips—''take something back.''

''And I came back a second time, too, didn't I?''

''You must be looking for something.''

''I told you, my brother left this—''

''I'm not looking at Randy. I'm looking at you, and I see a man who's searching. Your search brought you here, and I'm glad it did.''

''You would have liked him. He liked to talk the same way you do, about journeys and quests instead of just movin' on down the road.'' His eyes were alight with an elder's indulgence, but the light softened, misted by steam from his coffee, and shifted away in sudden shyness. ''You, uh . . . heading back to Rapid anytime soon?''

''I have to be there by tomorrow morning. I do have a job.''

''Lucky you.'' He flashed a quick teasing grin, which dissolved all too quickly. He leaned back against the edge of the counter. ''Where will you be next weekend?''

''I've been coming here most weekends, but I wouldn't have to.'' *Oh, right.* ''What I mean is, I might not. I'll be off for the summer soon enough. I plan to spend most of the summer here in Canton.''

''I do business in Rapid.'' Again the grin. ''I really do. Occasionally.''

''I believe you.''

''Maybe we could get together for supper.''

''What else do you like, besides lasagna?''

''I'm not asking you to cook for me. Company makes you nervous. I'm making you nervous right now.'' He gave her a look that dared her to deny it, and they both laughed. ''See? I made you nervous last night, didn't I?''

"Not at all." She tucked her hair behind her ear as she glanced away, betrayed by a girlish smile. "You were a perfect gentleman."

"Hell of a surprise, huh?" She blushed furiously and made him chuckle. "I thought so. Let's see how long I can keep it up. I'd like to take you out for supper. What do *you* like, besides lasagna?"

"Frybread."

"Frybread?" He eyed her, smiling doubtfully, then shook his head. "Not powwow frybread. That's probably all you've had, and that stuff's usually hard as a rock. Now you take my grandma's frybread, or even Auntie Cecilia's when it's still nice and hot . . ."

"How would I be able to do that?"

"Well, they don't hardly make it anymore. They're getting old." He dismissed his close brush with making a rash offer by downing the rest of his coffee. Setting the cup aside, he repeated his first proposal. "I could come down to Rapid on Friday. We could have supper. You'd still have the weekend for your . . ."

"I'd like that."

It was becoming more difficult for Zane to get away. The kids had gotten out of school right after lunch because some road crew had hit a water main. They'd come home chattering a mile a minute, flying high like two songbirds surprised to find the cage door open. Whatever Zane was up to, they wanted to join in. Jojo had noticed that the horse trailer was hooked up to the pickup, and the next thing Zane knew he and Martin had their hats on, ready to go. When he announced that he was on his way to Rapid City he found himself surrounded by pouty faces.

"A-*gain*," Sissy complained.

"We got a day off," Jojo said.

"You've got two more after this," Zane pointed out as he tucked his duffel bag behind the pickup seat.

He knew they hated being left behind when somebody was going some place. *Any* place, just to see a different patch of ground. He'd hated always being left behind when he was a little kid. Unci had always kept him close to home back then.

He promised to be back by Saturday afternoon. He also promised to take everyone to a show on Sunday. They were still pouting when he finally left. He figured he'd better try to make good on at least one of his promises.

He needed a little time for himself, and he wasn't going to apologize for that. Except for his Canton trips he'd been sticking close since Randy died, trying to allay the unspoken fears. He knew Cecilia was worried about losing the kids. The last time the social worker had visited she'd made noises about the meaning of the word *temporary,* as in temporary custody, about Cecilia's age and Chickie's responsibilities and the whole idea of children needing stability. There was also the matter of the lack of running water and central heating at the Tusk place, which Social Services found to be a major health problem. Zane wondered why it wasn't a health problem for the elders. Cecilia's name was somewhere on the waiting list for HUD housing, but technically she had no dependents, so she was not a high priority.

Zane had also thought about trying to call himself the kids' guardian. He figured his prison record wouldn't make him a good candidate, and he was afraid that any additional wrinkle might invite additional meddling— what Social Services might call "alternative placement." Auntie Cecilia thought it helped her cause to be able to say that Zane was part of her household. He was afraid she was kidding herself, but he went along with it. He was able-bodied, he was bringing in some income, and he was there.

But he had to be able to go off on his own every now and then. So he took care of the chores, and he made a barrelful of promises, and off he went. Hell, he'd be back. They didn't all have to give him that just-like-all-the-rest look every time he started up the pickup.

*   *   *

Michelle's nerves were wound tighter than a watch spring by the time she got home from school. Her second-graders were ready for summer, and so was she. Besides that, she had a date with a cowboy, and she'd been looking forward to it for a week.

She was tempted to surprise him by having a home-cooked meal ready when he got there, whenever he got there, but she'd decided to dress for dinner and let him take her out. She hadn't been out on a real date in almost a year, not since she and Harvey Johnson had decided to go back to being "just friends." Or to admit to each other that "just friends" was all they ever had been or would be. They were both teachers, had attended the same college in Aberdeen for three summers' worth of graduate courses, occasionally attended the same church, were acquainted with many of the same people. They should have made the perfect couple, but they didn't. There was no excitement, no zing in the blood when he touched her, no fire. Michelle had just about decided there probably wasn't such a thing.

But then she'd been kissed by a cowboy, and holy bucking bulls, talk about zing. There was surely such a thing as a stunning first kiss and the sweet anticipation of seconds. And maybe there was more.

Michelle had amassed a pile of rejected outfits on her bed and a stomach full of butterflies. This nervous energy was not smart, she told herself. She needed her wits about her with this man. She knew almost nothing about him, really, except that his smile was as disarming as a poster boy's, and his touch electrified her.

Maybe that was enough.

It certainly was *not* enough. She wasn't used to being electrified by someone she hardly knew. She seldom let people she hardly knew get close enough to generate even static electricity. There was nothing static about Zane Lone Bull, and she could very well end up getting singed.

Or stood up.

They'd talked about having supper, but not about supper *time*. By 7:00 she was feeling silly about the short, shiny polyester shift she'd opted to wear. What was the message here? Old maid school teacher offers an easy feel?

And what was his message? I'll get to you sooner or later, babe?

By 7:30 she was sitting yoga-style in her favorite easy chair eating potato chips with sour-cream-and-onion dip and watching a rehash of the day's Watergate proceedings on TV when finally there came a knock at the front door of her apartment. She sprang from the chair, skated across the newly waxed linoleum floor on stockinged feet to stash the snacks in the kitchen, then back again to answer the door.

She caught herself, straightened her dress, made her extremities settle down. She was not all that excited. She was not angry. She was not really expecting him anymore, and her pulse rate had not just gone from zero to sixty in two seconds flat.

"Zane." She smiled sweetly. More than sweetly. "I'd given up on you."

He glanced behind her, as if he thought "given up on" and "replaced" were synonymous. "Not hungry?"

She gave a slight-shouldered shrug and stepped aside to let him in. "I didn't know whether you'd forgotten, or I'd misunderstood or . . .''

"Last time I was early." He took off his black cowboy hat and pushed his fingers through his thick black hair, smiling a little sheepishly. "Last time I left home early, before anybody else was up. This time I waited too long." The sheepishness evaporated, replaced with mischief. "But I'm here now and hungry enough to boil up the neighbor's dog. You just point out the meanest one."

"Dog or neighbor?"

"It's up to you, sweetheart. My treat."

"I could call for a pizza."

"You don't wanna go out?" He gave her long legs and little dress an appreciative once-over. "Looks like you got dressed for it. You look very pretty."

"Thank you." And he looked handsome in his crisp white western shirt, like a young and eager beau. "We didn't really say a time, did we?"

"I thought about stopping to call, but once I finally got going I just wanted to get here." He scanned the apartment, the desk, the sofa, the TV, then dismissed the flickering image in favor of her eyes. "So now I'm here. I'd like to take you out, but if you don't wanna go out with me—"

"I do. I was just . . ."

"Pouting?" He tipped his head to one side, ostensibly to get her to look at him. "You done now? I can probably wait 'til you're done." He tucked a thumb into his belt while the other hand fished in his shirt pocket. "I haven't eaten all day, but that's all right. You take your time."

She tried not to smile. "I'm done."

"You sure? 'Cause I've got a couple of Life Savers here. I can go another hour on two of these." He peeled away the curling wrapper on the remaining candy and offered her the top one, along with a cocky smile. "Or I can spare one if it'll sweeten you up."

"Does this mean we only have half an hour left to find you some food?" She popped the candy into her mouth and sucked hard, hoping the peppermint would work fast on the onion dip. "I'm glad you got here."

"How glad?" He stepped closer, slipped his hand beneath her hair, and curved it around the back of her neck. His smile was in his eyes.

She sucked that peppermint for all it was worth.

He kissed her gently, generously, and even though she stiffened up and held her breath, she kissed him back.

"Damn, that sweetener works slick."

"Not as slick as your charm. I'll get my shoes."

He chose a downtown bar and grill, known for its ribeye steak and its all-country jukebox. Michelle ordered chicken, which seemed to disappoint him, so she made a point to tell him several times that the food was delicious. He persuaded her to try his steak, which he fed her from his fork, and she declared it the best she'd ever tasted. In truth, she could hardly taste anything. She sipped at her white wine, nibbled at her salad, and eyed the dance floor. She wasn't much of a dancer, but she'd always wanted to duck under the brim of a lanky cowboy's hat and slide around the dance floor in his arms.

Before she could drop the hint, Gabriel Starr, a BIA cop from Rosebud Reservation, joined them at the table. He'd already had supper, he said, but he accepted Zane's offer of a beer.

"Gabe's an old army buddy," Zane told Michelle. "We joined up together. He had sense enough to get out while the gettin' was good."

"You did all right for yourself over in 'Nam," Gabe said.

"You were in Vietnam?"

"Sure was," Gabe answered for him. "Zane was one hell of a soldier." Then, taking exception to Zane's reproving glance, he added, "Hey, that goes a long way with the ladies, buddy."

"Not anymore," Zane averred quietly before taking a sip of his beer and changing the subject. "What do you hear about Flynn's so-called murder investigation?"

"They haven't arrested anybody yet. I know they're still sniffing around, but . . ." Gabe shrugged, glancing up at the waitress who was serving his beer. "Even questioned a couple of the guys who were down at the Knee, after they threw in the towel."

Zane dropped a dollar bill on the tray and signaled for the woman to keep the change. "It's over?"

"Where you been, man? It was over three, four days ago." Gabe smiled at Michelle as he gestured toward his friend. "This guy lives out in the boonies, I swear to God. Barely comes out once in a while to indulge himself in a little socializing. How'd you two meet, anyway?"

"Through Randy," Zane supplied.

Gabe questioned Michelle. "You knew Randy?"

"I never met him face-to-face." Michelle explained the ad and the letters, touching delicately on Randy's interest in them without giving any details about Martin or his grandfather. "Are you familiar with the Canton asylum?"

Gabriel shook his head, then turned to Zane. "Ol' Randy was like a turkey buzzard sometimes. Once he latched on to something, you couldn't shoo him off. Persistent as hell. Last time I talked to him, it was land titles. He was trying to dig up stuff about old allotments, trying to find your grandma and your uncle in the agency records at Pine Ridge and Rosebud. He was all hot about challenging titles to some of the land that was sold before the Indian Reorganization Act of 1934."

Zane shook his head. "Cedric Kills Crow's bright idea."

"Cedric's into mineral rights and power company easements these days. Too many irons in the fire, that guy. But him and Randy, they said they had it all figured how we could use the courts to our advantage." Gabe braced his forearms on the edge of the table and gestured matter-of-factly. "Me, I'm a cop. I spend more time in court than I care to, and I don't know if it ever works to anybody's advantage. The best way is to mind your own business and stay the hell out of there. Right, Z?"

"Amen to that, buddy." Zane shared a knowing smile with his date. "Michelle's not interested in Indian politics. She's more into history. Indian ghosts."

"Ghosts, huh?" Gabe wagged his head. "Same caution applies. Mind your own business and stay the hell out of there." He shimmied his bulky shoulders in a mock shiver. "You don't wanna mess with the *wanagi*, Michelle."

"We've discovered"—she caught Zane's warning glance and nodded—"exactly that. Just what you said." It was her turn to redirect the conversation. "If nobody has any faith in this FBI agent, wouldn't the Indian police be looking for Randy's murderer, too?"

"Gabe's from Rosebud," Zane reminded her. "Different reservation."

"Same jurisdiction for the FBI," Gabe said. "And they handle murder on any rez."

"Or bury it in triplicate," Zane said, and the two men

chuckled. "Anybody get charged for Wounded Knee?"

"They worked some kind of a deal. There were a few outstanding warrants, so they took those guys in. Party's over." Gabe took out a pack of cigarettes. "The AIM members head back to the cities, and Pine Ridge is still left with Wilson as chairman. Part of the deal is that somebody's supposed to investigate the complaints against him and look into the charges of corruption in the BIA, but who's gonna do that?" After Michelle refused his proffered cigarette, Gabe pointed the pack Zane's way. "You got any ideas about Randy?"

"I'm no cop." Zane stuck the end of the cigarette in his mouth and leaned toward Gabe's match.

Cowboys don't ask permission, Michelle mused as she watched the two men go through the light-up ritual. His eyes caught hers as he dragged deeply. "I'll get some more Life Savers," he promised, slipping her that sly wink on the tail of a stream of smoke.

"I don't know who'd want him dead," Zane told Gabe. "All his big ideas about getting back what was ours, you know, it was just..." He shook his head, smiling wistfully. "It was just Randy. It wasn't serious."

"I think he was serious," Gabe said. "He wanted to impress you with it, Zane."

"Don't try to lay that on me. I've already heard it from his mother." Zane shifted in his chair. "Let's talk about something else. How'd you like to do some heelin' for me this summer, Gabe?"

"Team roping's an old man's event."

"We might be old men, but we always said we were cowboys first, last, and always." Zane reached across the table for an ashtray. "And that does impress the ladies. If you don't have a job, first thing they wanna know is, are you a cowboy?"

"This guy here's one hell of a good cowboy," Gabe testified artlessly. Zane laughed. "Good at a lot of things."

"Having a policeman for a character reference impresses the ladies, too," Michelle said.

"That's what I'm thinkin'." Zane invited Gabe's consideration with a characteristic chin jerk. "What do you say, old man? All I need is a partner. You rather head? I can catch either end."

"He can, too," Gabe confirmed enthusiastically. "You got a horse?"

"I'm workin' on one."

"You got one for me?"

"Jesus, Gabe. I got the pickup, got the trailer. If I have to come up with two roping horses, what are you gonna kick in?"

The policeman grinned. "Like I said, Michelle, I don't care what you've heard about him, the bad stuff ain't true. This guy never hurt nobody, and he's good at a lot of things."

"That'll do, I guess." Zane jabbed his cigarette into the ashtray as he slid his chair back. "How good am I at dancing, Gabe?"

"This guy's one hell of a good dancer."

"The dreaded Sioux circle dance?" Michelle asked.

"You kiddin'? Not within the city limits." Zane grabbed her hand and drew up from her chair. "Watch my back, partner."

Gabe saluted, then settled back to nurse his beer.

"Are you expecting someone to sneak up on you?" Michelle asked.

"Never know." Zane scooped her in close with one arm and tucked her against his chest, his big body nearly enveloping hers as he picked up the honky-tonk rhythm.

"Is it because of the war?" She looked and smiled wistfully. His hat brim was like a roof over her head. "Do you have nightmares or flashbacks?"

"Sometimes. But I don't worry about snipers poppin' out of the chandeliers, if that's what you mean." He leaned back, studied the look in her eyes, his full lips twitching slightly. "I'm not crazy, Michelle."

"I know you're not."

"How do you know *you're* not?" His eyes swept the dim, hazy, crowded dance floor as his hand tightened at the back of her waist. His muscular thighs slid against hers, sensitizing her as they guided her steps. "We've gotten one or two barefaced stares just since we started dancing. Would it bother you if one of your teacher friends saw you right now?"

"No."

"I'm not saying I think you're—" He swallowed the word, brushed her cheek with his and confided, "Indians aren't too popular around here right now. Some people say all that noise down at Wounded Knee just makes it bad for the rest of us."

"Are you one of those people?"

"I used to wear a uniform, and some people said I made Indians look good. I was a lifer. Army regulation, straight down the line. Good Indian soldier." He chuckled derisively. "Gabe's all wrong," he said. "I didn't do any good for myself or anybody else over there."

"What happened?"

"Nothing you'd wanna hear about. Nothing that didn't happen to all of us." He spoke softly, as though there were just the two of them, or maybe just him. "Out in the bush we used the term 'Indian country,' meaning dangerous territory. I said it myself sometimes, without even thinking. Like 'Indian country' was the worst place you could ever be."

He leaned back, looked down, let her know he knew she was there. "I had a belly full, that's all. I took off the uniform, decided if I was gonna be a good Indian soldier, I oughta be defending Indian country. Makes sense, doesn't it?" She nodded, and he laughed. "Pretty soon I'm the one gets accused of makin' it bad for everybody else. So now I mind my own business. I tried to tell Randy that, but it was like he thought I'd lost my nerve or something."

"Who do you think killed him?"

"I let myself start thinking about it, and I always end up back on that road with unfinished business, *somebody else's* unfinished business driving me—" He waggled his eyebrows, wagged his head. "See, that's why you burn their stuff and you don't talk about 'em. Otherwise they won't leave you alone." He moved his hand, spreading it along with its heat over the center of her back. "So, can we talk about something else? How about your kids?"

"My kids? How about *your* kids?"

"Sissy and Jojo?" He chuckled warmly. "I almost had to bring those puppies with me. They let school out early, and those two had all kinds of plans for me. What grade do you teach?"

"Second."

"Jojo's in second grade. He's having a lot of trouble with reading, though. He can't sound out words worth a damn. They want to hold him back. You think that's a good idea?"

He looked to her for an expert assessment, his eyes brimming with the full measure of paternal concern. She found herself wanting to be the expert, the teacher-sage, the Earth Mother, the one who would supply him with whatever his children might need, just because the look in his eyes said, *Can you help me with this, Michelle?*

"That depends on the child and what the cause of his problem is. How old is he?"

"Seven. Eight in July."

"Then he's on the young side for his grade. You'd want to make sure—"

A woman's voice interrupted. "They just announced a ladies' choice. That means I can cut in, doesn't it, cowboy?"

The request caught them both off guard, but the dark-haired woman only had eyes for Michelle. Predator eyes. Michelle's back stiffened as her hand instinctively tightened on Zane's shoulder.

His fingers stirred soothingly, rubbing the soft fabric of her dress over the base of her spine even as he offered the interloper a friendly smile. "Hey, Marla. Catch me on the next set, okay?"

"Catch you—"

"You wanna take a twirl with me, Marla?" Gabriel suggested, deftly inserting himself between the two women. "Sorry, Z. Took my eyes off your back for half a second there."

Michelle looked up at Zane as Gabe danced Marla off, into the crowd. "What was that you were saying about your lack of popularity around here?"

He shrugged. "Except when they see me on the dance floor. I don't know what it is."

Michelle did. She knew she'd just met the other woman.

They all converged on the table at the same time, but Gabe was the only one who took a seat. Marla postured a bit, lifting a hank of swept-back hair, dropping it in place again as she eyed Zane. "Introduce me to your friend, and I'll let you off the hook on the next set." Then on an impatient sigh she stuck out her hand. "I'm Marla Ferrell. I sell some of Zane's work in my shop."

"Zane's work?"

"His beadwork. He does exquisite—" She modeled her belt, slung low on her slim hips. Its unusual pattern, the swirl of color, and the superior workmanship made it a distinctive piece. "Like this. Isn't it beautiful?"

"It certainly is."

"Marla," Zane injected, "this is Michelle Benedict."

Marla spared Michelle a nod, withdrew her hand, and turned back to Zane. "Long time, no see, cowboy. I wasn't in at the store at all today."

"Neither was I."

"Oh." She digested the rebuff with a coy moue. "Picking up some horses, then?"

"Before I leave town, yeah." He braced the heels of his hands on the back of his chair. "How was your trip to New Mexico? You been there and back already?"

"Oh, yes, I found some great stuff. A new silversmith who does sort of an updated squash blossom, very clean lines." She smiled, pleased to add, "I also found a shop owner in Santa Fe who'd like to carry your work. Classy shop, one-of-a-kind pieces for discerning clientele."

"One-of-a-kind, huh? That means once in a while?"

"Artists are expected to be temperamental."

"How about cowboys?" Michelle asked.

"Definitely. I like 'em dark and brooding." Marla slid her a sidelong glance. "Is that your fantasy, too?"

"My fantasy is to dance the *kahomni* under a big Dakota moon," Michelle said airily.

Zane chuckled, his eyes alight with amusement.

"Did I say it right? *Kahomni*?"

"You said it just right." He slipped his arm around her shoulders. "You know where we can get some frybread this time of night, Gabe?"

"Hell, you can probably fry some up yourself, Z. All you need's a little flour, water, yeast, and something to do while the dough's rising."

"Ready to go?" Zane asked Michelle, and she nodded quickly. She was more than ready. "Good seein' you, Marla."

"Flour and water and what else?" Michelle asked as she kicked her shoes off inside the door.

"It'll take the rest of the night."

"We'll have frybread for breakfast, then."

"If you say so." He followed her into the kitchen. She was already opening drawers and doors, slapping stuff on the counters. It was a pretty little room, all yellow and blue, a cheerful place even in the middle of the night. "My big chance to cook with gas."

"Here's an apron."

"Cowboys don't wear . . ." He shook the folds out of the butcher's apron and smiled when he saw KISS THE COOK emblazoned on the top. "But this one I like. Yes, ma'am." He tossed his hat on the table and draped the neck strap over his collar. "Ready to kiss the girls and make 'em sigh."

"After you prove to be the cook." She reached around his waist to tie the apron strings. "You look like the cowboy who stole the apron."

"You want proof? I'll get my kiss, lady." He gestured expansively. "This is almost too easy with all this de-luxe rigging. Hell, running water, don't have to worry about running out of wood or . . ." Sidling up to her, he hooked his arm around her neck and held his hand in front of her face. "Left-handed, okay? For two kisses, I'll do it left-handed."

"A small price to pay." She ducked away and handed him the flour.

"You think so, huh?" He bounced the five-pound sack in his hands. "Wait'll you find out where I like to be kissed."

"Isn't it kisser's choice?"

"Not if we're playing by cowboy rules." He set the flour on the counter and laid a flour-dusted finger on the point of her chin. "Let's get it straight before we start. Cowboy cook, cowboy rules."

"Aren't they made for wild horses and wilder women?" she wondered innocently as she reached back into a cabinet.

"Cowboys or rules?"

"Both."

"Some are, but we won't use the ones that don't apply. It's my job to figure out—" He looked down at the next thing she'd set in his hands. "What's this for?"

"It's a bowl. For mixing."

"This puny little thing? Don't you have a washtub?" His arms formed a big circle, but he shrank it by half when she shook her head. "Okay, a dishpan. But I can't cut the recipe any more than that."

He didn't seem to have a recipe. He said there were only two spoon sizes, and he selected a coffee cup for its shape and used it for measuring larger amounts. He told her he'd learned his kneading technique from his grandma, who'd had no daughters to share it with. Watching his big hands work the dough, Michelle reveled in the wonder of him, filled herself with him, soaking up every word, every look, every laugh they shared. Even when his creation ended up looking exactly like the simple bread dough he'd said it would be, in her eyes he'd made a minor miracle.

Zane showered while the dough was rising, and

Michelle dozed on the sofa. Down on one knee he woke her with a soft kiss and a softer smile. "That one doesn't count in our bargain," he told her. "I just couldn't resist. Here, I'll take it back." A drop of water rolled off his hair and into hers as he kissed her again. "Some Indian giver, huh?"

"Some cowboy cook."

He was wearing a white T-shirt and jeans, and he smelled of shower water and aftershave. "My dough is up and ready," he said with a wry smile. "You wanna come on and light my fire?"

"Oh, dear." She hoped she knew how.

He did the deep-fat frying left-handed, as promised, lightly browning pieces of dough cut to look like square donuts. She opened the window above the sink, and the night air cooled her skin and fanned his fire. She could see it in his eyes.

Let the flames spill over on me, she thought. I'm ready to burn with you.

"There you go." He placed the last piece of frybread on the draining mat they'd made of brown paper bags. "Enough for breakfast for a week."

"Will it keep for a week?" She swallowed the last bite of the piece she'd shared with him, by turns feeding him a bite, letting him nibble her fingers a little each time, then taking one herself and licking the same fingers.

"Not at my place." He surveyed the walls. "You know what time it is?"

"Time for your reward. Almost time for sunrise. Would you like to go for a short ride?" She slipped her arms around him and rubbed her palms over his back, enjoying the feel of soft cotton over corded muscle. "I know a beautiful spot for kissing."

"You've got one all picked out?" He lowered his head slowly, tipping it to the side, nuzzling her hair aside and touching his lips to her neck. "I do, too," he whispered, his breath striking the spot of skin his lips had dampened. "Where's yours?"

"Not far." The delicious shiver he'd started in her

neck splintered into a thousand shards and scattered instantly throughout her body. "It's very . . ."

"Very what?"

"Very nice. Very, very . . ."

"Beautiful." His hands took the measure of her waist and slid upward, taking the loose fabric of her dress along with them as he breathed adoring kisses beneath the curtain of her hair. "Very beautiful. I wanna dance you in circles now, Michelle. 'Til you're so dizzy you can't think straight. Now you tell me." He caught her earlobe in his teeth, traced the edge of it with his tongue and whispered, "How far do you want to take me?"

"To my favorite—"

"How far do you want to go?" he demanded.

"As far as . . ." She pressed herself against him, full to bursting with a desire she wasn't ready to admit to. "I want to be close. I want . . ."

His hands bracketed her head as he threaded his fingers into her hair and kissed her. First a hungry tasting, soft-lipped and breathless, then a deep mating of mouths, a meeting of tongues. Her lips trembled when they drew apart.

"I want to watch the sunrise in your eyes, Michelle." He plumbed their depths now as he declared his intentions. "I want to see it through your bedroom window."

"Cowboy rules?"

"No rules. Only wishes. Do you have any?" She nodded. "I've told you mine. The rest are yours."

"How many will you grant?"

"As many as you make. You don't even have to say them out loud. But if I stray from the mark, just tell me."

"I will."

She took him to her bedroom and opened the blinds on the east window. It was still dark. The window overlooked a courtyard outside her second-story apartment. On the far side a child's swing creaked as the night wind played across its seat.

He stood behind her, swept her hair to one side, and unzipped her dress. He pushed it off her shoulders and let it slide to the floor. She turned to him, took him in her arms as he took her, and they lost themselves in a throat-searing kiss. And at first they devoted themselves to holding each other, pressing against each other, she lifting herself on tiptoe to match her hips to his while he ravaged her mouth as though her kiss was all he'd ever craved.

Then slowly, moving like mirror images, they stripped one another to the waist. Pale night light poured over them through the window. Her fingers explored the contours of his chest, while he chose to feast on her first with his eyes. Then he read her face while he touched her breasts, deftly drawing her nipples into tight knots. Her eyelids drooped and her lips parted, needing his kiss. He gave generously, lavishly, stroking her tongue with his. She was so slight, so sweet, so responsive, and she stirred him so profoundly that he wanted to give more and more.

He knelt to worship her with his mouth, each breast in its turn, until she swayed toward him. He steadied her hips while he burrowed his face between her breasts, breathing deeply of her soft scent, tasting her skin, peeling her pantyhose away like the skin of a delicate piece of fruit. How soft and cool she felt against his face. Without destination or plan he blazed a trail along her midriff with the tip of his nose, dipped his tongue into her navel. She gasped when he nuzzled the flattened nest that covered her private cleft.

She said his name shyly, more question than challenge, and suddenly he felt a little shy himself. She didn't move. She trusted. He couldn't tell her how much he wanted from her, how much he wanted to give. All he knew was that it was more than rhyme or reason would justify. All he knew was the need to uncover all of her and to know all of her and to favor and caress and make her his.

"Just a kiss," he whispered as he placed her hands on his shoulders, then again took her hips in his hands.

"Kisser's choice." He pressed his lips upon her and made little raids with his tongue until she called him by name.

He caught her up in his arms and laid her on the bed in a nest of her own clothes, telling her how wonderful she was and letting her taste herself on his lips. She clutched at him as though she were afraid he might leave her. He drew her hand to the front of his pants and helped her unsnap them. She started to jerk at the zipper, but he cautioned her against a hasty undoing.

"Nothing under my jeans but me," he confided. "Anything gets caught, it'll be painful."

"Oh . . . I'm—"

"No reason to be sorry," he said, kissing her fingers, then guiding her hand over his broad chest, sucking his breath swiftly when she flicked his flat nipple. "I want to make you wish for bigger and better things, sweetheart. Are you still wishing?"

She nodded and made a small, gratified sound as he touched her in kind.

"What are you wishing for? Show me." He guided her hand over his abdomen and begged her, "Touch me. Make me bigger and better for you."

She did, exploring her power to change him, harden his body even as she gentled his mind. "I wish you'd come inside," she said.

"I won't come until I'm inside." He shucked his pants and gave himself over into her hands. "Lead me, darlin'. This one time, I'm gonna let you lead me by the . . ."

"Zane, I'm not . . ." She put her mouth close to his right ear and whispered something he couldn't quite make out. His weak ear.

His weak *head*.

"I'll take care of it," he promised, and he reached blindly for his pants.

"I probably should have mentioned it sooner."

"I almost strayed from the mark, didn't I?" But he found it. "I forgot, you get nervous about having company."

"I'm not." The way she touched his face felt like an appeal to him, a shy plea. "Maybe I am, but I know what I want."

"I do, too." He rose over her, bracing his weight on his arm. "Grant me one wish, Michelle."

"I'll try."

"Don't be sorry later."

"Make another one." She reached for him, her body accommodating his every move, responding to every suggestive signal as they came together. "That one's already granted."

"Okay, one more then." His hands took charge of her hips, tilting them to him to ease his way. "Make me feel at home."

And she did. He felt as though a wayward part of himself had finally found its rightful place, a place that fit him flawlessly, where the rest of him already lived. With each thrust of his hips he was met by the soft underbelly of his own hardness, the budding of his root, all ready to bloom.

It felt better than good. It felt right. It felt like the perfect liftoff. He drove her ahead of him, playing with her like a balloon on a shaft of air, building his pace on the sound of her pleasure, and when she came to him, he joined her. They sailed together, and later, after the sailing stopped, they drifted together, then settled together, arms and legs entwined, each breathing the other's breath, each warming the other's skin.

It was a stunning surprise.

"Did I put this smile on your pretty face?" he asked finally, touching the corner of her mouth.

"Yes, you did." She turned her head slightly, kissed his fingertips. "You granted wishes I didn't even know about."

"Lonely old cowboys make good lovers."

"Must be all those wild horses and wilder women."

He chuckled wickedly as he smoothed her hair back from her face. "I've survived some real ball busters, all right, but this . . . you . . ."

"I'm not usually this messy." She lifted a wad of

fabric off the bed, then dropped it again. "I tried on everything in my closet. It all looked so ordinary."

"To you, maybe."

"I've never known anyone like you, Zane." She stroked his back, then made a bold foray over his buttocks, her smile turning saucy. "Z? Is that what the other cowboys call you?"

"That's what my brother called me." His finger traced the letter across the top of her breasts, cut a diagonal swath across the valley between them, then underlined their lower swells, branding her. "I want you to call me Zane, and I want you to say it the way you said it when I was kissing you between your legs." His invisible line tracked the midline of her torso.

She turned her face away from him and closed her eyes as his hand took firm possession of her mound.

"No, look at me, Michelle. Look at my face, and say my name."

"Zane." She lifted her face to him, but her eyelids grew heavy as his fingers delved deeper. "Oh, Zane."

"Open your eyes, Michelle." She did, immediately seeking his. He smiled. "I see another wish."

"Zane . . ."

"You taste so good to me." He licked her breast, then suckled in earnest, then blew on the wet spot he'd left and thrilled to the sound she made. "Everywhere. Every part of you tastes good to me. Say my name again."

"Za—"

He consumed the taste of the word on her lips, sipped it from her throat, sucked it off her tongue and said, "You make my name taste good, too."

"You're my only wish."

"I could grant that wish for you all day long and into the night," he whispered into her hair.

"Zane, you're the only Zane I've ever . . . I've never known anyone else like you."

"You already said that, and I believe you. And the truth is, darlin', I don't think anyone else has ever known you"—he lifted himself over her to look, to see, to love the way the starlight washed her skin and the moon glowed in her eyes as he said—"the way I do."

❧ 9 ❧

It was a relief to turn off the highway onto the familiar gravel road, the last leg of the way home. Zane felt like a drunk behind the wheel, hanging on, taking exaggerated pains with simple moves, fully expecting all hell to break loose any minute. He felt better and worse than he ever had in his life, and the woman on the other side of the pickup seat was entirely to blame for it.

She'd bewitched him. He had dozed off in her arms and awakened feeling like a new man, completely made over, with one single experience to his credit. He couldn't say it was the best sex he'd ever had, but that was only because he couldn't remember having sex with anyone else. He knew he had. More tasteless times, more faceless women than he cared to count. But he couldn't recall the details and didn't care to try. Lying there in her bed, her entire wardrobe carpeting the floor around them, the sound of her sleeping with her face close to his good ear, he had felt as contented as a breast-fed baby, or as contented as he imagined one might feel, never having been one himself.

But then he should have made her the same kinds of promises he'd made the kids, said his good-byes, and taken his contentment with him. He could have sailed all the way home on that feeling and some good old-fashioned country tunes if he hadn't complicated it all by letting Michelle talk him into taking her to meet his family. Then he'd told her that he had already promised to take the kids to the show on Sunday, and suddenly another invitation had flown out of his mouth. Stay until Sunday and go with us.

What in hell was he thinking?

Where in the hell was he going to put her?

Put her in a pumpkin shell, and there he . . .

God help him, that was about what he had to offer her. Two pumpkin shells. A six-fifty shack and a two-room log house.

They had always been enough. The two together made a place to stay. Randy used to call it their campsite. It was better than a bed in a dormitory or a barracks or a prison cell. It was where the people Zane cared about stayed, and that was enough.

Until he thought about taking a woman there. He'd taken Jesse there, but that was different. He'd known Jesse all his life. She had been part of his world, so much a part of it that he'd taken her for granted. He'd loved her in his way, but he hadn't missed her much until he'd finally realized that she was no longer there. Jesse had been part of his world until she'd gone to the next.

But Michelle was not. Quite suddenly she was part of him, but not his world. She wouldn't fit. Wouldn't want to. It was up to him to fit a piece of himself into hers. There were two halves of Zane Lone Bull, one for each of South Dakota's two worlds. He knew from experience that it was easier to divide himself than to try to mix the two. But making love with Michelle had turned all his experience into a haze, and here he was, crossing the line by taking her with him.

"What I'll do is, I'll have Jojo read to me a little," she was saying. "I'll be able to tell quite a bit just by—"

"We don't have too many books around," he said distantly as he guided the pickup over a washboard of ruts. "I bought a couple, brought them home, the dog chewed them up. I kinda think that one book was too old for Jojo, anyway. He liked the pictures, but . . ."

"I brought some books for the kids." She reached for the dashboard as a big bump bounced her forward on the seat. But it didn't shake her smile. "The old maid school teacher always has books for the kids."

"Old maid?" She looked more like a little girl on her way to the Fourth of July carnival, all excited, all dressed up in her nice blue jeans and her flowered blouse, hair clipped back from her face in a big barrette. She had him smiling, too. "I hear those old maid school teachers get kinda desperate."

Pleasure light danced in her eyes. "Desperate enough to take up with old cowboys."

"Take up what?"

"Take up . . . time?"

He nodded once. "Got plenty of that."

"Space, too, and I've suddenly got plenty of that."

"Yeah, well, I don't." The west wind made waves in the sea of grass that surrounded them. The four strands of barbed wire running along the right-of-way gave the only clue that there were people around somewhere. "Plenty of wide open spaces, but no place to, uh . . ."

She leaned closer, smiling impishly as she laid her hand just above his knee. "Having company makes you nervous, does it?"

"I never have company. Not like . . ." He drew a deep breath and let it go grudgingly as the pickup topped the crest of the last hill. "But we're here now."

"Any place is fine, Zane. I don't need a guest room." He laughed.

"Or even a bed, for that matter," she added quickly.

"My kinda girl." He tossed her a flirty wink.

Her comeback squeeze sent a jolt from his knee to his groin, and damn if it didn't give him a hard-on.

The rutted dirt road forked near the corral, which was where Zane headed first. He was glad he had to stop and unload the bay mare he'd picked up at the Hausauer place on their way out of town. He asked Michelle to help him, just to make sure the two little faces peering out the front window could see that he'd brought somebody with him. Right about now they were reporting the news to their grandma, who was telling them to hurry and get some of their stuff picked up while she cleaned off the table and made some coffee. He figured he'd give her a little time to put things the way she wanted them. They didn't get many visitors anymore.

Floppy-eared Soup leaped out from behind the wood pile to greet Zane. He was wary of Michelle until Zane slipped her a piece of the frybread from the paper bag on the front seat. She fed it to the big, shaggy dog, as instructed, and Zane assured her she had a friend for life.

He turned the mare loose in the largest of the three pens he'd fixed up since he'd moved back home. "I should try her out later," he told Michelle as he lit a cigarette. "See how much work she needs. Hausauer's hired man seemed to think she was some valuable piece of horse flesh and couldn't figure out why they'd be letting me take her out of his sight."

"You must have quite a reputation."

"That I do." He eyed her speculatively as he turned his head to let the wind carry away a stream of smoke. "Satisfaction guaranteed. Word gets around."

"I'm sure it does." She looked away, turning her attention to the mare trotting around the pen.

"I used to break horses when I was a kid. The wilder the better. I loved to just ride the buck out of 'em. Now I know better." He cupped his hand around her neck and rubbed the back of it with his fingertips, smiling when she finally looked into his eyes. "Horses are really touchy. It doesn't matter whether they come from some fancy breeding farm or straight off the range, it works a lot better if you treat 'em gentle right from the start."

"Why don't you try her out now? I'd like to see how you—"

"Uncle Zane, you're back!"

"Uncle Zane, can we run the horses in?"

Zane withdrew his hand just as the kids became two bowling balls hitting him from behind. Fortunately he'd braced himself. He hooked an arm around each of their heads and hugged them against his sides. "Not if you two break my legs for me."

Sissy squinted up at Michelle. "Did you break down or something?"

"No, but your uncle did," Michelle said with a smile. "I asked him to bring me here to meet you. You must be Sissy, right?" The little girl nodded. "And Jojo. I'm Michelle." The boy just stared until Zane prodded him to offer a handshake. "Your uncle's been talking about you two so much I just wanted to come out here and say hello. He finally broke down, and here I am."

Jojo looked up at Zane. "Where'd you get her, Uncle?"

"Rapid City."

"Is that where you took us to Reptile Gardens that time?"

Michelle burst out laughing.

"Yeah, but that's not where I got her, Jojo."

"There was one lady there, she had long hair just like yours, and she let this big giant boa constrictor crawl up her arm"—Jojo's hand simulated the snake's head as he demonstrated the motion on himself—"right into her hair."

"Wow," Michelle responded appreciatively as Zane buried the remains of his cigarette with his boot heel. He claimed the paper bag from the pickup and started them all moving toward the house. "I'm not really afraid of snakes," Michelle told Jojo. "But I wouldn't want one in my hair, would you?"

"Corky White says they pay a lot of money for rattlers down at Reptile Gardens." Jojo took the lead, walking backward. "I'm gonna catch me some and sell 'em."

"You're gonna catch you some hell if you start messin' around with rattlesnakes," Zane warned, scooping the boy to his side in time to prevent him from backing into the dog.

Jojo threw the front door open and bounded inside. Zane caught it and invited Michelle in with a gesture as he called out, "I brought you something, Auntie."

Cecilia greeted them at the door, wiping her hands on a stringy towel. "Looks like you brought us some*one*."

He introduced Michelle, then shoved the paper sack in the older woman's hands. "Made some frybread."

"You?" She opened the bag and sniffed at the contents.

"Michelle had me cooking all night." He slid Michelle a sidelong glance and enjoyed watching her cheeks color. "This woman can really put away the frybread. I told her I had old ones and kids to feed, so she left you a few pieces."

"You got this one to cook you frybread?" Cecilia glanced at her nephew, then checked the contents of the bag again, muttering, "Must be love."

"Uncle Zane found her in Rapid City, and she said she wanted to meet us," Jojo said. "Can I have some frybread?"

"Are you his girlfriend now?" Sissy asked tightly, shaking off the piece of frybread her grandmother offered.

"Well, we've certainly become friends."

"And she's a girl," Jojo said around a mouthful of frybread.

"That probably means we don't get to go to the show," Sissy said glumly.

"I've been invited to go along to the show, if that's okay."

"Can you ride a horse?" Jojo asked.

"I haven't ridden a horse in a long time, but I can. Can you?"

"Can we, Uncle Zane? If we share?"

"After a while. We just got here." He laid a hand on Michelle's shoulder and urged her toward the ancient woman sitting in the corner chair next to the cold wood stove. "Unci, I brought somebody to meet you." He pushed a tattered kitchen chair up close to the old woman's knees and indicated that Michelle should sit. "She doesn't see real good," he explained.

Michelle drew the chair up even closer as she sat down, leaning close, watching the woman's face for some signal that she'd found her in her field of vision.

Zane dropped one knee to the floor, positioning himself between the women as he spoke softly, introducing them to one another in a combination of their languages, explaining that Michelle was a schoolteacher in Rapid City, that she taught little kids, that they'd gone dancing, and she could *really* do the *kahomni*. Michelle gave him a quizzical look.

He covered the old woman's leather-skinned hand with his. "I met Michelle that time I went down to Canton. Remember that first time I told you about going down there?"

Something flickered in Beatrice's rheumy eyes. She straightened, leaned forward slightly, and squinted at Michelle. "No good," she announced finally. "No good, sonny."

Zane squeezed the woman's hand under his, rubbing her shoulder with the other. "This is my friend, Unci. I want you to be nice to her." He glanced over his shoulder at Michelle. "I think she's talking about me, not you. Lately everything's 'no good.' "

Beatrice surprised him when she grabbed his arm and spoke in Lakota. "Take her back. You can't have her."

It was more than his grandmother had said in months, and her worries amused him. Maybe she still had it in her to tease him a little. "Why not, Unci?"

"They'll take you away again."

"No, they won't. I'm not going away anymore." The old woman hadn't lost her memory, then, if she was afraid he'd go back to jail. Maybe she was thinking about Jesse Strikes. "Michelle teaches little kids like Jojo," he repeated. "Teaches them to read."

"No boarding schools," the old woman said. "No good."

"I know, no boarding schools. Michelle teaches at a regular school." He turned to explain. "She never wanted me to go to boarding school, and I guess now I understand why."

Michelle noticed the pieces of cotton fabric and the small pair of scissors in the old woman's shawl-draped lap. "What are you working on, Un . . ." She looked to Zane for approval, and he nodded. "Unci? What are you making?"

"They make star quilts. Unci used to be a damn good quilter. She cuts the pieces by feel." He gave his grandmother's shoulder a parting pat as he rose to his feet. "She doesn't usually say much of anything. You got her goin' a little, but don't worry about it. She didn't mean anything."

Cecilia offered coffee with the frybread. They were about to sit down to the table when the front door opened. Zane signaled Michelle with a subtle glance. There was only one person missing from the family circle, the one who had brought them together in a sense. Michelle had been privy to his past, and now the old man was about to walk into her presence.

Zane shook off a funny, foreboding feeling with a broad smile. "Hey, Uncle Martin. What a nose for frybread, this guy. Want you to meet Michelle." He took her by the arm and drew her closer to the door. "This is Uncle Martin."

"Pagla?" she asked softly, offering him her hand.

Martin stepped out of the shaft of light from the open door, the sound of his boyhood name attracting him to her blindly. His hand found hers on its own. He searched her face, his eyes brightening as they adjusted to the dim interior. The door stood open, and the room was quiet. The old man held her hand for a long moment, studying her as though he thought he knew her.

"We call him Martin. The other name is—" Zane felt a little awkward, hearing his voice break the silence, but the intensity in Martin's eyes was disconcerting. He didn't know whether he felt threatened by it or just embarrassed because the man wouldn't let go of Michelle's hand. He cleared his throat and thumped Martin on the back. "Uncle, this is *my* girl, so don't get too . . ." He caught the look of surprise in Michelle's eyes. "She's pretty, isn't she?"

Martin nodded, the ghost of a smile softening the lines in his face as he finally released her hand.

Zane prompted what little talk there was over coffee. When he pronounced it time to take a ride, Sissy and Jojo were out the door. He saddled up the new mare, took a few turns around the pen, and determined that she hadn't been ridden much. She was a little goosey when he got her out in the pasture, but she neck-reined well enough to use her to run the other two horses in. He put Martin and Jojo on the gelding he'd been riding for Tom Deiderich and mounted Sissy behind Michelle on his own well-broke sorrel.

"Today I'm the one in need of a teacher," Michelle told her saddle partner. "If I'm messing up, just tell me, Sissy."

Soup trotted along with them until he spied some movement in a patch of buck brush and took off after it. Martin pointed when he spotted the jackrabbit, but the dog's prey had a good head start. The horses were headed in the same direction, following a spring-swollen creek at a more leisurely pace. The late afternoon sun warmed their backs, and the wind toyed with their hair. It all felt good, and Zane realized that they made easy companions, the kids asking Michelle about her school, she wondering about theirs. It all felt fine.

They meandered down the draw, then climbed to the top of a ridge, which afforded them a view of both houses.

"Is this all your family's land?" Michelle asked.

"Most of what you can see belonged to Auntie Cecilia's husband, so now it belongs to her kids. Most of it's leased out now, but they used to have cattle. She kept a quarter section out for a horse pasture." Zane pointed out the fence line. "When I was a kid, we all lived in the log house. Back then it was all one big room. A lot of people got rid of the log houses, sold them, or cut them up for firewood when the tribe got the payments for the reservation land that got flooded out by the Oahe Dam.

"People built those houses," he explained, leaning across the saddle horn on his forearm as he nodded toward the little green house that was Auntie Cecilia's domain. "Six-fifty houses, we call them, because that's what the payment amounted to—six hundred fifty dollars apiece—and that's what that kind of money would build. But we kept the log house around, called it the bunkhouse.''

He turned, adjusting his hat against the sun. "Right, Uncle? It's a good bunkhouse for us two old cowboys.''

Martin smiled at Michelle and nodded.

Zane wondered what in hell that silent old fox was thinking when he looked at her with those big sad eyes and smiled that way, like some lovesick, cast-out stag. It occurred to him that he'd never known his uncle even to notice a woman. Not that he'd been around too many.

Michelle pointed to a circular structure near the house. It stood on cottonwood poles and sported a roof of leafy boughs. "That must be like a gazebo or something?"

"Never heard it called that," Zane said, chuckling. "Some people call it a squaw cooler. We call it a shade. It gets a new roof every spring. We just put that one up, Martin and me. In the summer we move the stove outside so the house doesn't get so hot. When it's warm enough sometimes we'll sleep out there.''

"Like camping out in the yard?" Michelle flashed him a bright, big-eyed smile. "Oh, let's do that tonight.''

"Me, too!''

"Yeah, me too!''

"You kidding?" Sun in his face, he stared at her, nonplussed. "You wanna sleep out on the ground? Do you realize how hard that ground is?''

"No, I don't. I never got to camp out in the yard. I had no sisters, no brothers, and no adventuring friends. Just boring girls, and all we did was stay in the house and play boring board games and do paint-by-numbers. Oh, Zane, let's.''

"We'll make straw beds," Sissy suggested, unable to stifle her enthusiasm.

"We got a whole buncha blankets," Jojo put in.

"And the mosquitoes aren't a problem yet." Michelle was truly pleased with her suggestion.

Zane felt the years drop away as he gave her a slow, affectionate smile. "Suits me fine."

Cecilia thought they were crazy when the plan was announced, but she just shook her head and dished up the soup she'd made for supper.

Later Michelle gave the children the books she'd brought for them. Sissy squirreled hers away in the back room "So the dog wouldn't get it," while Jojo chose one called *Old Hat, New Hat* and sat down at the table with it under the glare of a bare lightbulb. Michelle pulled up a chair and encouraged him to share his book with her, pictures first, then words, a phrase at a time.

A shadow fell across the page. Michelle looked up, half expecting Zane, who'd been helping out in the kitchen. "Oh. Did you want to read with us, Martin? I mean—" The old man sat in the chair across from them, and she leaned forward to confide, "Someone sort of told me that you'd rather be called Pagla. Not Zane, but someone else, sort of indirectly. Is it a secret name, like something people aren't supposed to use unless—"

Abruptly Martin extended his hand and set a curling, dog-eared old photograph on the open book.

"What's this?" Michelle straightened the softly shadowed black-and-white picture carefully. The eyes were more round, the forehead a bit more pronounced, but the shape of the mouth and the cut of the chin looked familiar. "What a beautiful woman."

"Where'd you get this, Uncle?" Zane asked, suddenly standing there at her elbow. He took the photograph from Michelle's hand. "I haven't seen this since that time I found it in Unci's—"

He looked up, peering into the shadows in the far corner of the room. The old woman sat bolt upright, as though she sensed some change in the air, some warning. "Look at her," Zane said, amazed. "Be damned if she doesn't remember. You took it away from me, Unci. How come you gave it to him?"

"Who is it?" Michelle asked.

"Some woman who got herself knocked up by some Indian guy." Zane studied the picture, a thousand dried-

up wishes and boyhood speculations rearing up in the
back of his mind. "This was my mother, or so the story
goes, and that's all I know about her. She whelped me
and left me with Beatrice."

"You don't know whether she might still be alive?"
He shook his head. "What about your father?"

He deferred to the picture with an indifferent jerk of
his chin. "He was her secret, I guess."

"She really is beautiful."

"She looks a little like you." He looked at Michelle
curiously, then back at the picture. "Long pale neck,
high forehead, big eyes."

"Other than those traits, she looks—"

"Nothing like me," he insisted. "Which means I
must take after the mystery man, huh?"

Michelle turned to the man across the table. "Did you
know her, Pagla?"

The old man moistened his lips as though he might
try to speak to her. But he didn't, except through deep-
set, glistening eyes.

"He thinks you look like her, too." Zane laid his
hand on Michelle's shoulder. He wasn't sure why his
uncle's response to her bothered him. Clearly the man
had actually seen his mother in the flesh, and Zane re-
sented that, too. Foolishly.

He forced a wry smile. "Some people say they all
look alike, Uncle, but that's not true. If this was in color,
you'd see the difference. They're both pretty. That's the
only similarity."

"But she's truly beautiful," Michelle said.

"You keep saying that." Zane slipped the picture into
his shirt pocket. "As far as I'm concerned, beautiful
women don't desert their kids. Right, Auntie?"

Cecilia was setting up her quilt frame in the kitchen.
She paused for a moment, glancing at Sissy, then Jojo.
Without comment she finished adjusting the height of
the frame.

"Did she just—"

"I don't know anything about it, Michelle. It happened way back in the Dark Ages."

Martin was watching him now, staring at his shirt pocket.

Zane returned the stare, but his was hot and angry, and he didn't know why. He snatched the picture from his pocket and flipped it across the table like a playing card. The two-toned woman lay in the shelter of Martin's shadow, staring up at him with sightless eyes, sharing his secrets in some strange conspiracy of mutes.

"You want it, Uncle? It's yours. It means nothing to me." Turning on his heel, he waved an arm and barked at Sissy as he headed for the door. "You kids find that whole bunch of blankets you were talkin' about?"

The girl nodded, all wide-eyed innocence, wondering, of course, what she'd done wrong. Zane tried to reassure her with a smile, but he knew he hadn't quite pulled it off. He managed to soften his tone. "I'm gonna have me a smoke, and then we'll break up a couple of bales and make ourselves a bed under the stars. Okay?"

Sissy nodded again.

Zane lit a cigarette, braced his back against the house's newly painted siding, and reminded himself not to put his foot against it as he dragged heavily on the smoke. Martin had done a nice job with the light green paint. By summer there would be mud splatters and hand prints around the bottom, but for right now it looked okay.

He'd brought the paint home from his second trip to Canton and put his uncle in charge of the project. Martin had been so proud, so careful, and Zane had made a point to praise his initial efforts lavishly, except for one small thing. He'd painted around the barn swallows' nests under the eaves. "That's okay," Zane had assured him as he'd smashed the wattle dwellings with a broom handle. It was his own fault. He hadn't *told* Martin to get the nests down first. "It needs two coats anyway."

He'd never forget turning around and seeing those big baby tears standing in his uncle's eyes. Worse than the look on Sissy's face when he'd snapped at her just now. Big baby tears, the kind he used to tease Randy about. Mama's boy, he'd called him.

They were tenderhearted, all of them. He had to remember that if he was going to look after them. He had to remember that about Michelle, too. He had to expect them to get all sentimental over old pictures and relations and names on tombstones. He ought to be able to keep a level head and let them have their fantasies. He'd been willing to let Marla have hers, kinky as they sometimes were. He'd understood hers better, appreciated them less. Maybe he was envious because he had none of his own.

A cold nose tickled his palm, broke him down, made him give a little. "I'm throwin' you into a tub of water pretty soon, you ol' soupbone," he told the dog as he scratched behind a floppy ear. "Trouble is, I can't decide whether to add soap or potatoes."

"He doesn't look too worried." Michelle closed the door behind her and moved to his corner of the house, arms folded, smiling that irksome wise-woman smile. "Something tells me he's got your number."

"I suppose you think you do, too."

She settled in next to him, back against the house. "I get a little touchy about my mother, too, sometimes."

"I'm not touchy. I told you, the woman in that picture means nothing to me."

"Your grandmother didn't tell you anything about her?"

"It's no good asking questions, she said." He drew deeply on the solace of a lungful of smoke, then sent it drifting toward the hazy blue horizon. "She said those were silver tears on the picture. Those mildew spots. Silver tears. I remember the way she said it, kind of melancholy-like. Never figured that one out. Unlike the rest of you, *that* old woman was about as sentimental as a fence post."

"I think the tears of a woman who had to give up her baby would be precious. Don't you?"

"I wouldn't know."

"I used to wish my mother would give me up," she confided. "I wanted to be adopted by a TV family, like the Nelsons. They needed a girl in the family."

"What Nelsons?"

"Ozzie and—" She shrugged. "Well, the family next door. Mother, father, two or three kids. My father left us, and my mother . . . well, she didn't have much luck with men."

"You turned out okay, looks like to me."

"So did you." She turned to him, pushed his hat back, made him look into her eyes, and invited a smile. "Looks like to me."

"This is crazy." He dropped his cigarette into the dirt, and she ground it beneath her tennis shoe while he took her hips in his hands and settled them against his own. "You know that, don't you?"

"What's crazy?"

"You and me."

"Are you and Marla crazy, too?" He drew an exaggerated frown. "Well, she *is* the other woman, isn't she? The one you said you were seeing?"

"That isn't crazy. It isn't much of anything, except an occasional . . ." He searched her eyes. "You don't want that. You'd be lookin' for a lot more."

"What do I want, Zane? Have I asked you for—"

"You asked to come here. I don't know why I let you talk me into it, but here you are. We've got kids and grandmas here. No mothers and fathers. Nobody next door to us but the coyotes. I never do this. I never bring my women home."

"Really?"

"Really. You've got me acting crazy." He slid his palms up her back and pressed her closer to him. "You've got me thinking crazy. What did you do to me this morning?"

"What did you do to me?"

"Something I . . . probably had no right to do."

Her response was a coy smile. "Maybe I had no right to do what I did to you, then. But it's done now."

"What? Did you feed me some kind of loco weed, woman?"

"You fed me. And then you—"

She jumped away from him like a guilty teenager

when the door flew open and blankets started popping out, landing one or two at a time on the wooden step. Then came a head, tipped sideways, dangling braids brushing the blanket pile.

"Is this enough, Uncle Zane?"

It was enough to make a straw-cushioned pallet. Zane rearranged the boughs overhead to give them a view of the sky, and Michelle told stories until the two children nestled between them finally fell asleep. Then they lay quietly for a while, listening to the breeze rattle the cottonwood leaves above them.

With no earthly light to compete with them the stars put on a dazzling display, glittering, Michelle fancied, like a mother's tears turned to silver by some sympathetic goddess so that mortals might experience the pathos without even knowing the story. Maybe they weren't supposed to know. Maybe it was too sad for a mortal heart to bear. Martin's heart had somehow lost its voice, but she'd glimpsed the sadness through the window of his eyes. Maybe the goddess had eased his pain by dulling his wits.

And maybe it was a good thing Zane was asleep. She eased onto her side, causing only a slight rustle in the straw. If he could hear her musings, he'd no doubt . . .

"Michelle?"

She tingled deliciously at the sound of his voice, deep as the darkness surrounding them. "Yes?"

"You warm enough?"

"Yes."

"You sure?"

"Mmm-hmm." Her gaze skimmed over the part in Sissy's braided hair and the cowlick springing from the back of Jojo's head to the shadowed contours of Zane's face, turned her way. "What are you thinking about?"

"Just thinking how good it would feel to hold you." Her heart swelled. "Just hold me?"

"Just hold you. For now."

"When did I become your girl? Early this morning?"

"Before that."

"When?"

"The first time I saw your underwear."

"Do you . . . is it customary for you to have more than one girl at a time?"

"No way. I like it one-on-one. Give me your hand." He stretched his arm out, laying it above the children's heads. She followed his lead, laying her hand in his. "What about you?" he whispered.

"There's no one else."

"So I won't have to worry about being bushwhacked by some jealous—"

"I don't think so." She caressed his thumb with hers. His skin felt thick and rugged. His hand was warm. "You're already in the habit of covering your back, so I'm sure you'll be fine."

He turned his hand, splayed his fingers, and slid them into the channels between hers. "I don't get to Rapid that often."

"How often do you get to a phone?"

"As often as I need to." His thumb slipped into the hollow of her hand, a suggestive titillation that soon had her sighing and him smiling in the dark. "See why I said this is crazy?"

"Mmm-hmm. Look! A falling star." Her finger, suddenly jabbing at the hole in the leafy canopy, described an arc, following the star's path like a single Magus. "Did you make a wish? Don't tell me what it is."

"Too late," he whispered. "I already told you what I'm wishing."

Michelle woke up feeling a little stiff, but the streaking pink and blue sunrise and the haunting sound of Martin's morning song soothed all discomfort. She found herself missing conveniences she'd always taken for granted, but she discovered that even without faucets and pipes, there was still water. People carried it, heated it, used it carefully, but still there was washing, cooking, drinking, cleaning. It took more time, more work, but the needs were met. She could feel Zane watching her sometimes, and she wanted to tell him, to show him that she was not there to judge. She was there to learn. She was there to meet his family.

At the Sunday matinee they saw *Sounder*. Michelle had a hard time convincing Jojo that she really enjoyed the show. Movies about kids and dogs always made her cry. That didn't make any more sense to him than the explanation that he couldn't ride with Uncle Zane to take Michelle home because he had school the next day, and Michelle couldn't stay because *she* had school the next day. He wanted to go to her school. He wanted her to come to his. Maybe next time, she said. But the look in Jojo's eyes betrayed his distrust of next times.

Michelle went into the house to say her good-byes to Beatrice, who was painstakingly fashioning quilt squares. The old woman didn't seem to know she was there, but Michelle told her that she had enjoyed meeting her. And then, since everyone else was outside, she confided, "I think I'm in love with your grandson. I'm not sure how he feels. I just wanted you to know about my feelings." She touched Beatrice's sweater-wrapped shoulder. "In case you had any concerns along those lines."

She jumped to her feet when the door hinges squeaked behind her. "Oh, Martin, I was just saying good-bye to Unci. I wish you'd gone to the show with us. I hope next time—"

The old man's eyes begged her to stop chattering and attend to him as he reached for her hand and filled it with tightly folded papers.

"For me?" She gave him her teacher's smile, the one that had rewarded many a seven-year-old artist struggling with his first crush.

But when she started to open his gift, he stilled her hand, folding it around the papers, the look in his eyes urging her to hold off.

"I'll take this with me," she said, pressing the token into the harbor beneath her breasts. Martin seemed to approve. "Thank you, Pagla. I'll be back to see you soon."

*   *   *

They spoke little on the long drive back. Zane took the back roads, a shortcut that skirted what few towns there were between his home and hers. Twilight shadowed the angular buttes and vast grasslands as they sailed along the narrow black ribbon of patched and potholed South Dakota highway. They listened to Johnny Cash and Willie Nelson until the Mobridge station faded out. Zane flicked the radio off and invited Michelle to put her head in his lap and take a nap. It was an offer she couldn't resist, not because she was sleepy, but because he'd suggested it, and because it was such an intimate place to lay her head, and because she wanted to hold on to him as long as she could.

It was a surprise to wake up and find that they were parked in front of her apartment complex.

"Some copilot I am," she said as she pushed her hair out of her face. "I didn't mean to pass out on you."

He flexed his shoulders and stretched his back. "What did you mean to do?"

"Turn you on so that when we got here you wouldn't be able to leave right away."

"Is that what you were up to?" He laughed, caught her hand, and spread it over the front of his jeans. "I thought you were just plumping up your pillow."

She caressed him sensuously until he dropped his thighs wide apart in complete submission. He hooked his arm around her neck and drew her head down, her mouth to his, her tongue to his, kissing her hard enough to steal her breath away as she had his.

His agonized groan ended the kiss.

"I should go."

"But you won't."

"I won't." He nipped at her kiss-juiced lips, spiked them with his tongue, sucked at them noisily. "You wanna do it right here, right now?"

"Yes."

"Don't tempt me, honey." He covered her hand with his and arched suggestively. "Either unzip me and have at it, or get off it and take me to bed with you."

"Let's go with plan B first," she said, sliding away. "Followed by A."

They left a trail of clothing, starting with her shoes inside the front door and ending with his jeans, trampled in the middle of the bathroom floor by two pairs of wet feet. They were two trying to become one and sharing everything in the process—soap and water, body and breath, desperate need and delicious anticipation, each doting on the feel of the other, the scent, the sound, the taste of the other and the joy of being the answer to the other's need. It was good to pleasure and be pleasured, good to come together, cleave together, shatter together, linger together, drift on the dream that the intermingled pieces could never again be completely sorted out.

"You wore me out," he said at last, his hand inching over the contour of her hip. "But I'm getting my wish now, holding you."

He was leaning over her, and she felt sheltered by him, cherished by him. She laid her hand on his cheek. She wanted to care for him, too. "I think it's time for you to lay your head down and go to sleep with me."

"Is that supposed to be some kind of a punishment, teacher? Put your head down, Zane. You've been a bad boy."

"You've been a very good boy." She patted her breast. "You get to put your head down right here."

"Every schoolboy's dream," he said, touching his lips to the pillow she offered him. "But I want to tell you something first."

His tone stilled the breath in her chest. Pale moonlight illuminated the moist fullness of his lips as she watched them, dreading what they might say.

"I've done time, Michelle."

"You've done"—ordinary, innocuous, it was none of the words she feared—"time?"

"Prison time." He gave the new word a moment to sink in. When she said nothing, he sighed. "I was convicted on a firearms charge, along with a few other things like destruction of public property and assaulting a police officer. I spent twenty-two months in the state pen.''

"Did he hurt you?''

"Who?''

"The man you fought with.''

"Police officer,'' he repeated carefully. "I was the one charged with assault, not . . .'' His mouth twitched, on the verge of a smile. "We both came out looking like we'd been in a bar fight, but I've got a tough hide. He hurt someone else.''

"A woman?''

"How'd you guess?''

"You wouldn't stand for that.''

"Don't be so sure.'' He rolled to his back, and she felt strangely bereft. "You don't know much about me, Michelle. I'm taking up space in your bed, and you don't know a hell of a lot about me.''

"Of course I do.'' She moved over him. "I know you're looking after three elderly people and two abandoned children. I know you're a good man.''

"All you know is that I'm a good stud.'' He caught her chin in his hand, touched his finger to her lips, forestalling her protest. "No, I mean it. Don't let yourself be too sure of anybody. You can get hurt real easy that way.''

"Have you been hurt that way?''

"I told you, I've got a tough hide. I just thought you had a right to know that I've got a record.''

"When did this happen?''

"Not long after I came back from 'Nam. Do you remember the county courthouse takeover back in the fall of '69?''

"I remember reading about it. There were a number of arrests, as I remember. A woman was shot.''

"She died.''

Michelle nodded. Like the Wounded Knee occupation, only the confrontation itself was front page news. The consequences were less visual, less sensational, less newsworthy.

"Were you in love with her?''

"I don't know. I guess I should have been." He tucked his arm beneath his head and stared at the ceiling while he continued. "Her brother had been murdered, beaten to death by a couple of well-connected young cowboys who said they were just out honkey-tonkin', having a good time. They were charged with involuntary manslaughter, paid their five-thousand-dollar bail, and walked away from the courthouse, which is where we took our protest. Figured there oughta be something else said, something more done, some kind of justice for Indians, too."

His voice became hushed, and he receded from her in every way but the physical. "There weren't supposed to be any weapons. I don't even know where that goddamn rifle came from, but somebody said, 'Zane knows how to use it better than anybody,' and all of a sudden I was armed."

"Just you?"

"Just me. Some big uprising, huh? The reporters said the protesters were armed. *One* of us was armed, one tin soldier turned Sioux warrior. One pitiful peashooter and I threw it away. I threw it down when I should have used it to protect her."

"From . . ."

"From the law." He shook his head, and he glanced at her, perplexed. "How do you like that? From the goddamn law. All she did was move. Deputy Sheriff Gunderson said 'Don't move,' and she moved. She was scared out of her mind, she started to turn towards me, and the lawman blew a hole in her."

"Oh, God."

"So that's who you're sleeping with, Michelle." Then he added nonchalantly, "I did my crime, and I did my time. Just thought you had a right to know."

"It doesn't sound like it was your crime."

"The jury said it was."

"I say I'm sleeping with a good man," she said quietly, shaken by his story. "I'm sleeping with Zane Lone Bull." She longed to put her arms around him and hold him close, but she knew that wasn't what he wanted right now. He wasn't ready to lay his head on her breast and take sympathy or even comfort.

So she planted a soft kiss in the middle of his smooth, expansive chest. "Where's your necklace?"

"What necklace?"

She traced a V from the high point of his collarbone to the place she'd kissed. "Somewhere between the front door and the shower I noticed a beaded medallion hanging right here. I don't remember taking it off you."

"You were too busy tearing off my pants."

"They were in my way at the time." He laughed. She tapped a persistent finger on his breastbone. "But the necklace wasn't. Is it one you made?"

"I've had it as long as I can remember. It's kind of a good luck charm."

"Your grandmother made it?"

"That's what I was told. I guess she did." He shifted his hips toward her. "Now I have to take back what I said. You know about as much about me as I do." He tucked her hair behind her ear, then slid the backs of his fingers over her cheek, just below the soon-to-be-dark hollows under her eyes. "And you have to get some rest."

"I slept on the way down here, but you . . ." She put her arms around his neck. "Will you be here when I get back from school?"

"No."

"When will I see you again?"

"I don't know." He sighed. "This ain't gonna be easy, honey. We got a lot of miles between us."

"Then I have to ask you about something. Did you tell Martin anything about me, other than the part about me being your girl? Anything about Canton?"

"Are you kidding?"

"Maybe it's just because he associates me with you, or because he thinks I bear a resemblance to the picture of your mother."

"He doesn't know too many white women."

"Well, he certainly knew her."

"Maybe he saw her drop me off on the doorstep."

"I don't think so. She was somebody very special to him, Zane."

"Not that special." He rolled away from her, snatched at the bedsheet, and pooled it into his lap as he levered himself into a sitting position. "No way, lady, not *that* special. He's not as old as he looks. Hell, when I was born he was only about . . . I guess he'd'a been about seventeen or eighteen, but not in his mind. In his mind he's never come anywhere near . . ." He snapped the bedside lamp on. "Why are you looking at me like that?"

"Like what?" She drew her end of the sheet up, too. "I'm just listening."

"Yeah, but I know what you're thinking, and you're dead wrong."

"I'm not thinking anything except that Martin treasures that photograph. Before we left he gave me some papers. More drawings, I think." She reached for her robe, which was draped over a nearby chair. "Should we look at them?"

"Jesus." Still hanging onto the sheet, he swung his legs over the bed. "I need a cigarette."

"Do you want to see them, Zane?"

"It's no good asking too many questions," he recited as he raked his fingers through his thick hair. "I ask him about Canton, and he starts in with these pictures. The ol' lady, she starts in with this 'no good, no good.' They were both goin' along from day to day just peaceful until you came along with your damn hospital records, and now they're both acting . . ." He turned, offering a wry smile. "Can't say crazy, can I? For us it's probably normal."

She cinched her robe at the waist as she approached him. "You can say anything you want, Zane, but I didn't come along with my damned hospital records. You came to me, and you were following a trail your brother left."

"I got no brothers. The only person I know, or at least I was *told* I was related to by blood was the woman in that picture. She was white. I'm a half-breed. That's all I know." He adjusted the sheet, eyeing her defensively. "You're trying to say he could be my father, right?"

"It's possible, isn't it?"

"No. No, it is not possible. It's bullshit. Why wouldn't somebody have told me?"

"He's trying to tell you something now. I don't pretend to know what it is, but I do think—"

"All right!" He glared at her for a moment, then sighed. "All right, show me what you've got."

She retrieved the drawings from her purse and looked them over while he put his jeans on and lit up a cigarette. She offered him an ashtray and joined him on the sofa with the packet of papers.

"This is almost the same as the one he gave you," she observed as they examined the first page. "Two people, bound, and it looks like maybe there's something over their mouths, like they're gagged. What do you think?"

He blew a stream of smoke to one side, then spared the paper a glance. "I think your guess is as good as mine."

"Zane, this man is trying to tell us something with these."

"Yeah, well, I got a real bad feeling about it."

They looked into each other's eyes for a moment. She started to fold the papers back up, but he stayed her hand, then took them from her, plugged his cigarette into the corner of his mouth, straightened the corners of the papers, and finally looked hard at the top one.

"You're right. Two people, bound and gagged." He tossed the first exhibit on the table and considered the next one.

"This is a big building," Michelle said, pointing instructively. He glanced at her, squinting through his smoke screen in mock surprise as he set the cigarette aside. She persisted with her pointing. "But notice there's a third person in the building in this picture."

"You think that's the woman in the photograph."

"Actually I'm thinking it's another man, but look—"
She directed him to the next page, which was a series of

scenes. "These two people—males, I think, the way they're dressed—they start out with long hair, maybe braided. This third one comes into the picture, another male. Now they all have short hair. The first two had their hair cut, don't you think? They'd probably do that at the hospital. But look at this." She pointed to a figure rendered considerably differently from the others. "Here's the woman. She wears a dress and shoes. The other three have no feet, but she has feet, and there are things on her feet. And look, these guys are tied up, but she isn't."

He looked the page over carefully. "I don't know. That could just be scribbling right there. You gotta remember, he's—"

"Childlike, I know. I have a lot of experience with children's drawings. They put in the details that are outstanding *for them*." She laid her hand on his knee. "Martin's telling a story about three males and one female. And he's taking a risk, at least in his mind. The drawings were folded up tightly, just the way yours were, and he was very careful about slipping them into my hand without letting anyone see."

Zane retrieved the first page and pronounced it, "Martin and his grandfather." He studied the other pictures. "I don't know who the third man would be," he mused. "Or the woman with the boxes on her feet."

"It's the woman in the photograph, Zane. It's your mother."

❧ IO ❧

Canton, South Dakota
Winter 1933

R achael Trainor's job at the Hiawatha Asylum for Insane Indians was turning out to be achingly frustrating. Neither her training nor any of her hospital experience had prepared her for Hiawatha. In her own mind she was beginning to question Dr. Tim's effectiveness as an administrator. Half the staff members were not on speaking terms with the other half. Everyone seemed to work independently of everyone else. Untrained attendants routinely made decisions with regard to the care of the patients, while housekeeping chores were performed so haphazardly that Rachael found herself doing many of them herself whenever she could find the time.

She had stopped looking to Head Nurse Ella Sims for direction. The woman almost never gave her a direct order. Sims made up the schedule, and both of them pulled long shifts since the professional staff was scarce. But Rachael found herself at work in a strange world where the ability to talk had atrophied.

She was exhausted most of the time. The improvements she'd once thought might be easily made now seemed less feasible. It was all she could do to meet the most immediate needs. Cold, snow, wind, and darkness brought on more influenza, more fever, more depression, and more problems with hygiene on the asylum wards. Most troublesome to Rachael was Dr. Tim's penchant for isolation and restraints.

According to Dr. Tim, it was Adam Lone Bull's resistance to control that made it necessary to confine him in total isolation. But he had spent so many days and nights in his own private subterranean cubicle, subdued by rigid restraints or heavy sedation, that it was hard to assess his condition. Rachael tried to visit him when she could late at night. She didn't like sneaking around, but there was no other way.

She had learned her lesson about pushing Dr. Tim too hard too fast when she'd asked him about allowing Martin to spend more time with the other patients. He'd angrily demanded that she show him her M.D., at which point she'd resolved to back off on any strategy for broaching the subject of Adam Lone Bull. But it was certain that he would never make any progress under such oppressive conditions. Confined to a dark, cold, abysmal cell, it had been some time since he'd even acknowledged her presence. Sometimes he consciously ignored her, but more often, lately, the drugs he'd been given denied him even that satisfaction.

She sat beside his bed late one night, her own shadow shielding him from the lamp light. He slept fitfully, mumbling in Lakota. When she touched his face his eyes flew open for a moment, but he was unable to focus. He mumbled something about gas, and the metal wristlet clanked against the bed frame as he tried in vain to lift this arm.

"It's all right, Adam. You're safe and secure." A wry understatement to be sure. His smooth skin felt warm and damp. "But I can't tell whether these are fever dreams or a result of the sedatives."

There were no notations about his medication in the daily log. Male attendants, when they noted anything about him at all, referred to him as "Mad Bull." Dr. Tim insisted that he and his appointed male attendants would be responsible for medical attention given to the violent patients. "I won't have my staff take risks that I wouldn't take myself," he often said. Where Adam was concerned, the doctor didn't seem to be taking many risks lately, or paying him much attention.

She opened his cotton shirt and began sponging his face and chest. The water seemed to revive him. He looked at her, apparently recognized her, then turned away. It felt like a rejection, and it stung her. She shook off the feeling, calling up pity in its place. He needed a change of clothing and fresh bedding, which she resolved to supply. She doubted that the attendants would notice.

"I've brought soup," she told him as she wedged her arm beneath his head. "I think you can drink it if you let me hold you up."

"Not hungry," he muttered. He turned his head toward her, pressing his cheek against her breast.

She could feel the heat and the dampness of his hair through her dress. "You're wasting away, Adam. I'm not leaving until you eat. I don't know why they bother with the restraints anymore." There was only one wristlet this time binding his arm to the bed frame. "You're not strong enough to fight."

"I can fight." The metal links clanked as he sought to prove his claim. Wild-eyed, he grabbed her arm as he strained to sit up. "Took my rifle. Need more shells." Trembling from his effort, he sank back against her. "Where's the . . . where's the goddamn . . . caisson?"

"It's all right, Adam, you're in a hospital now. We're going to take care of you, but you must eat." She laid her hand on his face, now misted with sweat. "I think you've come down with something."

He groaned, his chest heaving with each breath he took. "Is that you, Deer Woman?"

"If it is, will you take some of this soup for me?"

"Whatever you say." He opened his eyes, tried to focus on her face, gave up, and let them slide closed again. "Can't stay awake."

"The doctor wants you to rest." She took up the tin cup of soup and struggled to prop his head against her shoulder. "I want you to eat. I know it's the middle of the night, Adam, but this is the only time I can come."

"I'll make you come, Deer Wommm . . ." He gasped for breath, his head lolling against her shoulder. "I'll be the best . . . best you've had."

"Stop babbling and taste this," she whispered, tipping the cup to his dry lips. "I know you're thirsty."

With a groan he gave his will over to her by accepting the cup. She had to warn him twice not to drink the warm chicken stock too fast. Finally she held it away for a moment. "I don't want it to come right back up."

"You're a tease," he muttered.

"I'm a nurse."

He closed his eyes and turned his head, as though he would hide his face under her chin. "Deer Woman can trick a man so easy, so easy, Grandfather says. Don't care anymore." His warm breath tickled her neck. "Don't care who you are."

"You know who I am, Adam. Rachael Trainor. I don't know anything about Deer Woman." She shifted, trying to give him better support. "Do you want to tell me about her? Is she a real person?"

"Don't wanna talk. Just wanna . . ." His free hand groped awkwardly for a hold on her. "Ready to die in your arms, Deer Woman."

"Finish the soup now, and I'll let you sleep."

"It'll be better for you—" Sips of soup interrupted his ramblings, but only momentarily. "I'll do better . . . free my other hand. Let me use my hands, Deer Woman."

"I almost wish I could."

"You can. Deer Woman has strong medicine." He lifted his head, laboring to pour his husky whisperings into her ear. "Wash me again, Deer Woman. I'll get . . . get big and hard, and . . ."

He was already without breath, and she caught herself holding hers. Curiously stimulated by the wild images his suggestions conjured, she supported his head, soothed him, indulged him.

"Deer Woman?"

"Let me feed you first, Adam."

"Touch me so you can . . . fuck me and kill me, the way . . . the way you're supposed to. It's a good day to die. Good way . . . good way for us to end this . . ."

"Will you let me take your temperature?" Had she her wits about her, she would have laughed at herself as she set the cup aside and reached into her skirt pocket. She could feel the flush in her own face. "I know the sedatives can really throw a man off kilter, make him talk out of his head. I want to help you, Adam."

Like a rooting infant he turned his face to the row of buttons between her breasts. "You smell good. You can help me sleep."

"I'll help you—" She lay him down gently and held the thermometer against his lips. "Hold this under your tongue for me, please."

His eyes were closed, his slight smile the only sign that he heard her. His lips parted in sluggish submission. She steered the instrument where she wanted it to go, her free hand absently stroking his hair back from his forehead. "Don't bite too hard. If you break it, you'll have a mouth full of glass."

"Mouth full of . . ."

"Under your tongue with it and be—"

A key clattered in the lock on the door. Rachael turned, ready to have her hand caught in an unusual cookie jar. She knew just what she was going to say, too. This man was in their charge, and he needed . . .

"Well, well, well." Head nurse Ella Sims stepped in, leading with a lantern held aloft. She chuckled as she closed the door behind her and planted a fist on her ample hip, assuming a decidedly self-satisfied pose. "Dr. Tim's pet has a pet of her own, it would seem."

Rachael came to her feet beside the bed, breathing a ragged sigh. "I know I'm not supposed to be here, Miss Sims, but this patient is not eating, and I think he's physically ill."

Nurse Sims nodded pointedly toward the bed. "You'll have a better idea if you catch that thermometer in time."

A half-baked argument died in Rachael's throat. She turned, dropped quickly to Adam's side, and caught the glass stick. "Adam, hold this under your tongue." She probed, but the dark, full lips remained slack. "Adam, *please* wake up and hold this in your mouth."

His lips moved, again sketching a slight smile before they claimed the instrument. He positioned it with a suggestive flick of his tongue.

Nurse Sims chuckled again. "He's practically comatose, and still he manages to have a little fun with you. Remarkable, isn't it?"

Rachael turned, questioning the woman with a look.

"It's a sign of tremendous stamina, you know." Nurse Sims turned the wick down on her lantern, extinguishing the flame. "Their sense of humor," she explained as she set the lantern aside. "The way these people are still able to see the irony in all this as some form of humor."

"I really don't think he's joking. I think he's—" Rachael pulled the heavy army blanket over Adam's chest. "I don't understand why he requires so much sedation."

"Why who requires it? Not this poor fellow." The head nurse moved closer, arms folded, head tipped to the side as she surveyed the patient's situation. "It's Dr. Tim who sets the requirements."

"I met this man a couple of months before he was committed. Adam Lone Bull."

Rachael continued to fuss with the blanket, tucking it firmly around his shoulders, feeling obliged to protect him as long as she was so unsure of the woman hovering over her, the woman whom she'd supposedly been hired to replace. If Miss Sims was looking for some sort of advantage over her, she had it now. But it must not extend to their patient. He was suffering enough.

"Alcoholic, if I remember correctly."

"He did have a problem with alcohol, but he was quite sober when I first met him, and he showed no sign of . . ." She shook her head, gazing intently at the chiseled face, much thinner now, his masculinity even more pronounced in the sharper angles of its bone structure.

"I would never have thought a man like that would come to this."

"I knew you were sneaking down here. I almost reported it, and then I decided there was no telling what Dr. Tim Hubble might have put you up to, so I thought I'd see for myself." The stocky woman's shadow fell across the narrow bed as she stepped closer. "Even I don't interfere with the patients who have been singled out, like this one. Hubble would have my head. But apparently yours is safe."

"I wouldn't say that. I've been trained to follow the doctor's orders, not to question them." Rachael stood slowly, interposing herself between her patient and the obscure Nurse Sims. "But you and I know that there are things that should be, *must be* done for these patients. And we are not doing them properly. I'd rather do my job under the auspices of approved policies, but if I have to work outside those policies simply to provide basic care, some modicum of sanitation, then I guess I'm quite willing to—"

"You think I haven't been willing to do my job?" Nurse Sims challenged her with a piercing stare. "*He* says I haven't been, is that it?"

"I'm not one to carry tales."

"Of course not." The older woman sighed as she adjusted the auburn finger wave that dipped over the right side of her forehead. "I'll be leaving soon. You won't have to wait much longer."

"I'm not sure I want your job."

Ella Sims expressed her doubt with a quick glance.

"I really didn't know the job was filled, and at this point rank in this peculiar service is hardly foremost on my mind." Rachael bent to reclaim the thermometer. "A hundred and three." She dropped the instrument into its vial of alcohol and studied her patient. "I wonder if anyone's given him any aspirin."

Nurse Sims produced a bottle from her own sweater pocket. "Not yet."

"You've been looking in on him, too?"

"No. As I said, I followed you. Frankly, I thought

you might have intended him some kind of harm.''

Rachael stared, stunned. "Why?"

"Your brother is the agent at Pine Ridge?"

Rachael nodded hesitantly.

"I've heard that he's a close friend of our Dr. Tim's,"
Ella elaborated. "I, on the other hand, am anathema to
Dr. Tim. My complaints about the way he runs this place
have been heard in Washington. I won't be around much
longer, but neither, I predict, will Hubble. Roosevelt's
administration will be making some changes. Like
everything else generated in Washington, it will take
time before the effects finally trickle out here, but it will
come, and Hubble knows that." Ella eyed Rachael con-
sideringly. "So does your brother."

"My brother had nothing to do with my appointment."

"You're either lying, or you're incredibly naive."
Ella folded her arms and stepped back, surveying the
huge rough-hewn support beams overhead, the network
of pipes, the cobwebs. "What kind of a place is this to
keep a sick man?"

"It's not . . ." Rachael knew the answer. She simply
wasn't sure she trusted the woman posing the question.

"Could it actually be the latter?" Again, Sims eyed
her carefully. "Do you really disapprove of the way
things are run around here?"

"I would certainly like to see changes. Make some
myself if I can."

"When you get my job," Ella surmised wryly, dis-
missing any exceptions with a wave of her hand. "Never
mind. What sort of changes?"

"The record-keeping is abysmal."

"I agree. What else, besides, as you mentioned, sanitation?"

"I have a good deal of experience in psychiatric nursing. Dr. Tim's 'containment facility' philosophy is out-
dated. These patients need therapy, and they're not
getting it."

"I've said that, too."

"I haven't actually *said* it," Rachael admitted, "but

I have tried to work with them myself. Martin Lone Bull, for example This man's brother.''

Sims scowled, looking down at Adam as though he'd acquired a new head while he slept. "This is Martin's brother?"

"When I first met this man at Pine Ridge Reservation and told him I was coming to work here, he asked me to find out how his brother was doing. He hadn't seen Martin since the boy was committed." Rachael shoved her hands into her skirt pockets. "That's something else that should be changed."

"Family contact would be inconsistent with Dr. Tim's program," Ella reminded her.

"Not that this patient hasn't had some extremely violent episodes," Rachael allowed.

"Wouldn't you?"

The women shared a look, a wordless confirmation. They were both nurses, professional caregivers. If they were free to use their own good judgment, they could do better than this, not only for Adam Lone Bull, but for the patients locked in their rooms upstairs, most of them chained to their beds for the night.

Rachael nodded.

Ella responded in kind, then offered up the bottle again. "I think we should get some aspirin into him."

Rachael retrieved the tin cup, made sure there was enough soup left, then lifted her patient's head again. "Adam?"

"Deer Woman?" He forced his eyes open, his focus clearly fuzzy, the image of her swimming before his eyes. "Still here?"

She showed him the white pills. "This is nothing more than aspirin. It should help the fever." Lips pressed together, he looked to her for comfort, not more pills. "You have fever, Adam. I promise you, this is only medicine for the fever."

"Whose . . . medicine?"

"Mine. Not Dr. Tim's."

He let her put the tablets in his mouth, followed by a swallow of cold soup.

"That's good, Adam. If you want to get strong again, you're going to have to start eating."

"Deer Woman loves strong men." His eyes drifted closed, but when she started to move away, he grabbed her wrist. "I'll be ready for you soon," he whispered. "Soon."

"I don't know what he's talking about," she told Ella. "He probably doesn't, either."

"Oh, yes, he does. According to the Lakota, Deer Woman is able to transform herself. In her human form she seduces men, killing them in the throes of ecstasy. Then she flees the scene in the form of a deer, leaving behind her telltale cloven tracks."

"How flattering." She checked the contents of the cup. "Drink this, Adam. All of it. You need fluids."

"Like hell I do." But he looked up at her again, a spark of amusement in his eyes as he accepted another sip from the cup.

"I'd say Mr. Lone Bull knows exactly what he's about." Ella chuckled. "Many of them do, you know. Many of these patients should never have been institutionalized. Not in an insane asylum, anyway."

"Why are they here?"

"For lack of a better place. There's a woman who's been here for ten years because she got sick when she was visiting relatives in Canada—stroke, I believe—and the Canadian government asked the American government where they should send her. They were afraid no one would pay her bill, you see. Somehow she ended up here, fully recovered but committed to an asylum for insane Indians. And once they're in, they're in."

"Mr. Lone Bull was diagnosed with alcoholic dementia, and he admits . . ." *In confidence*, she recalled. He couldn't remember what he'd done, but he'd told her that in confidence. "He was certainly out of control when they brought him here."

"And now they have him under control." Ella squatted next to the bed and looked up at Rachael. "In your career as a psychiatric nurse, have you ever seen such a general application of restraints?"

Rachael shook her head. "These are outmoded devices, and the use of any restraint is generally not left to the discretion of attendants the way it is here. But you have to admit, our facilities leave much to be desired."

"Have you broached the subject of fire safety with the good doctor? Can you imagine what would happen with all these patients chained up at night if we had a fire?"

"Yes, I have asked about that," Rachael admitted as she withdrew her arm from supporting Adam's head.

"And what was his reply?"

Rachael sighed. She was so tired she could hardly stand. "He says that security is the greater concern."

"With our patients? Most of them are deathly docile, Miss Trainor. Surely you've noticed how quiet it is here compared with most institutions of this kind." Ella gestured dramatically. "This man is the exception. There's some fight left in him."

"Many of them have genuine psychoses, Miss Sims."

"Many of them do not, or didn't when they came in here."

"What about Martin?"

"His grandfather was a holy man. He didn't speak English. He tried to practice some of the dances and whatnot that have been outlawed. I don't think that constitutes insanity. As for Martin . . ." Ella glanced at the ceiling. "This place has been hard on him. He certainly suffers from depression, but he's no idiot."

"Do you think he's suicidal?"

"I don't know. I will say we've had a few." Sims shook her head as her weary gaze fell to the bed. "I suspect your friend here will be taken off the sedatives for a while. He's sick. He's weak." She touched Rachael's arm in a sympathetic gesture. "If you get caught down here, you're going to join me on the enemies list."

"And then I'll be . . ."

"Useless?" Ella gave a caustic chuckle. "The best improvement would come from shutting this place down, but Hubble is determined to hang on. So is the

city. And the state. This place is what they call a real
pork barrel."

Rachael surveyed the dingy basement cubicle. "Pretty
lean pork if you ask me."

"These are lean times, and any pork is better than
none." She squeezed Rachael's arm, converting com-
miseration into a plea. "We can help each other, Miss
Trainor."

"All I want to do here is care for our patients."

"That's what I've been trying to do all along. Maybe
your way is better. Through the back door and down the
cellar stairs, hmm?" Pleading with Rachael eye to eye,
Ella tipped her head toward the bed. "Let's see what
we can do for this one."

"One of you could hand me the damn piss pot," their
patient suggested. "Then get the hell out . . . let me sleep
it off."

During the next week, Ella and Rachael devised their
own schedule so that they could nurse Adam Lone Bull
in secret. Between their shifts they were able to tend to
him without any notice from the attendants assigned to
check on him. Dick Hollings and John Gatewood, whom
Dr. Tim affectionately referred to as his right and left
muscles, paid little attention to their patient's condition,
and their daily checks were brief. They offered him
food, let him relieve himself, left him alone as long as
he was quiet.

With Ella as lookout, Rachael was able to pay him a
nightly call, sometimes another visit during the day. She
broke his fever and his self-imposed fast but not his
despondency. More than once, when she asked him what
she could do to make him more comfortable, he asked
her to bring him a drink. His second choice was a cigarette. Not on an empty stomach, she told him. Finally,
when she had him sitting beside her on his bed and
taking a full meal of solid food, he said, "Tell me of
my brother."

She looked down at her hands, folded in her lap.

"This makes you sad," he observed. "What are you keeping from me?"

"You're doing so well."

"I've decided not to die here." He scraped the last of the pork stew from the bottom of his bowl. "It might be a good day, but it's a bad place. If I can figure out what they want from me, I'll give it to them, and maybe they'll let me go." He cast her a sideways glance. "Isn't that what you keep telling me?"

"Your brother hasn't spoken to me since the time we heard your voice. He actually said a few words to me then," she recalled, watching him finish the stew. "He knew who you were. He's not said a word to me since."

"Do you speak to him of me?"

"No, I don't. I don't want to upset either of you. You most especially because, as you said, *he's* not prone to violence."

"But I am." The spoon clanked as he handed her the empty bowl. "Fighting is the only way I know."

"No, you must stop fighting so that we can take these stupid restraints off."

"We?" He was shackled to a water pipe by a three-foot length of chain. "You said you couldn't take them off."

"I can't."

"I don't believe you, woman. The way you come and go here—" He gestured expansively, but his glance fell wishfully on the heavy wooden door. He turned to her, planted his knee on the thin mattress, and rose above her, blocking the lantern light. The blanket he wore over his broad shoulders made him look like a caped silhouette, an imposing night rider. "Bring me a piece of wire or a fork, and I'll make a skeleton key."

"Adam, if you broke out, you would be a fugitive." She reached for him but stopped short of touching him, instead crushing the ragged, unbound edge of his blanket in her hand. "When you get well, you'll be released, and you'll be a free man."

"What do I have to do to get well? I haven't had a drink in . . ." The blanket slid from her hand as he gestured. "I don't even know how long I've been here. But I'm sober. The fever is gone. What do you want from me?"

"Exactly what you're giving right now. Cooperation." She drew herself up, matching his pose if not his height. "You know I'm not assigned to—" It was time to give him one more reason to trust her, and she carried the reason in her pocket. "Let's just say, my visits to you are just like this little gift." She produced a pack of Lucky Strikes. "Off the record."

"I've known that, and I've kept your secret. I don't speak to anyone else, except to curse their eyes and their ancestors." She felt the slight tremble in his hand as it carefully descended upon hers. He looked into her eyes and favored her with a genuine smile. "But for this gift I gladly pay my respects to yours."

"You have to stop shouting and cursing, too, Adam. That's a sign of instability. It's a type of violent behavior."

"It was the right behavior when they wanted me to sail across the sea and shoot Germans." As he spoke he tapped the top of the package into his palm to tamp the tobacco. "Hell, I could curse their bowels as I pulled them out of their bodies on the point of my bayonet and earn a medal for it."

"I know." She tucked her hand into the pocket of her sweater, guarding the matches, watching him open the cigarettes. "I've seen what those memories can do to a man. At St. Elizabeth's Hospital in Washington, I've held their heads while they wept, Adam. Your fellow soldiers. I can do the same for you. You can tell me about—"

"Is that why I'm here?" Carrying the cigarette he craved, his hand stopped midway to his mouth, and he stared in disbelief. "I was a soldier a long time ago. Do I have to pay for that now?"

"In their own minds some men do," she said gently. "It's best not to keep it inside, but some men do. They hold all the suffering inside themselves and—"

"The cause of my suffering is all here." He gestured

with the cold cigarette. "It's all around me. Don't you
see it? This prison is the cause of my pain, Rachael. Let
me go, and let me take my brother with me. I can take
care of him myself."

"Neither of you is ready for that now, but I think you
can be ready soon."

"No one ever leaves here, they say. This place is
Iktome's best trick. Once he gets you in here . . ." He
plugged the cigarette into the corner of his mouth and
let her light it for him. He took a long, deep, gratified
pull on it and dammed the smoke up inside for a moment, just as she had suggested he was doing with his
emotions. *"Pilamaye,"* he said on the tail of a gray
cloud. "Thank you, my friend. I will defend you from
your enemies until my dying day."

"All the other patients are permitted to smoke," she
said, as if to explain her favor away.

"It's been so long, it makes me dizzy." He braced
his back against the cement wall, closed his eyes, and
savored another deep drag, chuckling as he exhaled this
time. "Feel like a green kid."

"Are you going to be sick?"

"Hell, no." He brought the cigarette close to his
mouth, looked at her solemnly for a moment before one
corner of his mouth betrayed him in a lopsided smile.
"If I am, it's okay. I've got my nurse here to hold my
head for me."

She blushed. He puffed on the cigarette again, engaging her with his eyes. Dark, compelling, exotic eyes. He
held out his hand, beckoning her, and she wanted to step
closer, for what purpose she didn't know. Closer was
not a purpose. It was a foolish impulse.

"Are the other patients permitted to have matches?"
His fingers curled, soliciting her. "How about a piece
of flint?"

She stared blankly. Then laughter bubbled in her
throat.

"I won't set the bed or myself on fire, and I'll hide
them well."

"Promise?"

He wiggled his fingers again, his eyes challenging her to trust him. She dropped the matches into his hand.

"Those two fools who stick their heads in here once in a while are easy to deceive. The real challenge is Iktome." He stared at the rafters above her head, as though he suspected the Trickster might be hiding there. "But I can find a way to beat him."

"I believe you can, Adam, but first you have to stop fighting."

"Let him think that I'm no longer a threat." He nodded once, considering the prospect. "I've learned to pretend to swallow the sleep drug when they give it to me, but sometimes I want to take it. It's like whiskey. It makes everything go away for a while." He shook his head as he brought the cigarette toward his lips. "Iktome at his best."

"Is Iktome anything like Deer Woman?"

"They're very closely related. Always up to some trick, using a man's weakness against him. Turning him on himself." He drew greedily on the shrinking cigarette, then flicked the ash into his hand. "But it's possible to beat them the same way."

"I'm sure it is. And you're a strong man, Adam."

"You're a small woman." He trapped her gaze with his, drawing her closer in earnest now with his deep, smooth voice. "Stand next to me and let me see if you're really Deer Woman's size."

She moved without thinking, without choosing. *Closer was not a purpose. It was a craving.*

He dropped the cigarette and the ash into his supper bowl, then put his hands on her shoulders. "She changes shape," he allowed.

"So do I. Once a month, I put on about five pounds." She looked up and saw her own surprise reflected in his eyes. Such a thing to say to a man. She lifted her shoulder beneath his warm hand. "But then I always lose it again."

"I think Deer Woman only has one season a year."

"Then she's one lucky doe."

"And you're pretty small, even in your funny shoes."

She dropped her chin. "Funny shoes?"

He chuckled, pleased with himself, lifting her chin on the curve of his finger. "Even now, as weak as I've become in this hellhole, I could lift you in my arms and carry you"—He turned her around by her shoulders and drew her back against his chest—"out that door, up the stairs, and out the next. Into the clear, crisp winter night. What would we find out there?"

"There were people skiing out there today." She swallowed, her stomach jittery, her muscles bunching everywhere, but still she didn't step away. "On the bluffs across the river. I understand they held the Olympic ski jump trials here last winter." She gave a nervous titter. "Who would have guessed? Here in South Dakota."

"This Dakota country is full of surprises." He draped his blanket around her shoulders, crossing his arms around her, anchoring his hands and the corners of the blanket on her shoulders. "I surprised you that first day, didn't I? I don't know what you expected, but it wasn't me."

"No, it wasn't." She closed her eyes. "Adam, you're my patient. I can't allow this kind of . . ."

But neither could she step away.

"Do you know how cold I feel sometimes?" he said huskily, close to her ear. "My nurse should keep me warm."

"If I bring you another blanket, will you hide it from the attendants?"

He moved his cheek against her hair. "I could hide you from the attendants. If they came in now, they wouldn't see you. I would hide you. I would not let them punish you for helping me."

"Adam, this is not . . ."

She could feel his desire for her. She knew every inch of his body. She had washed him, fed him, cared for him, and she knew exactly what her proximity was doing to him, but she could not move away.

"I could lift you in my arms and carry you out that door, Rachael Trainor."

"I believe you could."

"You know I could." His hands tightened on her shoulders. "Set me free, and I will carry you away."

"I don't have . . ."

"A piece of wire," he whispered. "That's all it would take."

It was his pleading tone that shook her. She had only heard it once before—when he had asked her not to come near him. It was a tone wrung from the depths of his shame. He was no more an animal than she was, no less a man than she was a woman, as her body achingly attested to her now. Yet he was chained to a wall.

"I should simply ask for the key," she said, turning in his arms, stepping back as he let her go. "I'm a nurse on duty here, and I ought to be able to take the damn things off if an untrained attendant can put them on." She adjusted the blanket on his shoulders. "But if I ask, they'll know—"

"You don't have to ask. You have only to do what you know is right."

Her head was spinning with the foolishness of the world outside his cell and the crazy wonder of the nearness of him. Her mind sought some possibility, some semblance of reason. "Dr. Tim will know it's right when he sees how well you're doing, and how calm—"

"I don't feel calm." His hand slid down her arm. "Give me your hand. I know you like to use a different instrument for this, but your small hand is better. It will tell you more." He drew her hand to his bare chest, his eyes intent upon hers. "How calm am I, Rachael?"

"You have a strong, steady heartbeat."

"Shall I sing a Strongheart song to steady my nerves? I may remember the one my grandfather gave me before I went to war." His heart thudded beneath her palm, and hers went wild in its cage as he lifted his voice in a hushed, haunting Lakota song.

"Is that one of the songs that's forbidden?" she asked when the last strain had been absorbed into the massive rafters.

"Anything sacred is forbidden." He rubbed the back of her hand, still pressed against him. "Anything that might bring us aid or comfort is forbidden."

"That song should not be. It's very powerful." Her fingers stirred over his skin. "I can still feel it deep in here."

"If I had a Lakota flute I would play a song that would take all your resistance to me away." He closed his hand around hers and drew it around his back. "Do you doubt me? Bring me a piece of cedar. I'll carve a special flute and play a love song for you. Even as pitiful as I look right now, you won't be able to resist me when you hear my love song." He lowered his head and whispered close to her ear. "Bring me a small piece of cedar and a small knife." Head up, he looked down at her and smiled. "And a piece of wire."

"And who is this trickster you spoke of?"

"Deer Woman."

"No, the other one. Iktome."

"Deer Woman ties me to the bed, and then she stands close to me and makes me want her." She pulled her hand away, and he nodded. "I must remember that she has always been forbidden."

"We must get you well, Adam." She jammed her hands into her sweater pockets. "For . . . your brother's sake. He needs—"

"Let me see him." She looked doubtful. "You can do that much, can't you? He's in this building somewhere. You can find a way to let me see him"— he caught his blanket as his absent shrug made it slip— "through a window or something."

"I don't think he should see you just yet."

"How bad do I look?" When she didn't answer right away, he smiled. "That bad? Why weren't you laughing in my face when I tried to sweet-talk you?"

"Sweet-talk me?" *Why, indeed?* "Somehow laughing didn't occur to me."

Rachael and Ella Sims became secret allies. While Rachael could not completely abandon her sense of duty to the hospital chain of command, she began making compromises. Private compromises. She made it a point to do her job as Dr. Tim laid it out for her, and to do it well. Her public discourse with Head Nurse Sims was businesslike, involving nothing more personal than the requisite "please pass the bread" at lunch.

She knew that Ella kept a journal, which she hoped to use in bringing Dr. Tim's administration down, and perhaps the asylum with him. Rachael would have no part in that aspect of Ella's plan, but she was willing to conspire to begin alleviating certain problems. Other than sanitation, with which Rachael was making gradual progress with Dr. Tim's tacit approval, isolation and restraints were the most pressing.

The doctor had not agreed to modify any of the procedures in those areas, but Rachael took heart one day when he finally allowed her to complete a sentence that contained a suggestion.

"It occurs to me," she said as she fingered the leather spines of a row of books on his office shelf, "that greater attention to some form of therapy might make our job easier in the long run."

"What form of therapy?"

"I'm not talking about any newfangled psychoanalysis," she assured him quickly, even though she nearly choked on the description. Beyond the walls of Hiawatha, psychoanalysis was no longer considered newfangled, and they had a number of patients whose thoughts were coherent enough to profit by it. She approached the desk. "I've been thinking of ways to broaden our occupational therapy, for instance. I've had a good deal of experience in that area, you know. Beyond your exercise program, which is truly an exemplary model, I think an expanded activity program would encourage more interaction among the patients, more talk."

"Talk?" He glanced up from his seemingly endless paperwork, sparing her a dubious look. "About what? What would they have to talk about?"

"They do talk, you know."

"Not around me." The wooden swivel chair groaned as he leaned back and peered at her above his wire-rimmed half-eyes. "We have the sewing room, which is underused because they really have no ambition, poor souls. And we have the farm."

"As a matter of fact, I've spoken with Mr. Brothers recently, and he says he could use more able-bodied help out there." She knew that Dr. Tim and hired farmer Albert Brothers were barely on speaking terms. "There are several patients I'd like to take out there one at a time, so that I'm sure I have control, just to see how they might respond."

"We have four patients assigned out there already."

"I know, but I think we could increase that number." She paused, then added carefully, "I was thinking of Tom Yells At Night and Martin Lone Bull."

"Martin?" Dr. Tim shook his head. "Impossible. Martin's condition is fragile."

"He's much better. I don't see any sign of—"

"Who's the doctor here?"

"You are, of course."

"Martin's infection is inactive because I keep him closely guarded, just as I do each of my charges. I do what's necessary for each one individually, and I think you know by now what a challenge that is."

"I do." Rachael drew a deep breath. Her stomach churned. If she looked at him, he would see her anger, so she stared at the floor the same way the patients so often did. "Perhaps I might take Tom down to the dairy barn."

"All right, Miss Trainor. You may experiment with Tom Yells At Night."

So far, so good. "I was also wondering about our patient in the dark ward." She cleared her throat. "Martin's brother."

"What were you wondering about?"

"It seems that such a long period of isolation"—she forced herself to look up, to form a plastic smile on her face—"has probably done wonders. We've heard none of Mad Bull's bellowing lately."

"He was a bit under the weather for a while there, but he must be on the mend. Otherwise I would have been called down."

"There's nothing in the daily log for him."

"There isn't?" He chuckled, rolling his eyes ceiling-ward. "Ah, that Hollings isn't much for book work, is he. My own records are complete, and that's what counts. I have to account for each addled head in order to justify every penny. Don't concern yourself with Mad Bull, Miss Trainor. Take Tom Yells At Night over to Farmer Brothers and see if he can teach a morose savage to milk a cow. See whether Tom has any interest in a teat." He laughed, then abruptly drew a serious face. "Forgive me, that was crude. That was very, very crude. Bumpkin humor. I ought to be ashamed of myself, hmm?"

"A sense of humor can be a sign of"—she tried to recall Ella's words—"tremendous stamina in the face of adverse conditions."

"Interesting observation, Miss Trainor." Dr. Tim smiled, peeled off his glasses, and set them aside, sprawling in his chair as though he owned the world. Or at least his corner of it. "Yes, I think you're right. It takes a sense of humor to persevere in this service, doesn't it? We'll have to see about putting Mad Bull to work, too."

❧ II ❧

In the dead of night Rachael carried only enough lamp light into the basement to keep her from tripping along the way to Adam's isolated cubbyhole. She knew the stairs and the passageways, but obstacles had a way of popping up in the dark. On various visits she'd encountered a feline mouser and its prey, a chamber pot that had been abandoned rather than emptied, a partially hidden whiskey bottle.

Tonight the way was clear, but the narrow tunnel to his cell seemed especially chilly and forbidding. It was a relief to push his door open and see his sleeping face. She was about to take a terrible risk, but risk-taking seemed to come more easily these days, what with the muddying of right ways and wrong ways and with sense and nonsense blurring at the edges.

"Adam, wake up. I've brought you something." She knelt beside him and gently shook his shoulder. He tried to roll away, but he could pull his right arm no more than eight inches from the bed frame.

Rachael eased his arm back down, insinuated her thumb between his wrist and the metal band, and rubbed his skin. "Did they give you something to make you sleep, Adam?"

"What?" He lifted his head, blinked hard, and dragged his bleary gaze over her face as he fought to keep his eyes from rolling back into oblivion. "Rachael? Are you really here?"

"I'm really here." She touched his cheek, testing its warmth. "You're not sick again, are you?"

"Dreaming about you," he muttered, his eyes drifting closed. "Drank something Hollings gave me . . . don't know how long I've been . . ."

"They've got to stop doing this to you," she grumbled as she took up the enamel pitcher she'd brought with her and poured some water into her hand. "Brace yourself, Adam. This is cold, but it should—"

"Hiya!"

His blanket flew in her face as he jackknifed off the bed, splashing more water in the process. She managed to save most of it as she toppled backward. Dripping, scowling, he'd sprung to the edge of the bed, and there he perched, ready to fly at her. For a moment, she thought he might try.

The wristlet clanked as he lowered his feet to the floor, his muscles relaxing one by one. He wiped his face with his free hand, then lifted a warning finger. "Don't try that again."

"I'm sorry." From her spraddled position on the floor she looked up, stunned, afraid to move.

"Hollings and Gatewood used to say it was to cool me off. It doesn't cool me off, Rachael." He closed his eyes, slowly retracting his finger into his fist. "It makes everything go red inside my head, like the smell of gas, or the sound of . . ."

"I only meant to wake you up. I didn't mean to . . ."

He looked down at his hand, opened it slowly, and studied it as though he wasn't sure who the trembling thing belonged to.

"I didn't mean to scare you," she said. "I would never do anything like that to you, Adam."

His eyes softened when they met hers. "I would never want to hurt you, either, but I could." He offered her his hand. "My head is full of cobwebs and spiders sometimes."

She nodded, taking his hand, holding her tongue.

"I'm awake now," he prodded gently.

She took a piece of wire from one sweater pocket, a fork from the other, and held them both in front of his face. "Which do you prefer?"

His eyes darted from one to the other, then met hers in utter amazement. "What brought this on?"

She laughed. "For heaven's sake, man, if I brought you a horse, would you count his teeth?"

"I wouldn't even count his legs." He chose the wire.

"Ella Sims is busy detaining the night attendant in the hospital building."

He was already working the wire inside the lock on the wristlet. She laid her hand over his, and he looked up expectantly.

"Just a brief excursion, Adam. Martin knows you're here, and I want him to see that you're all right. I think he needs that, and I think you should see him. That's all. You must promise me you won't try . . ." She pressed his hand with an urgent squeeze. "Because if you do, they'll put you both so far away from my reach and anyone else's who might possibly care what happens to you that . . ." She couldn't look him in the eye and demand that he submit to locks and chains after a few moments of freedom. "I'm afraid we're going to lose Ella soon."

"Is this a loss I ought to mourn?"

"I don't know for sure. I don't know anything for sure anymore, except that . . ." Except that this man did not belong here, and it was a crime to chain him up this way. She withdrew her hand, and he went back to scratching metal within metal. "You have to promise me you won't try anything foolish, Adam."

"Foolish? How about crazy?" He spared her a glance and flashed a truly bright-eyed, almost doting smile. "Tell me this, woman, how can you ask a crazy man to promise you he won't do anything crazy?"

"I'm not asking a crazy man. I'm asking you."

They heard a click and exchanged an exultant can-do look as he broke the horrible hoop apart. He rubbed his wrist, then took her face in his gloriously free hands, kissed her lips soundly, and promised, "For tonight, this one night, you have my word."

She led the way upstairs, dousing the lantern before she opened the door at the top of the steps. She made sure the coast was clear, then led him to his brother's brightly moonlit room. They found the boy asleep, one hand bound to the bed.

"Pagla," Adam whispered as he lowered one knee to the floor. "I'm here, Pagla. *Ena. Niciye kin.* Your brother."

The boy lifted his head, then pushed himself up on his elbows. *"Ciyewaye kin?"*

"Yes." Carefully Adam put his hand on young Martin's shoulder. *"Ohan."*

A strangled sound issued from Martin's throat as he threw his free arm around his brother's neck. Whatever he said was muffled in Adam's shirt. The boy's whole body shuddered. He gasped, struggled for breath, then finally wept freely.

Adam closed his hand slowly around a fistful of his brother's hair, lifted his chin, and desperately held on— to the moment, to his brother, to his own tears, which clearly threatened to destroy his fiercely guarded reserve, a self-imposed restraint more rigid than any steel bonds.

But he did not begrudge his brother's tears. He did nothing to try to stem their flow, but let them bathe his own skin. Tears for all the days and nights spent in this place, for the devastation of their family, for the loss of their grandfather, for all the sorrows the boy had borne alone.

Finally Martin lifted his face and whispered a tear-drenched appeal to his brother.

"Hiya," Adam ground out, his throat laden with emotional gravel. Rachael knew that the request was denied, and that whatever explanation followed in Lakota was heartfelt. Adam took the boy's slight shoulders in his own big hands, pressed forehead to forehead, and whispered a Lakota litany of what she was sure were reassurances. Martin returned some soft, sad disputation, and Adam responded by shaking the boy's shoulders

gently, then clutching him to his chest and exhorting him all the more.

She was glad she'd brought Adam up here. This was what the boy needed. So many words unleashed! Clearly Martin Lone Bull might well be reclaimed from the ravages of mental illness with the right kind of care, the kind Dr. Tim had no use for.

Adam reached for her hand and drew her close. "Rachael," he whispered as he made her part of the reunion, perhaps naming her as the brothers' benefactor. "Our nurse and our friend. *Kola.* You're our friend, aren't you, Rachael?"

"Yes, I am. Martin knows this." Lovingly she touched the boy's damp cheek. "Pagla, you know I'm your"—she looked to Adam for approval—"*kola?*"

"That's right," Adam said, but with a few more words in Lakota he had Martin crying again.

He turned to Rachael, his face distorted with anguish. "What can I tell him? What can I say? What can I promise that won't be a lie?"

"That you won't drink anymore?"

"Christ, I'm way past thinking about that." He tipped his head back and drew a deep, steadying breath. "He can't take much more of this, Rachael. His spirit is too gentle for this. He's going to slip away from me."

He hooked his arm like a shepherd's crook around his brother's head, drawing him into the pocket of his big shoulder. "I should have come for you, *misunka.* I should have come and taken you long ago."

"Please, Adam," Rachael whispered, disturbed by the emotions that threatened to engulf all reason, by words she couldn't understand. She tugged on a precarious rein. "You promised."

"For tonight only."

"All right, for tonight. We start tonight."

"Start what?"

"Facilitating your recovery. Your release, then Martin's. Ella says—" He turned his face away in disgust. "No, listen, Adam. Ella says that there are people in the Indian Bureau, President Roosevelt's new appointees, who have begun to advocate shutting this place down. She says it's just a matter of time.''

"Then you'd be out of a job.''

"I can find another job. I'm concerned about the patients here and what will happen to them. Many of them have been here so long that . . .'' She sighed. "I don't approve of much of what goes on here. This isn't the way the more progressive hospitals are run. But there *are* patients here who *do* need help.''

"I wouldn't know about that, would I? I never see anyone else.''

"And you shouldn't be here at all. You are not suffering from alcoholic dementia.'' She dropped her voice to a lower register, aping her boss. "When did you become a medical doctor, Miss Trainor? Are you questioning my professional judgment, Miss Trainor?'' And then, "Yessir, I believe I am.''

Adam looked at her as though she were the one in need of restraints. "Who're you talking to?''

"I'm talking myself into making a pact with two men who are not well served here.'' Saying it helped. It sounded right, *felt right*. She leaned closer to them, stroking Martin's back to soothe his silent trembling. "We really must be careful, Adam. They may decide to call you a criminal instead of a madman. You were committed because you assaulted someone.''

"So they say.''

"And you don't remember exactly what happened, which they'll use against you. You have to *show them* that you've fully recovered''—she took a deep breath and gestured sympathetically—"from a state you were never in. By the time a drunkard reaches the stage of dementia, his brain is generally pickled.''

"Oh, Christ.''

"And that's not to say it *can't* happen to you. If you don't remember what happened the night they arrested you, you were obviously in a sorry state, Adam, so it very well *could* happen to you.''

"No temperance lectures, woman. I've sworn off, all

right?'' He guarded his brother's tears as he eyed her cautiously. "What kind of a pact?''

"I'm not sure yet. You'll have to trust me." She searched his hooded gaze for some sign of assurance. "As I'm trusting you."

"For this night only."

"I'm proposing to extend that."

He stroked his brother's short hair. "I have to get him out of here soon."

"You must assure him that I'm going to look after him, and you're going to see him again, and it's going to be okay." Regretfully, she added, "I have to take you back, Adam. If we get caught, you'll be stuck in this place without me."

"I don't think we'd like that." He leaned back. "Right, Pagla? Little owl eyes, always watching for a chance to swoop down and mess with your brother's plans."

The boy looked up at him, his sad eyes full of expectation.

"I know," Adam said quietly. "You never harmed a living soul in your life, did you? Not even a field mouse. You'd starve first. That's why it was up to me to—"

"Adam, we have to go," Rachael pleaded. "Tell him something, so he'll know it's okay."

"Lie through my teeth, you mean?" He chuckled bitterly, for she finally had no ready answer. When he spoke to his brother in their first language, the boy grabbed his arm and responded in a voice that quivered with fear.

"No, shhh." Rachael stroked Martin's shoulder, her maternal instincts thrashing within her mercilessly. "I'll be back soon. Tell him that for me, Adam. Tell him I'll take care of—"

"I can only lie for myself," Adam said, his tone utterly flat. "I can't do it for you, too."

They returned safely to Adam's underground den, and there they sat, side by side on the only piece of furniture available. He washed his face and the back of his neck in the cold water she'd brought, trying to revive his senses. She was painfully silent, wrestling in her head.

"You're a good woman," he told her at last, as though he'd been listening to her mental doubts. "How did you get to be Trainor's sister?"

She was glad he'd given her an excuse to smile. "He's not so bad. A little stiff-necked, but he means well."

"I won't try to take that away from you." As he studied her face the emotions that crossed his were by turns killing and kind. "For a long time I thought you were the one who got me clapped in irons. I thought, maybe because I was alone with you."

"I didn't tell him anything about that."

"I wanted to see you the night I went to the agency, but when I got there, I knew what a stupid idea it was." His mouth twisted in a self-deprecating smile. "Decided I was better off with a bottle."

"I was glad to see you." She arched one eyebrow, surprising herself by confessing, "And sorry you chose the whiskey over a longer visit with me."

"I wanted more than just a visit. Does that shock you, Rachael?"

She laughed. "You've made much more shocking suggestions than that."

"I guess I have." Smiling, he touched curved fingers to her chin and lightly dragged his knuckles down the slope to the base of her delicate throat. "Have they shocked you? Or is there a better way to—"

"Rachael, it's me, Ella." The door yawned. The face appeared in the shadows. "You've got to come. Alice DeCouteau has gone into labor, and she's calling for you."

Rachael sprang to her feet. "Is Dr. Tim—"

"He's with her." Ella's hand beckoned nervously. "Without the restraints, she'd be clawing his eyes out. You've got to come quickly."

The two women hurried across frozen turf and moon-lit pillow drifts, scurried through dark hallways and up the stairs, but it was all over by the time they got there. The hospital building's seldom-used operating room

looked like the back room at a butcher's shop. There
was blood everywhere—pools of it, smears of it, tracks
of it everywhere. Bloody linens were strewn about the
place. Gory instruments lay on tabletop and tray.

Rachael stood in the doorway, aghast, choking on the
horror and her own breathlessness. But for the sound of
running water and her own pounding heart, the place
was deathly silent. Mother was bound in a blood-
splashed restraining camisole, child bound in the cord
the two still shared. Neither had survived.

Dr. Tim did not look up. He was busy washing his
hands. "I've never seen anything like it," he said
calmly. "The woman nearly turned herself inside out."

Rachael stared at the back of the man's head. Pomade
held his thinning, straw-colored hair perfectly in place.
Unruffled. Surrounded but untouched.

"Was it too late for a Caesarean section?"

"I'm not equipped for this kind of thing here," he
said quietly as he continued to roll the fat white bar of
soap over and over in his hands. "What did she mean,
getting herself pregnant here?"

"She didn't mean anything." Rachael approached the
long table, seeking communion with the face of the
woman who had given her new words. "She wasn't responsible."

"Of course she was." Dr. Tim slammed the faucet
shut and whirled away from the sink, hands and forearms dripping water on his blood-spattered black shoes.
"She was a woman, imbecile or not. She had no business getting herself pregnant under my—"

"Doctor, the woman is dead." Rachael stepped
around the table, blocking Alice's face from the man's
view. His anger would not disturb her peace now. "This
woman is dead, and so is her child." *And that is what
means something.*

"It's just as well he never drew breath." He jerked
his blood-stained white coat off his shoulders, sloughing
it off like outgrown skin. "Damn winter burials. They'll
have to break out the picks to get below the frost line,
and there'll be no end to the complaining. One hole's

all they need for the two. She can carry the poor little bastard for all eternity.''

Rachael's mouth went dry. ''Doctor, what about family?''

''She was obviously a disgrace to whatever family she may have had. They don't have to know.'' He turned to Ella, standing by the door, and assumed a wide stance that brooked no argument. ''No one has to know about this. God knows, and he did the merciful thing by taking her.'' Again he turned, throwing up a stiff arm as though blocking some imagined blow. His eyes accused Rachael. ''*He did the merciful thing.*''

''Yes, Doctor.''

Ella stepped aside. Hubble hurried out the door, hollering down the hallway. ''Gatewood, get in here and clean this mess up!''

Rachael's whole blood supply had dropped into her feet. Her knees had rusted. She might have fainted except that it was her duty not to.

Her stiff legs took her to a cupboard. What few supplies there were had been ransacked. Gauze, bandaging, a box of needles spilled, a bottle of denatured alcohol smashed. A sliver of glass bit her palm as she pushed the mess aside and reached for a sheet. Ella came forward to help her cover the two bodies.

''I couldn't see much,'' Ella said quietly. ''They wouldn't let me past the door. I heard the shouting, heard her calling for you. I thought they might send someone looking for you, which, of course, would have been . . .'' She squeezed Rachael's arm. ''You couldn't have done anything, either.''

Rachael frowned. ''I'm sure he would have let me assist.''

''Assist with what?'' Ella ground out. ''That man has no business—''

''Damn, I hate it when they die.'' Gatewood breezed into the room pushing a litter past the two women, who stood there looking at one another while he chattered. ''Whoever it was that said the only good Indian is a dead Indian didn't have to touch the dead ones. They give me bad dreams every time. I don't go anywhere near that cemetery unless I have to. And when they croak, that's when I have to.'' The rangy attendant lined the wheeled bed up with the stationary one. ''I'll move 'em, but I ain't cleaning up any blood. That's what they pay the cleaning woman for. I'm an attendant, by God.''

''Keep her covered.'' Rachael tucked the sheet under Alice's shoulders. ''If you don't treat them with respect, I understand they can come back to haunt you.''

Gatewood laughed nervously. ''Sounds like maybe you been here too long already, Miss Trainor.''

Ella took Rachael by the shoulders and directed her out the door. She kept her moving down the hallway, putting one foot in front of the other, shushing her when she muttered, ''What kind of a doctor is he?''

''Just be quiet, now. He's not a surgeon.''

''It doesn't take a surgeon to deliver a baby. A meat cutter could have done a better—''

''Don't ever say that,'' Ella warned quietly as they rounded the newel post on the stair landing, finding their way by the winter starlight that glittered in the windows. ''If we're asked, and we probably won't be, that is the one thing we can never suggest to one doctor about another. We are not doctors, and they will be quick to point that out.''

''But we are nurses, and we have—''

''Shhh.'' Ella pushed her around another corner. They stood before the door to Rachael's room. ''We must find a way to let him expose his own incompetency.''

''Is that what you've been hoping for, Ella? At whose expense?''

''Look to your own blind eye, Miss Trainor.'' Ella took a deep breath and sighed. ''There's a lot going on here that you have yet to see, that you won't see unless you keep your eyes open. Forget about what can and cannot be and start seeing what is. At whose expense,'' she mocked softly. ''I'll tell you something. Adam Lone Bull, for one, is not confined to this place for his—''

''Oh, my God.'' Rachael clapped her hand to her mouth. ''I forgot about Adam. I didn't lock him in!''

"I did." Ella eyed her pointedly. "If they caught him trying to take his brother out of here, they might just kill him."

Rachael was already edging away.

"Just keep that in mind, Rachael. And be sure he understands that, too."

Adam was lying on his bed, having a smoke and weighing his options. He'd made some gains this night that he didn't want to lose. If he walked out now and took his brother with him, they couldn't go home. If he got caught and Agent Trainor sent him to prison, who would look after Pagla? Their mother? She'd given up and gone to stay with her sister. There's trouble everywhere you look, she'd said. Can't do anything about it. Just keep to yourself and hold on to what's left. And she didn't have much left.

Neither did he. He'd tried the "progressive" road, the one advocated by the boarding school teachers, the recruiters, the agents, and many of the mixed-bloods. But the war was over, the cattle were gone, so much of the land was gone, everyone he cared about was either dead or nearly so, and the road itself led nowhere. An unreal place called Hiawatha Asylum for Insane Indians, which had to be nowhere.

Maybe he'd had it coming. He'd started down the same road his father had taken, knowing in his heart and mind that it was a bad road. It had led him to a bad place in the middle of nowhere.

His grandfather's road had been different—the old road, the ancient ways—but it had led the old man to the same place. Hiawatha Asylum for Insane Indians.

Nowhere.

But here in this nowhere was his brother. And here in this nowhere was a strange white woman whose eyes had somehow enchanted him from the start.

The start of what?

The start of nothing in the middle of nowhere.

Patience, he told himself when he heard her distinctive footsteps beyond the door. Whatever had started would be played out. That was all he knew.

"I forgot about the restraints," she whispered as she closed the door, making sure it was still locked. "I forgot the lantern, too."

"Did you come back to see if I escaped?" He swung his legs over the edge of the bed and sat up, pulling his blanket around his shoulders. "I thought about it. I could have."

"The door was locked. Ella locked it."

"I still have my key." He smiled as he drew the wire, remarkably, from his hair. "But I gave you my word for tonight."

"Is that all that stopped you?"

"That, and a brain that's not quite pickled yet." He took a final puff on his cigarette before dropping it in the water pitcher. With a gesture he invited her to come to the bed and sit beside him in the shadows of his dimly lit cave. "What happened?"

"They both died. Alice and her baby." She leaned back against the wall and closed her eyes. "A little boy."

"Was she your friend?"

"She was a patient. She taught me some Indian words." Pain strained her face and made her voice quiver. "She cried a lot."

He put his hand on her knee. It felt so slight, like a bird's wing hidden beneath her cotton dress. "Where's her man?"

"She's been a patient here for several years. Immaculate conception, I guess." She pressed her lips together, as though staving off the escape of more sarcasm, then sighed. "It's an awful thing, but it happens. I've seen it before. Even the most vigilant . . ."

He wasn't sure what she was talking about. Birth and death were everyday occurrences, and surely in her job she'd seen plenty of both.

"Oh, Adam . . ." A slow, deep breath fortified her. "The women are so trusting, so vulnerable, just like children. Employees come and go in a place like this, and some of them . . . because they find it easy, you know?" He just looked at her, and the tears finally welled in her eyes. "I'm sorry. You know better than I."

"I'm not a woman." His hand stirred. "I'm not a child."

"But a man in chains . . . would know."

"You've removed my chains," he said softly. "And Tunkasila has removed your friend's."

She nodded tightly. "Funny how two men can make nearly the same statement, but the meaning"—her tears spilled over her cheeks as she looked into his eyes—"is so different. I like yours better."

He claimed her next tear with his thumb and touched it to his lips. "Salt," he said. "The salt of the earth. A man cannot survive without it." He smiled wistfully. "I've gained wisdom since I became a madman."

"Share it with me, then." Her lower lip trembled like a little girl's as she mopped her cheek with her sweater sleeve. "I need some new wisdom. I'm feeling like an idiot."

"Was your friend an idiot?"

"She was . . ." The language of her old wisdom was inadequate. The words her profession used didn't fit. "She was a woman trying to bear a child."

"She wanted you to be there with her when her child came. That's an honor. She trusted you as she would her mother or sister."

"I let her down."

"You went to her when she called for you. You did not hesitate." He took her hand in his. "We'll make a song for her."

"I can't sing."

"And I *don't* sing." He shrugged and let her see the irony of that claim in his eyes. "That's what I said when I was trying very hard to become a white man. But we'll make a song for your friend and her child, Rachael. The *wanagi* will hear us and see that we mourn for them, and they will enter the spirit world with pride and honor."

"He butchered her," she whispered disconsolately,

staring past him, remembering. "Dr. Tim took her—"

"It's done now. She's free. He can't shame her in the
next world. He has no power there."

"I do . . . truly m-mourn . . ."

He lifted her hand, turned her moist palm to his lips,
and tasted more of her. More salt, more tang. He drew
back to examine the small injury. "Yes, I see that. You
bleed."

"I cut myself on a piece of glass."

He looked into her sad eyes and felt the stabbing.
With a quick nod he picked up the wire she'd given him,
drew back his sleeve, and gashed his forearm.

"Adam, don't hurt your—"

"This is what I have neglected, and my spirit has been
the poorer for it." He took her shoulders in his hands,
pulled her back against him and shared his blanket with
her. "You will wail while I sing. But softly, like this."

He demonstrated her part, then took up his. The keening came naturally to her, as did the sorrow and the
tears. The coal furnace and the boilers roared not far
away, masking the sound of their mourning for all but
those who no longer needed ears.

He held her the way he'd held his brother earlier. He
felt strong again, and it occurred to him that the singing
had truly fortified his blood. He didn't know where the
song had come from. His grandfather, maybe. The old
one's spirit was here on these grounds, and it was working on his head, waiting out his rage, then counseling
him in the ways of patience and cunning.

He remembered his days and nights in the vision pit
on the hill when he had been confined to a small space.
The walls had been drawn by a string, but they were
just as real as the gray stone that surrounded him here.
The land and the sky stood waiting beyond the perimeter, still the same wind rustling grass of the same
root. Still the same heart beating within the broader chest
of Adam Lone Bull, who was older now, but not much
wiser. Still proud, still angry, still less fearful of the
darkness around him than the dark place he carried deep
within.

He pressed his cheek against the woman's soft hair and blindly touched her face. "You're angry, too."

"Sorrowful," she contended.

"I can feel the heat of your anger in your tears, Rachael." He spread his hand beneath her chin and slid it over her throat, slipping it under the neckline of her dress, taking the measure of her delicate collarbone. "In your skin. Men die in battle, and women die in childbirth. Whether your skin is brown or white, this is the way of the world."

"I'm not angry. I'm trying to do a job here. I'm—" She covered his hand with hers and surprised him by pressing it, as though she accepted his unspoken claim on her. He could hear the tears in her voice. "I'm a good nurse. There's work to be done, and I could do it and do it well. It wouldn't be easy, but things could be made better. And it wouldn't have to cost a lot. Dr. Tim is just so set on *his way*."

"Our people fear this place. Did you know that?"

She shook her head tightly, and he felt another tear splash on the back of his hand.

"They do." He wanted her to know this. He wanted *someone* to know. "People whisper about this place. They're afraid to talk about it out loud. It's a bad secret, they say. A bad mystery. Don't ask questions or something bad will happen. First they take the dreamers, the *heyokas*, the ones the people believe are touched by the spirits. Pretty soon they've taken a child here, an old man there, and they've all been sent away. And no one knows who will be next. Maybe it'll be a drunk, like me, or maybe a child who can't get along in school. No one knows."

She groaned and tipped her head back against his shoulder. "It's supposed to be a place of respite, not a punishment. I don't know what to do anymore. I thought I did. Clean the place up, change some antiquated procedures, bring some light into the dark places and . . ."

She turned her head toward him. "I'm discussing these things with my patient." Her sigh tickled his neck, and he smiled. "Wonder of wonders, I have found a patient who understands what I'm talking about better than the doctor does."

"He's a damn redskin to boot," he said, chuckling as he shifted, bracing his back against the wall and settling her in his embrace as he spoke. "But I'm a prisoner here. I'm not a patient. I wonder how many others have there been, besides my brother and my grandfather."

"I don't know. Dr. Tim claims that Martin has tuberculosis, but there have been no tests, and he shows none of the symptoms. I was told that he couldn't speak, but obviously that's not true. When he saw you—"

"He wants to die."

She stiffened in his arms. "Wants . . . to die?"

"He wasn't asking me to take him out of here," he reported quietly as she looked up at him. "He was telling me that he doesn't want to live anymore."

"Not here, I'm sure."

"Not anywhere."

"Adam, if he's suicidal, then he *does* belong here, and we have to protect him from his own—"

"This is a bad place. *No one* belongs here."

She sighed and settled back into his arms, and he knew from her silence that she believed him now.

"Do they have places like this for white people?"

"Yes . . . no, not *exactly* like this, and not—" It amused him to think that he'd almost stumped her. "I can't think of one that's called an asylum for insane white people."

He had to laugh. "That's because they couldn't build one big enough."

She looked up at him, wounded. "What do you think of *me,* Adam? Do you think I'm insane?"

"Why, Nurse Trainor." He smiled as he laid a finger on the point of her chin. "Is that a sensible question to put to a madman?"

"You're not a madman." She pushed herself up, taking a closer look. "No, you're definitely not."

"Tell me when you're truly convinced. I'm doing my level best to act normal."

"But when you were committed—"

"I was drunk, I know." He glanced across the room, eyeing the small flame glowing inside the lantern's glass chimney. "I figured it didn't matter what happened to me anymore. I thought I didn't care. But I do. I don't want to live as a prisoner, and I don't want to die here." He held up the wire, turned it in the light, gazed at it as though it were made of gold. "Thanks to you I won't have to."

"I don't suppose there's any way I can take that back from you now."

He looked at her and smiled.

She looked at him solemnly. "I believe you'll soon be discharged, Adam. Promise me you won't try to take Martin and run."

"When I take him out of here, there must be no chance of them getting him back."

"Which means we need two discharges."

"I would trade my land." She looked at him quizzically. "The usual price is one dollar and consideration. Tell them our freedom is the consideration."

"Tell who?"

"Have you seen your brother lately?" he asked carefully.

"Not since last summer. Dr. Tim sees him on occasion, and he tells me—" He watched her closely as she spoke of her brother—or did not speak of him. She seemed genuinely confused. "What do you mean about trading your land?"

He shook his head. "I hope someone has taken my horse and my dog in, that's all. The horse could probably forage for himself in the hills, but that dog of mine is spoiled." Just as he would like to spoil her, he decided as he let his gaze wander from her sweet, puffy eyes to the little scar he noticed for the first time above her thin eyebrow, to her small-lobed ear. "I've thought about that dog a lot," he said absently. "Hate to think he died waiting for me to come back and feed him."

"I could try to find out for you."

"No, you couldn't." His eyes had hers entranced. "I don't speak to anyone. We've never talked, you and I."

"Not since you helped me that time I fell off my brother's stupid horse."

"I haven't laid eyes on you since. Or hands." He slipped his fingers into her hair and cupped his hand over the side of her head. "I've never kissed you."

She moistened her lips. "It wouldn't be right."

"It wouldn't be wrong if it never happened."

He brushed his lips against hers, nibbled them, parted them, and tasted them delicately. "Anything wrong with that?" he whispered into her mouth.

"With what?"

He opened his mouth over hers as he lowered her to the bed. The kiss that never happened exploded into loving that could not be, yet was. He wanted her, needed her desperately, needed her in more ways than he cared to count, needs that were hard for a man to claim. But right now there was only one way, one need, one woman. If she wanted a prisoner, she would have one. He was ready to be taken inside this woman and held tight and driven to the brink of life's sweetest form of madness.

He reached down and moved her under him, fitting her to him as he kissed her hungrily. With her small bottom filling his hand he rocked his hips against hers. She put her arms around his back, slipped her tongue into his mouth. Their clothing was all that kept him at bay.

He lifted his head and touched his forehead to hers. "Rachael, this can't happen unless you're as crazy as I am."

"I have to be crazier. Make me feel alive, Adam. Make me . . ." She started to unbutton her dress, but he moved her hand aside and popped the buttons open, all the way down to the hem. He kissed her cool skin until it turned to silky underwear, then slipped the satin straps over her shoulder and rooted greedily until he found her nipple. He took his time loving her thus, using his lips and tongue to make her sweet female flesh ache for him, make her nipples as hard for him as his male flesh was for her.

She gripped his shoulders while his hands glided over her hips and thighs, over and under slip, garters, panties, getting it all out of his way.

"Adam, this can't happen here. You said this was a bad place, and I'm afraid."

His hands stilled. "Afraid of me?"

"Afraid of this place."

"We're here, Rachael. You're here with me. We'll make it a good place." Bracing himself on his forearm he rose over her, tenting them with his blanket, stroking her intimately, coaxing her body to weep from wanting him. "If it isn't good, it never happened. Never saw, never touched, never knew each other."

"I need . . . I *want* to know you."

"Know this." He pushed his loose pants out of the way, and she gave way, and he made his way, slowly, carefully, lovingly. "Is this enough of me?"

"Not . . . no . . ."

"Too much?" Ah, it was good to have the freedom to move and the strength to savor the tension, the power to hold off, hold away just a little. "Tell me now. I can hear you if you tell me now."

"More." She arched up from the bed, up from the gloom of this place and into the joy of their union. "There's no such thing as too much of you."

"Are you my prisoner, Rachael?"

"Yes. Oh, yes, keep me . . . make me . . ."

"Mine. You're mine . . . mine . . ."

And he held her in a possessive embrace, his powerful shudders blending with hers. The moment brimmed so full that it burst wide open with the bittersweet flavor of its intrinsic transience. They both knew it, and they held each other all the more desperately for it.

"Now, woman, *my* woman—" He sat up, taking her with him, and she curled up, all rumpled and musky and unsteady, in his lap. He brushed her hair out of her eyes. "Have I made you feel alive?"

"My heart's pounding out a very lively beat. I feel beautiful." She ducked beneath his chin, seeking his refuge. "And scared."

"Then say it never happened. Can you do that?"

"It's easier for a man than for a woman. You're part of me now." She sought his hand, pushed it into her lap, and curled herself around it, making his big, rough hand her pearl. "It all happened inside me."

"You warmed me and hatched me, and I came to life inside you." He smiled. It pleased him to shelter her marvelous woman's place with his hand. "When you go, you'll take the fire with you, and I'll be cold again. How is that supposed to be easier for me, Rachael?"

"I've never known anyone like you."

"I've been alone for a long time, but I had a wife and child once. I know how to love a woman." He adjusted the blanket, cuddling her as he rested his head against the cold cement wall. "I need your help. I need an ally."

"I think I must talk to Edward about—"

"Not about me. Don't talk to anyone about me." He glanced down, found her looking up at him, found himself wanting to assure her somehow. "I'll speak for myself when the time comes. Until then I won't cause any more trouble. I'll let them think they've made me their trained animal."

"They need able-bodied men to work the farm."

"Able body, pickled brain." He chuckled derisively. "But they'd have to give my boots back, wouldn't they."

"I would have to say so."

"And you would have to say that I am able-bodied." She nodded, smiling. "But we don't know each other, Rachael. There's nothing between us." He touched the corner of her soft smile. "Not yet."

❧ 12 ❧

Late Spring 1933

There were no wheelchairs at Hiawatha, but Rachael had rigged up a cart for Mr. Blue, who had been confined to his room for several years. He seldom spoke to staff members, but, like many of the patients, he'd begun to trust Rachael. He'd complained to her of "too much bad breathing."

Agreeable breathing, she decided, was not too much to ask. She'd found a broken garden cart in the machine shed, and Albert Brothers had provided more parts and tools for her project. She was quite pleased with the results, and she proudly enlisted Peter Magpie to help her pull Mr. Blue and his new cart onto the porch. Bolstered by her achievement, she had then drawn a plan for a system of ramps to enable her to take those who were not ambulatory into the yard, but Dr. Tim had said that her plan would be too costly.

Out on the pillared porch Peter Magpie smoked his cigarettes while Mr. Blue swatted flies. Sightless Peter confidently declared a hit or a miss after each whack, and he was seldom wrong. When Rachael asked him how he did it, he claimed that he could hear flies squeal. She hoped he was teasing. Fly swatting was a popular form of indoor recreation, and the patients were always conspiring to keep screen doors open long enough to let a few flies in. There had been a couple of times lately when she could have sworn she'd heard a tiny squeak within the echo of a *thwack*.

She was going soft. Dr. Tim had advised her against taking a personal interest in the patients, but Ella had candidly warned her about "going soft." She'd said it would cloud her perspective and that the time was coming when she'd need a clear perspective and a level, unsentimental head.

Rachael missed Ella, but she'd had several letters from her since she'd gone to Washington D.C. Ella's experience and Rachael's recommendation had gained her a position at St. Elizabeth's Hospital. She was also tirelessly turning the door handles of the Office of Indian Affairs. But while Ella was working on executive branch bureaucracy, she also reported that Congress had its role to play, and that the South Dakota delegation would most certainly be looking after its interests in Canton.

The Canton asylum had been established more than thirty years ago by an act of Congress, and Congress had recently appropriated funds to keep the facility operating at full capacity despite the negative reports delivered by inspectors. Dr. Samuel Silk, a psychiatrist on staff at St. Elizabeth's, had described the asylum as a place of "padlocks and chamber pots." He had decried the use of antiquated restraints and isolation and pointed out that it was impossible to tell much from the records, but many of the patients did not appear to be mentally deficient. Those who were, he said, needed care and treatment that was not provided at the Canton facility.

More recently John Holst from the Indian Service's education division had said that those who were "herded into" the asylum were "practically forgotten," and that those who "sacrifice themselves to serve the unfortunates at the same time cut themselves off from the outside world in living burial." Nevertheless, the Board of Indian Commissioners under the Hoover administration had concluded that the asylum was a "necessary evil."

Ella believed that the appointment of John Collier as commissioner of Indian Affairs was cause for optimism.

President Roosevelt had tapped him for the job based on his reputation as a leading critic of Indian policy. The Silk report had suggested that, barring a major overhaul, the institution ought to be closed and the patients removed. Rumored changes in Indian policy were surely about to materialize.

The South Dakota congressional delegation contended that the asylum was ultimately the responsibility of Congress and that Dr. Hubble's problems had been caused by "employee discontent." Ella added, "I am credited with stirring up same, being unwilling to submit to authority, but now that I am out of the good doctor's thinning hair, that's all supposed to change. I intend to speak to Mr. Collier personally. I urge you to be patient, and above all, be careful."

It was one thing to be careful—a challenge, sometimes, but a manageable one—but being patient was something else. There were days when Rachael was overwhelmed by an oppression she couldn't name. It was a vague feeling of dread, as though the air felt unnaturally still or the wild creatures were behaving strangely. Secrets were troublesome, she decided. Sure passage to paranoia.

Adam's life had become easier since he's assumed the role of a model patient. He followed directions, grunted when he was spoken to, spent most of his waking hours preparing the cornfields for planting, and for that he was allowed to take his meals in the dining room and use the bathroom regularly. He was still locked down at night, and Martin, still presumed to be tubercular, remained secluded.

Without Ella Sims on the lookout, Rachael was, indeed, more cautious, and she begged Adam to follow her example. Dr. Tim's security system was heavily dependent on locks and restraints. At night a single attendant was usually left in charge of both buildings, and unless Rachael was on duty, night rounds were never made.

The first time she woke in the dead of night to find Adam standing over her, she would have given their secret away if he hadn't covered her mouth with his hand, then with his kiss. He swallowed her shock, her protests, her anxieties, everything but her pleasure, which he stoked with a stroking tongue.

Silently she drew him into her arms, moving over to give him half the bed. He kissed her again, then drew back, placing a finger on his lips as he turned to close the window that had given him access. Moonlight cast his lean body in light and shadow as he stripped off his clothes. Naked, he claimed the space she'd offered him in her bed.

"This is dangerous." She snuggled into his embrace and spoke to him softly, her lips moving against his cheek. "You must let me come to you, Adam. You're sure no one saw you?"

His hands slipped smoothly over her satiny nightgown, exploring hills and valleys of flesh far more yielding than his own. "I'm sure of nothing but a need that's so bad it makes me climb walls to get to you."

"That's all you're sure of?" She pushed her fingers through his hair and whispered close to his ear. "I'm sure I love you, Adam."

"We'll talk about that some other time. It makes no sense now." He settled her back, taking her hands from his nape and pinning them on either side of her head, their fingers bound together in a tight weave.

"Love always makes sense," she told him in a voice that might have belonged to a romantic sixteen-year-old. "Or it never does, I'm not sure which."

"Then there are some things you're unsure of, too." He loomed over her, smiling, admiring the way her hair made a silky, starlit pool on the pillow. "That comforts me."

"Why?"

"You seem to have everything right where you want it." He dragged her hand down and tucked it low between their bodies, pressing it over his erect penis. "Whenever you want it, or feel like coming for it, you know it's still there in the hole where you keep it stored."

She closed her eyes. Anticipating some protest, he watched her lips, the lower one pressing up slightly. He felt her hand do the same, but only slightly, and he knew that he had succeeded in hurting her. It was a wonder to him that he had the power to hurt anyone. Guilt pricked him, which was an even greater wonder.

He rolled to his side, sat up, lit a cigarette, and listened to the sound of her breathing, soft as a kitten, behind his back. Forearms braced on his thighs, he took a deep pull on the smoke, tucked his chin, and blew it into the cavity of his belly.

The head of his stubbornly hard cock mocked him. What was he doing? Blessing his tools before he did the job he'd come to do? His resentment of the fact that he wanted her was outstripped by the wanting itself, and that scared him as nothing else, *nothing else* did.

"I'll be ready in a minute," he said, as though her breathing came across the bed as a sound of impatience.

"For what?"

"Whatever you want."

"I don't understand, Adam."

"Yes, you do, woman." He took another long, deep, mean pull on the cigarette, but the smoke wasn't enough to drive the devil away. "Tell me what would excite you to start with. My finger? My tongue? What is your first wish?"

"I wish you wouldn't do this. I didn't ask you to come here tonight."

"I'm not welcome?"

"Welcome or not, you're here because *you* wanted to come."

"I wanted to see if I could still act on my own will." He gave a mordant chuckle. He was looking for pain, and he relished the sting of her words. "I wanted to open the door myself and take an unscheduled walk outside, prove to myself that I could leave this place whenever I wanted to."

His cigarette hissed when he dropped it in the glass of water sitting on her bedside table. He turned to her, touched the side of her neck with apologetic fingertips.

"Or that I could come to you, lie in your bed, be some kind of a man."

She turned her face to his palm, forgiving him with the brush of her lips, then looked up at him anxiously. "If you left here—escaped—where would you go?"

He glanced overhead as he raised a thumb and whispered, "Anybody up there?"

She shook her head. "Operating room."

"I'd go to Paris." He stretched out next to her, leaning back against the headboard. "I would not be taken for a madman in Paris," he said wistfully, tucking his arm behind his head. "If I wanted a bottle of wine, they would sell it to me. If I wanted to sing my grandfather's songs or dance the old way, they would leave me alone, or they might join in." The thought made him smile. "The French have always been friendly to us. Many of our mixed-bloods have French names."

"I've always wanted to go to Paris," she said distantly.

"Then why did you come here?"

"I thought I would be needed here."

"As it turns out, you are." He put his hand on her breast, laying claim. "But this is not what you had in mind, is it?"

On a breath her breast rose and fell while he stroked the satin gown with easy-riding fingertips. "I am breaking every rule, every code of proper professional conduct," she told him. "For a nurse to sleep with her patient . . ."

"I am not your patient. I'm your lover. And as long as I'm here, I'm your prisoner."

"No." She rolled her head from side to side in its pillow nest. "I'm not keeping you here. You could leave any time. We both know that."

She looked at him, and he nodded, confirming the notion for himself as much as for her.

"I'm afraid we're going to get caught, Adam. But I worry more . . ." She tipped her shoulder toward him and laid her cheek against his forearm, avoiding his eyes as she made her confession. "Each time I go to your room at night, just before I open the door, I say a quick prayer that you'll be there.''

''Tied to the bed?''

''No. Don't you know how much I've hated seeing you restrained? From the very first, I . . .''

''Not as much as I hate it.'' He captured her face in one hand, lifting her chin in the crotch of his thumb until their eyes met. ''I suffer your pity, Rachael. It makes me hate you. It makes me hate myself more.''

''Oh, no.'' She shook her head tightly. ''It isn't pity I feel for you, Adam, it's—''

''I *will* be a madman if I stay here much longer. Some of the others have gone that way. They've given in to madness.'' He watched his forefinger wander over her cheek, his thumb trace the line of her jaw, committing every subtle curve in her face to the annals of his memory while he still had one. ''You know that, don't you, Rachael? It's easier that way, to become whatever it is they want you to be.''

''I want you to be a free man. I want you to be whole and healthy and . . . I want you to be my husband.''

''Is that so?'' He smoothed her silky hair back and searched her shadowed face for a glimmer of the impossible. ''Can that truly be so? Would you ask for that kind of trouble, woman?''

''I'm not asking for trouble. I'm asking to spend my life with you. But you've never asked me to be your wife, so I guess it's presumptuous of me to say—''

''I have nothing to offer you.'' He knew what she wanted, what she thought she wanted, and he pushed it from his mind, insisting, ''I have nothing.''

She smiled bravely. ''Like it or not, you have me.''

''I came to you to give you pleasure. That's all I have to offer you.''

Maybe a child. He hoped to give her a child, even though he had no right to. Right and wrong didn't figure in anymore. It was a matter of survival. If he died in this place, he wanted this woman, *this woman* to carry some part of him away.

Even now she carried him away with her loving

touch. "You came for your own pleasure." Her whispered indictment warmed his chest, while her hand skimmed his flat belly. "You said so yourself, that you came to satisfy a need."

"A man's needs. I'm still a man."

"The most remarkable man I've ever met." She sampled the flavor of a remarkable man's broad chest with the tip of her tongue. "I do understand, Adam. I think I would hate me, too, if I were you."

"Only sometimes." He closed his eyes, delighting in the way her taunting tongue made his nipple stiffen.

"Then maybe you could love me sometimes." She slipped her hand between his legs and stroked him lovingly as she slithered down his side. "Let me try to make you love me."

"No." He saw the direction she was taking, and he knew she would unman him with it. "Rachael, no. You don't have to—"

"I know." She kissed the curve of his hipbone. "Do I have to restrain you, or will you let me nurse you?"

"Holy . . . sweet . . . woman, for God's sake . . ."

"No," she whispered as she discovered the most excruciatingly pleasant way to torment him. "No pity. You don't deserve any."

"I'm not . . . asking."

But he suffered only so much before turning the tables of his tongue and his tender touch on her. They filled their senses with one another, consumed each other entirely until they could have sworn they shared one heartbeat. When they'd exhausted each other with pleasure, they clung to the warmth of its embers, despairing of the steadily shifting pattern of starlight.

Reluctantly he gave the signal kiss. "I have to go."

Knowing where he had to go, she clung to him like a young child trying to postpone some inevitable punishment. "Let me talk to my brother, Adam. He's the one who sent you here. If he knew—"

"If he knew, I'd be a dead man. And you—" He drew the sheet up over her breasts, as though protecting her from prying eyes. "What would he say to his little sister?"

"I wouldn't tell him about us, Adam. Not yet."

Not ever, he thought, not if you're smart.

"I would start by telling him that you've made remarkable progress, and that you're ready to be discharged. Generally that's up to the doctor in consultation with the family, but in this case we've got this unusual, sort of a guardian relationship, I guess with the agent being—"

"Rachael." He lifted her chin and made her look at him, even though he wasn't sure she would understand even if he could find words to explain. "This agent, this guardian, this . . . whoever, whatever he is to me, it's something no free man wants or needs. Do you understand? He is no relation to me. He comes from somebody who calls himself my 'great white father,' and has the power to . . ." He shook his head. "But we know what he is to you. He's your brother."

"Which is why I think he might listen."

Again he shook his head, looking into her eyes, realizing that she truly believed what she was saying and that she loved her for her innocence. And that, God help him, he would vie with any man for his share of her trust.

"Your brother and I have not seen eye to eye on certain matters for some time. Indian land, for one thing. Soon there won't be any left. There have been some of our people, like my grandfather, who have warned the others against selling it. Trainor has done nothing to stop these sales. Sometimes he even suggests a buyer."

"I didn't think anyone had any money to buy land."

"There was more money in leasing, and for a while that's what people did. But then everything went dry, everyone went broke. The land just blew away, and the people went hungry. Now they sell it for little or nothing. Usually it's not for money; it's 'for consideration.' Maybe that's a cow. Meat for the winter." His hand stirred over her bare shoulder as he told her his side. He wanted someone to know *his side*. "I started to talk about holding on to the land, said some of the things my grandfather used to say—that we had been cheated out of the Black Hills, and now we'd lose the rest if we didn't watch out. Trainor doesn't like that kind of talk because he says we need to move on. And I say, move on *where*? And round and round it goes.''

"But that's not why you're here."

"I'm not saying it is. I'm just telling you not to speak to anyone about me, not even your brother. I have something to say to him, but I will speak for myself.''

"You once said something about trading your land,'' she reminded him. "But surely you don't think that you're being held . . . for ransom.''

"I don't know what I'm being held for, but if that's what it takes to . . .'' To appease the monster, he thought. To appease its insatiable appetite.

He remembered when his grandfather had compared the appetite of a legendary river monster to the white man's appetite for land. The difference was that as far back as the people could remember, the river monster had been satisfied with a reasonable offering. The *wan-agi*, too, those restless spirits, they would take their scrap of a man's kill and leave him in peace. All things had a place. All things claimed a share. It had been that way as far back as his people could remember.

Until her people had come, he thought, watching his hand pass over her shoulder like a shadow on the moon.

How could he love her?

He had befriended her, and what had she done? She'd stolen from him, as was the way of her people. She'd stolen his thoughts. Any time of day or night, it didn't seem to matter, she could steal into his head and take his mind off the worst circumstances imaginable. She had even taken his pain away, suffocated his anger a time or two. She had wrested his hard-earned hopelessness from him, as was the way of . . . a good woman. And she was a good woman.

How could he not love her?

He closed his eyes and rested his head back against the headboard.

She hugged him hard and uttered the most reassuring words she had at her disposal. "It'll work out. Edward can be terribly pigheaded, but he's an honest man."

And he's your brother.

"All I know is, I have to get my own brother out of here some way."

"We're going to get this Mr. Collier to help us. We're going to—" She looked up at him, her face full of infectious female expectancy. "I'm going to write to him. If I have to, I'll go to Washington myself."

"He works for the Indian Service, doesn't he?"

"He's the new commissioner."

"From what I've seen, one's about as bad as the next."

"You mean, like my brother."

He sighed. "I'm not talking against your damn brother."

"Ella thinks there's going to be another investigation, straight from the top this time. Dr. Tim simply isn't doing the job here."

Whatever that was, he thought. "If they get rid of him, will they let us go home? Or will they send someone else?"

"I think they'll have to do a complete evaluation of all the patients here. And that will turn up some very interesting findings. For one thing, they won't be guessing about who might be tubercular. There is not one sputum test that I can find recorded in any of the files."

He didn't know much about records and tests, but he knew tuberculosis. It had ravaged his people over the years. The answer for it—like the answer for everything—was always *take them away.*

"That's why my brother is kept apart from everyone else, isn't it?"

"Not completely," she said. "The other patients whom he *calls* tubercular are housed in their own section of the hospital building. Their dishes are not washed with the others. They're washed"—she sighed, troubled—"in the bathroom. But Pagla stays in the main building, and no one makes a fuss over his dishes or anything. And, really, he shows no symptoms that I can see. Not that I'm qualified to make that determination. I'm not a doctor.''

"We Lakota did well for a very long time without doctors to make these determinations for us.'' He gestured, indicating the structure surrounding them. "Without agents and schools and places like this. We did very well until they started hounding us for the land.

"Rachael . . .'' He looked into her eyes—not the eyes of a white woman, but the eyes of *his* woman—and he trusted her with his fear. "Rachael, if I give them what they want, I am left with no place to go. That's why they put me here. They'll bury me out there with my grandfather.''

"No.'' She touched his cheek and smoothed his hair back at his temple. "They won't, Adam. There are people who have more to say about this than Dr. Tim or my brother. People who will listen to Ella and me and . . .''

"And me?'' His humorless laugh rumbled deep in his chest. "Two women who are not doctors and one alcoholic Indian prisoner. Ah, Rachael . . .''

"They will listen. They have to. We have to give this Mr. Collier a little time to establish his authority. He was *just* appointed, just a couple of—'' She broke off with the talk of time out of respect for the kind of time she was asking him to give. Hard time. Humiliating time. Time spent in exile. "For the sake of all the patients here, Adam. Just a little more patience.''

"How much? There isn't much left of me. Look what's left of Martin. Look at the others. *Look at me.*'' And he forced her to, for he needed to see himself in her eyes. "There's not much here for you to love.''

"That's not true. There's so much.'' She looked deep into his eyes, seeing with her heart. "So much.''

"Hold on to it then. It's up to you.'' Unable to bear her scrutiny any longer, he pressed her head to his shoulder and held her fiercely. "You're the only one who sees it.''

"You're my secret," she claimed. "My big, beautiful, wonderful secret."

"And you are my only ally."

Spring turned all too quickly into summer, and the south winds took their toll on the dry land. The asylum's thick-walled brick buildings protected its residents' bodies from the hot, stinging, soil-laden wind, but not their ears, and not their minds. Relentless winds made for long, dull, cooped-up afternoons. It was too hot to keep the windows closed, so the staff hung wet linens over the openings to stop the blowing dirt, tying the corners down so that they puffed up like sails.

Nightfall brought relief from the wind and sometimes from the heat. Patients who'd slept during the day were restless at night, but the schedule did not change. It reminded Rachael of the Robert Louis Stevenson poem "Bed in Summer." But those were the lamentations of a child, and Hiawatha was the bane of a collection of miserable people of all ages who lay abed waiting for sunset, then waiting for dawn.

Adam was one of the lucky ones. Long hours of work during the day at the farm helped him to sleep at night, and his basement cell was cool. The attendants seldom bothered him except to take him out of his cave in the morning and lock him down at night. He and Rachael visited each other regularly, and occasionally when the nearsighted and slow-moving attendant Mrs. Williams was on night duty Rachael sneaked him in to visit his brother.

It was all becoming almost too easy.

Late one sultry night Rachael was about to check on Martin when she heard a noise in the bathroom at the end of the hall. The lights were out, and the patients had been locked in their rooms for the night. She hadn't gotten that particular routine changed yet, but she thought she'd finally persuaded the attendants to stop locking "noisy" patients, bound in restraints, in the bathroom at night. If she found poor Margaret Broken

Thumb, who was epileptic, put to bed on the bathroom floor one more time . . .

"Be quiet," someone hissed in the dark. "I'm trying to clean you up."

The voice was not Margaret's, nor was the anguished, barely audible response she heard. Rachael had never known Dr. Tim to visit the asylum at night unless he was summoned for an emergency, but the voice surely sounded like his. The door was ajar, and it appeared to be dark in the room. Rachael approached cautiously.

"I take very good care of you because you're my special one. Don't you realize that? Why do you look at me that way? Don't you love me, Martin? Don't you love your Dr. Tim?"

Martin?

Rachael pushed the door open. Her lantern, carried low at her side, cast its soft yellow glow across the linoleum floor. Martin stood to the side of the big slop sink with his head bowed, eyes closed, looking almost like a sleepwalker. His arms were restrained in a camisole, but he was naked from the waist down. Dr. Tim stood behind him. Rachael could see a towel, and it looked as though the doctor was wearing his bathrobe.

Awkward. Strange. Rachael's brain recoiled from pursuing her impressions to a conclusion as the doctor looked up, then froze.

"Miss Trainor." He glanced behind her, then cleared his throat nervously. He did not move. "This boy befouled himself, and there was no one readily available to do this nasty job."

"Do you need"—she glanced at Martin, who seemed totally lifeless, mentally removed—"help, Doctor?"

"I would not, certainly, ask a woman to attend to this. Our Martin is not a boy anymore. He's a young man, aren't you, Martin?" He waved her away with a snap of the towel. "I'll finish up here. You go about your—"

"Uh-oh."

Rachael jumped at the sound of the voice. She turned. Dick Hollings had crept up behind her.

"Sorry, Doctor," he announced. "I was just over in—"

"Hollings, get in here and, uh . . ." Hubble glanced at Rachael, but still he didn't move from his shadowy post behind Martin. Instead, the man who rarely explained himself began to chatter nervously. "Hollings sent for me because . . . the boy was quite agitated. Hollings couldn't, uh . . . couldn't find you, he said. But that's fine, that's fine. Our staff . . . it's hard to cover so much . . . much territory, much . . ." He scowled. "Hollings!"

"I think I heard somebody bawlin' over in the hospital building, Miss Trainor," Hollings said as he shouldered past her. "These hot nights, everybody's restless."

Rachael backed away, heading for the other building. Even though her immediate thoughts were unthinkable, they refused to be rejected completely. She told herself not to jump to any conclusions, but the question kept creeping back into the forefront of her mind, seeping back, like the blood of the innocent.

Alice's blood, her baby's blood. What was going on? *What was going on?*

It happens sometimes, she'd said. The women are so vulnerable, so easily used. Employees come and go. But the doctor? The man in charge?

Unthinkable. Martin was, as Dr. Tim had said, a young man. But a vulnerable young man.

A vulnerable *man*? Those were terms she rarely put together in the same sentence. Alice, her infant . . . and Martin?

An hour later she went to Martin's room. He was sitting up in his bed, wearing the camisole device with a pair of pajama pants. His face was bathed in sweat.

"Pagla," she whispered as she untied the blind arms of the camisole.

He refused to look at her, refused to look at anything but the bare wall.

"I'm sorry. I didn't mean to barge in during your . . . your bath, but I really didn't see—" Don't insult him by lying, she told herself. "I mean, I didn't look. I respect . . . your modesty."

He allowed her to remove the camisole, but he ducked away when she tried to touch his face. She sat quietly for a moment, marking the tremor in his every ragged breath.

Respecting what little privacy he had left, she avoided looking at him when she asked gently, "Are you hurt, Pagla?"

He twisted his hands together between his knees.

"It's all right to tell me," she assured him. "I won't hurt you. I won't touch you unless you want me to, but I want to help you. Do you want me to . . ." She glanced up and saw the tears gathering in his eyes. "If you could tell me . . ."

He grabbed both of her hands and squeezed them hard as he struggled to make her understand. "Not . . . hurt." He shook his head vigorously. "Not see. Not . . ." He tapped his chest with a trembling hand. "Not see."

"No. I didn't see. I didn't look; that would be rude." Because it was the only part of him he seemed willing to share with her, she clasped his hand between hers. "I'm sorry, Pagla. If Adam—"

"*Hiya*. No." He shook his head, searching for words, grappling with the need to speak. "Not Adam. Please. *Please*. Not tell."

"He wouldn't be angry with you, Pagla. He would be angry with . . ."

"Not see." He closed his eyes tightly, sending two tears on a path down his face. "Not see. Please."

"All right." She touched his wet cheek. He stiffened, but he didn't pull away. "All right, Pagla."

He opened his eyes. "Not tell?"

"I won't tell Adam." She shook her head as she wiped his tears with her fingertips. "I'll keep your secret, Pagla. Not see. Not tell."

She avoided the back stairs as she left the building. If she went to Adam now, he would know something was wrong, and she would be hard-pressed to keep this from him. There was no telling what he would do if he knew. She had to find a way to free them both—to free them all from chains and locks and secret lives.

Her head was dizzy with secrets, some sad, some cruel, but one unequivocally cherished. She couldn't tell Adam yet. She desperately wanted to share the joy of it, but not the fears.

Funny that there should be fear involved with such a beautiful secret. Such a tiny secret, capable of making her head spin and her stomach churn while it spun a silver web of hope deep in her womb.

Adam was admitted to Hubble's office while the noon meal was being served in the dining room. He clutched the felt hat they'd given him to wear in the sun. The back of his neck itched from sweat and grit, but he didn't move. Didn't twitch. He just stood there, waiting for the good doctor to acknowledge him so that he could say what he'd come to say. He was sure the balding little son of a bitch was purposely taking his time thumbing through his file drawer just to make him squirm. But he wasn't squirming.

"Mr. Brothers tells me that you're working out very well on the farm." Hubble closed the file drawer and swiveled his chair toward the big oak desk. "And now that you have regained some control, I hope to move you upstairs as soon as we have a vacant bed. Would you like that, Adam?" He peered over his reading glasses and forced a smile. "A room with a window, perhaps a roommate or two?"

"I would like to stay in the room with my brother."

"I'm afraid that's not possible at the present time. We're taking very good care of Martin, but he needs to be by himself." Hubble tapped his fingertips, one at a time, on the file he'd laid on the desk. "Now what can I do for you? Mr. Brothers said that you wanted to talk to me about some concerns you have over your property back home. There's something you want Agent Trainor to take care of for you?"

Adam cleared his throat and fixed his stare on the bookshelf several feet above Hubble's head. "There's some land that some of us might want to sell. Some of us Lone Bulls. If I could get out of here, I could talk to my mother, my uncle, a couple of other relations. Martin owns a piece of it, too. And I . . . wouldn't talk against some of the other neighbors selling if they want to.'' His casual shrug camouflaged the long, deep breath he required to calm himself inside and maintain his nearly expressionless tone. ''Like I was before. You know, I'd get drunk and talk against some of those white guys who bought up some of the land. But, hell, it's like they say. Might as well sell it to somebody who has some use for it.'' He swallowed hard, nearly grimacing over the bitter taste of bile. All he needed was something to eat, he told himself. ''So if I could get out of here . . .''

''Just you?''

''Me and my brother.''

''Your brother's quite ill.''

''I can take care of him.'' He could feel the way Hubble was studying him, judging him. For what, he didn't know. He pressed on, speaking softly, being as self-effacing as he could manage. ''Like you say, I've gotten control of myself now. Learned my lesson.''

''I see.'' Hubble tapped his fingers again, more slowly this time. ''I expect to meet with Ed Trainor very soon. I'll pass these concerns on to him.''

Adam nodded.

''You'd rather have your brother stay here in Canton than see him shipped off to Washington D.C., wouldn't you?''

''Why would he have to be shipped—''

''Well, I don't know, but that's the scuttlebutt.'' The chair squeaked as Hubble leaned back. ''However, you can count on Dr. Tim to oppose any such attempt.''

''You mean, they wouldn't just close the place down and let us all go home?''

''Let you all go home?'' Hubble chuckled. ''Where would you be without Dr. Tim? I'll tell you where you'd be, most of you. On a train to the East Coast, my friend, and that means you, too.''

Adam looked at him now, and Hubble smiled readily

this time. "That's right, you, too. But I don't intend to let that happen. The people of Canton . . ." The words gave him pause, a thought, and he repeated them more slowly, just to hear them again. "*The people of Canton. A delegation. Yes, indeed, a citizens' delegation.*"

"Trainor can stop this. Some of these guys here aren't, uh . . ." Adam clamped his jaw when Hubble shot him a warning glance. He could feel the who's-the-doctor-here routine coming on, and he didn't think he could stomach it. "Just tell Trainor he can have whatever he wants."

"Yes, yes, we can use his help, too. Citizens' delegation." Hubble snatched a pencil from a cup and made a note on a pad of lined paper. "You and Martin have a mother still living, is that correct?"

"Our mother's been staying with her sister."

"Ed would know how to find her, wouldn't he?" He made more notes. "A delegation from Canton, plus some Indians. Family members, yes. We'll get Ed here, have him bring your mother along, and we shall see." He tossed the pencil aside and looked up, his smile actually reaching his eyes. "So how about that room with a window, Mr. Lone Bull? I could move you upstairs.

"I like to keep to myself," Adam said quietly. "I get mad sometimes when I'm around other people too much. Their habits agitate me." It was a word he'd heard staff members use. They liked to fret over "agitated" patients.

"We don't want that, do we? We want you to be able to go outside and work with the animals. Mr. Brothers says you're very good with the horses." He gestured impatiently toward the door. "Go get your dinner, Lone Bull. You let Dr. Tim take care of all the rest."

When Edward Trainor came to Canton in August he brought Beatrice Lone Bull with him. He told her that some people in the government wanted to move her sons, along with the rest of the patients at the Canton asylum, to Washington D.C. If that happened, he warned, she would probably never see them again. Beatrice pointed out that she had not seen either of them since they had been taken away.

Dr. Tim took her to Martin's room, where she met Rachael, whom Trainor described as "the best nurse in the business." It seemed to please Beatrice to learn that the agent's own sister was tending her son. Dr. Tim explained that since the boy had been kept apart from the other patients and under his care, Martin had not suffered the symptoms of active tuberculosis.

Beatrice asked Martin several questions in Lakota— whether he thought he was sick, whether he wanted to stay in this hospital, whether he wanted to go to a different one. Martin did not speak to his mother in the doctor's presence and he did not see her outside his presence.

"You don't want him to go Washington and never come back, do you?" Dr. Tim asked as the group, minus Martin, returned to his office.

Martin was apparently lost to the woman, but at least now she knew where he was staying. She shook her head.

The thinly veiled threat made Rachael's skin crawl. She wasn't sure why she'd been included in this little meeting, although she was pleased to make Beatrice's acquaintance. The handsome, statuesque woman with jet black hair and deep-set eyes must have been a very young woman when she bore her older son, who looked more like her than the younger one did. Rachael longed to take Beatrice aside and speak to her alone, if only she could think of a way.

"Both of your sons are doing quite well with us," Dr. Tim was saying. "Isn't that so, Nurse Trainor?"

"Yes, Doctor," she heard herself obediently attest.

"And we'd hate to lose either of them, Mrs. Lone Bull," the doctor said.

Rachael turned to the window and watched the wind toy with the swings in the yard. She didn't want to be part of this, so she distanced herself by imagining herself on the swing while she listened. The two men took turns with their thinly veiled threats and sickening sugges-

tions. Back and forth went the voices. Back and forth
went Rachael's mind, battered by wind. Toes pointed
up, toes pointed back, pumping hard and getting nowhere.

"Now, the people of Canton are our friends—friends
of the Indian, friends of this hospital," Dr. Tim claimed.
"Some of them are going to Washington to speak to the
commissioner about keeping our patients here. They're
going to speak up for your sons."

"Led by the president of the Canton Chamber of
Commerce, from what I've heard," Edward added.

"That's right, the president himself," Dr. Tim said.
"I can't be involved personally, of course. I'm a federal
employee."

"Neither can I."

"But *you* can take part, Mrs. Lone Bull, as a private
citizen and the mother of two of our patients." Dr. Tim's
chair squeaked. "Now, in order to get anywhere with
this effort, someone has to petition the court. A lawyer
must be hired, a competent attorney. The lawyer will try
to secure what's called an injunction against removing
the patients. Lawyers cost money, and, of course, nobody around here has any money. They're having a heck
of a time raising the money to send four people to Washington to meet with the commissioner."

"As it happens, Beatrice, there is a buyer who's interested in your land," Edward said.

Rachael closed her eyes, wishing the motion would
stop now. She could always drag her feet. If she had
any nerve, she could bail out. She knew now where this
was going. Back and forth, back and forth.

"My land is on the Rosebud Reservation."

"Well, Butch is interested in that, too. But, you know,
your sons are not mentally competent, and they both
have land at Pine Ridge," Edward said. "And Butch
Hausauer's done all right for himself lately, what with
some sidelines he's gotten into since the cattle market
went to hell. Some fellas are bound and determined to
wait out the drought. I tell you, as worthless as some of
that country is out there, I 'spose a fella like Butch fig-

ures if he buys up enough of it, eventually he'll be able to catch up with his topsoil."

The joke amused Edward and Dr. Tim enormously. Rachael wanted to cry. She wanted to throw herself at Mrs. Lone Bull's feet and beg forgiveness for herself, her brother, the Indian Service, and the entire medical profession. But there were two men in the room who had the power to strip her of what little authority she had in this institution and restrict her access to its patients. It was a consequence she could not afford to risk.

"So Mr. Hausauer is willing to arrange for legal services for your son in return for patent fee reservation land that you have no use for anyway," Edward continued. "Nobody's buying these days, nobody's leasing. So it's a good deal, Beatrice. You'll have a lawyer who will represent your son, petition the court to stop the government from taking him out of South Dakota, taking him so far away that he'd never . . ."

"And the weather there would be very bad for his lungs, Mrs. Lone Bull," Dr. Tim said. "Probably kill him."

"What about my other son?"

Dr. Tim sighed heavily. "Well, you know, he's not as peaceful as Martin is."

"Drank himself crazy," Edward said. "You know that, don't you, Beatrice? Just like your husband did."

"But we can try to keep him here, too," Dr. Tim offered. "You might have trouble with him if he ever went back home."

"Never had no trouble with him."

"You've been staying with your sister lately. I don't think you know just how bad he got." Edward was filling his pipe. Rachael didn't have to look. She could smell the Prince Albert tobacco, and she closed her eyes to recall that once in another land, another life, her big brother had permitted her to light his pipe for him with a match from the box over the fireplace. "I always thought highly of Adam," he was saying, sounding completely sincere. "Hated to send him to prison, so I decided to put him here."

"And we don't want to send Adam away, either," Dr. Tim told the woman. "He's doing well here. When he behaves himself, we let him work with the horses we have here. That usually keeps him happy."

Back and forth, back and forth. Beatrice Lone Bull finally agreed to trade land for the services of a lawyer. Edward Trainor said that he would make the arrangements.

The air was hot and heavy that night, closing in on Rachael like a thick net. It was a relief to sink into subterranean coolness as she descended the steps on her way to Adam's room—the first inkling of relief since she'd left Hubble's office. Adam was right. She was his only ally. And perhaps, as her heart's mate, he was her only true kin. She'd had a brother once. "I know my brother," she'd told Adam. Well, she did now, and he bore no resemblance to the man their father had raised. Edward had his faults, she'd said, but he was nothing if not honest.

He was nothing. Nothing to her, anyway. She was still reeling from the gut-level shock of it, but most of the pieces were fitting together quite readily in her brain. The question was, What to do now? It was Adam and Rachael against . . . everyone else?

Everyone *here,* she amended, except the patients.

She trusted Ella.

Two women and one supposedly demented Indian man.

Oh, God, where was the sanity in this world?

Rachael set her lantern down by the door and quietly sorted through her keys. Too many secrets, she told herself. The secrets were killing her. She'd been counting on Ella to locate an ear that was open to truth—preferably an ear attached to a powerful head. But it was taking too long, and the secrets would not keep much longer.

"Making your rounds, Miss Trainor?"

Rachael's keys hit the floor. Dr. Tim stepped out of

the shadows with his hulking henchman, John Gatewood.

"Our patient is sleeping now." The doctor bent over
to pick up the keys. "He's had a long, hard day. I think
you ought to let the man rest."

"It's my duty to check on all the patients, Doctor."
Her throat was suddenly so constricted she nearly
choked on the words.

"Indeed. One of the reasons I've had little use for
nurses is that they can't seem to get it through their
simple little female heads that their duty is what I say it
is. We did fine without a nursing staff, didn't we, Gatewood?"

"We sure did."

"An unnecessary expense, I told them, but the Indian
Service insisted, and so here you are." He dangled the
ring of keys as he eyed her pointedly. "And while I
have no problem with your clandestine liaison—Heaven
knows we all need some diversion here in this god-
forsaken desert—I suspect your brother would be
shocked if he knew what I know about his little sister."

"I was—" Her quick gesture was simply a reflex, as
was her lie. "I heard a noise."

"Well, yes, so did I." He caught her hand, smiled,
and dropped her keys into her palm. "I've heard a lot
of noise about the conditions here at the hospital. Your
friend Ella Sims is making some noise, I believe. So is
John Collier and that meddling Silk who was out here a
few years back nosing around." He folded her fingers
around the keys. "I can make noise, too, Miss Trainor."

"I truly wanted to make this a better place," she told
him, risking a quick glance at Gatewood, Hubble's
shadow, who was leaning against the wall. "Cleaner,
more efficient, more effective. That's really all I intended . . . to do."

"Yes, that's very touching." Hubble chuckled. Gatewood provided a dutiful echo. "I don't know whether
you're using Lone Bull or whether he, knowing who
your brother is, thought he could use you. Maybe you're

using each other. Love works in mysterious ways, doesn't it?''

Rachael squared her shoulders as she pocketed her keys. ''What do you want from me, Doctor? I have no land.''

''I know you understand that it's incumbent upon us all to keep each other's secrets.'' He lifted his brow, staring at her, allowing the inference time to take root. ''They're sending Silk back here. I just received a copy of his letter of reintroduction, this time from Commissioner Collier. In the meantime, we have a court hearing set for October. We have a delegation of concerned local citizens waiting in Collier's outer offices at this very moment.''

''What is Dr. Silk's assignment?''

''He thinks he's going to remove my patients.'' Hubble smiled. ''*Our* patients, Miss Trainor. When Silk gets here tomorrow, you will want to be very careful what you say. I might be inclined to release that strapping young buck in there. But if I decide to sterilize him first, he won't really be a buck anymore, will he?''

''*Sterilize* him?''

''As you well know, Nurse Trainor, sterilization is standard procedure for the feebleminded.''

❖ 13 ❖

Late spring 1973

Cedric Kills Crow was obviously nervous about the meeting, even though it was his idea. He'd gotten in touch with Zane through Marla and said it was *really* important, but he wasn't too hot on driving all the way to Standing Rock on the northern state line, nor did he want Zane's pickup parked in front of his mother's grocery store on the Rosebud Reservation, hugging the southern state line. "Too risky," was the reason he gave. The halfway point was Pierre, where Cedric occasionally did research in the State Archives, and where neither of them would be likely to run into anyone who would recognize him.

Zane thought the whole plan was typical of Cedric. Big buildup, small substance. Which was why Cedric's revelation, fired across the table in a busy truck-stop café, surprised him.

"I saw Randy the night he was killed."

Zane's brow went up, coffee mug went down. "Where?"

"I met up with him at a bar in Mobridge." Cedric planted his elbows on the table and slouched forward, his head dipping into the trough between his shoulders. "I was headed up to the BIA office in Fort Yates, so I didn't stay long, but I had some information for him about something we'd been working on together. He'd

272

been down to see me just a couple days before that."

"When he went down to Pine Ridge," Zane recalled.

"Right. Well, he came to see me over in Rosebud first, then went to Pine Ridge. We were doing some digging around in the agency records in both places, trying to track down the history of some land sales. We'd been working on it for a while. I don't know if he told you."

"He said something about it, yeah." Zane wished he'd listened, not to involve himself with the issue so much, but just because he'd never have another chance, just to listen.

"I think we were on to something, Z. See, I've been working on utility easements and mineral rights, and I got Randy interested in this idea that we could be challenging the titles on some of the allotted land that was supposedly sold back before the Reorganization Act was passed in thirty-four."

"Kinda like chasing the wind, isn't it?"

"People challenge land titles in court all the time. You wouldn't believe how often you can find some kind of irregularity. Heirs nobody knew about. Heirs that just plain got screwed. Stuff like that. If nothing else, it can tie up a land sale for a while." Cedric's enthusiasm for the possibility glowed in his eyes like polished jet. "We gotta know the law, Z. We gotta learn to use it to our advantage."

"So you were giving my brother lessons." Zane glanced past the younger man, feigning impatience, knowing damn well he could intimidate him with a show of disgust. Pushing it off onto Cedric was one way to avoid the disgust he *knew damn well* he was really only feeling for himself.

Worse, he envied Cedric Randy's final investment of trust, even took a stab at denying it.

"I've heard a list of names of guys who saw him that night, and you weren't one of them."

"Like I said, I wasn't there very long. I had come across some more stuff after he left, and I was on my way through his stomping grounds, anyway, so I tracked him down. Wasn't too hard.''

"What time of night was that?"

"It wasn't too late. I didn't stick around. Like I said, I had copied down some information I found on some abstracts down in the Todd County records.'' The Rosebud Reservation, which made up virtually all of Todd County, was Cedric's home. He gave Zane a sympathetic look, inviting him to claim his own connections. "Abstracts with your grandmother's name on them."

Zane shrugged. "I figured she must have sold some land somewhere along the line since she doesn't get any lease money."

"Yeah, but aren't you a little bit curious about the circumstances?" Undaunted by the lack of a response, Cedric leaned closer. "She sold out back in 1933 for one dollar and consideration."

"*A dollar?* How much land?"

"Two sections."

"Jesus Christ." Zane tried not to sound too annoyed. After all, it was no real surprise. "What was the *consideration*?"

"That's not in the records. Probably depended on how hungry she was."

"So what good does it do anybody to dig all this up now?"

"The idea was to find out who bought the land, which I did. And since then, I also found out who bought your uncle Martin's land in Jackson County. It was the same guy and for the same price. And he still owns it. That and a whole bunch more." Cedric lowered his voice. "The guy's name is William Hausauer."

Zane's eyes widened appreciably. Couldn't help it. He hadn't expected to recognize the name.

"You know him?" Cedric asked.

"I've done some work for his son. They've got a place down in Rapid."

"They've got land in five counties down in the southern part of the state. And guess which counties." Cedric nodded, pleased that guesses were unnecessary. "In and around Rosebud and Pine Ridge."

"Butch is an old man. He's turned the reins over to Bill Jr., his asshole son. Drugstore cowboy who's—" Zane paused, a disconnected recollection suddenly coupling in his brain. "Butch said something about Bill trying to sell the land. Said he started out with a spread down around Pine Ridge and Rosebud, but his son was more interested in land deals and mineral rights than"— Zane's eyes connected with the gratified look in Cedric's—"livestock."

"There's a lot of interest in South Dakota real estate these days. A lot of deep pockets looking to invest, people from out of state, even foreigners. There's Middle Eastern oil money looking for a piece of the American Dream."

"Land ol' Butch bought off Unci for a buck."

"*And* consideration," Cedric reminded him pointedly. "Kinda makes you wonder, doesn't it?"

It did, he had to admit. "Was this what you had my brother wondering about that night?"

"I didn't have him wondering. *He* had *me* wondering, so I checked it out. And he was so hot to show this stuff to you, I thought he was gonna piss his pants."

"Show me what?"

"I told you, I copied all the information off the abstracts. Names, dates." Cedric reached into the black vinyl briefcase next to him on the booth bench and slapped an army green file folder on the table. "This is the stuff I got on your uncle's sale. I didn't know about this one when I talked to Randy, but I was thinking about it after that blind-eyes, no-ears FBI agent questioned me—"

"What did you tell Flynn?"

"I told him I met up with Randy in this bar up in Mobridge. I didn't tell him all this stuff about the abstracts, but I did tell him that Randy kinda got into it with a couple of white guys when he started talking kinda loud about getting the land back. Then they started in about AIM raisin' hell down at Wounded Knee. And

you know Randy.'' Cedric's enthusiasm drooped. ''I
mean, how he *used* to be. He had a mouth on him, but
no muscle to back it up.''

Zane simply stared, lacking the heart to laugh or to
say *you should talk, kid,* which was what ran through
his head. ''You told Flynn about this?''

''Yeah. He asked me to describe the two white guys.
I told him they all look alike to me.''

Now he had to smile. ''What kind of a lawyer are you
gonna make, Cedric? You can't even be a witness.''

''Flynn's not looking for any white guys. He's bound
and determined that Randy was on the outs with AIM,
so they did him in. Like we've got some kind of Indian
mafia going.'' Then, sheepishly, he added, ''Or you,
maybe. He asked me a whole shitload of questions about
you.''

Zane's stomach tightened. ''Real bloodhound, huh?''

''The thing is, Z . . .'' Cedric's hand flopped open on
the table. ''After Randy died, I kinda let his project slide.
Or tried to. It kept bothering at me, bothering at me. I
got to thinking about those notes I gave him that night.
They looked just like this.''

From the folder Cedric produced a yellow sheet of
blue-lined paper with names, dates, and land described
in numerical and directional terms with hard, deliberate
strokes of a soft pencil. ''Handwritten, same kind of paper. Only this information is from Jackson County. I
gave Randy some stuff on your grandma's land in Todd
County. He stuck the paper in his pocket, like so.'' He
slipped four fingers into his shirt pocket. ''Must've been
right there when they, uh . . . I mean, he just shoved it
in his pocket and left it there, as far as I know. Did
anybody ever say anything, ask you about some notes
in his pocket?''

Zane shook his head.

''You never got them back with his effects?''

''We didn't get much back. No clothes. We burned
everything we . . .'' Zane snatched the paper off the table
and scanned it. He remembered Michelle's letter, written
on fine blue stationery. ''Flynn showed me some papers

he found in the pickup, but nothing like this. I think he would have asked me about it.''

Cedric cocked a finger at his written work. "Randy didn't lose that stuff. He was too anxious to show it to you.''

"You think somebody took it off him?''

"I don't know." Cedric glanced away, his Adam's apple bobbing twice in his scrawny neck as he swallowed. "I don't know.''

Zane leaned back, cradling his cooling coffee mug between his hands. "So ol' Butch Hausauer bought Uncle Martin's land. Wonder what Uncle had to say about that sale.''

"See, that's it," Cedric crooned, heartened by Zane's willingness to ruminate over his findings. "Back in 1933 he would have been just a kid, right?''

"He would have been locked away." Zane eyed the younger man, enduring the twist in his gut that came with permitting the eager glow in Cedric's eyes to remind him of Randy. "You ever heard about that insane asylum they had for Indians in Canton back then?''

"Seems like I heard something about people getting sent to Canton. One of those better-watch-out places.''

"They closed it down back in the thirties, but Uncle Martin was there." Zane reached across the table and tapped his finger on the lined paper. "Right about this time.''

"So he wasn't competent to sell his land," Cedric concluded, scanning his own notes. "That's important—that he was incompetent. Was this land inherited from his dad's side?''

"Would have been, yeah. His dad was dead by then, and he from Pine Ridge. Unci and Auntie Cecilia are from Rosebud.''

"The agents had a lot of control over stuff like this back then. I'll have to do some more checking, find out who the agent was at Pine Ridge.''

"What for?''

"I don't know. Find out what he was like. I've got this theory, see. Back in the early nineteen hundreds they

finally got around to parceling out the reservation land
into the allotments, about a dozen years after they
rammed the Dawes Act down our throats so they could
dole out the 'surplus' land to homesteaders.

"So our people had their allotments, most of them
kind of together in family groups, and there was supposed to be a twenty-five-year trust period so people
could sort of adjust to the idea of individual ownership.
But then they passed the Burke Act in 1906—named for
this South Dakota congressman who was all in a sweat
to open up even more Indian land for white settlement—
and that pretty much kicked that twenty-five-year trust
period in the head. If the Secretary of the Interior or his
commissioners declared an Indian land owner 'competent,' he got what they call a fee patent—that's a land
title," Cedric explained patiently, "and he could sell his
land, which they did in droves.

"What they did, these so-called competency commis-
sions came out to the rez and held these big ceremonies,
big feeds, making off like it was some kind of an honor
to get your fee patent. And then, of course, the buyers
were all ready with their little bit of money or their trade
goods.

"So now, while Congress was grabbing up about five
million acres of our land—I'm talking all six Western
Sioux reservations, now—through these 'surplus' land
statutes, a lot of individual allotments were bought up
by white settlers, from about nineteen-ten on up to
nineteen-thirty-four, when the Reorganization Act made
it next to impossible to sell the land." Cedric's hands
measured the passage of time as he told his story. "Hell,
we might have lost it all except for the stubborn traditional Indians who held out against selling. See, the traditionals, they were still protesting the Dawes Act and the
taking of the Black Hills. Way back in the twenties, they
started writing petitions, hiring lawyers, and they never
gave up. Still haven't. But in that time, that twenty-five
years, we lost even more land."

"Sold it," Zane clarified. But he was listening. And

he was doing his damnedest to remember that this was all just hard, cold history.

"Yeah, sold it, for 'one dollar and consideration.' So my theory is, you had some collusion going with these land sales, maybe with the agents. Perfect opportunity for kickbacks. Just like, back in the early reservation days, you had the so-called Indian rings with the government procurement agents and the Indian agents and the cattlemen running paper deals on beef while the people were going hungry.

"You always hear people talk about what a shame it was at Wounded Knee or Sand Creek, killing women and babies, but nobody talks about what happened after that, you know? You ask most white people what happened to the Indians after nineteen-hundred. They don't know." Cedric sat up tall, his insight enhancing his physical stature. He hammered his left palm with the edge of his right hand. "They kept on stealing our land, Z. That's what happened. But it wasn't the spoils of war. They can't say that. It was more like, you put the prisoners in a camp, and you hold them down, and it's open season on whatever they've got left."

"Jesus, Cedric." This was the part he didn't want to hear.

"I'm not talking about some distant ancestors, Z. I'm talking about your grandmother and your uncle."

"Shit." He had the pieces in his hands, and he knew it wasn't going to take much. They were going to fit together somehow. "You're talking about my brother, Cedric. You're talking about Randy."

"You mean, because he left something unfinished." Cedric paused, then asserted quietly, "He won't leave you alone about it, will he?"

"Randy's dead, Cedric. It's not him."

"It's not?" Cedric slapped his hand on the yellow paper. "I felt like dropping this. I don't know why, but it scares the hell out of me. I wanted to just drop it, and I couldn't."

"Flynn's not gonna do anything."

"I know."

"And I'm a convicted felon. I can't even own a gun."

"I know." But he wouldn't give up. "All he was after was the truth. Find out what really happened and let it be known. If we could make a case and take it to court, even if we lost, at least we spoke out."

Zane said nothing. His temples were pounding.

"You know . . . *you know* there's something wrong when a guy like your uncle gets a dollar for nearly two sections of land, even back then."

"And consideration," Zane repeated tonelessly.

"Consideration?" Cedric leaned closer. "For who, Z?"

Zane blew a heavy sigh. There was only one word for it. "Shit."

Peter Worthington was not the kind of man Zane wanted to spend Saturday night with, but Rapid was only a two-and-a-half hour drive from Pierre. In the course of relaying his messages Marla had talked Zane into letting her set up a dinner meeting with her rich friend from Albuquerque. She'd piqued his interest when she'd mentioned that Worthington's appreciation for Indian art and jewelry had grown out of a lifelong fascination with the West, complete with the dream of owning his piece of it. He was willing to pay handsomely for a chunk of South Dakota.

He said as much over a plate of ribeye steak at the Cattleman's Grill.

Zane wondered offhandedly whether he'd done any serious shopping.

"Actually, I have, but these things take time." Worthington set his fork down and reseated his wire-rims against the bridge of his nose with a long, bony forefinger. "I want . . . I *envision*"—splayed fingers, all long, all bony, brushed the invisible canvas—"blue sky, rolling prairie, nothing but tall grass as far as the eye can see. Badlands, rugged, untamable, beautifully striated. A natural wildlife habitat. Coyotes, mustangs, rattlesnakes."

"Rattlesnakes?" Marla laughed. "Only Peter would actually plan on having rattlesnakes."

"In their natural habitat. And I want buffalo. No cattle. A huge herd of buffalo." Worthington's fingers flew, playing midair piano. "I can see them, grazing on the hillside. I'd give them the run of the place."

Zane spared a crooked smile. "Sounds like something that might've been done before."

"Yes, and we can have it back. A little piece of it, anyway." Worthington sidelined the dream as he reclaimed his fork. "I'm looking at a spread that's surrounded by Indian land. If I invest here, I plan to open a shop right here in Rapid City, which will be an excellent opportunity for Native artisans like yourself, Zane."

"You're gonna give Marla some competition, huh?"

"I'm going to expand the market. Santa Fe, Albuquerque, Denver, they're all growing art centers, flourishing because of the renewed interest in Native American art. Rapid City could easily be the next—"

"Hey, Pete, I didn't know you were in town."

The three heads turned as Bill Hausauer approached the table.

"Just checking up on you, Bill."

"What do you mean?" Bill glanced tentatively at Zane, then flashed Marla a good-buddy smile. "Are these guys runnin' me down, Pete?" He gave a smug chuckle. "I tell you what, if you ever need a horse trainer, this is the man for you, right here. How's that mare you're workin' for me now, Chief?"

"The name's Lone Bull."

"Well, sure, I know that. I was just being—" Another chuckle. "Do you have any connections to any Lone Bulls at Pine Ridge?"

"Not that I know of." But it was such an interesting question, Zane was inclined to invite the man to sit down if nobody else did. "But then, we're all related somehow. Who do you know down at Pine Ridge?"

"Well, names, you know. I grew up in that part of the country. But you're from up north, right?"

Zane gave a brief nod.

"Hell, if you're not a chief yet, they oughta make you one, the way you can handle a horse." Bill stole a chair from an unoccupied table. "You know, Pete, this guy's a damn war hero."

"He's a damn good artist."

"*Artist?*" Bill spun the chair on one leg, straddled it, and sat down, gripping the backrest and grinning like the kid who'd claimed the roller coaster's front car. "Well, wha'd'ya know?"

"A hell of a lot more than you think, Junior." Zane raised his beer glass in a mock toast, meeting Bill's eyes with a sardonic smile. "That colt's comin' along. When I'm done with him, he'll do whatever you want, long as you ask nice."

"Wha'd I tell you? Must be the artist's touch, huh?" Bill tapped the sleeve of Worthington's embroidered western shirt with the back of his hand. "Are you still interested in that deal we talked about, Pete?"

Worthington regarded the gesture coolly. "If you've got clear title to the land."

"No problem." Bill gripped the back of the chair again, smiling. "No problem."

"What about your father?" Worthington asked.

"No problem there, either. The torch has passed to a new generation. We're into hot-blooded horses and cool oil and gas leases. I'll be holding the mineral rights on that land, but everything else is for sale."

"Sounds like we'll need to do some negotiating. But not right now, Bill. Right now I'm interested in—"

The target of Worthington's interest was suddenly leaving the table. "You guys go ahead and negotiate all you want," Zane suggested as he dropped his napkin next to his plate.

"Well, well." Marla followed Zane's focus to the group of people the hostess was herding toward the dining room on the other side of the bar. Zane was getting the eye. "Do you have a little explaining to do, cowboy?"

"If that's what it takes."

"Who's that?"

"Her name is Michelle Benedict," Marla told Bill. "She's a teacher."

"Is she the one from Canton?"

"She's from here." Marla frowned. "Canton?"

"The name rang a bell. Something I read about a while back. Teacher of the year, maybe?" Bill signaled a waitress. "Let me buy you guys another drink."

Zane approached Michelle with a tentative smile. She looked pretty, her hair pulled back and falling behind her shoulders, her blue eyes wide with emotion, something akin to surprise, maybe mixed with a little hurt. He wasn't used to explaining himself, and he wasn't exactly sure how to go about it. But he knew she had the wrong idea.

"I was going to call you."

"To tell me what?"

"To *ask* you—" He had to smile. She was trying so hard not to look at the table and the woman he'd left behind, but damn if her eyes didn't stray. "—if I could stop over tonight."

"After . . ."

"Yeah. After." He stepped closer, so close he could smell the fresh bayberry scent in her hair. "The guy in the Roy Rogers outfit buys Indian beadwork. Marla sells it. I make it. And that other guy—" A waitress coming by with a loaded tray gave him an excuse to put his hand on Michelle's bare arm and draw her to one side. He liked her summery blue dress, except that he thought it was a little short. "He's got some land he wants to sell."

"You're buying land?"

"Yeah, right." He glanced into the room behind her. The people in her party were playing a little musical chairs, deciding who should sit where. A couple of plump women did a little rubbernecking, and a man in a bright yellow sports jacket lifted an eyebrow in Michelle's direction. "No, what I'm doing is . . ." Putting it into words made him laugh. "I'm playing detective. Do you believe that?"

"I might as well."

"Damn right, you might as well, 'cause you're the one got me started. I let Marla set this up because—" He moved her over, another step out of somebody's way, another step closer to the front door. He sighed, chafing under her skepticism. "Marla sets a lot of things up. She knows a lot of people. She's a professional go-between. And what's goin' on over there right now could be a real interesting land deal." Then, flatly, "I'm not with Marla."

"You're not?"

He glanced behind her. "Is there anybody over there that you're not with?"

"No."

"How about the guy in the banana suit? He keeps looking over here like he thinks I might try to drag you out the door any minute."

She shrugged innocently. "I'm with all of them. We always go out for dinner the last day of school."

"Those are your teacher friends?"

"Would you like to meet them?" Her smile was perfunctory. "I've already met Marla."

"I'd like to be the guy you take home tonight." He glared across the room at the nosy banana. "And that's how I'd like to be introduced."

She surprised him by slipping her arm through his and turning, tugging.

He laughed. "I was just kidding."

She looked up at him guilelessly. "I'll introduce you any way you please to anyone I know."

"How about your family?" he challenged, and once it was said, he wondered where in hell *that* had come from.

"My mother's all that's left." She smiled and nodded toward her friends. "Any time, Zane."

He glanced away, nonplussed. "I don't wanna break up your party."

"I didn't mean to break up yours."

Their eyes met, each one's reflecting the growing gleam in the other's. They both laughed at once.

"Come on." She slipped her arm around his waist and pressed him to escort her back to her table, where the speculative gaping was still hardly subtle. "Just a quick round of introductions—you can just tell they're dying of curiosity—and then I'll let you go back to—" She slid him a playful glance. "Playing detective, huh?"

"That's all." He gave her a quick squeeze. "Doin' real good, too. You got any other games in mind for me?"

"I've done a little more detective work myself, and I have a name for you."

"Don't start callin' me names, honey," he muttered under his breath as they reached the table.

"Everybody, this is Zane."

He'd soon returned to his dinner party and left her to hers. Bill Hausauer took the hint when Worthington expressed his interest in seriously discussing Zane's work. Bill left. Worthington talked and Zane listened, thinking seriously about the work he'd begun as a hobby, just to keep from going stir-crazy. Thinking seriously about the interest Marla's marketing had generated. Thinking seriously about the woman in the other room, being with her soon, being with her . . . being with her.

But the talk went on, and by the time Zane left the Cattleman's Grill, the teachers had gone. He was glad to find Michelle's car in its parking space behind her apartment building. He parked his pickup beside it, in someone else's parking space.

She was waiting for him.

His woman was waiting for him. It was a surprising pleasure to be expected, to be able to kindle a bright glow in her eyes simply by walking in the door. She greeted him with a kiss that tasted like a warm, sweet drink, soothing to a talked-out mouth.

He stepped back, just to admire her. The short dress she'd worn to the Cattleman's was gone, replaced by an old-fashioned ivory-colored number with a high neck, long sleeves, and bits of delicate lace.

Because she could see that he was enjoying himself

already, she smiled. "I have no right to be suspicious, do I?"

"*Right?*" He cupped her face in his hands and kissed her again. "No reason to be. She's business. Do you want to be business or pleasure?"

"Those are my choices?"

"The best I've got to offer." He pulled a long, narrow box gold-stamped with Marla's store logo out of his back pocket. "Got a present for you. How come you changed clothes?"

"I'm playing dress-up." Her long hair did a sassy swing as she pirouetted for him. "I've sorted through almost everything in Aunt Cora's attic, and I found some dresses from her younger days." She fanned the gently draped skirt. "Isn't this wonderful?"

"Can I play, too?"

"I don't have anything that'll fit you."

"Oh, yes, you do," he intoned as he opened the box. "But before I get us undressed to prove my point, I want to dress you up a little more." The pile of beads became a cascade when he lifted it by the clasp and tossed the box aside. "You like blue, don't you?"

Her eyes lit up as though he were dangling diamonds in front of her pretty nose. "I love blue. Oh, Zane . . ."

"It's just glass, but . . ." He held it up for her while she lifted the network of strands, examining the pattern as the beads caught the light. "I started doing this when I was in the pen. It was"—she glanced up, startled by the word, but her eyes were soft with sympathy—"something to do. My big, clumsy fingers learned to be patient with little things." He smiled into her eyes. "Pretty little things."

She slipped her hand behind his, drew it down, beads and all, and kissed his fingertips. "I love them."

"You haven't seen them on you yet," he averred softly, slightly hoarse.

"I've felt them on me. They're never clumsy and always patient."

"I made this for you, Michelle." He undid the clasp. She swept her hair up off the back of her neck and held it out of his way while he fastened the necklace blindly, lost in her smile. "I worked on it when I couldn't sleep at night for the need to come to you."

"Why didn't you come to me?"

"Because then I couldn't have made this." He took her shoulders in his hands, turned her, and pointed her toward the oak-framed mirror above the sofa. "Do you like it?"

"I do." Her fingers traced the intricate pattern of couplings and curves. "I love it. Isn't it just perfect with this dress?"

"It's nice with the dress. It's perfect with your eyes." He stood behind her, lifted her hair, and held it against the back of her head. "You do look a little bit like the woman in the picture."

"Your mother?" She turned, and her hair fell abruptly as she grabbed his arms, gave a quick squeeze, then dashed away. "I've found her name."

"My mother's name?" He sighed and sank to the sofa while she fussed around with some papers at the desk on the other side of the room. "The nurse. You still wanna think that nurse was messin' around with—"

"No, I don't. I don't want to think anything." She joined him on the sofa, proudly brandishing more of her multitude of folders. "This is what I found. Personnel records. And this"—she produced a small black-and-white snapshot—"certainly looks like the woman in Martin's photograph."

He scanned the page, full of statistics, then tried to get away with taking only a cursory look at the picture, but the eyes drew him in. His mother's eyes. She looked confident, relaxed, natural. "She cut her hair."

"And her name was Rachael Trainor. She was from Massachusetts, and she came to work at the asylum in 1932." Michelle peered over his shoulder at the picture. "She must have been a kind person, Zane. You can tell from the way Martin—"

Martin! He waved the inference away with an impatient gesture. "According to this, she was at least ten, twelve years older than he was. And he was—"

"There's another man in Martin's drawings," she reminded him patiently.

"His *grandfather,* for crissake. An old man and a kid. She must have been pretty hard up."

"A *third* man, Zane. Remember? Who could the third man be?"

"How the hell do I know?" He slammed the folder shut on the pretty young face. "Just another pitiful lunatic."

"We *know* they weren't all mentally ill. James Lone Bull was a holy man. Apparently Martin was committed because he ran away from school."

"Jesus Christ, Michelle, will you leave it alone?" He tossed the folder onto the lamp table, sending the empty jewelry box over the edge. "Okay, so now I know her name, I know where she came from, and I know she made an honest living. Thank you very much."

She looked hurt. This was her gift to him, this discovery of a name, and now she wanted to dig up another one. For his sake.

For his sake, couldn't she just drop it?

"What good would it do me to find out? Maybe some crazed patient raped her, got her pregnant, and she couldn't stand the sight of me. That's possible, isn't it? Or maybe, like you say, she had a thing for teenage boys who don't talk back, so she—"

"I didn't say that, Zane."

"She left me with Unci. Maybe I don't wanna know any more details."

She looked down at her pale-skinned hands, folded daintily against a pale skirt. "My father left my mother when I was four years old."

"And you've lived your whole life trying to figure out why," was his perfunctory conclusion.

"I know they didn't love each other, but that couldn't have been my fault, could it?"

"Not a chance." His hand easily blanketed both of hers. "They don't exist. If we didn't know them, if they never bothered with us, then they don't exist. That's the way I look at it. The people who stick by you, they're the ones who matter." Gently he asked, "Your mother stuck by you, didn't she?"

"I wonder if she ever met Rachael Trainor."

"Aw, Christ." He leaned back on the sofa and eyed her speculatively. "The real question is, would your mother want to meet *me*?"

She ignored the question. "She didn't get along with Aunt Cora at all, and I know she hated Dr. Tim. I didn't get to start spending summers with Aunt Cora until after he died. You know, I think my mother was jealous of—"

"Will you look at me, Michelle? I'm here. Right here in the flesh." When she did, he lifted an eyebrow. "What would your mother think about you and me?"

"I don't care what she thinks."

"Yes, you do." Her mother was as good a diversion as anything he could come up with. "Where does she live?"

"Sturgis. Less than a half-hour drive. I told you before, Zane, *any time*."

"Good."

It was her turn to challenge him. "When we visit her, what will we tell her about you and me?"

"Same thing we told my family. 'I've got someone I want you to meet.'" He leaned closer, slipping his arm around her, laying full claim. "I've *got* someone." He smiled as he touched the necklace where it curved over her shoulder. "Someone I want to be with. Someone . . ." He closed his eyes and touched his nose to her temple. "Someone who wants to be with me."

"Someone who loves you, Zane." He felt her fingertips skitter across his chest, causing his nipple to pucker beneath his shirt. "I love you."

He put his hand over hers, pressed it to his chest, and dragged it over his belly, his belt buckle, into his lap, then whispered, "How do you know?"

"I just . . . do. I want to be with you because I love you." Her shy fingers stirred over him. "Am I allowed to love you?"

"Oh, yeah," he whispered. "You're allowed."

"To *love* you."

He groaned when she took her hand away.

"I love you," she repeated, as though she were teaching him new words.

"I'm not sure I know what that means." He looked down at her, inviting her to read the candor in his eyes. "I don't know if it's because I'm a coward or just a plain, simple, selfish bastard, but I don't know a goddamn thing about loving somebody."

"I think you do."

"I know how to *make* love." He slid his hand up her side and cupped her breast. "Do you want me to make love to you, Michelle?"

"Do you want to?"

He looked into her eyes, lifted his chin slowly, lowered it slowly.

"Why?"

It was a woman's question. He had only a man's answer. "I can't get close enough to you any other way."

She blinked, and for one awful moment he thought that she might cry.

Just say the three simple words, you idiot.

He shook his head and drew her into his arms. "It's driving me crazy, you know that? The sight of you, the sound of your voice, just the *thought* of you. I want to put my hands on you, just your cheek or your shoulder, just touch you, just to show that I can. That you'll let me. And you know what's really crazy?"

"What?"

"I want your hands on me." He found her hand and guided it to him, around his waist this time. "Even out in public. You put your arm around me and I feel like—" *Three simple words.* "I feel good."

"You do?"

"Oh, yeah, I do." He looked down, and she lifted her face within an inch of his, hungering for more words, prettier words. He smiled. "But I'd feel better if I could get inside your skin. I'd feel better if I could just live inside you."

"You would?" Her smile made his heart swell. "Where would you like to live?"

"In your eyes. They're so blue, they look like heaven."

"Are you anxious to go to heaven?"

"Are you ready to take me there?"

She leaned close, and her breath felt warm in his right ear. He chuckled. "I can't hear a damn thing in that ear, honey, that's my—" The tip of her tongue traced the curve of his ear, and he laughed. "Sweet Jesus, it's a miracle. I'm hearin' you now. Speaking in tongues, right?"

"Speaking *of* tongues . . ." She took his face in her hands. "You want to live inside me? Let's start with your tongue in my mouth."

Gladly he covered that sweet mouth with his, savoring the warm, moist contact with the lips and the tongue that had formed the words. Formed them and said them and meant them. Her kiss tasted of the love he craved, the love he wished would simply absorb him into its fabric.

He drew back and looked down at her; his eyes pleaded for just that miracle.

She nodded. "I'm ready to move into another room."

He was ready to take her, to discover, finally, that he did know something about loving somebody. He wanted to know all about loving Michelle, and when she touched her lips to the scar high inside his thigh, he felt the heat of love. Healing love. It bathed all the raw places inside him, a soothing balm warmed in a woman's heart.

And he found his way inside her.

After breakfast he asked to use her phone, promising to pay for the long-distance charges. She told him he could wash the breakfast dishes.

Officer Obi responded to the call like a man who hated to be bothered, who barely remembered who Zane Lone Bull was. Randy's name stirred only slightly more interest. But, no, there was no handwritten page of notes found on the body. Zane's second call was to Cedric

Kills Crow, who told him he had found the name of the agent at Pine Ridge back in 1933.

And these names were beginning to repeat themselves.

"Edward Trainor," Zane reported to Michelle after he hung up the phone.

"Trainor?" she repeated in a small voice, then glanced away. "The agent? Why were you looking for information about the agent?"

"Because Randy was trying to find out what happened to their land—my grandma's and my uncle's. Him and this other guy, the guy I just called, they had some harebrained idea that they could dig up evidence of a land swindle."

Zane turned on the exhaust fan over the stove, then lit a cigarette. On a trail of smoke, he finally concluded, "Which turns out not to be such a harebrained idea. The trouble with Randy was that whenever he had an idea, he let everybody know about it. And I think he let the wrong person know about it."

"Do you know who the wrong person might have been?"

He studied the smoking ash on the tip of the cigarette. "I don't know how I'd ever prove it."

"That's Officer Obi's job. You should just tell him what you've . . ." She touched his bare shoulder. "Aren't you going to tell me?"

"Nope." He eyed her pointedly as he dragged deeply on the cigarette. She reminded him too much of Randy. He changed the subject. "I wonder if Rachael Trainor was Edward Trainor's wife."

"I don't think so."

"Why not?"

"Because Edward Trainor was obviously not your father."

"So what? That doesn't mean he wasn't her husband."

"He wasn't."

He looked at her skeptically.

"We can find out, Zane. I'll bet if we just called the State Historical Society . . ."

He laughed. "That's what I get for hookin' up with a teacher. A damn research project."

"I can do it for you."

"No, you can't. I don't want you going around asking questions. I'll do it my own way, in my own time." He wasn't going to let that hurt look in her eyes change his mind about it, either. He smiled, touched her jaw, rubbed his thumb over the point of her chin. "Okay? You let me take care of it. All you have to do is give me a grade."

❧ 14 ❧

That afternoon they drove to Sturgis, a pretty little town on the northern perimeter of the Black Hills. Michelle's mother lived in a shotgun house—basically three rooms in a straight line, front to back—on a quiet street in the middle of town.

The small, trim woman with short, unnaturally red hair answered the door. "Well," she said, her tone cagey. "Long time, no see. Has school let out already?"

"Yes, it has." Michelle did a half-turn toward Zane, who stood at the foot of the front stoop. "I brought somebody I want you to meet, Mother. May we come in?"

"Mother, may I? Yes, you surely may."

Zane took his hat off as he crossed the threshold, smiling at the woman who stood aside, back pressed against the front door as though she were preventing it from springing shut.

She returned the smile. "You're sure a tall, dark, and handsome drink of water."

Michelle introduced her mother as Meg Sandland.

Meg shook her head. "I've went back to Benedict now, officially. Sandland put me down too far." She gave a caustic laugh, then let Zane in on the joke. "In the alphabet. I work over at the veteran's hospital as an aide. You know how the government is. Everybody's alphabetized." She shut the door and turned to goad her daughter. "So what happened to Horny Harv?"

Michelle turned bright pink. "Harvey and I were never much more than friends, Mother. It's been almost a year since we stopped dating."

"That long?" Meg headed toward the back of the house, clearly counting on being followed as she went on talking. "Must be about how long it's been since you stopped by to see me," Meg announced over her shoulder, her bare feet padding toward the refrigerator. "Would you like something to drink, Zane? I've got pop and beer."

"A pop would be great."

"Nothing for me, Mother." Catching Zane's try-again look she amended, "Except a glass of ice water."

"So damn hot in here, and summer hasn't even hit yet. Let's go sit out back." Meg handed Zane a red can and turned to Michelle, who was getting her own ice. "Unless you'd prefer the *parlor*."

Zane glanced out the window. "You got a nice backyard. How 'bout we do this interview on the back porch swing?" It wasn't exactly a porch. More like a little hardpan patio shaded by corrugated green fiberglass. But there was a two-passenger lawn swing. He flashed Michelle a smile. "Kinda like the Nelsons."

"What are you interviewing for? You two wanna go steady?" Meg claimed a beer for herself and bumped the refrigerator door closed with her hip. "I'm a tough sell, as my daughter's probably already told you. As long as she lived under this roof, I was pretty strict with her and very fussy about her boyfriends." She popped her pull tab. "What do you do for a living, Zane?"

"Mother, *please*. Let's just—"

"I train horses, mostly."

"A cowboy." Mother toasted daughter. "Raise her up to be a lady, send her to college and all that, and what does she bring home?" She turned the salute on him. "A cowboy."

"I'm half Indian, if that helps any." He was busy ripping the ring off the pop can and avoiding the women's eyes.

"Oh, that helps tremendously." Meg laughed. "I'll tell you what does help. You're good-looking." Zane glanced up, and she nodded. "Much better than Horny Harv."

"Mother, Harvey wasn't—"

"Let's go outside so your cowboy can court you on the porch swing." She started to open the back door, but Zane reached past her and did the gentlemanly honors. She shoved on the wooden frame of the outside door, its sections of metal screen shaped like two sheets filled with wind. "First question is, can you make a living training horses?"

Sidling past him, Michelle muttered, "I knew this was a mistake."

"Piece o' cake." He smiled and gave his lady a subtle wink.

Meg sat in the webbed seat of an aluminum lawn chair, leaving the swing for her visitors. Zane offered her a cigarette.

"Thanks." She looked surprised, pleased when he lit it for her. She blew a cloud of smoke and sat back in her chair like she was holding court. "So, tell me all about how you two met, and how you've been keeping her so busy that she's barely had time to call her mother since Christmas."

"I've tried to—"

"I know. I know." The chair creaked as Meg crossed her bare legs. She was wearing knit shorts and a halter top. "I work shifts. It's not always easy to get hold of me." She glanced at Meg, then Zane. "I'm sorry. I'm being . . ." The apology had taken some of the edge off her tone. She shrugged. "Michelle says I always used to chase her friends away."

Still standing, Zane took a quick, hard drag on the cigarette he'd just lit. "I don't scare too easy."

"No, I can see that." She smiled. "Okay, I'm listening."

"The way we met is kind of a long story, Mother, and it has to do with Aunt Cora."

"Ah, your favorite aunt." She watched Zane take a

seat next to her daughter. "Did you know Cora?"

"No."

"Didn't think so. Cowboys weren't her"—Meg affected a snobbish tone—"*cup* of *tea*. And you're too young to have had anything to do with her dear husband's looney bin."

"Mother—"

"Sorry." Meg smiled, trying to be coy and cute, which was a tough act for a woman her age. The smile turned into a pout for Michelle's benefit. "What? Okay, I'm listening. Really."

Michelle sighed. "Forget Aunt Cora. I just wanted Zane to meet my mother. No explanations, no third-degree. Couldn't we just talk about the weather or something?"

"I already said it was hot." She glanced at Zane. "I said something wrong about the asylum."

"My uncle was a patient there."

"Oh." Meg sipped her beer, then raised it in distant deference. "Well, he has my sympathies if he was under Hubble's care for any length of time."

"He stays with me now, but he's still not . . . he doesn't talk at all."

"Neither do I. Hardly at all." She laughed, but it was quick and forced, faded fast. She sought consolation from her smoke, and on its tail she admitted, "I don't know much about that place. I know the town of Canton was all up in arms when they shut it down, and Cora said it just broke her Dr. Tim's heart when they took away his life's work." Her derisive tone turned sympathetic. "It's too bad your uncle can't talk. It might be interesting to hear somebody else's version."

"What do you think he'd say?" Zane wasn't sure why he asked. He *was* sure that she wanted to tell them.

"Behind those brick walls I'll just bet they had some names for Hubble that would burn poor Cora's ears." Meg's laugh didn't come across the way she wanted it to. The hardness had turned hollow. But she kept trying. "You've heard of Barney Rubble? How about Horny Hubble?"

"God, Mother, when did you get hooked on *that* expression?"

"It's a joke, Shelly." She shifted in her chair. "Just a joke. Personally, I didn't like the man. Everybody else did. I didn't."

"Because he took your sister away?" Zane asked.

"Cora was a lot older than me. We were never close." Meg's cigarette wobbled a little as she put it to her lips. A deep drag steadied her. "She left everything she owned to Shelly, which was fine by me. I let Shelly spend summers with Cora after Hubble died." Her voice drifted. "I used to spend summers with them, too, when I was a girl."

"Do you remember the asylum?" Michelle asked.

Her mother nodded. "Of course, I never went over there. I remember it being used as a prison farm, after they closed the asylum. Hubble was the doctor for them, too, but by that time he'd opened his own office in town."

"So you wouldn't have known any of the staff who worked at the asylum?"

"I was just a young girl, seen but not heard." Again, the bitter laugh. "Besides, Hubble had a policy of keeping his work separate from his home life. I remember they used to come to the house once in a while for ice, because they had no way of making ice over there. So, like, if one of the patients had a fever . . ."

She stared at the lilac hedge that surrounded the yard, squinting as though she were trying to see what was behind it. "I used to wonder what went on over there. Two big old brick buildings full of secrets and dangerous people, I thought." She chuckled humorlessly. "Man-oh-man, was I wrong. Turns out, I was staying in the same house with the dangerous person, the one who loved secrets."

Out of respect Zane stared.

But Michelle didn't get it.

"What do you mean, Mother?"

"Cora's beloved Dr. Tim"—Meg backed off with a

quick shrug—"was the devil incarnate, that's all. And Cora never, never knew."

"They had a wonderful marriage," Michelle argued, ignoring the subtle hand Zane laid on her knee.

"She thought she did." Meg looked at her daughter. "What are you going to do with that house, Shelly?"

"I haven't wanted to think about . . . selling it."

"Well, think about it. *Do it*."

Michelle drew a deep breath, then tentatively risked an offer. "Maybe you'd like to go down there with me and help me go through Aunt Cora's things."

Meg waved the suggestion away. "There is no way you can get me to set foot in that house." She took a last drag, then pitched the cigarette butt on the hard clay near Zane's boot.

Taking the hint, he flattened it, then repeated the ritual with his own smoke.

"When I sell it," Michelle was saying, "I want you to have half the proceeds. You can have anything you want of hers, Mother."

"I don't want anything. It's yours. She left it to you."

"She never wanted to shut you out. It was you—"

Meg's blue eyes flashed a little fire, but her voice was calm. "It wasn't *just me*. She made a choice. She went to the grave with her fairy tale all intact."

"Mother . . ."

Zane gave Michelle's knee a signal squeeze. "My uncle was probably about twelve or thirteen when they put him in there." He met Meg's detached stare with a look that offered support along with his subtle suggestion of another ally.

Meg nodded, glanced away, nodded again. Zane didn't have to look at Michelle. He could feel her concern for her mother, her need to speak in the woman's behalf as the words came harder. His fingers stirred over her jeans, counseling restraint.

"I was about that age when I started staying with them in the summers," Meg said, her once brassy voice now soft, almost childlike. "It was a lot better than staying home. There wasn't any money in our house. Even though we lived on a farm, food was hard to come by. I came from a large family. Mostly all gone now. Cora was the oldest. The only one who did well for herself, my ma used to say.''

She paused for a sip of beer.

Michelle drank her water, then set the glass aside.

Zane kept the cold can in his left hand, the warm leg in his right, grounding him in the moment. His thoughts were straying, taking him speculating, offering glimpses of a past that was none of his being, none of his doing. He wondered whether Meg had once looked like Michelle. Whether the boy Pagla had been slight and sweet-faced, like Randy.

Meg took a deep breath. ''So after a couple of summers of just me, my brother and I both went to stay at Cora's. And then the next summer it was just my brother.''

She paused, and Zane had to swallow hard to keep from warning her not to say a ghost's name. He already had enough of them to contend with.

Sure as hell.

''My brother Jake.''

''The one who killed himself?'' Michelle asked.

Meg nodded.

Michelle stiffened. ''Because of something . . . Dr. Tim did?''

Her mother nodded again. ''I've never told anyone. It was a secret, and Jake said we . . . had to keep it that way.''

''Did you ever try to tell your sister?'' Zane asked.

''I didn't know what to tell her. He was a doctor. He said he was just doing''—she gave a cheerless laugh—''what he was supposed to be doing. For our health, you know.''

She shook her head, and the look in her eyes revealed that part of her had drifted elsewhere. ''Cora was so proud of the fact that she'd landed a doctor. And he was always nice around her, always seemed to treat her well, I'll give her that. Better than . . .'' She shrugged. ''From what I saw, better than I ever got from any man. Who can figure?''

Michelle rose slowly, knelt by her mother's crossed legs, and took the woman's free hand in both of hers. Zane couldn't see Michelle's face, but he saw the flood of emotion in her mother's eyes. No tears. Just pure, raw emotion. The woman's whole heart was in her eyes as she set her beer on the ground and patted her daughter's hand.

"It's no big deal, Shelly. It happens, you know? Jake took everything hard. That was just the way he was. Me, I just figured it probably happened to . . ." She lifted her hand, shyly touched Michelle's hair. "I mean, it happened, it's over, and it was a long time ago." All mother now, eyes doting, fingers taking charge, Meg tucked a lock of hair behind Michelle's ear. "I wasn't gonna let it happen to you, though."

Michelle shook her head. She said nothing. Not a word. Not a sound.

Zane looked down at the scuffed toes of his black boots. His throat burned like crazy.

"In some ways I felt the same way you did about Cora," Meg said. "She was a special lady. She could set the prettiest table, and she always knew just what colors to put together. She knew all about history and music. But she never did have a daughter. I was the one"—she squeezed Michelle's hands—"who got the daughter. I made some mistakes, though, didn't I?"

Words finally came, soft but steady. "We all do, Mama."

"I never practiced what I preached. I wanted to protect you. I know I went about it wrong sometimes. But just try to remember that it's never all one-sided. Whether there's love or hate or a combination of both . . ." Meg looked at Zane. "There's lots of sides to every story."

He nodded.

She'd said nothing since they'd left her mother's house. Staring at the road ahead, she didn't seem to no-

tice the fact that he'd bypassed I-90, the fastest way back
to Rapid City, in favor of the scenic route through the
hills. Tall pines and rocky outcroppings lined the wind-
ing road. He knew where he was going—a secluded pic-
nic spot beside Rapid Creek—and when he got there, he
parked the pickup and quietly drew her into his arms.

She soaked the front of his shirt with the tears she
needed to shed, and through the tears she asked, "Why?
Why didn't she tell me, Zane?"

"When?" He smoothed her hair back. "When should
she have told you?"

"When I was going . . ." She took a swipe at her
eyes with the back of one hand, but they kept coming.
"G-going off to stay with Aunt Cora. She took me
there herself, and at first I wanted her to stay, too, and
she wouldn't. She could have told me . . . something . . .
so I wouldn't think it was . . . *her*."

"Maybe she didn't want to ruin it for you."

"After, *after* he died." She shook her head, sniffling.
Her lips trembled uncontrollably. "She never would let
me go when he was alive. But . . . but after a while, I
didn't even w-want my m-mother to go. I didn't care
because Aunt Cora was, I thought, m-more of a mother
to me sometimes than . . ." She squeezed her eyes shut,
the little girl filled with remorse. "What a mean thing
for a p-person to say to her own mother."

"You can have them both now." He kissed her damp
temple, tasting its saltiness. "One doesn't have to be
more or less than the other. You can love them both."

"But I didn't understand."

"You do now. Your mother couldn't tell her sister,
but now she's told you, woman to woman."

"It wasn't easy for her, was it?"

He shook his head.

"She's not as h-hard as she wants us to think, is
she?"

"Hard?" He brushed her warm, wet jaw with his
knuckles. "Or strong?"

"She's a lot stronger than I ever gave her credit for."
A long, deep, unsteady breath helped stem the tears.

"But she should have told me a long time ago." She pursed her lips and glanced up at him, sniffling guiltily. "Easy for me to say, huh?"

"It was a painful secret. She kept it where she thought it would do the least harm."

"He was a terrible man, Zane. Mama . . . my mother's right. I've got to get that house ready to be sold." She dragged the back of her wrist over her cheek and smiled a little, relieved. The decision was made. "You look as though you approve."

"It's not up to me. I was just thinkin' . . ." He shrugged. "Canton's too damn far away."

"So is Rapid City."

"Yeah, but it's closer than Canton."

"Not close enough." She straightened the flap over his shirt pocket, giving a tight little smile. "I squashed your cigarettes."

"I was gonna throw 'em out anyway." She glanced up. He smiled. "Gonna kick the habit and take up . . . I don't know, golf, maybe."

She chuckled. "Golf?"

"On weekends."

"I've applied for a new job. If they hire me"—she looked directly into his eyes—"I'll be Jojo's teacher next year."

He was stunned. She was thinking about coming . . . to him?

"I won't be crowding you, will I? I've always wanted to teach in a reservation school." Her lashes swept downward, relieving him of her scrutiny as her small voice asked, "What do you think?"

"I think they'll offer you the job." He also thought she'd be disappointed if she took it. Do-gooders generally were. He wondered how long she'd stay.

"Do you think I should take it?"

"It's not up to me." It was a cowardly answer, and he knew it, even though it was true. She really wanted to know how he felt about it, but that wasn't what she'd asked. "I think it would really make Jojo happy."

*   *   *

Zane went home the next morning. He had work to do. Between the wild goose he had no business chasing and the woman he had no business . . . chasing? Hell, yes, he was chasing her, and he was getting behind in the business he ought to be looking after. He had kids and old folks to look after, and he had . . .

Another complication. Chickie was back. Sitting in one of the folding chairs under the willow shade, watching Sissy and Jojo turn themselves inside out to entertain her with the cartwheels and somersaults they'd learned at school, Zane wasn't sure what bothered him more as he parked in the yard and watched through the windshield—the fact that the kids were trying just a little too hard for Chickie, or that they hardly noticed when he drove up.

Damn, he was touchy lately!

He greeted the kids and joined Chickie in the chairs set out under the dried willow boughs. They teased each other past the initial awkwardness, avoiding questions and explanations simply by kidding each other. The two children finally ran out of tricks and went off to play with the new kittens that were living under the house.

"Now that school's out, I guess I should take them with me," Chickie said as she watched them go.

"Back to Baker?"

"I moved to Miles City now. I've got a job. Melvin said I could bring the kids back with me if I wanted to."

He offered her a cigarette. "Who's Melvin?"

"Truck driver," she said, tucking the cigarette between her lips, leaning close to Zane's match. "Been with him since fall."

"Does this one like kids?"

"Sure." She squinted through a veil of smoke. "Don't you be judging me with that look, Zane Lone Bull. Mom says you're spending your weekends in Rapid City with some white teacher."

"I'm not judging you, Chickie. The kids are doing fine here. Doing okay in school. Making friends."

"They were glad to see me."

She stuck her fingers into the poufed hairdo, dated but

not unflattering. Not in Zane's eyes, anyway. He'd always thought she was pretty. The hard-life lines were
beginning to show in her face. Her body was a little
thicker than it used to be, and the fingers that primped
her luxuriant black hair were soap-and-water dry.

"You're their mother. They'll always be glad to see
you." He cupped his hand to shield his match from the
warm breeze, telling himself this would be his last cigarette of the day. He turned his head to let the wind
carry the smoke away. "Randy was your brother, too."

"I know." She dropped her hands in her lap and hung
her head, the little sister chastised. "I couldn't face it,
Zane. I wasn't . . . I was going through a bad time, and
I just couldn't get back then."

"You got the money I sent?"

She nodded, but she didn't look up. "I would have
made things worse here."

He didn't argue.

"Why would anybody want to kill Randy? I always
thought he'd be the one to really do something . . . make
something . . ." Her cigarette bobbed wildly as she
sucked on it for dear life.

One very short, very dear life.

"It's okay." Zane reached out, lifted her chin, made
her look at him. Smoke drifted from her lips. Her eyes
glistened. It was about as close as she ever came. He
gave a sympathetic smile. "Little Chickie-girl with her
hair full of feathers, it's okay."

"It's not okay. I should have been here. My *head* was
full of feathers." She closed her eyes and sank into a
slump-shouldered sigh. Rare tears appeared, one at the
outside corner of each eye. "And Randy's head was full
of dreams."

"You're right about that." He sighed. Crying women
turned his innards to mush, and he damn sure was getting his share of mush these days. "There was one in
particular he left behind that's . . . kinda got me going."

"Going on what?"

"Something kinda crazy." His thumb swept across
her cheekbone, and he smiled wistfully. "Silver tears."

"This is stupid." She brushed his hand and the telltale tears away. "I *never* cry."

"It's good for you. Cleans out the system," he said lightly. And then, impulsively, surprising them both, "Leave the kids with me, Chickie."

"With *you*?"

"With us. We're gonna get a house built. Running water, wiring so there's electricity in all the rooms, everything just like uptown." It was the first time he'd uttered the plan aloud, but it sounded good as he watched Jojo run around the corner of the house carrying a kitten. "Why shouldn't we?"

"Why *should* we? Why should we stay *here*. This place is like the armpit of the world."

"The hell it is. You don't know armpits from chicken feathers." Grinning, he popped several snaps and jerked his shirt open. The turtle amulet swung forward as he nearly ejected himself from the chair. "*This* is an armpit."

"Jeez, get that thing away from me!" She welcomed the antic, the chance to take a whiff of him, give a loud yelp, and push him away. "You smell like a white man. Where'd you get that stink?"

"That there's English Leather aftershave." He gave a two-fingered hat tip and cocky cowboy grin. "I smell like a white *English* man, so cheerio, Chickie girl."

She howled. "Maybe you oughta use it under your armpit *after* you *shave* the hairy thing."

Jojo popped up between them. "You gonna shave under your arms, Uncle Zane?"

"Hell, no. Guys don't have to, and your mom's just jealous." Zane hooked an arm around the boy and acknowledged the tabby kitten Jojo presented with a brief nod. "You wanna stay with me this summer? Help me break a few horses?"

"Where's Mom going?"

"Back to Montana," Chickie said. "I've got a job there and a . . ." She started to touch her son's hair, but he ducked away. She rubbed the kitten's head instead.

"You can come with me if you want to. You're my baby boy."

"Or you can stay," Zane said. "Us guys—us *men*—" He winked at Chickie. "We've got a lot of stuff to do around here, don't we?"

Jojo looked up at his uncle and smiled. "I'll stay with you."

It was going to be okay for Jojo and Sissy. Zane was going to see to it. His offer had surprised him as much as anyone. He'd made up his mind that he was going to take care of them as long as they needed him. But to *ask* for them—that was the part that surprised him. And to be *chosen*. That part made him smile as he headed off over the rise, looking for a light in the cabin window.

How many fathers got chosen by their kids? Not too damn many. If a woman couldn't keep her child, couldn't raise him herself, for whatever reason, then giving him to someone she could trust was a good thing. A brave thing, maybe. Maybe it was a hard thing, even for Chickie.

Maybe it had been a hard thing for Rachael.

Maybe.

Martin had left the damn door open again.

"You're letting the flies in, Uncle."

Whack!

Martin brandished the fly swatter. Two with one blow. Zane patted him on the shoulder as he closed the cabin door. Didn't take much to entertain the old man, he'd give him that.

The old man. Christ. Was Martin *the* old man?

If Martin hadn't always been this simpleminded, Zane didn't want to think about what it might have taken to bring it about. At the hands of a doctor. A goddamn *doctor*.

Zane peeled his shirt off and tossed it over a chair. "Where's the picture, Uncle? Can I see it again?"

Martin's triumphant smile faded fast.

"I won't take it. I just want to see it again."

Martin went to his room and came back with the photograph.

Zane studied it for a moment. Somewhere along the line his heart's shell had cracked, and the look in the young woman's eyes intrigued him. If they could see him now—the eyes of his not-yet mother, would-be mother, mother who never was—how would he look to her? What would she think of him? How would she speak to him? The sound of a voice that must have been registered sometime, somewhere in the primal part of his mind, what would it say to him now?

"Michelle looks a little bit like her, doesn't she? Pretty woman," he mused. He smiled, shared a man-to-man look with his uncle, and sang "Pretty Woman." He stopped short, then said the word, "Marry. I'd like to marry Michelle. Make her my wife."

Martin nodded slowly.

Ho-ly Jesus.

Zane laughed at himself, straight out. "I haven't told her that. Haven't told anybody. You're the first one, so it's just between you and me." He brandished the photograph. "And this pretty lady. But don't either one of you tell on me, now."

Martin grinned.

"Yeah, I think I'm in love. Feelin' kinda starry-eyed, like a kid." He grabbed Martin's arm and sat him down on the sofa. Sat himself down, too. "So I'm telling you, the way I might . . . tell my father, you know, if I had one."

If I had one . . .

"Do you remember that asylum where you stayed a long time ago, Uncle? Down in Canton."

Immediately sober-faced, Martin nodded.

"Do you remember, uh . . . Dr. Tim, I think they called him." Martin shifted his gaze to the photograph. "You do, huh. But you don't like remembering. Neither does Michelle's mom. See, Michelle's mom and Dr. Tim's wife were sisters, and she used to visit them. Not Michelle, but her mom, when she was younger, visited Dr. Tim."

Martin stared at the photograph.

"That doctor hurt Michelle's mom when she was a girl," Zane said quietly. "And her ... her uncle, too. I guess he was just a teenager then, her uncle."

Martin looked up. He understood.

"I guess that doctor was really no good."

Lips parted slightly, Martin leaned closer, and for a moment, Zane was sure he would speak. He wanted to. The longing fairly glowed in the old man's eyes.

Zane squeezed his shoulder. "Yeah. *Really* no good."

Martin nodded.

They let some long, quiet moments hang between them, sitting close. If it were possible to hear thoughts, they might have. The willingness was there. The air was thick with dreams and memories.

"Uncle," Zane said at last. "Was my mother's name Rachael? Rachael Trainor? Was she a nurse at the asylum?"

Martin's eyes glowed brighter with each question.

"She was, wasn't she." Zane looked at the picture and repeated his mother's name, dutifully honoring it in his heart. Then he looked up and pressed on. "Did you love her?"

Martin nodded.

"Uncle, did you love her ... the way I love Michelle?" No response. Zane drew a deep breath. "Where's my father, Uncle? Are *you* my father?"

Martin reached for the turtle amulet. Zane forced himself to sit still and permit the old man to lift the thong over his head, ducking as he took it off and away.

All his life the beaded turtle had been a keepsake at once treasured and scorned in Zane's mind, for it had tied him to his birth. It had suggested that he had—no matter how cold and gray the circumstances might have been—actually been born. His grandmother had presumably stitched a dried bit of his once-living connection with his mother inside *keya,* the traditional turtle, and wished him long life. Such had once been the practice.

So far, so good. He'd had occasion to run the race neck and neck with death, but still he lived. When a

split second or a scant millimeter had made the difference—not skill, not reason, certainly not merit—he had
been willing to credit the turtle with protecting him. It
had dangled next to his dog tags, warding off death like
the old ghost-dance shirt.

And when Martin took out his pocket knife and
started cutting the sturdy sinew stitches, Zane's arm shot
across the table. "Don't!"

Martin fended off the hand, made a calming gesture,
then touched silencing fingers to his lips.

"Guess I can fix it," Zane muttered as he watched,
trusting the familiar brown hands. His heart suddenly
thudded in his ears. Something metal.

It figured. One more kid-trust shot to hell. Another
goddamn myth, unless he'd had a tin umbilical cord.

Martin handed him the metal disk. It was an old dog
tag. "Adam Lone Bull, United States Army, K-477379,"
Zane read aloud. He rubbed his thumb over the raised
number as he lifted his eyes slowly to meet Martin's.
"My father?"

Martin nodded. *"Ciye."*

Holy Jesus. Martin was speaking!

"I'm your . . . *brother*?"

Martin laid two reverent fingers on the dog tag.
"Ciyewaye kin."

"Adam Lone Bull is your brother."

From the dog tag to Zane's shoulder, the old man's
fingers shifted, dug in. He studied Zane's face, and Zane
would have given his eye teeth to have seen himself
through those old eyes just then.

"Adam's . . . boy."

Zane swallowed hard. The burning in his throat was
worse than when he'd listened to Meg Benedict tell her
story. He cleared it and swallowed again. "Adam and
my mother . . . Rachael?"

"Look after . . . my child, *misunka.* M-my wife."
Martin nodded. His lips trembled as he quoted words
spoken to him long ago. "Live f-for me . . . *misunka.*
Care . . . for . . . them."

"What happened to him?"

Martin's eyes glazed over.

Jesus, don't go back in your shell now, keya.

"What happened to my father, Uncle? Where's my mother? Why didn't she—" Zane caught himself shaking the old man by the shoulders. He forced his hands open and patted, gently patted. "I'm sorry. I don't mean to scare you. Holy Jesus, you're talking to me."

Martin's eyes shone bright again.

Zane's eyes reflected the glow. Martin had found the key, dared to unlock the door, and *that* was the important thing.

"You're doin' real good, Uncle. I didn't know you could talk." He took the man in his arms and hugged him as hard as and as joyously as he'd ever hugged anyone in his life. "You can *talk,* Uncle. Damn, you can really talk."

Zane hoped that Auntie Cecilia might offer a few answers, but she didn't seem to have any. She was loading up the last of the dirty clothes into the pickup, which he'd agreed to take to the laundromat in McLaughlin. He had to make a couple of phone calls anyway. Chickie was in the house with Unci and the kids, and he figured he'd take Uncle Martin along with him, get him out of their hair. But for all of this, couldn't she cough up some little hint about his parents' fate?

"My sister didn't tell me anything when she came to stay with me. Only that she had finally gotten Martin back, but her other son was gone."

"Gone where?"

Cecilia said nothing.

"Dead?"

"Dead. Sure. It was a long time ago." She reached over the side of the pickup box and started messing with the flaps on the grocery box full of dirty laundry.

He laid a hand on her shoulder, urging her to attend to him. "You don't know how or . . ." He drew on the thong like a fishing line, pulling the turtle out of his shirt. He showed her the corner of the dog tag he'd hastily stitched back in place. "Did you know that Adam Lone Bull was my father?"

She grimaced at the mention of the name.

"What about my mother?"

"I didn't know your mother. Never laid eyes on her." She leaned back against the pickup and folded her arms over her middle, cupping her hands around her elbows. "My sister was always afraid for you. Two sons were taken away from her, and bad things happened to them when they were gone from her. We don't know how bad. We just know it was bad for them."

She squinted into the afternoon sun, remembering. " 'Just be quiet about it,' Beatrice would say to me. 'Don't let no one hear a word about it.' "

"A woman tries to keep her children safe any way she can. That's all she can do, you know? When she's alone and she has no man, she does what she has to do to keep them safe." She touched Zane's shirtsleeve. "Don't go digging up the past. Look what happened to my son."

"Do you know what Randy was after?"

"Trouble." She jerked her thumb sideways, toward the south. "Like the ones down at Wounded Knee, like when you and that one Strikes girl went into that courthouse. You can't bring back the dead. You can't get back what's been taken. All you get for your trouble is more trouble."

"I heard my uncle speak for the first time in my life, Auntie. He remembered for me. He was scared, and it was hurting him all over again, but he remembered some of it for me." He blew a weary sigh. "Maybe it takes some trouble to bring out the truth."

"How many must die for it? How many of our own?"

"I don't know," he admitted. "But if they died for something, seems like we ought to have some idea what it was."

He filled three washing machines with clothes and quarters, then got some more change for the pay phone outside the corner gas station and put in a call to Cedric

Kills Crow. "I need to know how long Trainor was the agent down at Pine Ridge," he said without any preliminaries.

"Into the late thirties. Seems like he had some friends in high places who helped him hang in there a while even after the tribe started filing complaints about him."

"What kind of complaints?"

"The usual. Looking out for his friends, excluding the full-bloods every chance he got. They never got him canned, though. Instead they say he drank himself to death."

"No shit?" Zane lit a cigarette. Figured he'd have three today, and this one was dinner. "Was he married?"

"Hell, I don't know."

"Can you find out? And can you check the Pine Ridge rolls for Adam Lone Bull? He was, uh . . . Martin's brother. He must've had some allotted—"

"You'd better back off on this stuff, man. I think it's . . ." A door closed at the other end of the line. Cedric's voice came on again, quietly. "Listen, somebody took a shot at me the other day."

"What?"

"I ain't shittin' you, Z. Big red pickup tried to run me off the road, but I hit the ditch and came right back up, slick as mud. I heard this loud pop. Hell, I thought it would be a good time to blow out some carbon, you know? Sounded like I was backfiring, so I tromped it and got the hell out of there. Got back to town, I had a bullet hole in the back of my pickup. Clean through one side, must'a ricocheted off the other side, 'cause there was a dent—"

Zane's smoke drifted over the unpaved side street. "Did you report it to anybody?"

"Who am I gonna report it to? This happened at Pine Ridge. I'm gonna tell Wilson's goons? They're just like your friend Flynn. Hung up on AIM. Any Indians getting shot at, it's gotta have something to do with AIM."

"Settle down, Cedric. You go talk to Gabe about this."

"Gabe Starr? He's with the *Rosebud* police. I told you, this happened when I was messin' around over in Pine Ridge trying to track down all this—"

"You think this has something to do with Randy's death, Cedric?"

There was a pause. "Might."

"I think so, too. I want you to tell Gabe everything, okay? Everything we know so far, about the land sales, about Butch Hausauer, about those guys in the bar, everything."

"What do we really know, Z?"

"A whole lotta nothin' until we put it together right."

But he knew now who his parents were, and he knew now that his uncle had not lost his voice.

He tried to call Michelle, but there was no answer at either place. She was going to Canton, probably on her way there now, and she'd be there alone in that house full of ghosts. White ghosts, dwelling across the road from red ghosts. Spirit people, gone to the grave with their secrets and their sins on their heads.

Living people were still hurting from those old sins. And living people were still profiting, hanging their hopes on secrets and lies.

Something told Zane he didn't want Michelle to be alone. It was one of those eerie feelings that nagged him once in a while, a fear without a face. One that would probably end up making him look like a fool, but so be it. He had to make sure she was okay, and that was all there was to it. Chickie had said she was going to stick around for a couple of days, anyway.

Damn ghosts. He was going to have to drive through the night. Michelle was going to think he was crazy, showing up at her door at the crack of dawn. He'd just tell her he had to see her, couldn't wait another day. Women loved that kind of talk.

Something told him he wanted to get a move on.

He called on Randy's old girlfriend, Patty Chasing Hawk, who lived in McLaughlin, for a favor. In return for gas money she agreed to finish the laundry and deliver it to Auntie Cecilia with a note, no questions asked.

Now there was just one more problem.

"You wanna take a trip with me, Uncle?" Zane slid behind the big steering wheel and turned to the man, who'd waited patiently and kept watch patiently.

Christ, for how long, now?

Zane owed an explanation, even though Martin didn't require one. He just sat there, open, willing, trusting.

"I'm worried about Michelle. She's all alone down at Canton. Where the hospital used to be?"

Martin's eyes widened with alarm.

"It's not there anymore, Uncle. They tore it down. The graveyard's still there, though. I've been there, and I, uh . . ." This was going to sound weird in English, so he spoke mostly in Lakota. "I've got a funny feeling that some spirit people there, they knew some things about me that I didn't know. It scared me a little, but they didn't want to harm me. They wanted to . . ." He paused, wondering at the magnitude and the utter craziness of what he was saying, wondering whether it could be, *how* it could be possible. ". . . tell me something, I guess. Maybe it's just what you already told me. Maybe it's more."

It was possible, he decided, simply because he felt it, and it felt true, and the *how* of it didn't matter.

"Anyway, I feel like I've gotta go make sure Michelle's okay." This, maybe for her sake, he said in English. He could see that his uncle understood. He understood every word. "Wanna come?"

Martin agreed.

They drove through the night. Daybreak had just begun to push against the night sky. The two-story house and its yard full of trees threw a dark silhouette against the dim canopy, and Zane was thinking about how good it would feel to hit the sack, especially the one warmed and scented by Michelle's body. He was homing in on the turnoff, ready to ease up on the accelerator, when a set of headlights suddenly lit up. A pickup was careening down the access road. The lights came on just before the vehicle did a jackknife turn onto the highway, fish-tailing wildly as it barreled past.

"Where in the hell did he come from?"

Zane knew the answer, of course, and he wasted no more time getting there. Michelle's car was parked in the driveway. The house was quiet, dark except for a side window in the back.

"Looks like something's burning in the kitchen," Zane said as slammed on the brakes before he reached the edge of the yard. "Damn, the house is on fire!"

Hands and feet moved instinctively—park, brake, ignition key, door. "Stay here!"

He called her name, but it took putting his fist through the window to wake her up. He used the little table on the front porch to break the rest of the glass out so he could climb in. The room was smoky. Beyond the bedroom door he could see flames licking into the living room. He flipped the lock on the window, raised it and swept the glass off the sill. His hand was already dripping blood.

She coughed. "Zane?"

"The house is on fire, Michelle! Shoes . . . there's glass—"

She was sitting on the edge of the bed, groggy, coughing. "Where's my purse, my . . ."

He couldn't see much but the hem of her nightgown and her bare feet. "Shit, never mind your—"

"Purse . . . on the chair . . ."

"Don't step!" He snatched some fuzzy blue things off the floor and tossed them in her lap. "Put these things on!"

She coughed again. His eyes were beginning to burn. He tripped over the chair. "I've got the purse. Here."

Glass crunched beneath his boot heel. He lifted her in his arms, pulling the coverlet off the bed with her. She was coughing wildly.

"Hang on, honey. Put your face against me." He shoved the coverlet out the window first, laying it over the sill to protect her. Then he lifted her legs through the opening. "House had nice big windows, didn't it? Out you go."

Fighting a coughing spasm of his own, he followed her out the window, then wrapped her up like a baby and bounded down the steps just as an explosion rocked the back of the house. "I don't know what that was, but the gas line's probably next."

He headed for the pickup. Both doors stood open. "Shit, where's . . . Goddamn, I told that guy to stay in the—"

Michelle pointed toward the side of the house as Zane lowered her feet to the grass. There was Martin, throwing his arm up to shield his face as he tried to peer into a flame-filled kitchen window.

"Uncle!" Zane's own coughing hampered his sprint up the driveway. "I've got her. We're okay." He grabbed the old man's arm and dragged him back. The heat threatened to blister them both. "Are you okay?"

Martin nodded, gesturing as they reached Michelle.

"She's safe," Zane assured him as he wiped the tears from his stinging eyes. "I'm gonna put you two in the pickup, then move the car."

"No, you're not! It's too—" More coughing.

"Give me the damn keys. Hell, I can—"

"Zane!" She fastened herself to his shirt front like a clinging cat. "It's just a car. It's—" She turned. Flames had begun to dance in the bedroom window. "My God, we were just inside there."

He moved her around the pickup door. "Where's the nearest phone? We'll call the police or something. Fire Department."

"Just let it go." She clutched the coverlet around her, couldn't take her eyes off the house. "It's what I should have done in the first place. Burn all their stuff. That's what you said." She nodded. "Let them go."

"Yeah, but you're not going with them," Zane muttered, his hand on her shoulder, easing her into the passenger's seat. "I'm keeping you here with me."

"Oh, Zane, if you hadn't come when you did . . ." She looked up at him, her hair tangled and tumbling around her shoulders, her eyes as watery as his. "How did you—"

"Somebody took a shot at Cedric Kills Crow. Somebody . . ." He turned, awed suddenly by the considerable force of the fire and the power, even more considerable, of the feeling he'd given up trying to explain away. He shook his head. "I don't know, I had this weird knot in my gut. I think we've got some ghosts . . ."

We.

Zane popped his head above the pickup cab and spun himself around like a periscope. "Where is he *now*?"

Across the street a lone figure, etched against the ever-brightening sky, drifted across parallel fairways, headed toward dark secrets and the promise of sunrise. Red lights flashed in the distance, sirens screaming down the highway.

"Should we let him be alone up there?" Michelle asked.

"No." Zane pushed the door back and drew her out of the pickup. "No, I think he needs us with him."

❧ 15 ❧

At the request of Commissioner of Indian Affairs John Collier, Dr. Samuel Silk paid a second visit to the asylum. His task was to examine the patients and report on their physical and mental condition with an eye toward facilitating their transfer to St. Elizabeth's Hospital in Washington. Dr. Silk spent most of the month of September at the asylum. In that time he and Dr. Hubble stayed out of each other's way.

Silk declared from the outset that he would not require much assistance from any of the Canton staff. He found existing records to be of little value in making his assessments. His contempt for Dr. Hubble was no secret, but inasmuch as they belonged to the same brotherhood, he made it quite clear that he was not there to mediate between the doctor and his staff. Barring any surprises in Washington, he fully expected their problems and their opinions soon to be moot.

Rachael was the exception to Silk's rule. They had not worked closely together at St. Elizabeth's, but she was a familiar face, and he knew her to be a good nurse. He tempered his strictly business tone when he conveyed Ella Sims's greetings to her and asked her if she'd like to have her old job back.

"I really have no interest in returning," Rachael told him privately over coffee in the employees' dining room early one morning. "This is a desolate place in many ways, but it's also hauntingly beautiful. And I feel as though I belong to these people now."

"If that's the case, you might as well pack up and come along." Steam fogged the portly doctor's glasses as he sipped his coffee. "The trip is bound to be difficult for some of them. Confusing. Frightening. They'll need you."

"I belong . . ." She glanced out the window. A clump of brown-and-gold prairie switchgrass, damp with dew, glistened in the morning sun. "I really belong here now, and so do they."

"You can't mean that, Miss Trainor. It's impossible for you to do your job properly under these circumstances, impossible for them to make any progress."

"Many of them don't belong in an institution at all." She had to know exactly where Silk stood, but she also had to tread lightly, so she hastened to add, "I'm not a doctor, and that's not a diagnosis. It's a simple observation. One you've no doubt made yourself."

"Yes, I have." He set his cup down and folded his arms at the edge of the table. "Hubble reports that some of these people were sent here because they had trouble at a school or some difficulty at the agency—maybe a fight, maybe just causing the agent a few extra headaches. That makes this place a peculiar catch-all."

"So you're saying that some of these people probably won't be transferred if the asylum is closed."

"*When* the asylum is closed." He leaned forward. "Between you and me, Miss Trainor, this place would be a major embarrassment if it weren't so far out of sight and out of mind. Of course, Commissioner Collier is the first one to say that our Indian policy has been a disaster, but that doesn't help these people much, does it?"

Silk drew himself up, squaring his shoulders under his brown pin-striped jacket. "I will recommend sending some of them home. Hubble claims that he would have done that himself, but in his judgment, there are those who must be sterilized first to keep them from breeding more problems.''

"Is that necessary, Doctor?" she asked calmly. She made a pretense of sipping her coffee despite the sudden protest in the pit of her stomach.

Silk sat back, offering an open-handed gesture. "The American Association for the Sterilization of the Feeble-minded and the White House Conference on Children *both* endorsed selective sterilization, what, two, three years ago now? You're familiar with—"

"Yes, of course, I'm aware of the case for steriliza-tion, but it seems an extreme measure that should only be used—"

"For eugenic reasons it's sound practice, I think." His hand went to his cup. "I understand Hubble's not much of a surgeon."

"I . . . I don't think so, no."

"He blames the facilities. There's an operating room here, but it's poorly equipped." He lifted his brow, looked up at her speculatively. "Nurse Sims told me about the mess with the baby."

She nodded, glancing askance as hard-soled footsteps sounded in the hallway. She waited until Hollings passed the open doorway, then offered, tight-lipped, "It was horrible."

"And quite unnecessary. Now *there's* a good example of the need for sterilization. Poor woman."

Rachael stared, befuddled. "But, Doctor, we can't go around sterilizing vulnerable people simply to make it more convenient for *other* people to prey on them."

"That's not the reason for doing it, Miss Trainor. It prevents reproduction, which, under *any* circumstances, is undesirable for mental patients. Don't you agree?"

"They're not all insane," she reminded him. "You said yourself, some of them are here for punishment for some vague or possibly even arbitrary—"

"At the behest of the *agent*." He drained his cup and set it down carefully as he considered his next question. "Are they arbitrary? Your brother is an Indian agent somewhere in the area, is he not?"

Rachael nodded. "Pine Ridge."

"Perhaps I should visit with him. I'd like to know
what the agent's perspective would be on the prospect
of taking some of these people back. From the records,
I can't tell—" He tapped one finger on the table at a
time as he enumerated the possibilities. "Is a fellow here
because he's chronically alcoholic, dangerously antisocial, or was it just some squabble that landed him
here? The history just isn't there, and some of them have
been here so long . . ." He shrugged. "Some of them
don't even speak much English."

"Maybe the families could—"

"Now, there's a pretty piece of irony. That injunction
business. They're asking for a court injunction against
transferring patients because it would deprive them of
family visits, which Hubble doesn't even allow."

"That request has been made in behalf of—"

"The mother of one of the younger patients, I know."
He chuckled. "And I'm supposed to believe Hubble
didn't put the woman up to it."

She wanted to confirm his suspicions. Lord, how
badly she wanted to! But if he challenged Dr. Tim on
her word, there would be the devil to pay. The devil and
Dr. Tim.

"Obviously, what's going on here can't continue, but
this is such a motley collection of, well, misfits, I'm not
sure where they belong," Silk admitted. "Have you
been to a reservation, Miss Trainor?"

"Yes."

"If we sent some of them back there, would they do
all right, do you think?"

"I think so, yes." *Depending on the agent.* "My
brother . . . you understand, he has a lot of power but a
very limited budget, and it may be that some people
have been committed for reasons . . ."

"I understand. It must be a difficult job, trying to do
what's best for your charges under such dismal circumstances. I'd be very interested in discussing some of
these matters with your brother sometime." He took his
watch from his vest pocket and flipped the gold case

open. "If only I *had* the time. I'd like to wrap this up soon."

"How soon do you think a . . . a plan of some sort will be formulated?"

"You needn't worry your head about the plans, Miss Trainor. Either way, your job is assured." He offered a patronizing smile. "I've got to get back to D.C. and deliver my recommendations as quickly as I can so that I can make preparations at St. Elizabeth's and arrange to transport the patients. There's still that request for an injunction pending, and there's that delegation from the burg of Canton camped on the commissioner's doorstep." He chuckled derisively. "But as soon as those little roadblocks are disposed of, we ought to be cooking with gas here."

Rachael was feeling desperate. Ella's letters counseled her to be patient, that it was only a matter of time before the whole Canton situation would be resolved. But Ella didn't understand that the matter of time was crucial to Rachael. She felt like a walking time bomb. Too many long, lonely days and nights, too many agonizing secrets, but the weeks had somehow piled up quickly, and she wasn't sure how soon her condition would become apparent.

Ella mentioned that Commissioner Collier had met a woman on his visit to a Pueblo reservation who had pleaded with him to secure her husband's release from Canton. The woman's story had impressed Collier, whom Ella described as an intuitive and sympathetic man. Rachael wondered how she might best plead Adam's case. She supposed that depended on just how understanding Commissioner Collier really was. Surely he could sympathize with a pregnant woman desperate to free the man she loved from bondage.

If only it were that simple.

She hadn't been able to speak with Adam since Silk had arrived. Hadn't dared. She would see him shepherding Tom Yells At Night out to the farm early in the morning, sometimes see him in the dining room at supper time, but they couldn't afford to take any chances while Silk was there. If Hubble decided to discredit her, all he had to do was catch them red-handed before Silk left.

But she'd been taking daily walks, watching the progress of the corn harvest. Adam was working in the far corner of the field when she managed to duck between the rows of drying cornstalks and catch him dousing himself with his drinking water.

"Now what will you do when you get thirsty?"

He turned, at once surprised and delighted by the sound of her voice. His wet hair glistened, blue-black in the afternoon sun. Water trickled over his bare brown torso. The sun loved his body as much as she did.

"Come here and let me show you," he invited as he tossed the water bucket aside. When she came within reach, he dragged her behind the wagon box he'd been loading, drew her into his strong, water-slick arms, and kissed her, slaking all thirst.

"Is he leaving soon?" he whispered against her mouth.

"Yes." She sipped a drop of water—or sweat, she didn't know, didn't care which as long as it tasted of him—from his upper lip. "Adam, I'm scared. They know about us."

He leaned back. "The doctor from Washington?"

"No. But Hubble knows." She laid her hand on his cheek, streaked with grit, warm and wonderful to touch. "Silk doesn't think much of Hubble, but if I try to appeal to him about . . ." She glanced away, wishing she didn't have to fail him this way. "Hubble can use what he knows to discredit anything I say."

"Deny it."

"I can't."

"Yes, you can." He took her shoulders in his hands, gripped them hard. "Think, Rachael. He can only ruin you at his own expense. He's the one who's responsible for what goes on here." He smiled, slyly lifting an eyebrow. "If one of the nurses has been sneaking into a patient's room and taking advantage of the crazy fool—"

"That's not funny."

"It is, a little bit." The smile in his eyes invited her to enjoy the irony. "Come on, it's also true. I *am* crazy for you." She doubted him with a look, but he wouldn't give up. "Would you care to examine me? I have all the symptoms."

She nodded, but her smile was too tight, too sad.

"Hubble won't say anything, and no appeals will be needed. This will be over soon." Impulsively he lifted his hand to her hair, but he saw the dirt imbedded in his skin and drew back. "They're going to release me after this inspection, or whatever it is, is over."

"They told you this?"

"I said I would sell them my land."

"Oh, God, I can't believe this is happening." She searched the sky. "It's all so deceitful and so . . . so *wrong,* and I should just blow the whistle as loud as I can. I should just—"

"You taught me patience. Now it's my turn to teach you."

"I'm afraid they'll try to hurt you, Adam. Before they release me, I'm afraid . . ." She caught his hand and held it tight, chafing his work-rough skin with her thumbs. She ought to tell him, she thought, but she swallowed hard and shook her head. "They might hurt you . . . somehow."

"What could they do that they haven't done already?" He dipped his head, searching her eyes for an answer. "No, they can't hurt me anymore. They'll have what they want, and I'll have my freedom, my brother's freedom. It will all be settled very soon."

She nodded fiercely. "It has to be settled soon so that we can be married."

"Married!" He laughed merrily. "Does that mean you're crazy for me, or just plain crazy?" Smiling, gripping her hand, he turned and leaned back against the tall wagon box. "Whether it's my world or yours, the man does the asking."

"Does he do it"—she planted her chin on his shoulder and finished softly—"before or after the baby's born?'' His head turned. She nodded, chin still stuck to his shoulder. "We're going to have a baby, Adam.''

"Are you . . . sure?'' Another nod. He stood stock still. "When?''

"In March, I think. Maybe even before that.''

"How long have you known?'' He turned to her, dipping his head to meet her nose to nose, his shoulder still resting against the wooden box. His free hand went to her shoulder, then stroked her arm, over the sleeve of her cardigan sweater. "Were you afraid to tell me?''

"Should I have been?'' She looked into his eyes. The answer was already there, but she asked anyway. "Are you angry?''

"With myself.'' He closed his eyes. "It is a wish I had no right to make.''

"You wished for this?''

"I did.'' He smiled, but slightly. "The way a boy wishes for wings.''

"Not quite. You *did* have the means to make this wish come true.'' She uncurled his fingers and spread his hand over her belly, hipbone to hipbone. "With my help.''

He bowed his head, pressed his forehead against hers. "Are *you* angry?''

"Not about this. Not about your wish and mine making this miracle inside me.'' Her eyes drifted closed. "I love you so much, Adam. So much, I can't tell you. All I can do is . . .'' All the blood in her whole being hammered it out in pulse beats. Love him, love him, love him. She smiled. "Any more wishes?''

"It's your turn to make one.''

"I wish to be married to this baby's father.''

"Then you will be.'' He caressed the cradle that contained his tiny hope. "I can give you that, if you're sure it's what you want.''

Silk went back to Washington in late September, and there was no word about the injunction. Hubble had been spending more time in town, stirring up concern for the future of the asylum, ingratiating himself with community leaders. Rachael tried to prepare some of the patients for the possibility of change. She talked about the beauty of large trees and the wonder of long trains and the prospect of less "bad breathing."

Adam had told her not to come to his room, to wait for him to make the next move, and she obliged, letting him teach her patience. A week went by, almost two, and still she waited, falling asleep each night bundled up in a chilly room, with the window raised just high enough to permit a hand to slip under the sash.

Finally one night he kissed her awake. "I've come to ask you to marry me," he whispered. "Tonight."

"Tonight?" She sat up quickly. "What's happened? Have they tried to—"

"Shh." He touched a finger to her lips. "Nothing's happened. I have convinced Albert Brothers that Hubble is our common enemy, and he's keeping me in the barn overnight to birth a colt." Moonlight flooded his smiling face. "I have been watching for a way to do this."

"Hubble hasn't changed his mind about releasing you, has he?"

"He's said nothing to me. He's like a coyote, pacing in the hills while he waits for the sun to set."

"He says that Washington's interest in this place has always been fleeting. He thinks this will all blow over, but I'm sure he's wrong." She fingered his collar. They'd given him a denim jacket to work in. "I just wish he'd let you go now."

He flipped her covers back and ran his hands over her flannel-gowned body—face, shoulders, breasts. Ah, yes, touch them, she thought, drawing up, expanding herself on a deep breath of the crisp night air scent of him.

"How soon before the child begins to show? I can see the difference already."

"Only because you know."

"Because I know your body." His arms went around her as he buried his face in the warm flannel-lined valley between her breasts. "It's been so long. If we'd been together these last weeks, I would have felt the difference."

She thrust her fingers into his cool, thick hair. "No one else gets this close to me."

"If Hubble is any kind of a doctor, knowing what he knows about us . . ." He drew a deep breath and sat up. "Before the sun sets again you will be married to this child's father."

"How?"

"Do you trust me, Rachael?"

"Yes," she said, without hesitation, following him to her feet. "Yes! Shall I wear a white dress? I just happen to have a whole wardrobe full."

"Wear some pants. You were wearing pants the first time I saw you. Find something like that, only shapeless and not . . ." He coaxed her toward the bureau. "We are going to do the impossible tonight. We are going to turn a beautiful woman into a pitiful-looking man."

"You're going to marry a man?" She stifled a giggle as she eased the top drawer open. "Now I think you *have* gone mad."

"We're going to ride the train." Her double take prompted him to add, "As uninvited guests."

"We are?" She forgot about the drawer. "Oh, how exciting. We're just going to hop into a boxcar and ride the rails?"

"It's not that exciting."

"You've done it before?"

"Many times. If I'd known there was a spur so close to this place, I would've come to . . ." He shook his head and leaned against the bureau, considering his neglectful past and his painful present. "God knows. Maybe I would've come. Maybe not. I guess the man I used to be was a damn poor excuse for a brother." He nodded toward the open drawer. "It's time I changed all that, Rachael."

She laid a pair of brown wool trousers on top of the bureau, next to her brush and comb. "Much as I'd like to, I can't be jumping off a moving train, you know."

"Do you think I would let you do such a thing? The train has its patterns, its habits, its feeding and watering and resting spots, just like a living thing. I've been

watching. The train that runs through here always stops
at the ski run.''

"Even now?'' She added a shirt and a pair of socks
to her choices as he confirmed with a grunt. "And, of
course, no one's getting on or off this time of year.''

"If you don't get moving, we won't be, either. Tomorrow is your day off, isn't it?''

She nodded. "Where are we going?''

"To find a color-blind preacher.''

"How will we do that? Do you know of one? I mean,
we can't just—''

"You can wish for one. Quietly.'' He hushed her with
two fingertips, a kiss, and a promising smile. "And I
can hunt him down.''

The harvest moon flooded the fields that lay between
the hospital grounds and the road into Canton. Like two
children playing midnight hide-and-seek they darted
from tree to tree until they reached the creekbed draw,
then made their way to the road and waited in the ditch
near the railroad crossing. When they heard the distant
whistle, Rachael clutched Adam's arm and bobbed up
and down on her toes. He laughed and pulled her down
in the grass.

She squatted next to him, childlike in wide-eyed anticipation. Indeed, with her hair tucked into his big,
floppy hat, her bulky sweater hiding her shape, she
looked like a young boy. He wished he might be taking
her on a real adventure. A wedding trip to Paris, maybe.
She'd never been there, and he wanted to be the one to
show her the sights. At the very least he wanted to be
able to take her to Sioux City by coach instead of boxcar.

"Here it comes!'' she whispered.

He chuckled. "Keep your head down until the engine
passes.''

The engineer sounded a warning in approach of the
crossing. The engine and the first few cars rolled by,
brakes sighing, wheels squealing as the train slowed.
Adam spotted the red glow of a cigarette in the first open

door that rolled by, so he let that one pass. The train slowed to a crawl. He dashed down the line, hopped into an open car, and quickly made sure it had no riders. He jumped down and signaled to Rachael.

The train didn't stop completely, but close enough. He tossed in the blanket bundle she'd brought, then hopped aboard and pulled her in after him. They hid in the back of the car until they passed through town and the train picked up speed. Then they nestled together in her blanket, a couple of crates for a bench, and watched the river bluffs and the open fields fly past the boxcar door.

"Now what do we do?" she asked, exhilarated by their success.

"Do?"

"It feels like we should...pull a caper or something."

He laughed, loud and heartily, and he hugged her. "For one thing, we can stop whispering for a while."

"Oh, golly, what a joy!" She hugged him back. "Let's sing."

"Sing?"

"Railroad songs. Do you know any?"

"Not a one. I know—" He sat up straight and crooned, "O-ver there! O-ver there!"

She joined him in a rousing chorus. He told her that he liked popular music, that he had built his own radio—a crystal set. They took turns suggesting songs, harmonizing on "Bye, Bye, Blackbird," "My Blue Heaven," laughing as they took liberties with the words to "When the Moon Comes Over the Mountain."

Finally Adam intoned, "Goodnight, sweetheart..."

"Mmmm, I'm not tired," Rachael complained, but she didn't object to lying back and cuddling with him.

"I don't want the preacher to mistake my bride for a raccoon."

She giggled.

"Rachael?"

"Hmmm?"

"Do you realize that I haven't been away from that place in a year?"

"Yes." She hugged him close. "You're an amazing man, Adam Lone Bull."

He looked down at her moonlit face and smiled. "What makes you say that?"

"You can still sing."

When they pulled into the Sioux City railroad yard, Adam pulled Rachael off the train before the yardman reached their car. It was still dark. The man gave out a half-hearted, "Hey you," but he had no urge to give chase. His shift was almost over, anyway.

They took refuge in a haystack near a boarded-up farm house and shared the biscuits and ham Rachael had taken from the staff kitchen. They watched the stars fade and the night recede slowly to make way for their wedding day. She unrolled the dress she'd brought in her blanket bundle—pale blue with a white lace collar. He helped her with the buttons, and he tied the narrow belt in back.

"I brought some money," she said, hoping he wouldn't take offense. "Would you like to get married in a new shirt?"

"I got us here, woman." He squinted up at her, grinning. "The wedding clothes are up to you."

When the stores opened, she gave him the money to buy the red western shirt he admired in a window, along with a pair of new Levi's.

"Does he work for you?" the clerk asked Rachael as she rang up Adam's purchases. The woman spared him little more than a glance when he handed her the money.

"We both work for the government, actually. The Indian Service." Rachael slipped her hands into her sweater pockets. "We're just passing through. On our way to Washington."

"Just the two of you?" The pinch-mouthed woman lifted her chin slightly and sighted down her nose. "That's a long trip."

"That's the nice thing about working for the government. You get to do some traveling.'' Rachael smiled. Adam coughed, cleared his throat. Hinges creaked. ''Better get going. Thanks.'' Rachael hurried to catch the door behind him.

''We both work for the government,'' Adam echoed, castigating her with a glance as they crossed the street. ''Rachael, when you're on the run, you don't want to be noticed. You don't say anything that won't be forgotten right away. You don't even talk if you can help it, don't look them in the face, don't hang around once you've got what you came for.''

''That makes sense.'' She skipped along to catch up with him. ''This is my first time being on the run.''

''Yeah?'' He shoved his hands into his pockets as he stepped up on the curb. The blanket bundle he'd tied and slung over his shoulder tapped against his side. He carried it for her, figuring it was more his style. He looked like a bindle stiff, but Rachael . . . ''Do you feel like turning around and running the other way yet?''

''Away from you?'' She slipped her arm through the loop his made. ''Not a chance, Mister.''

''Don't touch me, Rachael. Not—'' He stopped, swung around to face her, leaving her with an empty arm, her hand extended toward him. He glanced up the deserted sidewalk. ''Not right out here on the street.''

''I'm sorry.'' She mistook his apprehension for masculine reserve and flashed him a tolerant feminine smile. ''Do you realize we're eloping? I've always thought it would be the most exciting and romantic way to get married.'' When she smiled she lit up the whole damn dusty, dilapidated street. ''I was right.''

He was glad she thought so. This day was all they had, and for her sake he wanted it to be a good way, a good *day* to get married.

All he had to do to locate the right official was find the right part of town, the right little clapboard church. The Reverend Billy LaPointe was part Winnebago, part black, part French, and all preacher. The only questions he asked were whether Adam and Rachael would take each other as husband and wife and whether there was a ring to be blessed. To Rachael's surprise, Adam produced one from his pocket. It was the first time he'd smiled since he'd watched her get dressed in the haystack.

"I made it from a shell casing," he said proudly. "Been doing some horseshoeing. Brothers says I'm pretty good at it." He slipped it on her finger, and after they were pronounced man and wife, he kissed his new bride.

And she, like all brides, held her hand up to the sunlight and tilted it this way and that, awed by the richness of the promise in that circle on her finger.

"Oh, Reverend LaPointe, have you ever seen a more beautiful wedding band?"

The old fellow smiled. "Can't say I have."

That night they returned to Canton the way they had come, but they were much changed. They didn't sleep. They couldn't get enough of touching each other, talking with each other, learning, memorizing each other. They talked about the future. Not the immediate future, but the future beyond Adam's release. It didn't matter that he would give up his land to secure his freedom. He was good with his hands, and there were many ways he could support his family. They didn't have to go back to the reservation, he said, but she said she would like to work in an Indian hospital.

But they could live anywhere he wanted to, she said.

Anywhere she wanted to, he said.

They held each other close and listened to the clicking of the wheels and the passing of the miles, and they both wished they could ride the train beyond morning, beyond Canton, beyond the limitations of tracks and time.

But neither of them wished aloud.

Late in October Hubble finally had his answer. The request for an injunction against the transferral of Indian patients from the Canton Asylum was denied.

"Well, Miss Trainor, it seems we have our assignments," he told Rachael in his office. He tossed a piece of paper across the desk. "You will accompany these sixty-nine patients on a special train, which the Indian Service will provide. Silk is sending a physician and a score of attendants from St. Elizabeth's to help you. You have a new job waiting for you."

She picked up the list of names.

"I am to be without a job once these assignments are carried out," he said. "The government is closing the asylum."

Rachael looked up after scanning the list twice. "What about the rest of the patients?"

"You don't see the names you're looking for?" He gave her a cagey look. "Some are too ill to travel. Others may be released in the custody of the agents of their respective reservations as soon as arrangements can be made with the agents."

She stared, waiting.

Hubble smiled. "Your stud may be returned to his pasture soon, Miss Trainor. His younger brother may join him sooner or later, once all the legal hurdles are cleared. But he'll remain in my care a little longer. It's been a very trying month."

Pushing some folders aside, he took a seat on the edge of the desk, his eyes purposefully meeting hers. "You know, I really don't like the idea of turning loose ends"—he folded his arms—"loose."

"I really don't want to go to Washington."

"And I don't blame you. You've gotten yourself into a very sticky predicament, Miss Trainor." Again, the heartless smile. "Nothing to say in that regard?"

Nothing you'd remember to use against us, she thought. *You don't talk if you can help it.*

"Have you thought of appealing to your brother?" He chuckled. "Of course you have. He has his own secrets, Miss Trainor, but I haven't told him about yours. Not yet."

She glanced away.

"So, you see, anywhere you turn, there we are. Now, I don't know what you plan to do when you get to Washington. And I haven't decided exactly what I'm going to do when you leave. But as long as I have cus-

tody of your secret, I believe mine is safe. I don't think
either of us wants any secrets to get out." He tapped his
fingers on the desk, then rose abruptly. "To tell you the
truth, I suspect this entire program will one day be a
secret."

"The asylum?"

"Not an official state secret, of course. It's not that
important. The Indian question is no longer a matter of
national security, and what's been done about it over the
years . . ." He shrugged. "It's just something we won't
have to talk about much longer. This country's crazy
aunt in the attic, you know? No one ever sees her, and
we just don't talk about her."

Yes, she did know. Now, finally, she understood why
there were so many problems at the asylum that would
never be addressed. The answer to the "Indian problem," at least in part, was turning out to be the most
monstrous kind of profit-taking. What Hubble didn't
know was that he was talking about her *husband*, not
some temporary secret lover. He had no idea that he was
talking about her *family*, including her brother-in-law
and her unborn child.

He was also talking about a group of displaced people
being further displaced, and she couldn't go with them.
She couldn't take the train to Washington. She wasn't
going anywhere without Adam and Martin.

Adam came to her room that night and told her that
he'd heard the news from Albert Brothers, who'd said
he was out of a job.

"I was going to go to your room tonight," Rachael
said, taking him in her arms. He smelled of dusty alfalfa
and horse sweat. Perfectly wonderful.

He kissed the top of her head. "I've been told that
I'll be free to leave once I've signed some papers and
had my discharge examination. They're saying my
brother will probably be discharged in a couple of weeks
and that my wife is leaving for Washington."

"Your wife?"

"My words, for your ears only." He lifted her chin.

"My lawfully wedded wife. When were you going to tell me?"

"I'm supposed to accompany the patients Dr. Silk designated for transfer. They need me, too, and I wish I could go with them. It's going to be a difficult journey to a strange place. It's going to be frightening for them."

She laid her hand on his cheek and looked lovingly into his eyes. "But my place is with you. I'm not going to Washington, and you're not going to submit to Hubble's 'examination.' We have to leave here now, tonight, and we have to take Pagla with us."

"Why?"

"Hubble has managed to keep him here for the time being, but I don't know what the final disposition will be. And he isn't going to just let you go."

"The agreement on my land will be among the papers they give me to sign. I've been told this, although not in so many words."

"Other patients will be released, too, but . . ." How to say this to a man like Adam. The idea was absurd, but Rachael had begun to realize that absurdity and reality had become partners in this place. She sighed. "In what condition, I don't know."

"Condition?" Adam chuckled. "Does the runt think he's going to work us over first?"

"I don't know what Hubble and his goons have planned." She paused, then added, barely audibly, "Sterilization has been mentioned."

Adam shook his head, his quick laugh rumbling soft and deep in his throat. "They'd *geld* me, would they?" It took a moment, but then the partnership hit him, too. Absurdity. Reality. "Like a . . . like one of their farm animals?"

"You're a mental patient. It's accepted practice. Even Dr. Silk . . ." She rested her forehead on his shoulder and spoke disconsolately into the chasm between their bodies. "I thought . . . I don't know why I thought Hubble would just go quietly, or they would put someone else in charge, or . . . or somehow some court or some

official would step in and see that this was all handled
... properly.''

"Properly?" Adam felt the blood rise to his face, hot
with shock. Coming from a woman he trusted, the word
made no sense, even in a senseless context.

"Silk himself could see that some of the patients
should never have been sent here, that some terrible in-
justices . . .'' She looked up at him, her face full of tears.
"But I had a secret, too, you see, and because of that
. . . my word is useless against Hubble's."

He held her up, his hands bracketing her upper arms.
If he let go of her, she would collapse against him. He
could feel the terrible shuddering taking hold. Her secret
had brought her shame and left her powerless in a way
she couldn't stand to be powerless—a woman no longer
credible. If he let go of her now, she couldn't stand at
all.

He tucked her under his arm and led her back to her
bed. "So we have to take Pagla *now* and go, because
they can hurt you more," she was saying through her
tears. "They *can,* and there's no power to protect—"

"Shh." He smoothed her hair back from her face as
he sat her down. "You can't go anywhere until you
settle down. Where do you keep your handkerchiefs?"

She pointed to the bedside table, but when he leaned
toward the drawer, she grabbed his arm. "Adam, we
have to take him with us."

He nodded, only half listening as he pulled the drawer
open.

But she went on, sniffling, trembling, struggling to
explain when he'd already made up his mind. "Oh, God,
I'm afraid if I tell you . . . and he's afraid, too, he doesn't
want you to know, but I can't keep it . . . Oh, God . . .''

"Shhh." He eased her back down on the bed. "Lie
down for a little bit."

She shook her head, still trying to speak.

"No, here. Shhh." He captured her flailing hand and
kissed her fingertips. "You'll scare the baby. He's right
here, under your heart, listening to you. Feel—" He
placed her hand between her breasts, pressing it over her

heart. "It's beating too hard, little mother." Stretching out beside her, he kissed her above her eyebrow, again at the tearful corner of her eye. "*Ina.* That means mother."

"Adam, please listen." She drew a deep, shuddering breath. "Just before Dr. Silk came, I saw . . . I saw Hubble . . . in the bathroom late at night . . . with Pagla."

Unwanted, the image formed in her mind. Unreal in its secrecy, given voice it became real.

Unwelcome, the image formed in his mind. Sadness and rage warred in his tortured groan.

"I didn't see anything, really, I don't know . . ." She rolled her head back and forth, rejecting the image that wouldn't go away. "Pagla asked me . . . when I went in to see him later, he told me . . . he said, 'Not see, not see.' And I tried to assure him that . . . I had not seen him in any"—she breathed, trying to steady herself—"bad way. He's very, very modest, you know, and I . . ."

Numbing calm stole over him. He had made up his mind, and now there was no question. "You kept this from me?"

"He begged me not to tell you, and I promised not to." She wiped her eyes with the corner of the bedsheet. "Because I thought, okay, it's bad now, but it's going to be over soon because we're going to be . . . be discharged."

"We?" He knew it was true, that she was in this with him, but her release would not be decided by Hubble. It was up to him.

"But not this way, because Hubble could . . ." She closed her eyes and whispered frantically, "Oh, Adam, Pagla has kept his secret, and I have tried to protect mine, so that you . . . would not try to . . ."

Hands fluttering around his face, she thought to coax him. "But now we have to run, Adam. We *have* to. I'm sorry. I wanted to, to tell you, but I couldn't, and Hubble didn't dare . . . I think, as long as Dr. Silk was here, Hubble stayed away, so . . ."

He smoothed her hair back as he hooked one leg over

both of hers, pinning her down. "Lie back and don't talk now." Calming her with stroking hand, soothing voice, he reached for the handkerchiefs. "Breathe," he said, kissing her softly. He drew her arms up, over her head. "That's good. Just breathe."

He rose over her, immobilizing her, banding her wrist with one of the handkerchiefs.

Her eyes widened, like a child betrayed.

He whispered, "No, lie still now, and trust me."

"What are you doing?"

"I'm going to do what we both know I must do." He knotted her wrist to the brass rail above her head. "What I should have done long ago."

A small, incredulous voice sounded beneath him. "What?"

"Run. I'm going to take my brother as far from this place as we can go."

"But I'm going with you." She wasn't fighting him. She thought her intention, her wish was enough.

"No, you're not. You're no good at being a renegade." Securing her other wrist, he smiled sadly, thinking how pretty she looked in the starlight, her moon-bright hair pooling against the cloudy pillow. "*Lila sica*. Very, very bad. You're almost as clumsy at running as you are at riding a horse, my sweet wife."

"Adam, don't do this to me." The look in her eyes nearly broke him. He might have been holding a gun to her head for the utter dread he saw there. "It wasn't me who chained you to—"

"I know. Shh. Don't fight the bonds. That's what you told me, remember? Don't fight."

"I won't try to stop you. Just let me go with you."

"This cloth won't hurt you as long as you don't"— he touched her wrist with loving fingertips, hoping to soothe as he smoothed the lacy manacle—"don't twist yourself up and rub . . . rub yourself raw the way I—" He shook his head, the words nearly choking him. "Remember the patience you taught me."

"No," she groaned. "No, Adam, I'm your wife now. You promised to—"

"It's only for a little while. Someone will find you, but give me until sunrise before you make any noise."

"Please don't leave me."

"I can't have you"—he dragged himself off her—"I can't have you with me this time. We could change your hair, but not your skin, and not your beautiful eyes. Don't cry, now." He swept one twinkling tear away with his thumb. "I don't want to leave you crying."

"Then don't leave me, Adam. Take me—"

"I love you more than that." He gathered her nightgown above her hips, lowered his head reverently, kissed her belly, and worshipped her skin with the breath of a whispered vow. "I love our child."

The soft, quivering intake of her breath pierced him to the quick. He sat up, drew away. If he touched her again, God! He made himself look at her, see what he had done, and he forced himself to speak to her softly, moderately, as though tying his wife to the bed were a perfectly sane thing to do.

"I want you to ride the train to Washington, watch over your patients, and get them to their new place." He covered her with her nightgown, touching only the hem. "And have the baby there."

A small sob escaped her throat as she shook her head.

"Yes, Rachael, find a safe place and have our baby. Then come back home, after this place is closed down and they've sent Hubble and Trainor packing. In the end they will finally do this. I'm sure of it. Then it will be safe for us to go home, Pagla and me, to our mother. You'll look for my mother?"

He leaned over her, wishing he could drink her tears, drink her sorrow, just drink all of her and be saturated with her, never apart from her, never again. He let his hand drift close, feeling her warmth but not quite touching, not daring to touch . . .

"You'll go to Rosebud, where her people are," he said. "You'll ask for Beatrice Lone Bull. If I'm not there, she'll know where to find me."

"You're not going to cover my mouth? What if I—"

Before he could stop himself he had covered her mouth with his. He had to tear himself away, gasping for breath like a drowning man on his way down for the third time. "If you call out too soon, I'm a dead man," he warned her. "I trust you not to betray me, but I can't trust you not to follow me. This is the only way I can protect you now." He drew her blanket over her. "I'm counting on you, Rachael. I want this child to live."

"Then don't leave us."

Pushing away from the bed, he leaned close to her ear and whispered, "My heart will never leave you. I swear."

❧ 16 ❧

Late spring 1973

Martin's high-pitched, heartfelt song signaled the birth of a new day. The brilliant colors of sunrise outstripped the blaze that licked at the roof of the Hubble house. Zane and Michelle were mesmerized. He stood behind her, arms around his bewildered refugee wrapped in the coverlet from her bed, and together they watched the flames consume the house.

It was a matter of containing the blaze at this point. After Zane had let them know that there was no one inside, the volunteer firemen had saved the car, but the house was a lost cause. Michelle closed her eyes and tipped her head back against Zane's shoulder. He tightened his arms around her. Holding her hard against him, touching her hair, experiencing the texture of her skin against his cheek, all served to reassure him. He could feel his heart tagging along in celebration with Martin's song. Michelle was safe. He had pulled her out of that place full of dark secrets, and she was safe in his arms.

Not by chance, either. It was no coincidence that he'd gotten there when he did, no accident that he'd left most of the clothes his family owned in a laundromat and driven through the night to get to her. A skeptic by nature, he wasn't about to try to explain his "funny feeling" to too many people, but he knew what he knew. He was standing on sacred ground, looking up at sacred sky. And somebody up there liked him.

Martin's song was over. He touched Zane's shoulder.

"Is my father here, Uncle?" Zane scanned the neatly mowed grass with its orderly row of telltale dips. "Is Adam buried here? His name isn't on the monument, but maybe—"

"*Lala,*" Martin said softly.

"Grandfather's here. You're right about that. Your grandfather, my *great*-grandfather. Here's his name." He turned to the monument and pointed to James Lone Bull. "Can you show me where he's buried?"

Zane and Michelle followed Martin to a corner of the cemetery, but Zane could have led the way. He'd been there before, paid his respects, even shared a smoke. Maybe he'd done something right that night. For a skeptic, he'd been getting along with the *wanagi* pretty well ever since.

"See, Uncle? Look over there." Zane pointed to the big barns that stood on the site of the old asylum, their gambrel roofs darkly etched against morning gold. "That bad place is gone."

"So is the other bad place," Michelle said with a sigh. Then she blinked, grabbed his outstretched arm, and examined his bloody knuckles. "Zane, you're hurt."

"It's nothing." He grinned as he put his unscathed arm around her. "Had a little fight with a window."

"And you didn't even lose your hat."

He glanced up at the black brim, smiled, and gave her a flirtatious wink. "Sign of a real cowboy."

She nodded, but her attention strayed quickly, back to the commotion across the road.

"I'm sorry about the house, honey."

"It's all right. Those perturbed spirits will be put to rest now, won't they?" She looked up at him. "I have some of the records and some of Aunt Cora's things at my apartment. Maybe I should burn it all. Maybe . . ."

He could feel the shiver shimmying through her as she

looked back at the house. "They almost took me with them, Zane."

"I think they had some help. We passed a pickup." He gestured southward, beyond the small, rolling fairways and short-clipped greens to the road, where a sheriff's deputy was restricting gawkers from the turnoff. "Came around that corner like a bat out of hell. Cedric Kills Crow said the pickup he had a run-in with was red." He glanced over his shoulder. "Remember that pickup we saw down there at that corner, Uncle? What color was it?"

Martin pinched a piece of Zane's shirt sleeve.

"*Sa?*" His shirt was black and red. With the addition of a few blood stains he figured it was mostly red. "It was red, wasn't it?"

"Red shirt," Martin said.

"Yeah, but the pickup was—"

Holding an imaginary pencil Martin pretended to draw on his palm.

"I might have some kind of paper in the pickup. Did you notice something about—"

"*Niyate kin . . .*" Martin pointed to the burial ground. ". . . *hiya.*"

"He says my father's not buried here," Zane translated for Michelle. "He's dead, though, right?"

Martin nodded solemnly.

"Where did they lay him? *Tokiya?*"

Martin stared at the burning house in silence.

"I think that's why he wants the paper, Zane. He wants to tell you more."

"I wanna know more about that pickup," Zane muttered. "The thing is, Uncle, we've got a house burning down here, and some jerk in a red pickup who might have—"

Martin declared his contempt for the house with a scornful glare.

"Besides, Michelle needs to see a doctor." Zane nodded toward the Canton clinic, not far from the barns. "Is that where we should go to get you checked out?"

"I'm okay," Michelle claimed.

"I want to make sure. You took in a lot of smoke."

"So did you. Are *you* all right?"

"If I lay off the cigarettes for a while, it'll all even out." He adjusted the coverlet around her shoulders. "You sure you're okay?"

She was more interested in the congealing blood on the back of his hand. "This is what I want checked out."

"It's nothing."

"It's your hand." She bowed her head over it, dabbing at it carefully with the corner of the quilted coverlet. He saw her press her lips together. Her chin quivered. Then the belated tears came.

"Okay." He tucked her under his arm, and she pressed her face against his neck. "Okay, honey, we'll both have ourselves checked over, and we'll get you some clothes. You're shaking all over."

"Aftershock," she said tremulously. "Relief, gratitude . . . oh, God. Thank you." She turned, holding out her hand. "Thank you, Pagla. Thank you for coming."

The old man nodded soberly as he shook her hand.

They walked back across the fairways. The sheriff had spotted them, and he met them halfway. Zane told the man what had happened, described the pickup. He told the fire chief as much as he could about the fire—where he'd first noticed it, how quickly it had spread. In a matter of a few minutes, on the way to his pickup, he'd said what he had to say to both men. He didn't want to keep Michelle standing around in her nightgown. There were too damn many men around.

As soon as they pulled into the clinic parking lot, Martin panicked, muttering his fears in Lakota. Zane tried to reassure him, but Martin was having none of it.

"He doesn't want us to go in here," Zane told Michelle. "I told him this wasn't the same place, but he's always been afraid of doctors. He can smell one a mile off."

Martin turned to Michelle. "Not take . . . Adam's

boy . . . here." He gestured toward the windshield, facing west. "Rosebud."

"Rosebud?" Zane scowled. "That would be the closest Indian hospital, but that's never mattered to him before. A hospital's a hospital."

"He's afraid they're going to keep you here, Zane."

"You're right. He knows exactly where we are, even if the landscape's changed." Zane studied the sign on the unassuming building. It said nothing about keeping people. It wasn't an insane asylum for Indians. "The third man in his picture story must have been my father. So my father was here, my mother, my uncle, and my great-grandfather. Too many of us."

He'd been here, too, he realized. Some thought, some form of him had been here. He was part of that *us*, not as a foundling, but in blood and bone. He flexed the hand that rested on the steering wheel, purposely reopening the wound by stretching the skin over his knuckles. "Too damn many of us. I think I'll just let it bleed."

"We don't have to go in here, Zane. We'll get something to bandage you up with, get me some clothes, get us all something to eat"—she laid her hand on his thigh and rubbed him a little—"and head home?"

Rather than wait until the stores opened, Michelle called on a friend of Aunt Cora's who was the chairman of her church's annual rummage sale. Together they found a dress and a pair of sandals, which, Michelle declared, would get her home in fine style. Zane tethered Michelle's car to the back of his pickup on a rented tow-dolly and drove them to a truck stop on the outskirts of Sioux Falls, where they claimed a corner booth and ordered breakfast.

After the coffee had been poured, Martin flipped a paper placemat over and started drawing on the blank side. He drew the asylum, the same way he'd depicted it before, boxes within boxes. He drew himself, locked in his room, tied to his bed. Another man came into the room. Martin pointed to the middle of Zane's chest, where the turtle amulet lay beneath his shirt.

"My father, right? Adam?" His hand hovered over his chest as though to protect a sensitive part of himself.

Martin continued to draw.

"He came to your room. Came to take you out?"

Martin looked up, his questioning eyes glistening with sadness.

"It's okay to tell me about it, Uncle. We're not going back there." He jerked at a snap on the front of his shirt and drew the amulet forth. "I need to know about my father."

Martin nodded and went back to work on his story.

"Two guys . . . looks like they caught him, caught my father," Zane read. "Looks like . . ." He looked up. "He killed one of them? Broke his neck or strangled him, looks like."

Martin drew a pistol in the other intruder's hand.

"The other guy . . . shot . . . my father?"

Tears stood in Martin's eyes.

"He died? You . . . were with him, Uncle?" Martin closed his eyes and nodded once. "What about my mother? What about Rachael? Where was she?"

Martin took Michelle's place mat, turned it over, and drew the woman, a box, and a train . . .

She had claimed her husband's body. She had ridden the train with him once again, but this time Adam rode in a pine box, while his silent, shattered brother held his widow's hand all the way to Rosebud, where Beatrice waited for her sons. She showed Rachael the proper way to mourn her Lakota husband, but no amount of keening separated the wife's spirit from her husband's. She hid herself away until her time came. Then she expended her remaining earthly strength, along with much blood, giving birth to her son in her mother-in-law's cabin. Before the sun had risen on another day she joined her husband.

Martin remembered it all for their son, and he told it in stark, straightforward, profoundly moving drawings. "Live for me. Look after . . . my child, *misunka*," he recited with much effort. Then he slid the drawings across the table and spoke briefly in Lakota as he tucked them under Zane's hand.

"He says it's my turn," Zane translated. "Are they together somewhere?" he pressed, remembering the information Cedric had given him from the abstracts. He wanted to know that wherever his parents' bodies were, they lay side by side. It was a shamelessly sentimental notion, he told himself, but he didn't feel like apologizing for it. He looked into the eyes beside him and those across the table. Nobody expected him to.

Zane cleared his scratchy throat. "Trainor didn't take her away, did he?"

Martin shook his head.

"Damn, it's got to be that land Unci sold to, uh . . ."

"To whom?" Michelle coaxed.

"Old man Hausauer." Zane looked across the table. "They're buried at Rosebud, right, Uncle?"

Martin touched a finger to his lips.

"It's a secret, though. That she died in childbirth? Was that a secret?"

Martin nodded.

"I have a feeling *you* were a much-cherished secret," Michelle said. "I wonder if her brother ever knew about you."

"He was the agency superintendent at Pine Ridge, which is where I should be enrolled. According to Cedric, Trainor died in the late thirties. Meanwhile, Unci took us up to Standing Rock, probably to get away from him."

The waitress appeared with three plates of food, which her three customers regarded with wordless antipathy.

"I got the orders right, didn't I? A Belgian waffle and two combos?"

"Everything's fine," Zane assured her, but after she walked away, he chuckled humorlessly. "Just great. My great-grandfather and my uncle get put in this insane asylum for God knows what. Somehow my father ends up there, takes up with this nurse, gets himself killed trying to get his brother out.'' He stared disgustedly at the bacon on his plate. ''Meanwhile Butch Hausauer gets title to their land. Then my mother dies. Martin and me are all Unci has left, so all the while I'm growing up, that poor old woman's worried about somebody taking me away, so she doesn't tell anybody, including me''—he looked up, wagging his head—''where the hell I came from. God*damn*.''

Michelle laid her hand on his shoulder. ''But now you know who your parents were, and you know that they didn't leave you by choice.''

''They were taken from me. Just like Randy. Just like—'' He lifted his arm over her head, put it around her shoulders. ''We came damn close to losing you last night.''

''We?''

''Uncle Martin and me.'' He smiled and squeezed her. ''*Me*. I'm not gonna lose you, too. Not that way.''

''It was an old house, Zane. Old hookups, old wiring. Probably a hundred things that needed work. And kids are always racing their pickups down these roads. It's . . .'' He was shaking his head. ''You really think somebody set it on fire,'' she concluded.

He nodded.

''But why?''

''Why?'' he repeated thoughtfully. ''*Why* is a better question to start with than *who*. We figure out why, we'll know who. The house belonged to Hubble. Randy and Cedric were making noises about some land that now belongs to old man Hausauer. I'm wondering what those two had to do with each other.''

''You could ask Hausauer.'' She shrugged off his dubious look. ''Why not?''

''He's not gonna tell me anything.'' Reluctantly he picked up his fork. ''He probably bought up more allotments back then than he can count. The name Lone Bull rang a bell with him, but he didn't remember why. Just another Indian name.''

''You think Hausauer might have actually conspired with dear old Dr. Tim in some way?''

"Cedric's talking like that's what he thinks," Zane mused as he took a stab at his scrambled eggs. "They used to have what they call 'Indian rings.' They were circles of conspiracy, I guess you could say. Lotta times the Indian agent was involved because he controlled the access. To the Indians, the government money, the land, whatever. Big Indian ring down in the Southwest involved some big-time cattlemen, government beef contracts, politicians, agents, the whole works. Crooks got rich while the people went hungry."

He took a bite of eggs. They tasted like cellophane. He pointed the tines of his fork at Martin's plate. "You guys better eat. We've got a long drive ahead of us."

Michelle reached for the syrup. "So you think it was more than just Hausauer and Hubble."

"I'd say the agent's got something to do with this. That's Trainor. My other uncle, I guess. *Jesus.*" Zane shook his head, wondering at the irony. "I suppose as the Indian agent—back then that was like a damn guardian or something—he could commit people. Hubble's putting them away. Hausauer's buying up their land like there's no tomorrow." He shrugged as he buttered his toast. "Just a guess."

"What's Hausauer like?"

"The old man?" He set his knife on the edge of the plate. "Seemed like a straight-shooter to me, for a guy who probably swindled a lot of poor people out of their land. I bet he doesn't even think there was anything wrong with it. The Indian people weren't gonna use it. Hell, they wanted him to have it. They really needed that buck." He laughed derisively. "And some kind of *consideration.*"

But out of consideration for Michelle, whose family ties were as tangled as his, he wanted to drop the subject.

Out of appreciation for Martin, he told himself that he would never use the term *uncle* to refer to Trainor, his mother's brother. He had always considered Martin to be childlike, had tolerated his weak mind, congratulating himself whenever he'd managed to be patient a few minutes longer than he was inclined to be. But Martin had been patient with life, surviving the secret battles of an insidious war in abject silence. His silence was his defense. In silence he had kept his promise to look after Adam's boy, and now that silence had been broken in Zane's defense.

Zane had never been big on traditions, but now that he knew who Martin was, he realized that he owed him another sign of respect. More than *Leksi,* uncle, Martin was his *father's* brother. In the old way, father and father's brother were both the same. Zane offered Martin his hand and called him by the proper name for the first time.

"*Ate.*" Father.

Michelle had an idea that she might be able to weasel a few more pieces to the puzzle of the past out of Butch Hausauer. She had an excuse built into the research she'd been doing all along. She had her uncle's papers. When Zane came down to see her this weekend—after he got a few things straightened out he'd stop in for supper and they'd make some plans, he'd said—she wanted to be able to give him just the piece he needed. Some recollection from Hausauer about Trainor or Hubble, preferably both.

And all she had to do was say that she'd been going through her uncle's papers . . .

Bill Jr. came to the door. She tried to ignore his intense stare as she introduced herself. He was looking at her as though he thought he ought to know her from somewhere. "We've never met," she told him airily. "But I'm here to see William Senior. You don't look like a William *Senior.*"

"My dad's the senior. You don't look like any of his cronies."

"Nevertheless, he *is* expecting me. I'm doing some research on local history, and your father agreed to let me interview him."

Bill invited her in. "You a reporter or something?"

"Teacher." She offered a pleasant smile. "I'm taking some summer classes."

"Well, my dad's living history, all right."

The elder Hausauer appeared in the doorway to the living room. "Is this the girl who wants to know all about the Dirty Thirties?" he asked jovially as he extended his hand and offered a craggy smile. "Butch Hausauer. Come on in here and have a seat. I got stories. I got pictures. I got anything you want to drink. What would you like?"

Old Butch was clearly pleased to have a guest. Michelle agreed to a glass of lemonade and joined him on the sofa amid the rustic hunting lodge decor. They talked about her being interested in South Dakota history and him being part of it. He showed her old photographs of people he kept telling her were "gone now," but she recognized many of the names.

Finally she took out her pictures.

"My mother. This was the family's farm. They almost lost it, I guess."

"Where was this?"

"The eastern part of the state, near Sioux Falls. This is my mother with her older sister, Cora." She glanced up, looking for some sign of recognition. "My mother came from a pretty large family. By the time my mother was born Aunt Cora had already left home. She went to college back east, married a doctor. They ended up coming back to South Dakota. To Canton."

"Canton," Butch repeated. "Nice little town."

"Aunt Cora taught school there, while her husband—" She produced another photograph. "Here's one of Aunt Cora and her husband, Dr. Timothy Hubble. Do you remember him at all? He was in charge of the Indian hospital in Canton. The insane asylum? I think he was probably pretty well-known in that part of the state."

Butch studied the photograph without offering any comment.

"Aunt Cora died last year, and I inherited boxes and

boxes, just a wealth of material. That's where I came
across your name, in my uncle's papers.''

Butch looked up, surprised.

''I know it was a long time ago, but I'm really interested in my family history. That's why I'm doing this
project I mentioned.'' She reached for her lemonade. ''I
just thought you might remember some little anecdotes
about my aunt and uncle.''

He looked at the picture again. ''Met him a couple
times. Don't remember her. I met him through Ed
Trainor. Indian agent, down at Pine Ridge.''

Michelle forced herself to go right on sipping her
lemonade. She set it down, nodded, smiled. ''That
name's familiar. I got the impression, from, I don't
know, something I read in some of those old papers,
that the three of you were partners of some kind.''

''Partners?'' He shook his head, sparing an accusa-
tory glance at the picture. ''I don't know where that
idea could've come from. Trainor put me onto some
land deals. Back in those days Indians could just sell
their land outright, and most of them didn't know what
to do with it, anyway. The government had a cattle program for a while, but they sold off all their stock during
the war and then—'' He gestured helplessly as he gave
the picture back to her. ''They're just sittin' out there,
can't farm, everything's blowing away. They were better off selling out and moving into town.'' He
shrugged. ''Not a white town, of course. They had their
own little towns. Still do.''

''The reservations are a lot smaller than they were
around the turn of the century. I guess that's because
they just sold their land whenever they had the
chance.''

''Sure. Nobody was leasing anymore. Nobody had
any cash. Before they changed the laws on us back in
the mid-thirties, a guy could pick up a quarter section,
half section without putting up any cash, or hardly any.
Let 'em butcher an old steer or charge up some groceri-
ies on your account.''

He passed off a tongue click as some kind of sympathy. "Times were hard back then. Every man did what he had to do to get by—cattlemen, farmers, Indians, everybody. People traded for what they needed, gave up whatever they could do without. Some of us came through okay, others fell by the wayside. You had to be tough."

"Which you must have been," Michelle allowed.

"Damn right. These young guys, now, they don't appreciate the value of a dollar. Gotta have a new pickup every year, air-conditioned tractors, fancy hay machines. We put up hay by hand. We—"

Bill walked in flashing Michelle a friendly grin. "So you're related to Dad's doctor friend who ran that loony bin for Indians down in Canton."

"Hubble was no friend of mine," Butch said. "I don't know much about the man. He was Trainor's friend."

"Did you ever actually see the asylum?" Michelle wondered.

"I was there once. Trainor took me with him one time. What I saw there taught me a lesson I'll never forget." He looked up at Bill. "The land is everything. A man puts down his roots and builds his foundation in *land*. Lose it, sell it, you cut off your roots, and then what happens?" Butch jabbed a finger into the air, punctuating his answer. "You go crazy. The brain can't get any nourishment. You're bound to lose your mind that way. Maybe even your soul."

"We've got more land than we can use." Bill shoved his hands into the pockets of his western-cut polyester slacks. "Everything's for sale, Dad. You taught me that."

"Not the land. You don't sell your foundation."

"Looks like we've got more company." Bill peered out the front window. "Well, what a coincidence. It's my horse trainer. I think you know him, teacher. Name's Lone Bull?" He turned to Michelle with a squint-eyed smile. "Sure, you do. You know him pretty well."

"How would you . . ." Michelle rose from the sofa

to get a look through the window for herself.

"Saw you talking to him at the Cattleman's Grill not too long ago. I was sitting with Marla Ferrell. His ex? She kinda filled me in." Bill shrugged. "He's just picking up another horse. You wanna go out and say hello?"

"I don't know Marla Ferrell, and I don't know what she told you, but he's not—" She checked her watch. "I really don't have time."

"It won't take long." He grabbed her by the arm, reached behind her, and jerked a door open. "Wait in here. I want to tell him you're here first, just so he doesn't get the wrong idea."

Grinning, he shoved her into the closet before she was able to utter much more than a yelp of protest.

"What the hell are you doing?" Butch demanded as he dragged his slow-moving joints off the sofa.

Bill locked the closet door. "You stay out of this, old man. Seems you and your partners left a few holes in your land deals. Holes which I intend to plug up."

"What are you talking about?"

"I'm talking about some smart-ass Indian kid going around saying he's challenging some land titles. *Our* land titles. The lawyers tell me that kind of a challenge can get tied up in court for months, and I got a buyer who's willing to pay more than the appraised value of the land and let me keep half the mineral rights. But, see, this Indian kid's got a big mouth." Bill used the index finger gesture he'd learned from his father. "And there's only one way to handle an Indian with a big mouth. One less Indian. Who cares? Who notices?"

Butch moved closer. "What have you done, son?"

"Nothing you wanna stick your nose into, old man. You stay put." He jerked his thumb over his shoulder, indicating the closet door. "This woman's probably going to end up going over a cliff in a pickup with her boyfriend at the wheel. Sure is a damn shame, people will say. You'd think she'd know better than to get in with some drunken Indian."

*   *   *

A tall cowboy approached the pickup as Zane rounded the corner of the rail fence that surrounded the yard. "You the guy that's comin' for the horse?"

Zane touched the brim of his hat and flashed a toothy grin. "Don't you remember me from last time?"

"Yeah, sure. Bill told me to put the colt in the barn." The cowboy tucked his thumbs into his belt and ambled on over to take a closer look. He ducked, peered into the cab, got that smug look in his eyes. "You been celebrating a little, chief?"

Zane pushed his hat back with a forefinger and kept right on smiling. "I was early. Stopped for a few drinks on my way over."

The cowboy smiled back. A loaded smile for a loaded Indian. Easy target. He pointed to the barn. "We'll load him out of that back door. I'll get the gate and move my pickup so you can back right up to the door." He gave the door of Zane's pickup a loose-knuckled tap. "Take it easy, now."

"No problem." Zane kept the foolish grin going strong as he pulled away and swung around the house. "Shhhit." The grin dropped away like quicksilver when he saw Michelle's car parked behind the house. "What the hell is she doing here?"

He had a plan, and her presence could only screw it up. Smartest move would be to forget the whole thing. But how was he going to do that? He wasn't going to drive away and leave her in this viper's nest. Why in the hell . . . ?

He shifted the pickup into second gear and his brain into overdrive. Michelle didn't know these people. They must've gotten her over here on some pretext.

Damn. Why would she fall for something like this on the heels of the fire? He shouldn't have left her alone, not for a couple of days, not even for a couple of minutes until he had this thing nailed down. But he'd had to go down to Rosebud, and he wasn't sure it was safe for her down there.

Obviously she wasn't safe anywhere. Not until he had this bunch *nailed down tight* one way or another.

The hired hand parked a red pickup next to the fence, stuck his arm out the window, and waved, signaling Zane to drive through the gate he'd just opened. Zane followed the instructions. He parked the pickup, got out, and shut the door, staggering slightly as he circled to the back of the horse trailer. He lifted the outside latch but left the back doors shut.

From out of nowhere Bill Hausauer came moseying around the side of the red pickup. "How're you doing, Lone Bull?"

Zane offered a handshake and a sleepy-eyed smile.

"Feelin' pretty good, are you?" Bill asked.

"I'm doin' good, yeah."

Bill nodded toward the back of the house. "You recognize that car, don't you? We've got a friend of yours up to the house visiting with my dad."

"Oh, yeah?"

"You know Michelle Benedict, don't you? I thought sure I saw you talking to her at the Cattleman's Grill that night you were there with Marla Ferrell and Peter Worthington."

"Oh, yeah, Michelle. I went out with her a couple times." Zane folded his arms, teetered slightly, smiled. "I remember first names and telephone numbers, s'bout all."

"She says she's into local history, and, of course, the old man's a genuine South Dakota dinosaur."

"What I oughta do is, uh . . ." Zane made a production of giving the house, the car, the woman's name, and his footing on flat ground some careful consideration. "I oughta go up to the house and just say hello. See if maybe she'd like to go have a drink with me. I could come back and pick up the colt later."

The barn door slid open. The hired hand stepped out, cradling a rifle. "This guy's in no shape to be hauling that colt, Bill."

"He's not interested in any colt right now. He's got his mind on riding a certain little white filly. Right, Lone Bull?" Bill signaled for his henchman to move in closer. "I'd say he's in fine shape for that kind of a ride."

"You mean, we gotta do her, too?" the cowboy asked.

"I don't know whether you sent her here or what, Lone Bull, but I couldn't have planned this any better. You even brought me a trailer to load you up in." Bill laughed, shoved his hands into his pockets, and eyed Zane. "I was sorry to hear that the Tusk kid was related to you. I just found that out not too long ago. You're a damn good horse breaker. Not too many around like you."

"You killed Randy," Zane said quietly.

"He was just some big-mouth redskin troublemaker who was tired of livin'. You Indians are making so much trouble all over the state, nobody's too surprised when one turns up dead. One here, another one there. No big deal."

"No big deal," Zane echoed, again quietly. His blood was running ice-cold. The rifle pointed at his back, the two men, the odds didn't mean shit. All he had to do was stay cool and be ready. He had what he wanted now.

"That pretty little teacher should have known better than to get mixed up with a drunk like you, but then"—Bill was moving toward the horse trailer door—"she's kind of a do-gooder, ain't she? Digging up hospital records, trying to track down the relatives of a bunch of dead Indians, and what does it lead to?"

The barrel of a police service revolver poked out between the two trailer doors. An arm snaked around Bill's neck, and the nose of the revolver touched his temple.

Click.

"Leads to a goddamn murderer, looks like to me." Gabe Starr pushed the door open. "You'd better drop that peashooter, there, cowboy. I'd hate to splatter your boss's brain all over my clean shirt."

The cowboy eyed Gabe up and down, noting the blue uniform. "What kinda cop are you supposed to be?"

"The kind with the gun."

"Why don't we all put our guns down?" Butch
called out as he and Michelle emerged from the house.
He carried a .22 caliber pistol, pointed at Michelle's
back. They came through the corral gate, walked up to
the back of the horse trailer, and formed the third leg of
a precarious triangle. Three guns, three hostages, three
nervous trigger fingers.

Michelle looked at Zane, her face white as milk, her
eyes filled with terror and regret.

The odds had just changed. Zane could have sworn
the ground had just shifted beneath his feet, but he
didn't let it show.

"I don't want my son dead," Butch announced,
"and nobody likes to see a pretty woman get hurt. So
let's all just—"

"That's right, Dad." Bill eyed Zane askance.
"You're the one who's holding the ace."

"And I say we let them all go, son. According to this
young woman, they think they can prove that I stole
some land. So I say we let them try to prove it in
court."

"You guys wanna see her go first?" Bill licked dry
lips. "Hold her, Dad. This guy's not gonna risk it. Obstacles, standing in the way of honest, hard-working
men. Isn't that what you said Indians were, Dad? Obstacles to be removed."

"By buying them off," Butch said.

"Or paying someone else to remove them for you.
Settlements don't come as cheap as they used to."

"Dick, put the gun down," Butch ordered the cowboy. "We'll go to court, and we'll see who's got the
best lawyers. That's what it comes down to."

"I ain't goin' to court," Dick said, backing away
from Zane. He tucked the butt of the rifle under his arm
and slowly drew an arc with the barrel as he edged toward Butch and Michelle. "And I sure as hell ain't
goin' to jail, least not without taking somebody else
with me. And who do you think that would be, old
man?"

"You won't go to jail, Dick. Think!" Butch pleaded. "We can have the best lawyers in the state . . ."

"Getting your son off, yeah." Dick edged closer, reaching for Michelle. "You're coming with me, Missy. You let her go, old man. I need a hos—"

Gabe exerted a little pressure, and Bill made a strangling noise.

Dick turned toward the sound, hesitated, then laughed. "Hey, go ahead and shoot the sonuvabitch. Then you got no witnesses. You got no—"

Zane launched himself like a rocket, hitting the cowboy from behind as he knocked the rifle out of his hand. He could feel the wind whoosh from the man's lungs as they crashed to the ground, Zane on top.

"Hot damn, Z, you oughta be a cop," Gabe hooted.

Zane claimed the loose rifle and turned it on the sprawling cowboy. "Get up real slow," he said through clenched teeth. He was beginning to see red, hear his heartbeat again, feel the heat of his blood. "Wouldn't take much to set me off . . . *Dick*."

Dick groaned.

"Hell of an offensive tackle!" Gabe cheered. "Knocked that sucker's bad breath clear to Canada. Didn't you make it to state or all-conference or some damn thing, Z?"

"I never played football." Zane lifted his eyes slowly to meet Michelle's. Hers were wide and wonderful, bright with emotion, most of it meant for him. "You okay?"

She nodded tightly. Butch's pistol was no longer pointed at her. The man was staring at his son as though he were looking utter defeat square in the face.

Zane glanced at his partner, offered half a smile. "You were supposed to watch my back, Gabe."

"I was watching every move that sucker made. If he'd'a shot you, I'd'a plugged them both."

"Thanks a helluvalot." He nodded to Michelle. She edged away from the old man. "Put it down, Butch," Zane said. "It's all over but the mop-up."

The pistol slid from the old man's hand and fell to the ground next to his feet.

"Kick it under the trailer," Gabe ordered, and Butch complied.

"Did they hurt you?" Zane asked Michelle.

"Nobody hurt her," Butch said, and Michelle confirmed it with a tight head shake. "She said she was doing some kind of research project."

"Oh, she's a great one for research projects." Zane regarded her, his feelings for her filling his eyes. The color was beginning to return to her cheeks. A little embarrassment, he thought, because she'd stuck her neck out, and he'd caught her red-handed. God, he loved that woman!

"Remember those Lone Bulls from down around Pine Ridge you asked me about, Butch?" he asked off-handedly as he held out his hand to Michelle. He smiled as she skirted his sprawling prisoner and came to stand by his side. "Turns out, that's who I am."

❧ Epilogue ❧

A warm South Dakota wind whipped Michelle's hair across her face as she hiked up the brown slope, the reed grass swishing against her bell-bottoms. When she'd heard Martin's and Zane's voices echoing a doleful Lakota song, she knew the search was over. They'd found the spot. She'd waited a while before following the haunting sound. It drifted on the crisp autumn air like a freewheeling hawk, visiting the grass with a brief shadow. But the shadow had flown, and her husband was waiting.

"You found them?"

"We found them," Zane said quietly. He stood, head bowed over two long, narrow depressions in the ground, similar to the "big divots" at the Canton cemetery, except that these two were blanketed by natural prairie sod. "They're up here, side by side. They're comfortable here, and I ain't movin' 'em. Which means Butch Hausauer's got another fight on his hands."

The old man had lost the first one. His son and their hired hand had been indicted for first-degree murder, and no high-priced lawyer had been able to get the judge to set bail.

Zane turned away from Michelle as she approached, adjusted his hat, then dragged his shirt sleeve across his face. "Damn, this is embarrassing. Cowboys don't cry."

"Cowboys' wives don't tell."

He laughed as he turned to her and let her see him as he was, shaken by his discovery, his dark eyes glistening.

She put her arms around him, sliding her hands underneath his denim jacket. "I love you, Zane Lone Bull. You may be *one hell of a good cowboy,* but you're also a caring man, and that's what I love most."

"I love you, too," he told her, hugging her back. "I love you for taking on a ready-made family—old folks, kids, a soon to be over-the-hill husband."

"I've heard that life begins at forty."

"We'll see, come March. I think mine kicked in at thirty-nine." He nodded toward Martin, who was retreating down the hill, giving them a moment alone. "He says the house was down there on that flat. He's going down to have a look." He looked into her eyes, shifting his stance to give her some shade. "I want to build our house on my dad's land, west of here at Pine Ridge."

"Anywhere, any time," she reminded him. "It's yours now."

Cedric had discovered that Adam Lone Bull's name had been removed from the agency records at Pine Ridge, presumably by Edward Trainor. Hausauer had ended up with Adam's land. They had been able to establish Adam's identity and verify his allotment through the military and BIA records in Washington.

"Hausauer didn't contest my claim. My father never sold his land." He scanned the distant horizon. Clear blue sky, brown-gold hills, a handful of cattle grazing on the flat below. "We're taking Hausauer to court for this piece, too, and for Martin's. I think old Butch would just as soon take back his lousy dollar at this point, but his lawyers say it would set a bad precedent. Butch says he remembers letting the old woman stay here through the winter after she gave up the land, so

I guess we're lookin' at my birthplace. Anyway, Trainor arranged the sale, and my grandmother was supposed to be getting legal counsel for Martin out of the deal, but that was a sham.''

"The request for the injunction was denied,'' Michelle recalled.

Zane nodded. "Crazy Horse once said, 'My lands are where my people lie buried.' He was right. This rightfully belongs to my grandmother and her family. We'll see if the laws apply when it comes to protecting Indians.'' He looked doubtful. "Cedric thinks they do. We'll see.''

She stepped away, catching him by the hand. "We have a long drive ahead of us.''

"Sissy and Jojo are probably driving your mom crazy by now.'' He smiled. "Some honeymoon.''

"We promised Jojo Reptile Gardens, and that's where we're going tomorrow. We'll have plenty of honeymooning after that,'' she promised, tugging on his hand. "Starting on the train.''

"I don't know why you've got your heart set on this train thing. Rapid City has a perfectly good airport, and there are plenty of flights to Canada.''

"Bo-ring,'' she teased. "We're going to ride the train straight on 'til morning, and getting there is going to be half the fun.''

He chuckled. "I used to hop a freight once in a while when I was a kid, just to be going some place for a little while. I'd come home smellin' like a box car and catch holy hell from Unci.''

"This time you have a ticket.'' She lifted her hand to his smooth cheek, trying to imagine what he'd looked like as a boy. She'd find out sooner or later, she assured herself. Their babies would favor their father. They'd have his smile in their eyes. "I've never ridden on a train. It'll be an adventure. The perfect way to start a honeymoon. When they showed us that brochure, I just knew that was what I wanted to do.'' There was a promise in her smile. "Make love with you in a sleeper car.''

"I-I-I'll be workin' on the raaail-road," he crooned. He moved her hand to his lips, kissed her fingers, then drew back to admire the ring he'd placed on her third finger. The one his mother had asked Martin to keep for him, along with the photograph, the marriage certificate, and a cameo pin, which he'd also given to Michelle. Everything else had been burned long ago in the traditional way.

"I've decided not to buy you a new ring," he confessed.

"Good. I like this one."

"I'm going to make you another one to wear with it, like an extension. I've got a design in mind, and I found a place where I can use the smithing tools. Another Indian jewelry maker." He'd met with Peter Worthington again, who was bound and determined to call Zane an artist and introduce him around to other artists.

Zane figured it was something to do, and if people wanted to pay him for it...

He smiled. "You'll see. It'll be a honeymoon ring instead of an engagement ring."

"That'll be beautiful. The ring your father made for your mother along with the one you'll make for me." She stepped back, giving his hands another tug. The kids were waiting. "I know it'll be beautiful. You're so good with your hands."

He nodded. "Trademark of a lonely old cowboy." Didn't matter what they called him. He knew what he was. *Who* he was. And he knew his loneliness was a thing of the past.

"I hear they make good lovers," she said, raising her voice into the wind as she dragged him down the hill.

"Oh, yeah?" He grinned, giving her playful resistance as he raised his voice to rival hers. "You takin' up where Gabe left off? Tell the world, why don't you?"

"Hey, world! This guy's a damn good—"

He grabbed her by the shoulders and hauled her into

his arms, chest to chest, for the kind of kiss that proved her claim, like the granting of a wish for wings.

The wind gave voice to the grass on the hill above them. Two voices, in fact, softly whispering their approval.

❧ Author's Note ❧

At first glance it might seem like a pleasant spot for a cemetery. It's surrounded by a rustic rail fence, recently replacing the shrubbery that surrounded it for many years. The grass is well tended. People visit the site all the time, generally to recover the golf balls they've hit out-of-bounds. Rarely to pay their respects to the 123 former patients of the Hiawatha Asylum for Insane Indians who are interred there. The articles I used in my research didn't agree on the number—one said 119, another 120, still another 121—but I counted the names on the monument. There are 123. The gender of some of the names is unclear, but there are at least thirty women, at least eighty men, and at least two infants who died between 1903 and 1933.

My husband Clyde and I noted one name in particular—F. C. Eagle. We don't know who he is or where he came from, but seeing the name prompted us to recall the place where Clyde's parents and others of the Eagle clan are buried, on a windswept hill near Wakpala, South Dakota. That land was given for a cemetery by an ancestor, the legendary warrior and leader Gall (Pizi). There the graves have been marked by family members as they saw fit, and the prairie sprouts its buffalo grass, little bluestem, prickly pear, prairie rose, and the like, just as it always has.

Quite a contrast.

The Canton setting is laden with irony. Without knowing anything about the history of the asylum, you can sense it, you can *feel* it as you approach the monument. Here is a place where one culture rolled over another. It would seem that true motives and intentions, possibly a mixture of altruism and expediency, along with names on the monument, may have been lost in the shuffle of history. Respect for the dead is certainly forfeited between two par-four fairways. But this is where the storyteller's spark that became *Sunrise Song* originated, during a pilgrimage to a peaceful, sunny place that felt haunted.

Something, surely, was out of place.

The Hiawatha Asylum for Insane Indians was opened in 1902 as a result of legislation introduced in 1899 by South Dakota Senator Richard Pettigrew in the interest of bringing economic development to his young state. Even though the facility was billed as an insane asylum, from the outset American Indians were admitted with a variety of diagnoses, including mental illness as it was understood then. Reports made by federal inspectors indicate that as time went on, however, Indian people were sent to the Canton facility for other reasons. Few who were admitted were ever discharged.

The asylum had only two superintendents from 1902 to 1934, and both of their administrations ended with scandal. The first one involved the pregnancy of a young patient and "other affairs." The second superintendent, Dr. Harry Hummer, held his position for 25 years despite constant complaints and repeated negative reports from federal inspectors. In 1909 a feud erupted between the doctor and thirteen of his employees who charged that he failed to provide proper clothing and food for the patients, that conditions were unsanitary, and that patients were restrained or confined in isolation unnecessarily. An investigation resulted in the recommendation that Hummer be removed, but a clerk in the Office of Indian Affairs managed to forestall the action until the disgruntled employees either resigned or were transferred. The asylum was forgotten for a while.

More problems erupted in 1914 and 1915 concerning Dr. Hummer's relationship with female employees, but once again the investigations brought about no changes. In 1925 Commissioner of Indian Affairs Charles Burke visited the asylum and reported that conditions were appalling. He suggested increasing the budget so that "modern," more humane restraints could be purchased—many of those being used at Canton were the type used in prisons—and more attendants could be hired. Hummer replied that such extravagant expenditures were unnecessary. The matter was dropped until more feuding erupted in 1926 between Hummer and his nursing staff. One nurse in particular voiced her opposition to his methods. Hummer countered that he could get along fine without a nursing staff. The feud continued to simmer, with complaints countered by reprimands.

In 1929 Dr. Samuel Silk was sent to inspect the asylum and to report on the changes needed to bring the facility up to the minimum standard of the average state hospital. Silk's report was an indictment against Hummer's administration and the deplorable conditions at a facility he described as "a place of padlocks and chamber pots." He found that patients received poor medical care and that virtually no useful medical records were kept. He decried the general use of restraints and indefinite periods of isolation with patients whom he described as "quite well behaved and very few show any special combative tendencies." He said that the asylum was twenty years behind the times in the treatment of the mentally ill, and that, in fact, many of the patients were not insane. Some of them had been sent to the asylum, Hummer admitted, because of a squabble, a fight with a white man, some problem in school, or other "antisocial behavior." (During this period any practice of Native American religion was considered to be antisocial behavior and was illegal.) Most of the patients had been committed by reservation superintendents (Indian agents). Hummer told Silk that he would have sent some of them back to their reservations, but he didn't have

the proper facilities to perform the sterilizations he
thought necessary. When Silk again inspected in 1933
and found that no improvements had been made, he rec-
ommended that the institution be closed, which was finally done by the Superintendent of Indian Affairs over
the objections of the citizens of Canton and the South
Dakota congressional delegation, who voiced their concerns about the impact on Canton's economy.

Sunrise Song is a work of fiction firmly grounded in
historical setting. I have spoken with Lakota people who
remember the threat of Canton, the fear of being taken
away or sent away, either to that institution or one of
the others meant to "Americanize" the first American.
Little has been published about the Canton asylum. Except for the monument, the depressions in the grass that
mark the graves, and the memories of a few relatives,
the place has virtually been wiped off the face of the
earth. The state acquired title to the land and eventually
gave it to the city of Canton.

Among my sources for this story were the following
papers: Dr. Samuel A. Silk's 108-page report to the
commissioner of Indian Service following his inspection
of the Canton Asylum in 1929; Dr. Silk's 16-page report
following his visit in 1933; memoranda in response to
these reports from Superintendent of St. Elizabeth's
Hospital Dr. William White, Commissioner of Indian
Affairs Charles Burke, Secretary of the Interior Harold
Ickes, Secretary of the Interior John Collier; correspon-
dence (some handwritten) between Drs. Silk and White;
the *Congressional Record; The History of Lincoln
County, SD; The Meriam Report: The Problem of Indian
Administration* (1924); newspaper reports; and "The
Canton Asylum for Insane Indians, 1902–1934," by
Diane T. Putney in *South Dakota History Journal*.

Sometimes planning a wedding—
picking out the dress, the flowers, the favors—
takes on a life of its own! And when your daughter
is getting married it's important to get it right.

But what happens when the man you love—
the father of your child—comes back into your life
and you begin to think, "what if . . ."?

Once Upon A Wedding
by
Kathleen Eagle

**In hardcover
from William Morrow**

It's a story you'll never forget—a bold, breathless
romance that celebrates the power of love.

OUD 1002